Obsessed in Blood

OF BLOOD AND DREAMS
BOOK FOUR

KIM ALLRED

STORM COAST PUBLISHING, LLC

OBSESSED IN BLOOD
Of Blood and Dreams, Book 4
KIM ALLRED

Published by Storm Coast Publishing, LLC

Copyright © 2023 by Kim Allred
Cover Art by Dark City Designs

Print edition December 2023
ISBN 978-1-953832-29-0

No one changes the world who isn't obsessed.

Billie Jean King

IT WAS A NEW DAY, and my spirits couldn't be lifted any higher. The sun spread its early morning light through the condo I shared with Ginger, bathing everything with a touch of gold. Classic rock from the seventies and eighties blasted over the speakers. I danced through the kitchen, grinding coffee, adding water to the coffee pot, and laying out the ingredients for one of my special tossed omelets, which was nothing more than eggs, cheese, and anything else I could find to throw in.

While I wouldn't exactly call it a Cinderella moment, bluebirds might have twittered around my head as I set the table.

I jammed an air guitar solo, and when I twirled around to bring it home, I jumped in surprise when a disheveled Ginger appeared with one eye closed from eye crusties, mismatched knee-highs, and a sour expression.

"What in all that's holy are you doing so fricking early? Trying to wake the dead?" She stopped at the entertainment center and turned the volume down.

My lips twitched involuntarily. "One look at you says I accomplished my task. Didn't we both go to bed at a normal hour last night?"

"Lucas called around midnight, and we talked for hours." She shuffled to the table and collapsed into a chair. I filled a mug and then pushed it and the bowl of sugar toward her. Once the first sip was down, she wiped her eye until the lid popped open, and she gave me a typical Ginger smile. Her gaze twinkled. "He sounds so much like his old self again. We laughed, and he told me how stressed he'd been." She held the mug with both hands, savoring each sip as I chopped onions and avoided rubbing my own eyes.

"He'd been terrified the House might fall, and if he didn't have a choice of a new House, he was considering his options of going rogue."

I stopped chopping. "Oh my god. I had no idea. That's a big decision for a vamp."

She nodded, then her sunny smile returned. "But the House is safe. At least for now. He wanted to tell me everything he was going through as it was happening, but Simone and Sergi had everyone on strict orders of silence."

I rolled my eyes. Once the cadre discovered Devon was on the Poppy again, and his car was at the scene of a Council member's murder, the House had been in disarray. The Council had been eager to close the case as quickly as possible, with threats of sanctioning the House. It was an all-hands-on-deck moment, and even Lyra, as the temporary House leader, had difficulty keeping the cadre from enforcing marshal law. It was a tense week.

If that hadn't been bad enough, they wanted me on ice until everything had been resolved. It would have gone much easier if they'd trusted me. After everything I'd done for them since first landing on their doorstep, I'd thought I'd earned it.

"Well, that's over for now." I poured eggs into the skillet and placed toasted English muffins on the table along with the butter and jam.

"What's with the happy homemaker? You haven't cooked in ages." She nibbled at a muffin and eyed me suspiciously as I flipped the omelet. Then her gaze widened. "You got lucky last night."

I grinned as I slid the omelet onto her plate. She cut it in half, pushing one of the halves onto my plate while I dumped the skillet in the sink and plopped into a seat across from her.

"I brought Devon to a construct."

She grimaced. "Was he mad?"

"He was a bit confused about why I chose for us to talk it out in a dream." I savored my first bite and washed it down with a swig of coffee. "We still have a lot to talk through, but we've formed a tentative peace."

"I think you did a bit more than talk."

I winked. "You know what they say about makeup sex."

She giggled. "I think I'll get a reminder this afternoon. Lucas is taking me to the city for a couple of nights."

We clinked our mugs together before focusing on the rest of breakfast. Everyone needed a few days to decompress, and I was thrilled Lucas was finding time for her. And while I felt good about where Devon and I left our own wacky relationship, I was a bit unsettled with how the cadre would deal with me.

"So, what will you be doing today?" Ginger picked up the dishes and rinsed them before stacking them in the dishwasher.

I followed behind her with the condiments, sliding a couple of them into the fridge. "Anna is restarting our study of the Houses, and Devon wants to reestablish a training schedule. He's serious about getting back to the mission."

"A routine will help with his mental fugue."

"I was thinking the same thing."

She bumped my hip and gave me a quick hug. "Hopefully, everyone has learned a valuable lesson that we're stronger working together than apart."

I snorted. "Something tells me the cadre might need more than a single lesson before it sticks. Sometimes they don't know as much as they think they do."

She sighed. "We can only work with what we've got. I'm going to take a nap and then a long bath. Lucas said he'd pick me up at three."

"Have a great time, and keep in touch. My transport to the manor will be here soon. I'll see you in a few days."

DEVON STRETCHED out on the sofa in his office, though it was currently Lyra's as long as she remained the leader of the House, which was why he didn't sit at the desk. He could have used the one in his bedroom, but he needed a change of scenery and had scheduled a private meeting with Lucas.

The blinds were open, and the mid-morning sun washed the room with a bright light that only improved his mood. He should be more upset with Cressa's continued stubbornness, but after their dreamwalk the previous night, he couldn't argue her logic. His sleep had been the deepest and most restful since the beast had been put to rest. And though he hadn't tested it, his mental state seemed clearer this morning.

He stared at his tablet. The first thing that morning, he'd written down everything he could remember of what Cressa had shared about the symbols on the medallion. If this Colantha Dupré was to be believed, there was a strong tie between vampire and dreamwalker. He'd never heard of such a thing in his younger days. After Lyra had her psychotic break, he'd stumbled across an old myth of dreamwalkers in his search for something to help her. The medallion made it all the more real...as if the reality of shared dreams wasn't enough.

Sergi hadn't found any background on Colantha. Was that because this was all some sort of hoax? A group of psychics playing games? Or was it possible the Council had hidden a devastating secret so deep that after centuries, with part of their history unknown to them, its simple existence could tear the vampire world apart? If he'd never heard of dreamwalkers in his five hundred years, than whatever occurred to wipe them from written history happened with a Council centuries ago, possibly before his father's time.

He refocused on the tablet and pulled up his task list for the mission, adding a note for further investigation into Colantha Dupré. This covert assignment would belong strictly to Sergi. If the meanings of the objects on the medallion were legitimate, this discovery would be highly sensitive information.

When the knock at the door came, he switched to his notes about the illusive book, *De første dage*. The title was Danish for "the first days" and had been cataloged at the Renaud Library. It was now missing, as was the museum's curator, Philipe Renaud.

"Morning." Lucas sounded chipper for the first time since Devon returned home. He assumed Ginger had something to do with that. "Can I get you another?"

He glanced at his empty cup of espresso. "Yes, thank you. Is the car on its way?"

Lucas glanced at his watch. "I sent Mateo with a second car as a backup for Jacques." He raised his voice over the sound of the espresso machine. "They should be on their way back."

Devon smiled, curious at what Cressa's mood would be like when she arrived. Either way, an hour or two of intense training should shake out any remaining irritation she had with him.

Lucas set the cups on the coffee table and dropped into the chair next to him. "It will be good to get back to a mission."

"Have you told Ginger?"

He shrugged. "I told her I had a job that might take me out of town for several days."

"It could be weeks or months."

Lucas sipped his espresso, refusing to meet Devon's gaze. "I've heard back from some old contacts of Philipe's. They're willing to meet, but until we know more, there's no reason to upset her."

Devon laughed. "Are you not giving her enough credit to be monogamous while you're gone, or have you become so smitten you've discovered you'll be the one struggling with a long-term separation?"

When a light blush touched his bodyguard's cheeks, Devon relented. "How confident are you with these contacts?"

Lucas opened his tablet and turned on the LCD above the hearth to allow Devon to see the list of names. There were twenty of them, and next to each name was a city.

"That's going to take some time."

The door opened, and Lyra stopped when she saw them. "I'm sorry. I didn't realize you had a meeting."

Devon held out his hand. "Come sit. I should have mentioned it. Old habits, I'm afraid. We're reviewing a task I'd like to send Lucas on, if it's all right with you."

She closed the door and sat next to Devon on the sofa, her gaze reviewing the names on the display. "I recognize some of them."

"Where from?"

"Father, I think. I don't remember meeting any of them, but I'm sure he mentioned them at least once or twice. It was a long time ago."

"My first step will be determining the last time any of them have seen Philipe." Lucas lifted his cup, and Lyra shook her head. "Maybe they can share some of the locations he used to haunt. Then I thought I'd ask them about the book and see if I get any flicker of a response. But I wanted your opinion and approval. Just asking about the book might be problematic. It could leak to the wrong vampires."

"What book is that?" Lyra asked.

Before Devon had a chance to answer, the door burst open. They turned to find Sergi standing in the doorway, his face pale. He shot a glance at Lyra before turning his glazed eyes back to Devon.

"There's been an accident."

~

THE SCENE of the accident was barely ten minutes away. So close to home, yet Devon wasn't able to prevent it.

A dozen of his vampires blocked the street. Whoever had done this selected a stretch of road with stands of fir trees on both sides. One small side street ran west to the point, a location popular with bird watchers and the occasional surfers. Cars, as few as there were on this residential street, were either asked to turn back, or vampires ushered the vehicle past the debris if they lived on the road.

"I've spoken with the SBPD." Sergi drove the sedan past two other cars. "They've agreed to let us handle this as long as the road is cleared in thirty minutes."

Devon lowered the window moments before the burnt husk of the car became visible. The acrid smoke clogged his senses, and he struggled to keep the beast down. He understood his beast's rage. Beneath his own anger, his heart clenched, and his breathing grew tight. She couldn't be in there.

The sedan hadn't stopped before Devon was out and marching across the blacktop, with Sergi rushing to keep up. Four vampires circled the remains, one at each corner of the vehicle.

"They were either sloppy or didn't have time." Sergi glanced around, then nodded at a vampire standing off to the side with two others. "The sedan was hit mid-section from the cross street. The fire started in the engine compartment, and we believe it was set rather than a result of the crash."

Devon glanced at the vampire approaching them. "What happened?" He kept his tone level, waiting to hear Mateo's report before making any judgment.

"We were about a block behind Jacques. There was no one following us. A semi pulled out in front of us, and we narrowly missed it before stopping. Shots were fired from the cab, pinning us down. Rafael was able to go around and take out the shooter, but it took time to move the semi. I called Jacques once the gunfire started. He acknowledged the warning before I lost connection."

"Did he survive?" Devon asked.

Sergi grimaced and nodded. "Half his body is burned. They gave him blood. He should be at the safe house now. The healer is on her way."

Fire was not a vampire's friend and was one of the worst ways to die. But if one survived, the healing process, while painful, was quicker than for a human and didn't leave scarring. The restorative powers of fresh blood and healing herbs would repair the skin. Jacques would be out of commission until he healed. Which, with the amount of flesh burned, would be about two weeks.

Bella would be a mess over this and was probably already at his side.

He took a deep breath and moved toward the vehicle, terrified of what else might be in the scorched remains. When he grew closer, he breathed a sigh that the back passenger seat wasn't as badly burned. He was six feet away when he spotted Cressa's backpack. When he noticed how singed it was, he was seized by an uncontrollable rage.

The beast roared. And his chest ached. The beast seemed to be shaking his ribs like bars to a jail cell, demanding release.

He dropped to his knees as if someone had rammed a sledgehammer into the side of his head. Sergi was by his side, but he held out an arm to stop him. The pain was excruciating, as if his brain was swelling inside his skull with nowhere to go, ready to burst through.

He grasped his head with both hands, the pressure continuing to build. Then, with one last push, there was a sound like the popping of a balloon.

All was quiet, and fresh air filled his lungs. He blinked several times.

Sergi was on one knee; his brows squeezed, a hand resting on Devon's shoulder.

He stared at him in wonder, which made Sergi's forehead wrinkle more. He couldn't explain it, but his mind had cleared. It was as if all this time, he'd been struggling to breathe, then suddenly, out of nowhere, someone flipped a switch, and the bag over his head vanished. Instead of a slow stream of thoughts returning, it was a raging flood, erasing his previous foggy mental state and replacing it with complete clarity.

For now, he pushed the staggering experience aside and rose to his feet, stepping next to the open door of the back passenger seats. They were black with soot and wet from the foam of fire extinguishers. Bits of burnt leather had curled from the heat, and one of the windows had shattered, but the rear half of the vehicle hadn't burned.

"This is similar to another accident." Sergi stuck his head in as he surveyed what was left. "At least from the pictures I've seen."

"Lyra won't take this well." Devon glanced around, searching for anything that might have been missed. "I'd like the healer to meet us at the manor when she's done with Jacques. Bella can stay with him for now."

"What are you thinking?"

His thought was that the only thing that kept the beast at bay was that Cressa was still alive. She wouldn't have had time to wander away on her own with Mateo close enough to have put out the fire. The driver of the second car was also missing.

His laugh was harsh and full of menace. "There's only one answer. Cressa's been taken. And there's no question as to who took her."

"Lorenzo."

"And this time, he's gone too far."

Chapter Two

Devon raced up the steps of the manor, the front door opening like magic as he stormed through. The vampire behind the door kept their head down, so he couldn't be sure who it was, but it was clear that everyone had heard the news. Which had likely already spread to Oasis. "Where are the cadre?"

Sergi kept pace. "Simone is on her way. She should arrive in twenty minutes. Lucas is in your office. Bella is with Jacques."

Rage filled him, and he pushed it down. Not all of it. The beast wouldn't let him extinguish it all. It rode just under the surface—not pushing—but not relenting. He found it somewhat comforting. As if he wasn't alone with his fear.

Lucas was at the bar, typing into his tablet while speaking low. He was on his headset, gathering intel. He glanced up when Devon entered but didn't stop his conversation, only nodding and holding up a finger.

Devon paced behind his desk. "Did anyone call Decker?"

Before answering, Sergi glanced at Lucas, who, even as he continued his conversation, shook his head. "No."

"See if he has time to stop by."

Lucas finished his call, picked up his tablet, and took one of the chairs that surrounded Devon's desk.

"Where's Lyra?"

"She's in her room." Lucas glanced at Sergi, who had his head down, scrolling through his tablet. "She went there once news came that Jacques was taken to the safe house."

"Is the healer here?"

"She left a short time ago."

"Already?" Sergi piped in.

Lucas appeared paler than normal. "She spent five minutes with Lyra then left, complaining about wasting her time for someone who clearly doesn't want her help." When Devon sighed with exasperation, Lucas continued. "She left a few vials." He nodded toward the bar where a small box sat. "Then she returned to the safe house. Do you want me to call Bella in?"

Devon shook his head. Bella wouldn't be able to concentrate until she knew Jacques was recovering, and until they had more information she might as well provide as much comfort as she could. "She can stay there until she's needed."

He strode to the door. "Gather as much information as you can and notify me when Simone arrives." He took the stairs two at a time until he reached the third floor. Two guards were at Lyra's door. Standard protocol when a member of the House was attacked.

He paused, wishing he'd taken the time to think this through more. Lyra must be aware enough if she kicked the healer out. Had she returned to her manic state? She had come so far in the last few weeks. If Lorenzo's attack had set her back, Devon wasn't sure he'd be able to contain the beast.

It had been put away, settled, yet it hovered as if it knew there were scores to settle. The beast held affection for Cressa, and until she was home, it would remain close to the surface. He would need blood to keep it at bay.

He shook off his concerns for Cressa and refocused on the

matter at hand. The guards knocked on the door as he approached. No answer. He waited, deciding whether to knock again or just go in.

"Stop fretting and come in, brother."

He lifted a brow. Apparently not manic.

He closed the door behind him and took tentative steps until he could peer around the divider to glimpse the main room. Clothes were strewn everywhere, and three easels were positioned in front of the windows, each facing a different part of the backyard.

Lyra stood at the third easel, positioned to face the ocean. She wore a black, full-body, sleeveless leotard with a paint-stained apron tied around her waist. Sun streaked across the room, adding a touch of gold to the scene. The canvas was one of her larger ones, and it was smeared in broad red strokes. A shadowed figure stood just off-center, its gender undetermined. She dropped her paintbrush and picked up another. This one was heavy with blue paint, and she added short bursts at various spots, ending with long trails like the tail of a comet.

He watched her until she set the brush down then wiped her hands on her apron.

"Is she alive?" Lyra stared out the window.

"As far as I know. She wasn't at the scene, and the fire hadn't reached the passenger area."

She took a huge breath and let it out. "Lorenzo."

It wasn't a question, but he responded anyway. "That's my opinion. The sedan was rammed from the side. A semi blocked the escort car."

"How is Jacques?"

"The healer and Bella are with him. He should make a full recovery in a couple of weeks."

She nodded and rubbed her hands together—over and over. "I understand why you asked Madame Saldano to visit, but she shouldn't have left Jacques."

"The request was to see you after she was finished with Jacques."

She nodded.

"How are you, sister?"

A long moment passed. She was either unsure of her answer or didn't know how to put it into words. He couldn't begin to imagine what was going through her head.

Then her arm swung out and the canvas she'd been working on flew across the room, the easel crashing to the ground. She turned to him, and her eyes glowed with blue ice. Her body visibly shook, and he almost took a step back.

"I'm filled with rage. It's all I can do to keep the beast at bay."

The breath he'd been holding rushed out, and he smiled.

"You find this humorous?"

He shook his head. "I'm relieved."

She opened her mouth and then shut it. Her return smile settled his own beast. "You were worried I'd lost it and had returned to my other self."

He nodded. "Can you blame me?"

"Of course, not. But that time is behind me. I can't say the voices have stopped. They've been stronger since we were told of the accident, but the painting has helped."

"Do you feel good enough to join us?"

She glanced at the canvas that lay broken against the wall. "Perhaps not yet."

He chuckled and went to her, grabbing her shoulders and kissing her forehead. "I'm sending a blood donor up. Be gentle."

Devon raced down the stairs, eager to begin the investigation and determine where Lorenzo had taken Cressa. He had a good idea where it was, and if it were true, they would have one helluva time getting her back. Not without inside help, though he had an idea about that as well.

He was a few steps from the office when Bella appeared.

"What are you doing here?" He'd expected her to remain at Jacques's side.

"Sergi called a meeting." She would have brushed past him if he hadn't held out an arm to stop her.

"He wasn't supposed to call you. I assumed you'd want to be with Jacques."

"I called him, and Jacques is sleeping. The healer gave him enough sedatives to knock out an elephant."

"That doesn't mean you can't stay with him."

Her dark-brown eyes lit with fire and the inner glow of her beast. "I won't be left out of this. Lorenzo needs to pay."

He was surrounded by raging women...and he hadn't even seen Simone yet. "You won't be left out. I wanted to give you time."

She blew out a breath and stared at the wall to the left of him. Bella rarely showed her emotions, and it must be killing her not being able to hold them in now.

"Let's go." He pushed past her and marched into his office.

Everyone was there, including Simone. Her face was a blank canvas. If she was dealing with emotions, it was impossible to tell.

He dropped into his chair behind the desk. In all rights, he should have left it empty should Lyra wish to join, but now wasn't the time to worry about etiquette.

"From this point on, our only mission is recovering Cressa. Except for where we have previous commitments, all our resources will be to that end. The first order of business is to have more blood donors brought in from Oasis. Jacques will need a constant supply for the next few days, and I want the rest of us fed regularly."

"I'll take care of that." Simone opened her tablet. It was rare for her to take notes during a meeting, and it gave Devon an inkling of the inner turmoil she kept hidden.

"What do we have so far?" He turned to Sergi.

"The cars and semi have been taken to the warehouse for processing, but we've already traced the car the kidnappers used to an elderly couple who lives on the south side of town. They reported it stolen early this morning."

"Most likely it was taken last night while they slept." Lucas's leg bounced with nervous energy. "Mateo will ensure everything is dusted for fingerprints, but I doubt any were left."

"I agree." Sergi scrolled through a report on his tablet. "The semi doesn't seem to have an owner that we can find. It was hot-wired, so we'll check with SBPD and see if anyone has reported it stolen."

"They'll be dead ends." Devon picked up the white crystal from his desk and tossed it back and forth. "I'm declaring a level three security alert with security details rotated every four hours. I don't think Lorenzo will do anything rash after this attack, but we'd be fools not to be prepared."

Sergi nodded. "Do we suspect Lorenzo is aware Cressa is a dreamwalker?"

Devon took a moment to consider it. Lorenzo had only seen Cressa a handful of times, and nothing recently. "No. I think his intention was two-fold. He believes her to be my Blood Ward and suspects we have a deeper relationship. He wanted to take that from me in addition to proving he can strike a blow at the House whenever he wants."

"We should hit back hard and fast." Bella was pacing, as was her usual style. He understood her need for immediate action.

"No. We'll stay silent on this." When it looked like she would object, he lifted a hand. "He'll expect me to do something rash. I think he questions my stability after the Poppy. I need to prove him wrong. That doesn't mean we won't poke at him, and I'd appreciate your opinion on the best way to do that, but I want it to be nothing more than an irritating distraction. I want him guessing as to whether it's me or not.

"Before we can do that, I need a full report on his latest activities, any information on who he's met with since the week before Boretsky's murder and when I was dosed with the Poppy. Any scrap of data, even if it appears mundane, I want to know about. Reach out to your normal contacts. We'll meet again after dinner."

"How's Lyra?" Sergi asked.

"Raging. I sent a donor up to settle her beast."

"That's good." Bella stopped near the coffee bar but did nothing more than play with the dials on the espresso machine. "It's better than the alternative."

"Agreed." Devon set the crystal on the desk, nudging it several times until he felt it was in the right position. "And I don't want anyone acting any differently around her. She is still the leader of this House." He glanced at each of them, waiting until they nodded.

"What about Ginger?" Lucas asked. "She should be brought to the manor."

Devon rubbed his face. How could he have missed that? Cressa would be so angry he hadn't thought of her friend. "Of course. Do you want me to talk to her?"

Lucas shook his head. "I'd like to drive over to the condo and tell her. We had plans to go to the city so she'll be expecting me and is already packed."

"As if she would pack for the city like she would for spending time here." Bella's chiding was a welcome sound. Even in the face of adversity, he could depend on the cadre to remain calm and settled.

Lucas's expression shifted as he considered her statement, and a slight blush touched his cheeks, finally adding some color to them. "I guess we'll need time for her to repack, and then I'll bring her back here."

"Agreed. That's all I have for now."

Bella was out the door before the others stood. When they filed out the door, Devon called out for Simone.

"Can you stay a minute?"

She kept her back to him for a long moment before nodding and turning around to take a seat in front of his desk. Her fingernails tapped a steady beat on her tablet, but she never glanced up.

He waited until the last of the cadre had closed the door behind them. "You were quiet during the meeting."

"You didn't need me to pat your back." Her head tilted a fraction of an inch. "You seem different. Better. You're not second-guessing yourself or looking to Sergi for approval."

He grimaced. "Was it that bad?"

She let the thought of a laugh flutter her lips. "It's good to have you back. Have you fed recently?"

He swiveled around to stare out the window. From his vantage point, he could see a portion of the sycamore tree. "I dreamwalked with her last night. It was a construct. That's what she calls these scenes, worlds... Holy hell, I don't know what they are. But it was something she'd created on her own."

"She hasn't done that before?"

"I don't think so. She dreamed of the garden at Oasis before she ever saw it, but I think that was a prescient dream. She didn't even know what she was at the time. This was different. It was a combination of different places she'd been with disparate objects."

"Something she learned while in New Orleans?"

He nodded. "She was so proud of herself. We talked for some time, and after she closed the construct, I had the best sleep I've had since putting the beast away. I felt better this morning, but there was still a haze I couldn't quite get past, although I wasn't aware of it at the time. I just knew I wasn't a hundred percent.

"When I was at the accident scene, I couldn't stop staring at the burnt husk of the sedan. I hadn't been told yet of what happened to the passengers or how little the passenger seats had been burned. I was filled with such rage. I got this blinding headache like my brain was a balloon and something was filling it with air. The pressure was so intense, I thought my head would explode."

He stopped, remembering the moment as if he was still on his knees in the middle of the street with Sergi's hand on his shoulder. Simone didn't say anything, and the silence was comforting.

"It's difficult to explain. I'm not positive about what happened. But when I didn't think I could take any more, and the edges of my sight became shadowed, I thought I'd pass out, and then there was a pop. Like someone or something burst the balloon, and just like that—" He snapped his fingers and swiveled around to Simone. "Instant clarity. Like the world was reborn again, and all my senses increased at once—smell, sight, hearing."

He almost laughed at her dumbfounded expression. "I know what that sounds like, but it's what happened."

"I don't believe we know nearly enough about Cressa's powers or what her blood can do." Simone leaned back in the chair and rubbed her face with both hands. "I haven't been a very good friend to her lately."

"You were focused on caring for the House."

"It was more than that. I was relieved when Sergi took her to New Orleans. But she was the one who questioned why Lyra wasn't considered to be the next leader of the House."

That surprised him. No one had mentioned it, and he'd never thought to ask after his ordeal, assuming Anna or Lucas had reviewed the succession laws. He chuckled. "After all her complaining about Anna's lessons."

Simone grinned. "She learns fast, even when she's distracted."

Silence descended, and Devon gave her time. But as time passed, and she didn't say anything more, he gave her a gentle prod. "It's just me, Simone. No judgment here. From everything Lyra and the cadre have shared with me, you've been an exceptional leader the last couple of weeks."

She shook her head. "I disregarded one of our most valuable

assets. I tried to tuck her away so I wouldn't have to deal with her outrageous ideas."

"And you learned firsthand that she couldn't be controlled."

She nodded. "I knew she was scared and worried for you. Sergi was concerned about her interest in the beast."

"As was I."

She growled, and the tips of her fangs dropped. "That day she went to the mill to offer the beast her blood, she sneaked out of her room the evening before and escaped past all the guards."

He wouldn't have expected any less from his talented little thief. "We should have her added to our security reviews."

"I want her to do more than that. I want to run drills as she discovers ways around our security." She bent her head. "I want her to feel more welcome."

Devon rose and took the chair next to Simone, grasping her hands. She tried to pull away, but he held firm. "I know she tests you. But I also know she considers you a friend. I'm aware how difficult that is for you, and this next part will be even harder." He waited until she looked him in the eyes. "She felt abandoned by the cadre." He squeezed her hands when she tensed. "There's nothing to do about that now."

Her tawny eyes glowed with the bright yellow of her beast. "But there is. We will get her back. We'll prove to her that she's one of us. That she belongs to the Family of House Trelane."

His smile was one of his more wicked ones. "And we'll use all our resources, whatever it takes, to do just that."

Chapter Three

DEVON'S EYES SNAPPED OPEN. Long shadows crossed the room. It was late afternoon, and he'd been dreaming, but it had been an old dream. He'd been with Cressa in his private garden at Oasis. It was one of their first dreams. He'd hoped she might reach out to him from wherever she was, but she hadn't.

He popped up.

Had she been wearing her medallion when she was taken? If so, Lorenzo would have certainly discovered it. With everything that had happened while the beast consumed him, he'd forgotten about Lorenzo's search for the necklace. Devon told the cadre Lorenzo had no idea Cressa could be a dreamwalker. But what if Cressa had been wearing the medallion that morning?

He jumped from the bed and dressed quickly. Lucas should be back by now with Ginger. He raced down the stairs. Cressa's backpack had been left at the accident site. An oversight in the kidnappers' rush to leave? It was hard to say.

He found Sergi in his security office, and the stench of burnt material permeated the room.

Sergi glanced up. "I thought you were resting."

"I was." He looked around the office. "Where's Cressa's backpack?"

Sergi nodded toward the far corner where the pack sat on the wood floor, most likely so it wouldn't damage the oriental rug. It was stained with soot and foam from the extinguisher. Devon would buy her a new one.

"Have you searched through it yet?"

"I was waiting for you." Sergi stood and moved to a bookcase. The top half held shelves filled with various books on historic battles, technical manuals, and the complete set of House security protocols. The bottom half was cabinets and drawers. In the middle, there was a thin drawer that ran the length of the bookcase. When Sergi pulled it open, legs automatically dropped to form a table. He opened another drawer and pulled out a laminated board that he placed on top of the table, then waved for Devon to bring the backpack.

Devon couldn't fault his security chief for his predilection for cleanliness and order. But sometimes he had to wonder. He set the backpack on the covered table while Sergi pulled on latex gloves.

"Do you think she'll mind?" Sergi asked.

"Probably, but she'll also understand."

Sergi began with the main compartment and laid out her tablet, a notebook, a set of workout clothes, and a dogeared paperback mystery novel. Sergi set the tablet aside. No doubt he'd go through it. Then he flipped through the notebook.

"It's not a diary, but it seems to be written like one."

Devon swiped it from him. "I'll take a look."

Sergi didn't smile, but it was close for someone who didn't do it often. He opened the smaller compartment pulling out lipstick, Chapstick, a comb, two pens, a pencil, a card key, and her phone.

"Is that all?" Devon picked up the phone and put it in his pocket.

Sergi checked the bag again, feeling along the fabric in case she'd added hidden pockets. "That's all."

"She travels light."

"Most thieves do."

"Excellent point."

"What were you looking for? I have a feeling it's not anything we've found here."

"Her medallion."

"Ah. Maybe she was wearing it."

"I hope not. Is Ginger here?"

He nodded as he returned all the items—minus the tablet, notebook, and phone—to the pack. "She arrived a couple of hours ago."

"How is she?"

"I can only tell you what Lucas reported. She won't allow anyone but him in her room, and she refuses to come out."

Devon lifted a brow. The two of them were supposed to leave for San Francisco for a well-deserved weekend. Even if he didn't require Lucas to assist in Cressa's return, there wasn't a chance Ginger would go anywhere with Cressa missing. He didn't know Ginger as well as he should, and he couldn't fathom how she was taking the news.

Sergi continued to provide Lucas's report. "One minute she's inconsolable and unable to stop crying. The next she's in a terrible rage throwing things and stomping around the room vowing vengeance."

Devon laughed despite the situation. He might not know her that well, but Sergi's interpretation of Lucas's report sounded just like Ginger. He picked up the notebook and strode to the door but stopped. "Have a sedan brought around. One from the motor pool."

Sergi considered the request then nodded. "Do you want company?"

"Lucas will be enough and most likely the only one that can keep Ginger calm."

BEFORE GOING to Ginger's room, Devon retreated to his own and dropped onto the sofa in front of the cold hearth. He opened the first page of the notebook. The words were something you'd find in a diary, just like Sergi said. He read a page then snapped the book closed, feeling like a voyeur. As House leader, he had every right to read the notebook, if only to see if Cressa had been some-place or mentioned someone that might provide a clue to her whereabouts. But she could have written things she'd prefer he didn't read, and he had to respect her privacy—even now. Maybe it was best for Sergi to have a look... But then a better solution came to mind, and he set the notebook on the coffee table.

He turned on the phone. No voice messages. No text messages. He scrolled through her contacts. After his name, Ginger's, and each member of the cadre, the list was short—Harlow, Trudy, The Wolf, April, and her mother. It was an odd list of people, and he pushed down the irrational jealousy that had overtaken him when he saw Remus's personal number. But hadn't he given Remus her number in case of an emergency? It still rankled.

He stared at the phone numbers. Should he call her mother? He had nothing to share other than to add a new worry after the recent death of her husband, and preferring to wait before contacting Harlow, he dropped the phone on the coffee table. He picked up the notebook and strolled down the hall to Ginger's room.

He tapped once but didn't wait long as Lucas opened the door before the echo of the knock subsided.

"We've been expecting you." He stepped back and glanced at Ginger, who was on the sofa gripping a blanket that had been wrapped around her shoulders.

Her face was tear-streaked, and her mascara had smudged, giving her a sultry exotic look. Countered against the tears that began again, she looked like a terrified Siamese cat. If you pushed too hard the claws would come out.

"I'm sorry, Ginger. It's my fault for not protecting her better. I should have never allowed her to leave the mansion."

She stared at him. The only change was her eyes. They were truly the doorway to the soul. Several emotions flickered in them, moving at breakneck speeds—grief, fear, anger... No, not anger—rage. A dangerous combination.

He sat in a chair next to the couch. One minute she was sitting near him, the next she was on the arm of his chair, her arms circled around his shoulders.

"This isn't your fault. You must feel ten times worse than me. And ten times angrier."

She held him, her head bent to rest on his shoulder. This frail young woman, who had to be terrified for her best friend, was comforting him. He glanced up at Lucas, who didn't seem to find Ginger's behavior strange.

After a moment, she returned to the sofa and curled up in her blanket. "Do we know for sure it was Lorenzo?"

"No specific proof, and there probably never will be. The accident was similar to the one my parents died in, but the fire hadn't reached the passenger section by the time our security arrived to douse the flames."

"How's Jacques?"

Lucas would have told her, but she seemed to have a script of her own. And if that's what it took to keep her feet on the ground and head in the game, he'd take her lead.

"Jacques will have a difficult two weeks, but the healer is staying at the safe house, and I'm sure Bella will be by his side whenever she's not working." He fingered the notebook in his lap, then handed it to her. "This was in Cressa's backpack. I think it best if you read it. I'd like to know if there's any information that might help us. It doesn't matter how insignificant it might seem."

She ran a hand over it. "Thank you. I'll read it tonight." She turned silent and seemed to shrink into the sofa. Whatever she'd wanted to say or learn had been fulfilled, and the adrenaline that had kept her going was receding.

"I slept for a couple of hours this afternoon." Devon watched her expression.

She didn't seem to understand why he was sharing the information, but then her gaze went wide. "Did she bring you into a dream?"

"No. And if she were being held against her will, I would think she would at least try."

"What does that mean?" Her eyes took on that look that said she might be barely holding it together.

"You think she's been mesmerized." Lucas sat next to Ginger and put an arm around her.

Devon nodded. "It makes sense. Cressa wouldn't go willingly and wouldn't be a meek captive. Even if she'd decided to be compliant until she could find a way out, she'd try to contact me."

"So she either doesn't have her medallion, or she might not be aware she's a dreamwalker." Ginger's tone was calmer. "But she was able to contact you before without the necklace."

"Yes. When her emotions were high, specifically her anger."

"We need to go back to the condo." Ginger jumped up and grabbed her purse. "If she wasn't wearing the necklace, then there's only one place it could be."

"Do you know why it wouldn't be in her backpack?"

She was already at the door when she swung around. "From what she told me of her visit with Colantha, she was either to wear it or keep it in a safe place. She wouldn't consider her backpack safe."

Devon rose with Lucas. "The car's waiting out front."

❧

A VAMPIRE GREETED them at the door to Ginger and Cressa's condo.

"Hello, Rafael. I wasn't expecting to see you here." Devon hadn't seen anyone downstairs and had assumed Sergi canceled the security teams.

"Sergi asked for the door to be guarded."

"Place discreet monitors inside and out and then take a couple of days off. You have nothing to prove. No one could have predicted the accident."

Rafael's smile never reached his eyes. "Yes, Father."

Devon patted his shoulder. "Find a donor and spend some time with Jacques. I understand from Bella he's been asking for you."

"Thank you. I'd like that."

Devon waited while Ginger passed the card key over the screen. "I appreciate the precautions." She took a deep breath before opening the door.

His first surprise was the spotless condition of the living space. He hadn't expected that, considering how messy Ginger seemed to prefer her room. He must have appeared shocked because Ginger smirked at him.

"I woke up this morning to find Cressa making breakfast, and she'd cleaned the entire place." She dropped her purse on a table and headed down the hall. "Follow me."

She led them to the bedroom on the right. It had been difficult to find a condo with two master suites, but Lucas had suggested it so the women wouldn't fuss over who got a room with a bathroom. Ginger would have felt obligated to let Cressa have the larger room, even though she'd be spending the majority of her time at the manor. Devon had agreed it made sense.

"We each have a hidey-hole." Ginger walked straight to the closet.

"There's a safe in each of the rooms."

Lucas laughed. "I remember Cressa saying safes weren't safe enough for the really important things."

Ginger's return laughter echoed from the closet. "So typical for a safecracker."

Devon shook his head. "What magical place did our thief find?" He expected she'd find a spot under a floorboard and was surprised when Ginger grabbed a footstool and, groaning, shoved the safe that rested on the third shelf six inches to the right. It would have taken some muscle to do that.

The back wall of the closet was covered with strips of cedar planking. It gave the room a pleasant woodsy smell and was meant to keep moths away. Ginger tapped along the wood until she hit a section that sounded hollow. She pulled on a corner and the cedar strip peeled away.

"When did she have that put in?" Devon asked.

"The first week we moved in. She had one put in both of our closets."

"Smart. Who would think to look *behind* the safe for the good stuff?" Lucas seemed in awe, and Devon was right there with him.

Never underestimate the mind of a thief.

Ginger brought out a long, slim metal box. He was surprised Cressa wouldn't require a key, then shook his head when Ginger pulled a necklace out from under her blouse that held several charms. One was a tiny key. She opened the box and peered inside. He held his breath as she smiled, stuck her hand in, and lifted the object up so everyone could see it.

Another key.

"You're kidding, right?" He wasn't sure why he asked the question out loud and felt the idiot when Ginger rolled her eyes.

"In the mood to visit a laundromat?"

Twenty minutes later, Devon was closing in on the Hollows, a less reputable neighborhood in Santiga Bay. It was originally the home of the wealthy, but time had taken its toll and the rich had moved out decades ago, leaving behind the houses that once upon a time were considered mansions. "I don't understand the runaround."

"It's not much of a runaround for a paranoid person." Lucas stared out the window from the backseat. "We'll probably find another clue at this place."

Ginger snickered, but her face was gaunt. It had only been hours since the accident, and Cressa's disappearance was already taking a toll. He'd have Simone set up a rigid schedule of training and regular meals for her. She needed to stay busy because she wasn't going to find quick closure.

He reached across the middle console and took her hand. "You have to prepare yourself for a long recovery plan. This won't be fixed in a couple of days. Lorenzo won't harm her. It's not the point of his message. He's hoping to turn her against me. If he's mesmerizing her, it will take some time before it gets to a point where it will be extremely difficult to reverse."

Her face paled. He'd gone too far and knew it but hadn't been able to stop.

"How long?" Her words were nothing more than a whisper.

"Two weeks. You need to be strong for her."

Quiet descended for barely a minute before she yelled, "Stop here!"

She pointed to a second-rate laundromat. Young men loitered in the parking lot, most likely selling drugs. Across the street, a group of six men leaned against the wall of a mom-and-pop grocery store. They eyed the sedan coolly.

Devon parked in front of the laundromat, and Lucas jumped out to open Ginger's door.

"Stay with the sedan." Devon tossed him the keys.

Lucas leaned against the car and stared at the men. They attempted a look of intimidation until Lucas flashed his fangs. The group dispersed.

Devon never got tired of that reaction. While most humans

knew nothing of vampires, it was different in the Hollows where vampires, shifters, and humans mingled.

Ginger led the way, seemingly unafraid of the men in the neighborhood, and paused to wave at one of them who returned her wave with a nod and a smile. She pushed open the door of the laundromat and waltzed inside.

A dark-skinned man the size of a small bus turned around, and she ran to him, her sobs easily heard over the sounds of washing machines and dryers. He caught her as she launched herself at him.

"They took Cressa. She's gone. We need to get her back." It came out in a rush of breath that could only come from someone desperate.

The man held her for a bit, eyed Devon, then set her down. "Slow down, girl. What do you mean they took her?" He turned to Devon.

"She was taken this morning." Devon leaned against a washer and quickly scanned the room for security monitors. There were several. "Someone rammed into her transport and then tried to set it on fire. My driver sustained serious injuries, but Cressa was gone." He didn't see a reason not to be honest with the man. They might need something from him someday, and Cressa would be upset if he weren't polite.

"You know who took her?"

"Yes."

The big man nodded and glanced down at Ginger. He was gentle as he ran a large beefy finger down her cheek. "It will work out. But you tell me what you need."

She wiped her eyes and gave Devon a quick glance. "Right now we just need access to Cressa's box. I have the key." She fiddled with her necklace. "Oh, this is Devon. Devon, Bulldog."

The two eyed each other, and then Bulldog nodded and unlocked a door to another room.

"You know the rules. Ten minutes. No exceptions."

"Understood." She entered first, and Devon followed behind.

When the door closed behind them, Devon took note of the additional security monitors and then the rows of boxes that filled the walls. Impressive diversification for a drug lord.

Ginger went straight to a box without bothering to check the numbers and used Cressa's key to unlock it. She placed the metal box on the table but didn't open it. When she glanced up at Devon, her eyes were shiny.

"I know the two of you have had a troubled week that strained your relationship." She lifted her hand when he opened his mouth. "That's behind you now. I just wanted to say that this morning when I woke up, she was the happiest I'd seen her in a long time. She felt good about the dream she pulled you into last night." Her cheeks turned a lovely shade of pink, and Devon understood exactly how much these two shared. "She wanted us to move to Oasis."

If he had a chair, he'd have fallen into it. Instead, he leaned against the table. "She never mentioned it."

"She knew she was stretching your security by being at the condo, but she still needed some space. Oasis seemed like the perfect compromise."

"It would have been." His eyes burned, and he turned away to stare at the wall of boxes. That compromise had been for him, and it meant the world that she wanted to be at Oasis. He rubbed his face and spun around. "Let's see if she left us a path to find her."

Ginger took a huge breath and opened the lid. "She used to keep this in a safe deposit box at a bank at City Center, but once you set us up in the condo, she decided to move her treasures back to the Hollows. She never said why, but I think she wanted to keep a connection to this neighborhood."

She pulled out a cigar box covered with a patchwork of a child's colorful drawings and placed it on the table. It was filled with what looked like Cressa's childhood treasures. He studied each item Ginger withdrew—pieces of colored ribbons, a seashell, a bead bracelet, other cheap trinkets that would only mean something to Cressa, and a short stack of envelopes addressed to her. The return address was the same but with her mother's name as the sender. They had their own difficult relationship.

After everything had been removed, the only thing left was a ring box. Ginger's fingers shook as she lifted the lid. They both stared down and simultaneously sighed.

The medallion and silver chain lay curled up in the soft velvet lining.

Chapter Four

DEVON STARED AT THE MEDALLION. It was a cool evening and all the windows in his bedroom were opened, yet a low fire burned, casting an orange glow over the necklace.

"Are you going to stare at it all evening or do something with it?" Lyra was wrapped in a thick blanket on the sofa next to his chair, her feet tucked under her. Her tight grasp on the wineglass stem was the only indication of her stress.

"Is the healer on call?"

"She's still at the safe house with Jacques." She twirled her glass in a slow circle, took a sip, then twirled it again. "I know you've recently recovered from a great mental strain. It's not difficult to understand your hesitancy. The medallion is very strong. If you prefer, I can try to reach her."

"No." He gave her a small smile. "I need to do this."

She nodded and turned her attention to the fire. "You try first. I'll call Madame Saldano at the first sign of trouble after I've ripped the medallion from your neck. But if nothing happens, I insist on giving it a try."

"That seems fair." He wasn't exactly scared to put it on, though he had no idea what would happen if the medallion sensed a vampire or someone completely untrained. He was nervous about what he'd find if he connected with Cressa. She had to be okay. If Lorenzo had wanted her dead, they would have found her body in the wreckage.

He set down his glass of single malt and picked up the medallion. "I need to be asleep, right?"

"Not necessarily. A meditative state should be sufficient." She set down her wine and stood, letting the blanket drop to the floor. "Get up." He stood, and she pulled his chair around so it directly faced the fire. "Sit down, and then put on the necklace."

He drained his glass then sat down.

"Is the necklace touching your skin?"

"Yes."

"Start with staring at the flames. Let your mind drift until the flames become out of focus, and then close your eyes."

He did as she asked as her fingers slowly massaged his neck and shoulders. The tension drained away as the fire blurred, and he closed his eyes. The gentle touch stopped, and he let his mind drift. Simone had taught him the basic tenets of meditation, though he rarely used the practice. But now her guidance returned, and he flowed with where his mind took him.

He stood in the garden at Oasis. He raced to the grotto, but Cressa wasn't there. He walked the entire garden before something pulled him toward the lake. A shadow of a person sat at the small knoll and watched the ducks come to rest on the water for the evening.

"Cressa?"

The figure turned its head then disappeared like mist in the sun.

"Cressa!"

He turned in a circle, arms outstretched, but there was no one there. Just the cool evening breeze and the sound of a crackling fire.

His eyes popped open. "Dammit."

"What?" Lyra sounded worried.

He looked around, expecting someone else to be in his room, but it was only his sister.

"What happened?" Her tone was more demanding.

"Nothing. I thought I saw her, or a memory of her. But it only lasted a few seconds."

"Try again."

He did. But it was only him in the garden and then by the lake. He shook it away and took off the necklace, tossing it on the table.

"Change places with me."

~

LYRA PICKED up the medallion and pulled the necklace over her head. She sat in the chair and followed the same instructions she'd given Devon. Well-practiced at meditation, she fell easily into a trance.

She was in her room upstairs and was painting. It was an island scene with lush vegetation and tall palm trees. The sand was a pure white and along the border of the jungle, a lone sycamore tree, completely out of place in the tropical scene, stretched its branches to the heavens. A picnic basket was on a checkered blanket, and instead of the man she usually painted, the light image of Cressa sat cross-legged next to it. Her image was as transparent as a ghost. She picked the flowers that appeared next to the blanket—rose bushes filled with dark blood-red blossoms.

Lyra glanced around, but there was no one else in the room. Without thinking, she called out.

"Cressa!"

For a moment, she thought the figure on the blanket looked up, but it was so quick it might have been her imagination. Then the faint outline of the woman rose. She picked up a pair of sandals and walked toward the jungle until she disappeared.

Lyra came out of the mediation slower than Devon.

"Well. Did you see her?"

"It was the strangest thing. I was in my room painting." She moved to the sofa where Devon sat and picked up the blanket to sit next to him. She described the dream in detail, then snuggled into him.

He put an arm around her. "We need to find another way."

"You know what you need to do."

"There's no guarantee she'll see me."

"It's worth the time. There's nothing else for you to do while the cadre completes their investigation."

"Thank you for taking the risk of putting the medallion on."

Lyra took the necklace off and laid it on the table. "I've worn it before, but I have to admit I was concerned who might greet me. I purposely focused on my room. Cressa and I have had the most wonderful talks there."

They stared at the fire for some time. Lyra thought he might have fallen asleep, but then he released a long sigh. She patted his leg, knowing he'd come to the right decision.

He hugged her close and kissed her temple. "I'll leave for New Orleans in the morning."

DEVON JOGGED down the stairs and dropped his travel bag in the foyer. He was on his way to the office when the front door burst open. He spun around to find Decker racing in.

"Sorry. I got tied up." Deep creases marred Decker's forehead, and dark circles punctuated his haggard look. For the last month, he'd been showing up late to everything. It wasn't like him.

"Are you getting enough sleep?" Devon studied the shifter. He'd been gaining weight but now seemed to be losing it again. Light tremors shook his hands.

"Plenty."

When the shifter grew closer, he stank of cigarettes. Then Devon understood.

"Are you going cold turkey or just slowing down?"

"Both, depending on the day."

"It's not easy when you own a bar."

"Tell me about it. I've moved most of my office home, and I don't keep any alcohol there. Sabrina keeps me solid at the club. I just have to find my balance again."

"What brought this on?"

Decker gave Devon a long look, his eyes burning with old wounds. "When I heard about the accident."

He nodded. "It's only been a day."

Decker ran a hand through this hair, leaving it looking even more disheveled. "Maybe it's been since the beast incident. I'd already been cutting back then."

Devon laid a hand on the man's shoulder. "You don't have to explain it to me. Lorenzo's days are numbered. He just doesn't know it yet." His friend wasn't just having problems sleeping; he was remembering, and that never bode well. "Let's get this done. They're already prepping the plane."

When they strode into the office, everyone was already there. Lyra sat at his desk with the cadre circling it. Devon walked to the bar, but not before stopping to lay a hand on Bella's shoulder. She leaned her cheek against it while grasping his fingers, where she placed a light kiss.

He dropped onto a stool as Decker pulled out the other one, leaning back, his elbows resting on the bar.

Lyra's brow rose when she glanced at Decker, worry in her gaze, but it disappeared when her focus dropped to the paper in front of her. "We've been going over our security plans again. With you and Sergi in New Orleans for a couple of days, Simone has agreed to handle the security details."

"I'll stay at the manor while you're gone." Simone was dressed in her tactical gear. Black cargo pants, a black sleeveless turtleneck, and a light Kevlar vest. Two knives were visible in addition to the short blade she wore at her hip. "Oasis is on full lockdown with perimeter security on high alert. The dogs are patrolling."

"Dogs are good, but this might be the time to bring on those rogue wolves I've told you about." Decker gave the cadre a wicked smile. "They've been trained by the best. I've shared their profiles with you already. They might be rogues, but they all have good reasons for it. Remus uses them on occasion. You could put them on the outer perimeter where they can cover more ground than dogs. Keep the dogs closer to the buildings as part of your inner security."

"The Wolf uses them?" Sergi asked. "Why would he use rogues?"

"Because they're rogues. No allegiance to any pack, which means no one would suspect Remus's involvement. He doesn't look at rogues like outsiders do. Sure, they come with some baggage, but we all do. Unlike vampires, who consider rogue vampires untrustworthy because they refuse to commit to a House, the wolves are pack animals straight to their bones.

"Rogue vampires are loners, maybe working for a House or two as consultants. Rogue shifters tend to congregate. They make their own pack, but there's no hierarchy. They look out for each other, but it's more like a commune where each shifter can come and go as they want. They don't stay long because they like to roam. And they don't start families. When they get the urge to settle down, they reapply for pack status."

"You say these particular rogues have been vetted?" Simone asked, her eyes shifting between Devon and Sergi.

"By me, yes." Decker swung a leg back and forth. "I suggest you do your own security check. If you don't want them at Oasis, test them out here at the manor or at your safe houses. They have my full confidence, but I understand you need to do your own background check. But I can assure you this. They have one thing in common with everyone in this room."

"What's that?" Devon asked.

"They all have a deep hatred for Lorenzo."

"I can run background checks on them while I'm in New Orleans," Sergi offered.

Simone nodded. "I'll arrange an interview with each of them."

Lyra made notes on the page she was holding, then moved it aside and picked up another paper. "We need to determine Lorenzo's defenses. It appears we keep track of him on a regular basis, but he's most likely made changes since the accident." She made a note then glanced up at Devon. "We don't have a definitive answer as to Cressa's whereabouts, though it makes sense Lorenzo would have taken her to Shadow Island. But we should check his other known safe houses."

"Agreed," Simone said. "The one thing we've never been able to accomplish is finding someone on the island willing to feed us information."

"I've been giving that some thought." Lucas set down his cup of espresso. He had more of an addiction to the beverage than Cressa. "No one is going to be brave enough to give House Trelane any information. Lorenzo wouldn't just kill them; he'd torture them first. But there are a handful who have friends amongst the Boretsky House."

"You know this for a fact?" Simone asked.

Lucas nodded. "I've been keeping in touch with Asher, helping him with realigning his House security. He mentioned there were a few who'd made friends within House Venizi, and he wasn't sure how to handle them. He thought their relationships were with lower staff members, so I suggested putting them in less secure areas. Keep them on the fringe without them feeling like it."

"Very good." Sergi seemed pleased by Lucas's suggestion.

Devon had to agree. Lucas had a knack for seeing things from a different perspective, maybe because he'd shifted Houses several times and understood the Family dynamics from a variety of viewpoints.

"See if you can nurture those relationships, but run it through Asher." Devon stood. "He needs to know who he can trust, and this would be a good test." He walked to Lyra and kissed the top of her head. "Be safe, sister." He strode to the door, and Sergi followed. "Keep us updated. We'll return as soon as we can."

He stopped next to Bella. "I'm checking on Jacques on the way to the airport. Do you want a ride?" He glanced at Lyra. "Assuming it's alright with you."

"It is. Simone can brief her on any changes."

Bella's relief showed, and she trailed behind Devon as they left the study.

"Anything special you need from me?" Decker called from his seat at the bar. He would stay and speak with Simone about the rogues. The old shifter had become somewhat of a papa bear within the rogue community. He didn't realize it, but Decker was becoming his own pack alpha.

"Keep Remus informed. I'll want to meet with him when I return. And I want to know the status of the blood tests."

They were jogging down the front steps when Sergi asked, "What do you hope to discover with the blood tests?"

"I want to know if there's a link between Cressa's blood and mine. But more than that, I want to know the full effect of her blood when combined with the Poppy, other than knowing it can put the beast to rest."

"Is there something you're not telling me that I need to know?"

"I'm hoping I can answer that after we find Colantha."

Chapter Five

MY EYES briefly fluttered open before I squeezed them shut. It wasn't from too much light. Wherever I was, there was little of it. It was my head. It felt like someone had trampled over it—with spiked boots. When I tested other parts of my body there was pain, but it wasn't as intense. My right leg, hip, and arm throbbed and were probably bruised. I wouldn't know more until I stood.

I raised up on my elbows, which increased the pain in my head, but I got a look at the room before I fell back against the pillows. It wasn't a familiar setting. The only source of light was a lamp on the dresser and a fire in the hearth.

Then I lifted my head and did a double take. A man stood in front of the fireplace. His shape and size said male, though with the firelight behind him, he was nothing more than a shadowed figure. A memory of such a man danced at the edges of my consciousness. When he moved toward me I expected long ash-blond hair and crystal-blue eyes.

What stepped away from the fire wasn't that man.

This one had silver hair, cut short but stylish, and a similar physique to what I'd expected. But, as he stood over me, his eyes were almost black. My first inclination was to put distance between us, but something made me lean forward instead.

His smile was warm, almost provocative, as he stared at me. He sat on the edge of the bed and took my hand before I could pull it away.

"How are you feeling, Cressa?" His voice was almost a purr, and I wanted to wrap myself in it.

"Do I know you?"

His features saddened, and if he hadn't been holding my hand I would have reached out to smooth the lines on his forehead.

"I was afraid this might happen. You don't remember running away?"

Now it was my turn to furrow my brow as I tried to remember anything before this moment. I knew who I was—Cressa Langtry. But there my memories ended. No. That wasn't exactly right. This man was a vampire, and while it should scare me, it didn't.

"I don't remember much of anything."

He nodded and squeezed my hand. I couldn't seem to stop staring into his eyes—as black as a deep well yet somehow enchanting. "The healer thought you might have difficulties remembering. It's not uncommon for the trauma you experienced to make you want to forget."

"I'm not sure I understand."

He scooted closer to me. "Of course not. Let me help with some basic information. Or perhaps I should ask the obvious. Do you know who you are?"

I nodded.

"That's an excellent start. I'm Lorenzo Venizi, leader of the House Venizi. We've known each other for some time, though you've been living at House Trelane as a Blood Ward."

The name triggered a flash of fear. A man who seemed more beast than human. Maybe not human—another vamp.

"Trelane is a hard man, feared by many, and treats his women with disrespect and severe beatings when they get out of line. Do you recall any of this?"

I shook my head, careful of the jostling as it still throbbed. The vamp sounded horrible, and I was grateful the memories eluded me.

"Something happened the evening before last. I don't know the details, and you haven't been able to recall them, but one of my men found you running down the street in a torn nightgown. You were bloody and had been beaten."

I sat up, pushing myself against the headboard. How could I have ended up like that? "That doesn't seem possible. I wouldn't be with someone like that."

"Not if you had a choice. You did seem to remember one piece. I believe you owed a debt."

Flashes of another man with a tattoo of a cobra on his face. "Ginger!"

"Who's Ginger?"

"My friend. I took on a debt to get her out of trouble."

"Ah, yes. I believe Trelane has her as well."

"No. We have to get her back."

His smile widened. "Of course, we do. But we have to be careful. And I'm afraid I've taxed you too much for one night." He ran his hand down my cheek and brushed my lips with his thumb. "You need your rest to heal. Soon your memories will return. And if not, I'll help you once you're ready. Sleep now, Cressa. Sleep deeply."

Then the darkness reached out for me.

I WALKED THROUGH THE TREES, the grass tickling my bare feet. Everything was in black and white, and darkness bordered the edges of my vision. It was like one of those old horror flicks with Bela Lugosi. But it was more than that. Someone had thrown a gauzy material over the world, giving everything a milky hue.

Even so, the lake was beautiful with the moon's reflection floating on the calm water. It was disrupted by two late-night ducks gliding smoothly along as if a wind pushed them. I turned at the sound of footsteps, but when no one was there, I leaned against the rough bark of a tree and stared at the lake. Tears fell, but I wasn't sure why. I was close to remembering something and at the same time a thousand miles away from grasping it.

I must have been transported someplace else when I closed my eyes because I was in a room when I opened them. A huge bedroom, or maybe a penthouse suite. Paintings were everywhere —hanging on the walls, leaning against the walls, or stacked on a table.

A woman stood at an easel, a brush in her hand as she considered her palette. I was behind her, and though I couldn't see her face, her figure seemed familiar. Everything was like the earlier image—the same black-and-white setting, the same milky gauze, and the same eerie feeling that I should know this person.

I stepped closer, but the woman either didn't hear me or chose not to turn around. I peeked over her shoulder. She dabbed little spots of dark, crimson red on the canvas, making delicate roses. The only spot of color in a sea of monochrome. A woman knelt by them. But on a second look, it wasn't the complete form of a woman. It was a transparent figure, as if the painter had drawn a soft outline but hadn't gotten around to adding the paint. The figure stirred and glanced up.

The face was mine.

No. That wasn't possible.

Transfixed, I stepped closer, and the closer I got, the more obvious it became that I was staring at myself. The figure stood, picked up a pair of sandals, and walked toward the jungle before disappearing beyond the canvas.

I stumbled back and felt something flatten under my foot.

Blood-red roses lay on the carpet—crushed. The woman was still painting.

An odd sound spun me around.

A dark figure loomed. The scene was no longer in black and white, and I wished it had been. It was in stark color, and the first thing that caught my gaze were the pasty-skinned fingers in the shape of claws. It was tall, bulky with muscle, and had a hunched back. Its eyes were a piercing ice blue that caught me in its gaze and didn't let go. He bent down as if to kiss me, but instead, bit my neck.

I screamed.

~

I TRIED TO SIT UP. My dreams felt like nightmares, though I couldn't remember any details. I wiped my eyes and glanced around. A vamp stood in the far corner, and I pulled the covers up to my chin. He tapped his ear and his lips moved. Telling the master I was awake?

I shook my head, not sure where that thought came from. I'd only just met him, but Lorenzo seemed attentive. He seemed genuinely concerned for my health and welfare. But why?

I tried to remember anything before I woke in this room, but other than my name and recalling Ginger, nothing else came to me. I didn't even know what I did for a living.

Wait.

Lorenzo said something about being at the House Trelane. Houses were vampire Families. I was there as a Blood Ward. I didn't know what that was and didn't think I wanted to.

My leg twinged with a stab of pain. I needed to see the damage but all I wore was a silk nightgown. I didn't want to know who had dressed me. The gown wasn't the one they found me in because Lorenzo said that one had been torn.

The vamp hadn't moved.

"Can I have some privacy? I need to pee."

He didn't even look at me. I searched the room and found a thin robe lying on a nearby chair. Irritated, I swung my legs out of bed then froze as the pain shot through me from multiple locations, all on my right side. When the worst of it passed, I stood, reaching for the nightstand and bed as I tested my legs.

Weak but working.

I inched my way to the robe, knowing how flimsy my gown was. Once I was properly covered, I stared at the vamp again.

"Getting a good view?" It was daytime, but I couldn't guess the time. Sunshine leaked under thick velvet drapes with long gold tassels that ran from ceiling to floor. The vamp ignored me, though he glanced my way, just as he had when I walked to the robe.

"Can you at least tell me where the bathroom is?" When he didn't respond, I added, "Who do you think will get to clean up the pee? Me or you?"

He nodded toward the far wall. I wandered over, not seeing anything until I was right on top of it. The door all but melted into the wall and was basically invisible unless you were looking for it. That was disturbing for some reason. I opened the door, relieved to see a bathroom, and even more relieved when I noticed the lock.

I slammed the door shut. Or tried. The damn thing was so heavy, only a vamp could slam it with enough force to satisfy. The lock clicked into place, and that was enough. I turned on the lights, and my jaw dropped. The room was enormous.

Twin sinks, an oversized tub with jets, a shower with two showerheads, and a walk-in closet as large as some apartments. A flash of a tiny rundown apartment made me think of Ginger. I shook my head and turned on more lights. A full-size mirror stood in a corner, and I stepped close to review the damage. My right eye was turning into a pretty good shiner. I shifted to the left and discovered a matching dark bruise from my right upper thigh to my shoulder. Something made me think it wasn't the first time I'd had bruises.

He said I'd been beaten, or at least made it sound that way. The black eye made sense but why beat the right side of my body? I suppose there's no explanation for someone who abused women.

A knock made me jump. Good grief. Couldn't I have a few minutes to myself?

"Yes." I wasn't sure what else to say.

"Are you alright?" It sounded like Lorenzo.

Can't a girl pee?

"Just another minute."

"I had breakfast brought up. You don't want it to get cold."

Of course, not. I took the opportunity to relieve my bladder. I hadn't been lying about that. After splashing water on my face, I wrapped the robe tighter and opened the door.

Lorenzo was sitting at a table by the window. The drapes had been pulled back, filtering the room with golden light. Stalker vamp was serving breakfast. Who knew he'd turn out to be an all-purpose babysitter?

"Come here, my dear. Let me get a look at those bruises."

I waited for the vamp to finish serving then walked over to him. He took my hand and pulled me close. Without asking, he pushed my robe aside and lifted my nightgown. I pushed his hand away, and he grabbed my wrist. Those dark pools locked with my gaze, and I fell into their depths.

"Don't ever push me away when I'm trying to help. Understood?"

I nodded. For some reason, I didn't want to disappoint him.

He ran his hand up my leg as he pushed the nightgown up. His fingers were warm against my skin. He ran a thumb over the bruise. "I can get you some ointment to help that heal faster." His hand moved higher until it reached my hip.

"I'll need you to stay in your room for another day, then you can move around the house. I don't want you to over-exert yourself."

His eyes never left mine throughout the entire exchange, and I leaned into him. His scent was an earthy musk, and my nose wrinkled. Not my favorite. Yet, something drew me to him, and I was quite aware that his hand was on my naked hip. It gripped me tight, sending small shivers through me.

He smiled. "Let's eat."

He removed his hand in one swift motion, and I stared down at him, not understanding what happened. My cheeks grew hot when stalker vamp held out his hand for me to sit. His gaze was heated as it roamed over my body, and he didn't seem to have any issue with Lorenzo seeing it.

Once I was seated, he went back to his corner like a good little robot.

Lorenzo entertained me with stories of his childhood. He was raised a spoiled little rich kid. Who was he now? He lifted a napkin and dabbed at the corners of his mouth. It was a sensuous mouth.

I licked my lips, and his gaze followed the motion.

Then he stood. "I have several meetings today so I won't be able to see you again until dinner. Remember you're to rest today."

"I remember."

He kissed the top of my head and lingered, his hand running over my shoulder and down my arm. "Be a good girl."

He opened the door, and I glanced at stalker vamp.

"Can't you take this guy with you?"

Lorenzo glanced at his vamp and then back at me. "He's here for your protection."

"Can't he do that outside in the hallway? It's a bit creepy waking up to see him standing in the corner. I won't be able to sleep."

That seemed to do the trick. He nodded at the vamp, who immediately walked out the door but not before giving me another one of his lecherous glares.

Lorenzo strolled back and lifted my chin with a finger. "I can't take a chance that anyone will hurt you again. I want to make sure you're safe so you can forget the past and concentrate on our future."

Then he was gone.

My body shook, but not from the thought of his fingers running up my leg. I caught his words. He didn't say to concentrate on *my* future. He wanted me to concentrate on *our* future. And as much as one part of me was excited by his statement, another part of me, way deep down, was terrified.

Chapter Six

SERGI DROVE through the quiet streets of the Garden District while Devon watched the passing houses. The yards were canopied by ancient oak trees, and a wide array of colors burst from crape myrtles, bougainvillea, and magnolias. The sweet, cloying scent mixed with the sultry air, and he made a promise that he'd bring Cressa here. Just the two of them.

"Lafitte only spent a minute with me and Cressa. Perhaps this will be the same." Sergi had said little since they'd left Santiga Bay.

"I hope so. I didn't come here to spend time pandering to another House leader, especially one who was quick to put distance between our Houses."

"You can't blame Lafitte or any other House leader for taking a step back until the Council ruled. And he didn't put distance between us. Only you."

It shouldn't have bothered him. He would have done the same thing. Betting one's House on a single vampire with strong evidence against him would have been foolish. And Girard Lafitte, leader of the House, sounded gracious if not somewhat demanding that he stop by. Considering it was dusk, it most likely meant they'd have to stay for dinner.

"You're right. If this were any other time, the invitation would please me. Our time is limited if Lorenzo is mesmerizing Cressa."

"We'll only have to stay for a few hours. If Colantha wishes to meet with you, it won't be until much later."

Sergi pulled into a driveway and stopped at a video monitor. "This is Sergi. I'm with Devon Trelane of the House Trelane."

Within seconds, the wrought-iron gate opened, and Sergi followed the narrow lane to a short circular drive with an ornate fountain in the middle. The manor itself was of Greek-revival style and sat on property that covered an entire city block. There were two garden cottages and a koi pond in the back, and lush vegetation spread throughout the estate. Lafitte also owned a fifty-acre estate outside Baton Rouge and spent equal time at both manors. This was where Devon had gotten the idea of building Oasis. The only difference was that everyone knew Lafitte had a second home, and only Family knew of Oasis's existence.

Two vampires waited for them. One took the keys from Sergi while the other walked them up the steps and through the manner to Lafitte's reception room.

Mingled voices preceded them walking in, and he was surprised by the twenty or so vampires enjoying drinks and appetizers.

Just his luck to have arrived on the same day as a dinner party. The question was whether Lafitte invited him to cement their relationship in front of allies or as a simple obligation. Lafitte didn't make them wait long as he strode toward them.

He was a couple of inches shorter than Devon, with a lean build. He still sported his signature goatee and white suit, but there was gray at his temples that blended into his coal-black hair. Had it been that long since they'd seen each other?

"Girard." Devon held out his hand, and Lafitte grasped it tightly in both of his. His shake was vigorous and strong.

"Devon. I can't tell you how good it is to see you after that unfortunate business with the Council." His smooth Southern voice was melodic. "The whole matter of Boretsky's death was quite worrisome. And this Magic Poppy is a danger to our entire species." He waved his hand in a grand gesture. "Now you've been absolved, though I must say, I'm not happy with how the Council handled the situation. They seem to have abandoned long-established policies."

He nodded at Sergi. "It's good to see you back so soon." When Sergi returned the nod with a warm smile, Lafitte continued as he strolled with them across the room. "Your timing seemed most unfortunate, as it's been some time since we've fished on the lake and talked, but sometimes things work out. It will do both our Houses good to have people see the two of us at such an event."

"We certainly didn't mean to intrude. My business here is of an urgent nature and not related to any of your interests."

"Of course not. I only invited you because I wanted to see you. How's Lucas?"

"He's a critical member of my cadre and shows great potential."

Lafitte laughed. "I always knew he had the potential for cadre."

Devon slapped his shoulder. "And I appreciate everything you taught him. Tell me, was that a red Ferrari Spider I saw parked outside?"

"Don't worry. Romero is eager to meet with you as well."

"I suppose I'll have to apologize for luring Lucas away from his House."

Lafitte gave Devon a wink. "If Romero didn't think moving Houses would be the best for him, it would never have happened."

Devon laughed. "I suppose that's one way to look at it."

The dinner party was exactly what Devon needed. Not only did he confirm long-established relationships with two Houses, he also relaxed. He had to remain aware of the ticking clock, but he didn't have to be ruled by it.

Now, Sergi drove the backstreets toward the French Quarter. He parked the car at their hotel, and they walked the rest of the way. Even with their casual stroll through the Quarter, it was easy to see they weren't tourists, though they stopped at various clubs that Sergi thought were critical in making their presence known to Colantha.

Their last stop for the evening was the jazz club where Colantha had invited Cressa to meet with her. They stopped in the entryway, and Sergi pointed to the black-and-white picture on the wall.

"That's Josephine Baker."

"I recognize the face. I've heard some of her music." Devon found the woman to be bewitching. The image caught her with the same expression Simone and Bella presented when everything was going their way—confident and proud.

"Keep her face in mind. Colantha could be her twin."

"Good to know."

They sat in a booth at the back and listened to the music. They spoke little of current House business, preferring to talk of old days on the battlefield. Sergi didn't have to mention it; they both knew a storm was coming. The culmination of centuries of secrets would soon be coming to light.

Was Devon the tipping point, or was it Lorenzo and whatever secrets he held?

At two in the morning, Devon had enough. It had been a long day with the flight and the dinner party. They walked back to the hotel, agreeing to meet in the morning for breakfast before paying a visit to the Renauds.

Devon entered his room but didn't bother with the lights. He stopped to relieve his bladder then walked into the main living area of the suite. A small lamp had been left on, presumably by the maid service.

He was in the process of removing his tie when he stopped short.

He was thankful Sergi had shown him the portrait. Her face held the same flawless beauty, and her hair was pulled back, a white magnolia blossom over her left ear the only decoration. She perched in one of the chairs as if she were royalty, and her voice was buttery smooth with a light French accent.

"Hello, vampire. Welcome to New Orleans."

DEVON STEPPED FARTHER into the room and tossed his tie on the sofa.

"Colantha, I assume."

She smiled but said nothing.

"How did you get in here?" He stepped closer, his anger rising. He'd played enough games hopscotching to every jazz club in the Quarter. When she continued to stare with her fathomless eyes, he got to the point. "If you're not Colantha, you're wasting my time. Cressa has been taken, and I need help finding her. Tell me now that you can help or get the hell out of my room."

Her smile widened, and she crooked a finger to bring him closer. Her dark eyes were locked with his, and he wasn't sure he could break free if he tried. He was a foot away from her when she lifted her hand, opened her palm, and blew out a breath.

A red mist hit him in the face, and before he could cough or wave it away he dropped like a stone.

DEVON'S HEAD hurt like he'd been fifteen rounds with a heavyweight boxer who used him like a punching bag. He blinked and looked around. He was on the floor in a dark room with no windows. A single lit candle burned ten feet away and two feet above his head, casting shadows on the wall.

He stretched his legs but could only extend them halfway. When he lengthened his upper body, his head hit another barrier, and he braced for the pain that never came. He pushed himself up and stared at the candle that was now at eye level. The floor had been raised, but when he scanned the room, that seemed wrong. If he had to guess, he was sitting in a pit.

He stood and toppled to his right, throwing his hands out and catching himself on the edge of the floor. The room spun, and he closed his eyes. He didn't remember having that much to drink.

"It's best if you remain sitting until you regain your equilibrium."

He spun around, reaching out for the edge of the pit again. A soft spotlight shone down on the woman who'd been in his hotel room.

"Where am I, and what did you do to me?"

Her chuckle was low and sultry. "You're a long way from your hotel, vampire. I required you to be asleep to transport you. It's been a very long time since I've had reason to trust your kind."

"You mean a dreamwalker doesn't trust vampires?"

"It wasn't like that over a millennia ago. But that is a story for another time. You said someone took Cressa. Do you know who this person is?"

"Yes."

"And what do you think I can do for you?"

Devon unbuttoned his shirt until the medallion could be seen. "He's a powerful adversary with strong defenses. I've tried reaching out to her to assess where she's being held, but I can't sustain the connection, even when I wear the necklace."

"The medallion wasn't meant for you. That doesn't mean you can't use it if she's brought you to constructs before, but without training, it's very difficult. The fact you reached her at all without my assistance tells me something has changed in you."

"What do you mean?"

She picked up a glass of what looked like juice and took a long swallow. He hadn't seen it a moment ago, but he couldn't be sure it wasn't there all along. She tapped a fingernail on the table and gave him a long look. "Cressa mentioned the beast. Did she cure you?"

"Yes."

"Was the beast brought on by the Poppy?"

"If you mean Magic Poppy, then yes."

"And she gave you her blood."

It wasn't a question, but he nodded anyway. "You seem to know a lot."

She laughed. "You don't know the half of it."

And he was pretty sure he didn't want to. "So what next?"

She turned and hit a button on the wall. The door opened, and two vampires walked in. He stood straighter but had to widen his stance against the feeling he was standing on a floating dock. Whatever the red mist was, its effects were slowly dissipating.

"Relax, vampire. This is Frederick and Jamison. They're here for my safety."

He gave her two bodyguards a long perusal. They appeared more diligent than threatening, and he leaned against the wall of the pit. He had to trust that Colantha wanted to help Cressa, even if it meant lowering his guard with two unknown vampires.

"Step out of the pit."

She took his place and sat cross-legged. Her face relaxed, though her posture remained rigid. She pulled out her own medallion, rubbed it, then focused on the candle. He wasn't sure what to expect, but if she began to sway and mumble foreign words it wouldn't have surprised him.

He leaned against the wall and waited.

Fifteen minutes later, she blinked and stood. One of the vampires helped her out of the pit.

She stood in front of him and met his gaze. Her dark eyes appeared worried, which increased his own anxiety.

"How committed are you to finding her?"

"I'm not leaving without reaching her."

"Jamison, take him to the cabin." She walked to the table,

lifted the glass, and drank the last of it. "The cabin is sparse but has food, water, and this juice in your kitchen. The juice provides the mental clarity required for the work we need to do. It will be physically and mentally challenging. Are you prepared?"

"Yes. But I need my phone to contact my cadre."

"Your vampire has been told to wait. You will be returned to him once we've accomplished our task."

Jamison held the door open for him.

"Did you reach her?" He needed to know she was all right even if she'd been mesmerized to believe him her enemy.

"Not in the way you think. The connection was fuzzy. If I had to guess, I'd say she's been deeply mesmerized. We will need to work quickly."

Jamison led Devon across a small expanse of the courtyard. He opened the door to a small cabin and then left after reminding Devon of his thirty minutes. The place was indeed sparse, but Devon didn't think he'd be spending much time in it.

He checked the bedroom and found a black martial arts gi in a drawer and he changed into it, surprised they fit well. He found makings for coffee but decided to drink the juice as requested. It was surprisingly refreshing, and within minutes, colors appeared more intense than usual. By the time he walked back to the central cabin, he was eager to start.

He followed Jamison to the room he'd been in before, which was most likely the training room Cressa had spent time in. The only light came from the spotlight over the table and four candles that had been placed at even distances around the pit where a blanket covered the bottom.

He turned when the door closed and found Colantha standing there. She wore a long caftan over a full-body leotard, similar to what Simone wore for everyday wear. She walked into the center of the pit and sat down.

She waved at him. "Come join me."

The pit was barely able to hold both of them as they sat cross-legged, their knees touching.

"This first attempt will be what you might call a joy ride. I'll be bringing you to various constructs. We'll visit a few and see how it goes. If it appears you're having difficulties with the transitions, I'll stop."

"Do I need to be wearing the medallion for this?"

"No. But it won't bother me if you do. I'll be in control."

"All right. Do we need to hold hands or something?"

"Only if you're scared."

He scowled.

"Prepare yourself, vampire."

ONE SECOND they were in the pit, the next they were at an upscale lounge. The chairs were plush leather, and Colantha sipped a martini. A cold porter was sitting in front of him, and he picked it up, taking a taste.

"That's good. Where are we?"

"The Buswells Hotel in Dublin."

"Why there?"

"You looked like you needed a good beer."

He laughed, then noticed she wasn't in her caftan anymore. She wore a raspberry-colored silk suit with a blouse a lighter shade of pink. Her hair was in braids, and she appeared twenty years younger. Although, whether it was being a dreamwalker or her genes, she always appeared timeless.

He'd been dressed in a brown tailored suit that fit to perfection. The tie was the same color as her suit. He took a long swallow of beer, unsure of how long they'd be there. "Is this a place you've been before?"

"Several times, but only through constructs. This is a favorite hotel of a fellow dreamwalker. He tells me the beer is the best he's tasted."

"He's not wrong." He waited until she took a couple more sips of her martini. It was apparent she was waiting for his questions.

"Tell me what the connection is between vampires and dreamwalkers."

Rather than being shocked at his brazen question, she threw her head back and laughed.

"The two of you are peas in a pod. Both want to get to the end of the story without bothering with all the gooey middle. The journey. The education with all the pitfalls."

"She asked the same thing?"

She shrugged and picked something off her blazer before straightening her sleeves. "It was more about controlling the medallion. But she was interested in the symbols as well."

"But you didn't answer her questions."

"Not all of them. Not most of them."

"You'll answer mine."

Her smile was sickly sweet before the darkness came.

DEVON MADE a slow turn as he searched the darkness. Vampires had excellent vision, but even they required a fraction of ambient light to see. There was none.

He was naked. The deep chill and earthy smell told him he was either deep in a cave or a cell. He reached out and took a tentative step. The dirt floor was scattered with pebbles, but he managed to find a craggy wall.

"Colantha?"

When there was no answer, he followed the wall to see how far it stretched. He counted his footsteps as he went, eventually finding where the wall ended. He turned left and continued counting. By the time he'd made it to the fourth turn, he calculated the room was twenty-by-twenty feet square. He wasn't disturbed that he was in some sort of cell. No. The troublesome part was not finding a door.

"I get your point. You're in charge, and you'll answer what questions you deem appropriate. I'll listen."

~

Bright light hit him, and after being in complete darkness for what he estimated to be thirty minutes, he lifted his hand to block out the blinding sunshine. Kids screamed with laughter. The scents of hot dogs, sugary sweetness, and suntan lotion were overwhelming. But the air was warm, and he glanced down. He wore boardshorts sans shirt.

Once his eyes acclimated to the light, he glanced around. He was at Coney Island if he had to guess, and he sat at a picnic table. The woman across from him was in a strapless white sundress. She held an amused expression as she viewed his chest.

"Now I see why Cressa is so enamored with you."

"That seems a bit sexist." It was far from the first time a woman had ogled him. In his early days, he spent most of his time bare-chested while training. But he suspected she was trying to keep him unbalanced. She'd have to try harder.

She tsked but couldn't seem to stop smiling. "I was talking about your time in the pit. You didn't panic. Your first instinct was to gather information before proceeding."

By leaving him shirtless, she'd set him up. He admired her guile.

"I've fought many foes over the centuries, and while it's been a long time since I've stood on a battlefield, I'm tested daily by Houses that wish to destroy my Family."

"You can't blame a woman for finding out for herself. There's a battle coming. I thought it might still be years if not decades away. Whether by manmade design or the force of spirits, it doesn't matter which. The genocide the vampires once attempted can no longer be hidden. Your journey to the truth is far from over, yet it must be completed before you're ready for the final test."

"You mean Lorenzo?"

She shrugged a shoulder. "Who's to say? But if it's him, he won't be alone." She twirled an umbrella in a blended drink that wasn't there a second ago. After giving it a moment of consideration, she took a long swallow and sighed. "This is the only place I can find sangria smoothies that have just the right amount of rum."

"I need training on how to use the medallion. There must be something that can be done to break through the mesmerizing."

"I have made two additional attempts to contact Cressa, but the same barrier is blocking me. We need more familiarity, a stronger bond if you will, in order to find a crack."

"And how will we do that?"

"You are still missing information critical to your mission. You must learn the secrets of the dreamwalkers and their connection to vampires. You are close. But you have far to go to find the one object that can bring more allies to your side."

"Aren't you the one to help me with that?"

"I will come to you when the time is right. Until then, go home, vampire. I'll leave you with one thing to help you take the next step."

She leaned over and crooked her finger, beckoning him closer. And like a fool, he leaned in.

She was swift when she raised her palm and hit him with the red dust.

He shut his eyes, but it was too late. This time the dust stung, and when he tried to stand, he fell. He waited a moment then opened his eyes and blinked.

He was on the floor of his hotel room, and his head ached to the beat of a drum solo. The pressure built like that day at the scene of Cressa's accident. When he didn't think he could take any more, there was a pop, and in an instant, his mind cleared. All traces of pain were gone. He stretched his body then stood, almost stepping on something.

He bent over and picked it up. It was a bloom from the Blood Poppy.

Chapter Seven

DEVON AND SERGI sat next to each other on the flight home. The Blood Poppy sat in a domed clamshell container on the polished wood console between their seats. The red-tipped edges appeared to drip down the sides of the white petals like blood. Devon had only pulled it out of his bag after he told the flight attendant to give them privacy.

Sergi had slid away from it, which, even though the seats were spacious, wasn't far since he still had his seat belt on.

"Where did you get that?"

"Colantha paid me a visit last night. She was waiting for me in my room."

"Did you try reaching Cressa?"

"Colantha tried several times, but she didn't have any more luck than me. She agrees Cressa has been mesmerized." And that confirmation didn't sit well with him. They had to get to her before Lorenzo charmed her too often and too deeply.

"The whole event was unnerving." He wasn't sure what to think, especially when he could have sworn a full day had gone by, not just a couple of hours. He thought he could tell the difference between a construct and reality. He'd been positive he'd been at her compound or whatever she called it. He remembered walking from one cabin to the next, changing into the gi, and drinking the juice.

He explained the entire night, starting with the red dust blown in his face, waking in a pit, walking to a cabin, and then shifting to other constructs. After she gave him a cryptic message about a coming battle, she'd hit him with the red dust again before he woke in his room with the Blood Poppy.

"Your description of the cabins and her compound is accurate, yet I agree that it seems inconceivable that everything you experienced was from your hotel room."

"Did Cressa ever mention red dust to you?"

Sergi's gaze never left the flower sitting between them. "No. And I think she would have."

"I agree." He tapped the top of the clamshell container. "What do you make of this?"

"I think if anyone knew we had it, the Council would rethink your involvement with Magic Poppy."

Devon's laugh was menacing. "We've always assumed the Poppy came from the Blood Poppy, but there's never been any proof. And it makes me wonder. Is Lorenzo growing his own, or is she a supplier?"

"She doesn't seem the type to be involved with Lorenzo, but at the same time, she's hiding something."

"Or she's being extremely cautious until she knows all the players on the board."

"Plausible." Sergi leaned closer to the flower and nudged the container so it turned in a partial circle. "It is a beautiful flower."

Silence settled over them until they circled the Santiga Bay airstrip.

Sergi pushed the flower toward Devon. "Colantha is extremely powerful. If there are more like her, I can see why vampires might have feared them."

"There's more to it. I just can't connect the dots." Devon took the container and placed it back in the white shopping bag he'd gotten from the hotel's gift store.

"What do you want to do?"

"I'll call Remus. He should have preliminary lab results from my beast's blood and the vial of Magic Poppy we took from Gheata's basement." He tapped the bag. "And I'd be interested to see what his lab can make of this."

~

DEVON TESTED the wine and nodded to the server. The merlot was the perfect end to a long day. After arriving home the day before, he'd spent most of his time in his room reviewing the various security and investigation reports compiled during his absence.

He had a quiet dinner with Anna and Ginger, the only ones in the manor who weren't away on assignment. Anna hardly said a word while Ginger was highly animated—a pile of nervous energy without Cressa or Lucas to calm her. Devon tried to be that bridge, but he'd failed miserably. He chuckled as he remembered her kissing his cheek and whispering, "Thank you for trying," before rushing off to her room.

He hadn't slept well, staring at the ceiling, unable to focus on anything but Cressa. Was Lorenzo treating her well or keeping her in one of his dungeon cells? Although they were illegal now, the law was new within the last century. Many of the old Houses still had them, and the Council had to take their word they weren't being used for their original purpose.

He'd risen at four a.m. and spent a couple of hours with Cook, listening to the local House gossip while making bread and blueberry scones. His idea to investigate the library afterward seemed wise at the time. He spent hours reviewing the books, excited when he found an old one he hadn't read before, hoping it might yield some seed that would grow to a larger lead. Then despair settled in when he found nothing. Hours of wasted searching. He should have known his father wouldn't have placed anything dangerous in the library where anyone might discover it.

He sipped the wine and looked out over Santiga Bay. Far off in the distance, he thought he caught the lights of Shadow Island. If only he could touch Cressa's mind. Maybe his timing was off. Lorenzo would have to touch her two or three times a day to keep his hold over her. The thought rankled, and he pushed it away. It would only make the beast angry.

Lorenzo would want to connect with Cressa first thing in the morning when his evening's touch wore off. Then sometime midday. He might do it less as the days wore on, believing his hold was growing stronger. Colantha had seen the same transparent figure that he and Lyra had. If that were the best they could achieve when Lorenzo's mesmerizing was at its weakest, then it would be almost impossible to reach her. There had to be a way to slip under his spell.

"Is that the first bottle you've had opened?" The Wolf pulled out a chair as the server rounded the table to pour a glass and refresh Devon's.

"I did consider coming early, but a clear head prevails."

They gave the server their order and waited for the door to close behind him.

"Decker told me about Cressa." Remus gave Devon a studied gaze. "I was sorry to hear the news, but she's a fighter. What can I do?"

"I could use eyes on the boats running to the island. I have my own, but we can't get close to the dock."

"That's easy enough since we perform our own monitoring of Venizi's schedule. There's a rogue who works for the harbor master maintaining the docks. He gets rather close to Venizi's boats and feeds me information when he can."

"He's trustworthy?"

"I believe so. He's smart. An alpha with a mate and too many pups. They keep to themselves and live by human rules, which keeps them out of pack trouble. The family goes to the mountains when they need to run. He'll be given Cressa's description. We'll also gather details of everyone that enters or departs the island."

Dinner came, and they discussed general topics relating to current world events. When the server took the plates away and left them with a bottle of scotch, the discussion turned back to business.

"I never asked you about a cryptic message I received from Cressa the morning I dropped her off at the paper mill. She suggested the packs shouldn't plan any birthday parties, specifically the Humboldt pack. Can you explain that?"

Devon was blindsided by the question. He hadn't made a decision on how to tell Remus that Cressa was a dreamwalker. But if it was The Wolf's lab doing the testing, he had to be told. Devon would soon confront the Council, and he required the shifter's support. If he didn't trust Remus by now, he never would.

He leaned back and twirled his glass before taking two swallows. "What have you heard about dreamwalkers?"

Remus's eyes widened. "So, it's true?"

"That puts us at a bit of a stalemate." It wouldn't hurt to hear what Remus had to say if he offered it.

"I have my suspicions, but I'll let you go first." His smile was wide and full of teeth. It was the kind of smile that welcomed you in just before he took a bite.

Devon gave a quick grin, then it slipped away. "I'd heard the rumors centuries ago when I was a kid. But they were considered fairy tales. After my parents were killed, and I came home to find Lyra in a melancholic state, I began my research. I can't tell you why I thought of dreamwalkers. Maybe it was the voices she claimed to hear or the nightmares that were so bad she refused to sleep. Either way, I began an earnest search. It got derailed my first time on the Poppy. But when I recovered and came home, Lyra wasn't any better."

Devon gave Remus a long look. "Then, a few decades later, a business associate brought me a thief in trade for a debt."

"Ah, good Christ." Remus fell back, shaking his head. "How did you know?"

"I didn't. Not at first. But then the shared dreams began. They felt real, and it was apparent she remembered them, though it took some time for her to admit it."

"Were you feeding from each other?"

"No. I'd considered a blood bond, but there hadn't been any exchange of blood. Everything had been strictly business. But then a dream would come, and I'd find myself somewhere that should be unfamiliar to Cressa, yet she recognized it. And she spoke as if we'd known each other for some time."

"Prescient dreams?" Remus leaned forward when Devon nodded. "When I was a young pup, there were stories of a species of people who could steal your dreams. But they lived long ago, and most say they were nothing but myths or fables. Stories we tell the pups in the hopes of keeping them close to the fire at night."

"Cressa thought I was the one creating the dreams, until the night of a ball where she was supposed to steal something for me. A few hours before the event, I had a dream that she would fall out of a second-story window and would require my blood to survive. It turns out she had the same dream, and everything we'd seen came true. Our foresight was unable to prevent it."

Remus sat back and stared at his drink for several minutes. "She had a dream about the wolves?"

"We both had the dream. It was a birthday party for someone in Elijah's pack. Then the rogue attack in L.A. happened. From what Sergi reported, it sounded like the dream we had, just a different pack."

"You didn't say anything."

Devon shook his head. "Sergi was investigating the Poppy situation, and we'd only heard of one case in the area. Then Boretsky was murdered, and with my addiction, it would have been too dangerous to keep Poppy on the street." He ran a hand through his hair. "I'm sorry for not sharing this piece sooner, but I'm not sure how that conversation would have gone."

"Cressa must have suspected something different about her blood, which was why she believed she was the only one capable of putting the beast to rest."

"She had a dream that she saved me." His chuckle was dry. "Even Lyra said Cressa would save me."

"Lyra? Can she dreamwalk?"

"No. At least, that's what she tells me. Did you find anything with the bloodwork?"

Remus reached into his jacket's inside pocket and pulled out a folded piece of paper. He pushed it across the table to him. "There's something definitely different in all three samples. The sample from the beast is, as we would expect, the most similar to yours, but the markers are a bit different—elevated if you will—and we see a variant that matches the sample of Magic Poppy you supplied. We've never collected blood from your beast before, so we had no baseline to work from. Overall, based on other vampire and beast blood we've tested, there is definitely an anomaly in the samples we got from you, which we expect to be the Magic Poppy.

"We compared the blood samples to the dead rogues from L.A. We see the same marker that we saw in your beast's blood and believe it's the Magic Poppy. However, with only one sample for comparison, it's not foolproof. But our conclusion is that vampires on the Poppy killed the rogues."

Devon stared out the window to the dark sea beyond the lights of town. He had expected these results, but it was quite different to have the truth in black and white. "What about the last sample?"

"That was the interesting part of the tests. The blood you donated after you returned to Oasis didn't include what we believe to be the Magic Poppy marker. Instead, it was contaminated with a different marker we can't explain. The lab has never seen it before."

"Contaminated?"

"It's not what it sounds like. Any foreign substance introduced to the base sample would make the sample contaminated. That doesn't mean bad or good—just different. I think it's safe to say that the additional marker came from Cressa's blood. At a minimum, we believe it's what returned you to your normal form." He shrugged and refilled glasses. "Who knows what other properties the marker might impact."

"My mental fugue might be a side effect."

Remus took a swallow of scotch. "That's more difficult to determine. You were given what was likely an injection of the Poppy and fed tainted deer for a couple of days. Add in the fact you remained in beast form longer than normal. It's not inconceivable that your brain simply required rest after the experience. Which I believe is what Madame Saldano told you."

"So, we know there's something different about dreamwalker blood, though we're not sure of its effects. It always comes down to the blood."

"When Cressa returns, we'd like to get a sample of her blood. It might tie up some loose ends."

"She'd most likely agree to that."

"Does Lorenzo know anything about Cressa other than she's your Blood Ward?"

"Like what? He wouldn't know she's a dreamwalker."

"What about her being a thief?"

"I don't know. Lorenzo had Underwood, Cressa's stepfather, searching for a medallion. Underwood knew Cressa had it, and also knew she had sticky fingers. I don't know if he shared any of that with Lorenzo."

Devon didn't like where this conversation was going and wasn't prepared to discuss the medallion. It wasn't Remus's fault. He should have already considered all the possibilities and determined contingencies, but he was too busy with how to make the medallion work. The mental fugue was gone. He was sure of it. But it didn't mean he was thinking smart.

Remus finished his glass and set it aside. "While we wait for word on Cressa, what's next?"

Devon drained his glass then poured another finger, swallowing it down immediately. He bent to retrieve the white shopping bag and set it on the table between him and Remus. "You might have to wait for Cressa's blood to finalize your analysis, but this might keep your lab busy in the meantime."

Remus lifted a brow and pulled the bag closer. He tipped it toward him and glanced in. He flashed Devon a glance before pulling the clamshell container partway out of the bag. When he spoke, his voice was filled with awe. "Is this beautiful flower what I think it is?"

"Yes. And you won't want to be caught with it."

Chapter Eight

THE FOLLOWING MORNING, I strolled through the walk-in closet filled with linen pants of every imaginable color along with matching blouses and blazers, dozens of casual dresses, party dresses, and evening dresses. A three-tiered cabinet held four dozen shoes. I counted. And two dressers held nothing but sweaters.

It was every girl's dream, and I couldn't find a damn thing to wear.

No jeans, no leggings, no sweatshirts, workout clothes, or tennis shoes. This wasn't going to work.

I rubbed my right hip. It was still sore, but even so, I dropped to the floor to run through a martial arts program. What did Lorenzo want with me?

It was strange. I'd begun remembering little things. Like an odd rundown apartment I shared with Ginger. But each time Lorenzo visited me, I became irresistibly drawn to him as I hung onto his every word. Once he was gone, the feeling faded within an hour, and I was left feeling dull and confused.

What I needed was fresh air. I needed to get out for a long walk through the gardens. I scrounged through the wardrobe and found a pair of wide-legged pants that would allow movement. A short-sleeved silver blouse that went with a black pantsuit was sufficient for what appeared to be a gorgeous day.

The one feature that made this experience tolerable was the second-floor balcony that looked out over a well-kept garden filled with flower beds, willow trees, and firs. For some reason, I expected to see a sycamore tree, but if there was one on the property, it must be in the front yard.

I turned when the door opened. That was another irritation. No one ever knocked. Not Lorenzo and not the guards. I wasn't fooled. They weren't there for my protection. That was fine, but not having privacy was a whole different matter.

This time it was the guard who liked to see me sleep and walk around in skimpy clothing.

"Master Venizi wants you to join him for breakfast."

"And what if I don't feel like joining him?"

"Then I'll take great pleasure in dragging you down the stairs and across the marble floor in front of his entire staff before dropping you at his feet."

That was fairly specific. Like he'd been fantasizing about doing just that. I walked past him and out the door.

"I was just checking."

The walk to the dining room gave me a chance to review the floor plan. I wasn't sure why I did it. A natural curiosity or something more ingrained—a need to know where the exits were. The dining room, like all the other rooms I'd seen, was something one would expect in a castle. It was tasteful and elegant and made me want to sit on one of the antique chairs, put my feet on the table, and eat popcorn just to see what they'd do with all the mess.

The staff were dressed in uniforms, and two stood sentinel against a wall behind Lorenzo while two vamps stood on opposite sides of the long dining table that sat thirty. He was reading something on a tablet, and his brows were furrowed. When he glanced up, he appeared irritated. Whether it was at me or what he was reading was difficult to tell, and if I didn't know it before, it was clear to me now.

This was a dangerous man. A man who owned things. Controlled things. And I seemed to be one of his new toys. I don't know why I thought that, considering how often I wanted to do anything he asked of me. This yo-yo behavior around him was driving me crazy, but the easiest thing to do was to play along until I learned more.

"You're late. I was expecting you a half hour ago."

Okay. He was irritated at me.

"I wasn't aware you expected me at a certain time."

His gaze flashed to the vamp behind me. "There must have been a miscommunication." He eyed me from my head to my toes. He didn't seem impressed. "I'll have Millie lay out your clothes from now on. She knows what I prefer."

I dropped into the chair next to him since it was the only place setting available. Coffee was poured, and breakfast was a simple egg-white omelet with spinach and a bowl of fruit. For some reason, I knew vamps ate organically, almost vegan, but something made me crave blueberry scones, and I wasn't sure why.

"I have an appointment off the island today and won't return until this evening. Mrs. Newbridge will see to your etiquette train-ing. I have no idea what Trelane has been teaching you, but I'm sure it's not up to my standards. I'm having a dinner party in four days with my closest allies, and I expect you to be stellar in your comportment."

Island. Did he say we were on an island? Claustrophobia clenched my stomach. It was a strange feeling because I usually didn't have an issue with small places. I spent a good portion of my childhood in them. Funny how I could remember that. Yet, the thought of being stuck on an island with this man terrified me.

"Is there something I've done to displease you? Other than being late for breakfast." I kept my head down. Best to play meek at this point. This man had my entire day planned out for me.

He tossed his napkin on the table. "I've had some unsettling news from the mainland. You'll learn to temper your behavior around me once we get to know each other better." He grabbed my wrist, and my eyes flashed to his and locked.

Whatever my earlier concerns might have been drained away. I leaned in. "How long will you be gone?"

His eyes glowed a dark red that I found pleasing and dangerous at the same time. He rubbed his thumb across my wrist and lifted it to kiss the soft skin underneath. He stood and pulled me up with him. Then his lips were on mine, crushing, bruising, his tongue forcing its way in as he tugged me closer.

Then he released me to drop into my chair. He bent low. "I'll give you time to think about how good things can be between us. On the evening of my dinner party, you'll be mine—body and soul."

He strode out, the two vamps following behind.

It took me several minutes to recover. There was a tightness between my legs and a desire to race after him. An image of him naked in a large ornate bed fit for a king with me naked under him flashed in my head. Then another image superimposed it. I was lying on the grass in a lush garden. A man with startling blue eyes stood over me. He knelt and ran a hand down my cheek. His eyes changed, glowing with an icy blue that warmed as he bent his head.

Dishes clattered as I snapped out of wherever I'd been and noticed my plate had been removed.

"I wasn't finished with that."

"You'll learn to eat when the master eats or not at all." My vamp bodyguard lifted me by my upper arm and all but dragged me out of the room. "First, you'll go up and change into what has been laid out for you. Then you'll remain in your room until Mrs. Newbridge comes for you."

He kept his grip on me all the way to my room. He took a

different route, which gave me more rooms to add to my internalized floor plan.

The vamp, who I decided to call Asshole, led me to the bed. He glared down at me. "You should understand something. Master Venizi is an exacting vampire. He expects only the best out of his Family. He can lavish you in the finest clothes and treat you like a queen as long as you do what he wishes. The moment he gets tired of you, he'll pass you on to one of his cadre or someone lower."

He bent his head until his lips touched my ear. His voice was nothing but a heated whisper. "I'm hoping he'll tire of you quickly. As your security, I will have first dibs. And I'm already planning how to use your splendid body." He pushed me onto the bed then turned and stormed out.

I shook with anger and fear. Obedience and domination seemed to be the rule at House Venizi. It was hard to believe life at House Trelane was worse than this. Because I was pretty sure a firm hand or slap was nothing to these vamps.

My fingers touched silk, and I looked down. It was one of the silk blouses, and next to it were rose-colored pants with a matching blazer. Four-inch heels were on the floor. Ugh.

I changed and walked out to the balcony. Now that I was looking for it, I saw the blue ocean beyond the trees of the garden. How big was the island and how many ways off it? But then where would I go? I had no money, and for some reason, I couldn't remember anything about House Trelane. All I recalled was a large mansion where I grew up. And something told me not to go there.

I was stuck.

The door burst open, and a sour-faced woman with gray streaking her black hair strolled in. "Come. You're late for your first lesson."

I was the one late again. How did that work when I was told to wait in my room? It was like everyone wanted me to fail. I took a last look at the bed. Thoughts of Lorenzo lying in it, beckoning me to go to him drew a shiver through me. I swallowed and turned to follow Mrs. Newbridge out the door. Asshole kept his eyes on me as I passed, and for the moment, I was simply grateful he didn't follow us. It appeared Mrs. Newbridge was my watchdog for the day.

I SIGHED at the outfit Millie, my vamp lady's maid, set out for me. This time it was a chartreuse pantsuit—pants, blouse, and jacket all the same horrid color. I tried not to gag when I put it on. No mirrors for me today.

This was day two of etiquette training. Somehow, I'd passed the first day with flying colors. No one was more surprised than me when I easily demonstrated eight different table settings based on various vamp engagements that included personal gatherings, social gatherings, formal dinners, and banquets.

Mrs. Newbridge grudgingly accepted my performance, though she tried hard to find something wrong. Today, she decided to punish me by stepping through every painful and boring task of how the house was maintained. I watched the staff polish silver, clean chandeliers, make beds, and then back to polishing—this time shoes. It seemed Lorenzo had a fetish for a high sheen on everyone's feet.

When we marched into the kitchen, I expected to see an urn for coffee. But there wasn't one, and I wasn't sure why I'd anticipated it. The smells were even different.

I stopped in my tracks. A splitting headache hit me, and I grabbed the counter.

"What's wrong?" Mrs. Newbridge asked in one of those tones that reflected irritation at something disturbing her routine rather than any concern for me.

"Nothing. Just a twinge from my bruising."

She tsked. "It's important you don't show weakness. Master

Venizi expects everyone to be at the top of their game at all times. Mistresses included."

Mistress. Was that what everyone thought? Great.

I grimaced in response as the headache faded. I smelled a fresh omelet, one where you tossed in whatever's left in the fridge, but when I searched the kitchen, nothing was being cooked, baked, or fried.

A group sat at a heavy wooden table, and we joined them so I could watch them make elaborate grocery lists.

"Is there any coffee?" Other than breakfast with Lorenzo, I always had to ask for it. It was obvious no one liked me, and I had no idea why.

"You can use the single-serve pods." Mrs. Newbridge pointed to the far corner of the kitchen.

That's when I noticed everyone had dropped their gazes. Maybe it wasn't that everyone hated me. They were just following Mrs. Newbridge's orders. Or perhaps her general feelings. The more loyal one was to Lorenzo, the less they liked me.

They went back to their menus and lists while I strolled to the coffee maker. It was on a counter at the back of the kitchen near a delivery door. I grabbed a clean cup from a nearby stack and popped a pod into the machine, tapping my fingers while I waited.

There was a corkboard above the little island, and I read announcements, calendar reminders, staff rotations, and a delivery schedule. I don't know why I did it, but I reviewed the schedule, which listed mobile containers that were moved on and off the island. Supplies coming in and garbage going out. It made sense. What else would they do with garbage on an island?

I grabbed my coffee when it was done and spent the next hour bored out of my mind as the group continued with their menu planning.

The next stop was the laundry. I trailed behind Mrs. Newbridge like a good little soldier, occasionally asking questions when I thought it was appropriate and remaining respectful. The time spent in this area was short as most of the laundry—bed linens, towels, and staff uniforms—were sent off-site. However, I had the opportunity to review more schedules—staff rotations and deliveries that involved industrial liquids required to clean and maintain the manor. What I hadn't expected, and took note of, were the multiple outbuildings—cottages, maintenance buildings, the pool area, and barracks for Lorenzo's large security staff.

I memorized the map of the island while Mrs. Newbridge reviewed the cleaning schedule that was divided into daily chores, weekly chores, or special requirements when guests were due to arrive.

When I was finally released before dinner, I requested to have coffee in my room so I could rest, claiming my bruises were still painful. They weren't. Not really. I'd had worse, though the incidents of previous recoveries were vague at best.

Once I was in my room, I took out a pad of notepaper and a pen I'd swiped from a desk we'd passed by and copied down all the delivery details I could remember from the kitchen and laundry. Then I drew two maps. The inside map was everything I remembered of the floor plan and the second what I remembered of the island, including the location of the boat dock.

What I needed was to get outside and see the island for myself. And there didn't seem to be a reason for Mrs. Newbridge to be agreeable to that, which left Lorenzo. But that would be a dangerous ask.

It was obvious from everyone that was allowed to associate with me, that I was supposed to be his mistress. He'd certainly made that veiled threat obvious with his comment about the upcoming dinner party, which was only three days away.

I stared down at the pieces of notepaper in front of me. Why would I have collected all this data? There was an innate need burning within me to have a clear understanding of my environment in addition to all possible exits. I just didn't know why.

I grabbed the papers and took them to the walk-in closet. I

circled the room, considering it from various angles before dropping to my knees and pulling out the lowest drawers in a corner cabinet. The third drawer down held an array of belts and had weak points along the edges where the bottom met the sides. I tucked each piece of paper along the edges. The bottom drawer held winter scarves, and I exchanged them for the belts, placing each one in the exact order I removed them. Then I slid the drawer back into the third cabinet slot. I replaced the scarves that neatly covered the notes and slid the drawer into the bottom slot.

If I only understood what I was doing or why.

Five minutes later, Millie rushed in.

"We must get you ready for dinner. The master is home, and he brought a friend for dinner. He wants you dressed appropriately."

Great. I could hardly wait. This time I followed her into the closet. I might not be able to vote on what to wear but I'd be damned if I didn't get to pick the color.

Chapter Nine

DEVON WOKE and glanced at the bedside clock. Four a.m. Just as he'd planned. He reached for the medallion resting on the bedside table and pulled the necklace over his head. This probably wasn't the best of ideas, but he had to try again. He settled back into the pillow and stared at the ceiling, his fingers running over the medallion, feeling the ridges of the imprint that formed the Blood Poppy, ibis, and Dagger of Omar.

He didn't believe in magic, except perhaps for the mysticism of the shifters and their ability to morph between man and animal. But that wasn't any different than the beast that lived inside him and all vampires. He'd be foolish to ignore the power he sensed in the medallion. While he might not have been aware of it the first time he'd held it, he was convinced of it now.

Maybe Colantha had something to do with that. Not in giving him the ability to possess the power, but to awaken to it. Every construct he'd been in was as real as the bed and room around him. That was true power. A magical energy so intense it would send tendrils of fear throughout vampire society.

Was that why they'd been persecuted, their entire society all but erased, and their very existence hidden from all vampire knowledge? What had happened for the Council to make such a horrific decision? More importantly, he had to learn the truth of why the two races had once shared a symbiotic relationship.

He closed his eyes, his fingers still wrapped around the medallion. He thought of his private garden at Oasis. The scent of roses and honeysuckle. The sound of bubbling water from a fountain surrounded by ferns and white camellias.

He turned around, searching for the path that would take him to the grotto. The sharp edges of the gravel path bit into the soles of his bare feet. He ignored the pain as he ducked under the branch of a young maple tree.

There was no one at the grotto. The blood-red roses that cascaded around the lone stone bench were in full bloom. Their scent permeated the air, and he stepped closer, gently running his hand over the fragile petals until their fragrant smell washed over him. He found a new bloom and picked it. He'd lifted it to his nose and froze.

A presence drew closer. He was almost scared to turn around. Would it be her? Would she still be nothing more than a ghost?

He released a breath and turned.

She wasn't in full color, but neither was she the transparent aberration. The answer was that she was somewhere in the middle, like one of those black-and-white pictures that was remade into color. Her once vibrant persona nothing more than a muted duplicate.

But she was here, and that was more than he could have hoped for.

She'd been gazing at the foliage and flowers, her hand reaching out but not quite touching. Her expression was one of awe until she lifted her head and saw him. She stopped and took a step back.

"Please," Devon said. "I mean you no harm. Don't go. I've been searching for you. I wanted to make sure you were all right."

She stayed where she was and tilted her head in a way he was familiar with, as if she might be considering his statement, determining if his words rang true.

He lifted the rose. "The last time we were in a construct—one that you made—I gave you a rose similar to this." He lifted it to his nose and took a long sniff, closing his eyes as he relived the memory.

When he opened them, she was a few steps closer.

"Who are you?"

The question squeezed his heart and sucked the air out of his lungs, but it confirmed one thing. She'd been mesmerized.

"Devon Trelane."

She took a step back, a look of fear on her face.

He didn't move. This next step was critical. He had to move slowly and build trust.

"You are Cressa Langtry. You've been a member of House Trelane for a few months. You were at the condo with Ginger until a car came to bring you to the manor to continue your training. Ten minutes from the manor, your car was rammed and set on fire. Jacques was severely injured, and you were taken."

She shook her head. "You beat me."

Shock and anger filled him at the lies Lorenzo was feeding her. He held up his hands in a pleading gesture but allowed some of the anger and fear to show.

"I've never laid a hand on you." He couldn't help but smile and soften his voice. "Except for when they caressed you."

A blush crept over her cheeks, and she glanced away.

"Lorenzo must have told you he and I are enemies. I can't make you remember the truth, but he's been mesmerizing you. His touch while holding you in his gaze allows him to manipulate you. You won't believe what I'm saying, but I ask that you remain diligent and be wise."

He held out the rose. "Let me give you this as a reminder of this moment."

He wasn't sure she'd take it, but with the slowest of movements, she took three steps and then stretched out her hand. Her feet remained firmly planted as she leaned toward him, her fingertips barely grasping the stem.

Then she stepped back.

"Try to remember, Cressa. You're greatly missed. The beast howls for you."

He wasn't sure he should have said those last words when a look of horror passed over her face as if she recalled the beast.

His eyes opened, and he was back in his bedroom. He wasn't sure he could call the dream a success, but she had taken the rose. It was a good start.

I POPPED UP, hand on my chest. *What the hell just happened?*

That wasn't a normal dream. It was too real—except for the hazy vision. Like someone had dropped a veil over the lens, leaving a muted version of the original. Dreams should be more disjointed, shouldn't they? A simple representation of one's subconscious. But this dream had been an actual conversation, right down to the tactile feel and scent of the rose.

Devon Trelane. That was the vampire who'd beat me. Yet, he claimed I'd been in an accident. That I'd been taken. That Lorenzo was an enemy. For a brief second, I smelled burnt leather, and I grabbed my head and shook.

What was true? Had my own subconscious created the dream? That was more likely. The stress of being under Lorenzo's care with nowhere else to go was more than enough to impact my dreams. Devon admitted he knew Ginger and that I'd been living in his House, which was what Lorenzo had told me. It would make sense my brain would use that information to conjure dreams. But that was where stories changed. Devon made it sound like we'd been lovers. Was that true, or had I made that up?

A flash of skin, ash-blond hair, and ice-blue eyes interrupted my thoughts. That could be anyone. And if that memory had been Devon, it wouldn't be unusual for a domestic abuser to lie and pretend nothing happened. That it had all been in my head. Yet, I didn't remember the beating. Lorenzo had provided those details.

It all came down to the bruises. They could be consistent with someone slammed against a car door or a beating. I reached for the bedside lamp.

"Ouch!"

Something pricked me. I jumped out of bed, turned on the light, and stared at my chest.

A small circle of blood stained the satin nightgown just below my breasts. I pulled down the neckline and found a tiny red pinprick. That was strange.

I looked at the bed but didn't see anything until I pulled back the covers and leaped back.

A single red rose lay on the bed.

What the hell? I picked it up and noticed a small stain of blood on one of the thorns. Well, that explained the prick and blood on my nightgown.

I made a circle, staring into the shadows. No one was there. I turned on every light I could find, confirming I was alone.

I laid the rose on the nightstand, stripped off the nightgown, tossed it in the hamper, and grabbed another one. The drawers were like bottomless pits. Every time I removed something, there was always more underneath.

This nightie was cobalt blue and fit better than the last one. I picked up the rose and sniffed it. It was the same scent as the dream, and I was clueless how it ended up in my bed. One thing was for sure, I couldn't let Millie, Mrs. Newbridge, the Asshole, or Lorenzo find it. I hadn't been allowed outside yet, and there hadn't been any live flowers in the manor except for in the foyer, and it didn't have any roses in it.

I went back to the dressing room and searched the drawers for the best place to hide it. Even if I tossed it, somebody would notice. Not that I wanted to. I ended up sticking it in the pocket of a winter coat. Spring was turning into summer and there shouldn't be any need for it. It would be ages before anyone found it. I bent and gave the pocket a quick sniff. The scent calmed me.

I moved around the room, shutting off lights. The clock read four twenty. My eyes grew tired, and once the last of the lights were off I climbed back into bed.

This time when the dreams came they were the disjointed mess I would have expected—a silver necklace, a white flower, its edges dipped in red, and a man out of someone's nightmares with glowing ice-blue eyes, his arms circled around me. Instead of being terrified, it felt like home.

The dream changed.

Fire was all around me—hot and intense. Someone grabbed me. Hot leather on the back of my legs. The smell of burnt flesh. Someone screamed in agony. I screamed, too.

My eyes popped open. Lorenzo stood over me.

He reached out, placed his hand on my arm, and stared into my eyes. I jerked away, averting my gaze. The first dream roared back with Devon's warning about mesmerizing.

"Is everything all right?" He sat on the edge of the bed and moved closer, once again taking my hand. "I was leaving my room to take a business call and heard you screaming."

I wanted to curl up but didn't think it wise to pull my arm away again. "It was a nightmare."

He nodded. "That's to be expected with the recent trauma." He waited as I stared at the bedcovers, searching for any remaining blood stains while I picked at a loose thread on the sheet. "Look at me, Cressa."

Shit. I braced myself and glanced up, once again caught in his gaze. His eyes glowed for a brief moment, and while I felt myself drawn in, his pull wasn't as strong. I leaned in like I usually did. He ran his fingers down my cheek, and I forced myself to remain still.

He bent down and kissed me. His lips were warm, and his

tongue traced the outline of my mouth. Then he pushed his tongue inside while a hand moved to my hip. He squeezed—hard. At least it was on the left side where there wasn't any bruising yet. The pressure brought tears to my eyes.

When he leaned back, his eyes still glowed. "Soon, Cressa. You'll be mine, soon." He kissed my forehead, and I waited for him to stand. I glanced up, still swooning, though I exaggerated most of it. I would be lying if I claimed he didn't have some magical pull, but now that the seed had been planted, all I could dwell on was that I'd been mesmerized.

And while his kiss wasn't half bad, it didn't compare to another's. And though I couldn't conjure a face, ice-blue eyes flashed in my mind.

Chapter Ten

DEVON DIRECTED the meeting from his office chair at Lyra's insistence. Her headaches had increased in the last couple of days, and she preferred to lie on the sofa and listen. He suggested she stay in her room and he'd report to her later, but she insisted on participating.

The cadre was in attendance, including Bella. Four days had passed since the accident, and Jacques was making remarkable progress. Most of his skin had healed, and he'd be approved for light duty in another couple of days.

He picked up the white crystal and scanned the group. "Have we heard anything from The Wolf on what's happening at the midtown docks?" Someone had to have seen or heard something. They needed confirmation Cressa was on the island, or they would be entirely dependent on her remembering who and what she was.

"Nothing specific." Decker sat in his usual place at the bar. He wasn't part of Devon's cadre, but they were at the point in the mission where constant sharing of information with The Wolf was their only ace. "But they've seen a change in Venizi's routine. He leaves the island each morning and doesn't return until late. His security around the docks has also increased."

"It appears my distractions are working." Bella sat next to Decker, her legs swinging back and forth while she picked through the bowl of nuts left on the bar, mostly likely searching for cashews.

"It's not enough." Simone was still on edge, and if Devon didn't find a target for her soon, he'd have to find a task for her to work out her frustration. "We need someone inside."

"That would be impossible," Lucas said. He split his time between keeping Ginger occupied and volunteering for extra security details, admitting he needed to feel more useful.

"Why is that?" Simone asked.

"Perhaps I should have said it would take longer than we want. The staff is vetted quite thoroughly, and Venizi is extremely careful with who he allows on the island. We would need time to build a solid cover story, and then it would likely take months before they were trusted enough to find a position where it would be of any help. The delivery company employees aren't even allowed on the ferry. The vampires move the supplies on and off."

"Let's give Remus's people a couple more days." Decker searched the cabinets behind the bar before pulling out a plastic container and pouring more nuts into a bowl. He was eating them by the handful and chasing them with ginger ale.

Devon glanced at Sergi, who had been more quiet than usual since they'd returned from New Orleans. "Anything to worry about with security?"

Sergi shook his head. "We're following the plan, changing shift times and routes every day. But it's quiet." He scrolled through his tablet, then glanced up. "I would advise against calling Venizi. That would only play into his hand."

"What makes you think I'd do that?" Devon wasn't sure whether to be irritated by Sergi's insight or by the glances he got from the rest of the cadre.

Before he had time to respond, Sergi's phone buzzed. He

glanced at the cell then answered it. "Yes?" He listened for a few seconds before shifting his gaze to Devon. "There's a limo at the gate. Colantha Dupré and her two vampires are with her."

Lyra popped up to a sitting position and held her head for a second. "Let her in. Lucas, can you ask Greta to prepare three rooms?"

"They won't stay," Devon said.

"Maybe not. But I'd rather be prepared."

Sergi kept his gaze on Devon, who shook his head. "Don't look at me. Lyra is the House leader."

"And we don't have a choice." Lyra stood and reached into her pocket, pulling out a familiar medicinal tube that Madame Saldano would have given her for her headaches. "Besides wanting to meet her myself, I believe her to be our only hope in getting Cressa back." She drank half the vial then replaced the stopper before shoving it back in her pocket.

Devon rose and offered her the desk chair while he moved to a barstool on the other side of Decker. When they passed each other, Devon took her hands.

"Are you sure about this?"

"We won't get on that island in time. Cressa needs to remember who she is and find her own way back to us."

"Do you need us to wait elsewhere?" Simone asked.

Lyra looked to Devon. "Will it be too overwhelming for everyone to be here?"

"She's come to us. This is our House. But I will warn all of you. She is quite powerful and might want to converse with one or more of us in a dream construct. If that happens, you'll do nothing." He wasn't sure how else to warn them, unsure of Colantha's plans. He was shocked she came without any warning.

"How will we know if someone is in one of these constructs?" Bella asked. She hadn't paced during the meeting, but she was at the edge of her seat as if ready to take flight.

"Because they'll look frozen in time. As will I."

Everyone turned to the door they hadn't heard open.

Colantha Dupré stood in the doorway, regally dressed in a red linen, tailored pantsuit. A matching red head wrap was accented with gold threads and beads. Her two vampires hovered behind her.

Lyra stepped from behind the desk and smiled as she opened her arms wide. "Welcome to House Trelane."

When the three visitors stepped forward, one of the vampires shut the door and locked it.

Sergi and Simone rose, and everything went dark.

A flame burst to light. It came from a single candle and grew until most of the room was aglow. The candle sat on a stone table, and Devon was surprised to see everyone who had been in his office sitting around it dressed in long, forest-green robes with hoods, though their hoods were down.

Colantha presided at one end of the table. Her vampires were nowhere in sight.

Everyone glanced around, and then Sergi and Simone rose as one but, within seconds, fell back onto their seats of stone.

Colantha wore a white robe, and her medallion lay around her neck, plainly visible.

"What is this?" Simone asked, clearly irritated, her struggles to rise slowly quieting.

Devon sat across the stone table from Colantha. Lyra was to his right, then Lucas and Bella. Simone sat to his left with Sergi next to her and then Decker. He waited, letting Colantha answer since she was clearly in control of the situation.

"I could have waited, but time is of the essence, and rather than try to explain what a dreamwalker can do, it seemed easier to show you." Colantha's wicker chair looked a great deal more comfortable than the stone chairs. At least they had armrests.

"Where are your vampires?" Sergi asked.

"In Devon's office with the rest of us." She lifted her hands in a calming gesture. "They are there as protection since our bodies will appear unresponsive." She sat back and studied Lyra. "I sense you've dreamwalked before."

Lyra, who smiled as if enthralled by the change in scenery, nodded vigorously. "Several times."

"And not just with Cressa."

Her smile faded. "No. Not just with Cressa.

"Our bodies were left defenseless in the office?" Simone gripped the arms of the chair and though made of stone could be easily crushed.

Devon laid a hand on her arm. She didn't remove her hands, but her grip lessened.

"Quite so," Colantha answered. "Which is why Frederick and Jamison always remain behind."

"Have you been able to connect to Cressa?" Devon hadn't shared his last experience with anyone. He wanted to speak with Lyra first, but he was still processing it, almost believing it had been a true dream rather than a construct.

"I haven't tried. But you have. And I believe your latest attempt was more fruitful."

He shrugged and ignored the stares from the others. He squeezed Lyra's hand, and though her expression was more than curious, she squeezed back. "I'm not sure I was successful."

"I believe you were." Colantha glanced down at her hands, her brows furrowed. "I don't think most of you are ready to hear what I have to share, but as I said, time is of the essence. Dreamwalkers have a connection to a psychic nexus that can turn energy into matter. Some believe it to be spiritual in nature, others believe it comes from the links that form the constructs of the dreamworld. Who's to say which is correct? I believe it's a bit of both. Those with great power who have practiced their art and honed their skill, can, under the right environment, connect with other dreamwalkers to share a construct. If powerful enough, they can sense another dreamwalker and gauge their connection to the nexus."

She glanced around the table, and Devon followed her gaze. The initial concern and confusion had been replaced by curiosity, except for Sergi and Simone, who still appeared unsettled.

"From what Devon tells me, and by my current demonstration, this next part should already be evident. It is possible for a dreamwalker to bring what we call an Outsider, someone who isn't a dreamwalker, into a construct at will."

"What if we choose not to participate? There must be a way to break free of your hold." Lucas appeared more curious than fearful, but his question was key, and Devon was just as interested in hearing the answer.

Colantha sighed and focused on her hands for a minute before facing the group. "It is difficult for an Outsider to remove themselves from a construct without the proper training or a more powerful will. I feel one of you now on the edge of breaking free." Her gaze turned to Simone. "And it was the knowledge of this single ability that vampires began to distrust us. I will admit, there were a handful of rogue dreamwalkers who took advantage of that ability." Her face turned as hard as the stone table. "But rather than wait for us to bring those dreamwalkers to punishment, the Vampire Council acted hastily." Then her voice lowered and muttered, "To their own detriment."

She took a deep breath as if to calm her rising anger. "But that is a discussion for another time. I simply mention our abilities for two reasons. First, to be open in our communication as to what dreamwalkers are capable of. Second, I have reached out to Cressa to test her connection to the nexus. In my first attempts, it felt smothered, which I assumed was a side effect of the mesmerizing."

She turned her gaze on Devon. "You dreamwalked with Cressa again and found a time when Venizi's mesmerizing was at its weakest. Even under Venizi's spell, she has a strong connection to you. I believe wearing the medallion increased the rate of your success.

Though the mesmerizing continues to impact her abilities, I sense an awakening."

"Then why are you here?" Devon asked.

Her grin was wide as she rubbed her medallion. "To help power your connection to her."

Chapter Eleven

I woke and pulled the covers to me, rolling over to watch the intense blue sky out the bedroom window. Puffy clouds promised a splendid spring day, but I wasn't feeling it. For a reason I couldn't explain, I thought there would be another dream last night, but there hadn't been.

There were remnants of the strange dream with Devon Trelane, but I was fairly certain that was my own subconscious playing tricks with me. As if trying to force me to determine fact from fiction. I wasn't going to find out anything sulking in my room, so I threw the covers off and sat up. I stretched and considered a workout, but that would be problematic.

From what one of the human servants told me, the only gym was in another building used by Lorenzo's security teams. There wasn't a chance Lorenzo would allow me to go there. I'd have to be satisfied with my martial arts routine and ask if I could go outside for a walk around the grounds.

The clock said I had an hour before I was expected for breakfast, so I found the largest empty spot in the room and stood straight, arms at my side, and closed my eyes. I thought about martial arts, and a series of images came to me. After they repeated,

I joined in, letting my body move languidly from one pose to the next. Before I could question them, additional movements urged me on.

I followed each one with precision, moving faster—ducking, jumping. When I dropped and rolled, I ran into an end table, knocking the lamp off. I grabbed it just before it hit the floor and hugged it to my chest while I lay flat on my back, staring at the ceiling and breathing hard. The laughter couldn't be contained. It sprang out of me and seemed to release a pressure valve I hadn't known was there. I jumped up and set the lamp on the end table, feeling energized when the door burst open.

I spun around to find Asshole giving me a nasty scowl. He scanned the room, searching for a threat, then marched to the bed and drew back the bed covers, tossing them back when he saw nothing was there. He spun toward me, his face an angry mask, and instead of being afraid, I planned which moves to use if he came at me. I wish I had my dagger.

I froze and stared at my hands. Why would I expect a dagger to be in them? Did I keep one with me to protect me from Trelane? If so, I would have given as much as I received. But I didn't have any cuts or scrapes. At least, not recent ones. I did have scars. Something didn't feel right. Nothing made sense.

"Where is it?" Asshole took a step closer.

I refused to budge. "Where's what?"

He looked like he wanted to strangle me. "The phone."

I snorted. "I don't have a cellphone or a tablet." I spread my arms wide. "But feel free to search the place."

"Then who were you talking to?"

I considered the last half hour. "I wasn't speaking to anyone."

"I heard laughter."

Wow. All this because I laughed. My early childhood days of avoiding trouble or making excuses for any I caused rushed back, and a lie came easily to my lips. "I stumbled when I got out of bed, over-corrected, and stubbed my toe. I hit the end table so hard the lamp fell over, and I barely caught it before it crashed on the floor. I don't know about you, and I really don't care to know, but it made me laugh. I suppose that's something a proper lady isn't allowed to do."

"You have a sharp tongue on you. Perhaps Lorenzo needs to increase your treatments." He turned away, his gaze falling to the floor. He must have realized he'd said too much.

I wasn't aware I was on any treatments unless he was talking about the mesmerizing.

"Take a shower. I can smell your stink from here. It's almost time for breakfast."

What a charmer.

He all but slammed the door behind him. Did Lorenzo know how he treated me? Maybe it was expected in order to keep me in line. One thing was a given, I didn't want to face the master's wrath this morning. I took a quick shower, and when I came out of the bathroom, Millie was laying out my clothes—this time a knee-length skirt with a matching blouse and blazer. She barely glanced at me until I startled her by exerting what little control I had.

"No. That color won't do. Bring me something in sage green."

"I SHOULD HAVE MENTIONED HOW lovely that shade of green looks on you." Lorenzo spread marmalade on his toast, his gaze more on me than his task. "I'll have to commend Millie for her eye to detail. It seems to be improving." He took a bite and chewed as he continued to study me.

It required all my self-control not to tell him I had chosen the color and that Millie might as well be color-blind for as much effort she put into her selections. But I played the noble card.

"It was helpful you asked her to assist me. I'm learning a lot." I sipped the coffee rather than chug it as I preferred.

"I'm sorry our dinner guest wasn't a very exciting conversationalist."

Now, Lorenzo was playing the diplomat. His guest was as riveting as checkers on a Saturday night while listening to a documentary on the invention of toothpaste. The vampire kept talking numbers and probability analyses for something they were testing in a lab. Lorenzo continually steered him to other topics, but the man was singularly focused. But as much as Lorenzo feigned disinterest, his eyes glowed for an instant when the man said the formula was almost complete. I had no idea what formula, and it seemed to be in my best interest to appear bored. It didn't slip my awareness that I could simultaneously listen to every word, capture every emotion, and memorize anything worth stealing in the room while maintaining a disinterested posture.

I wasn't sure where the last thought had come from other than the sheer tediousness of the evening. And I couldn't have been happier when Asshole retrieved me after dessert.

Lorenzo touched my arm, pulling me out of my reverie as I picked at another egg-white omelet. He rubbed the edge of the linen jacket, then ran his hand higher, gently brushing the tip of my breast before caressing my cheek. "I'd hoped to come to your room last night to see how your day went."

"I guess you had a lot to talk about." I somehow managed to sound part agreeable and part hurt. Was that my own reaction, or was he pushing his feelings onto me?

"I'll see if I can't make it up to you this evening." He took a last bite of his toast, swallowed it down with coffee, then wiped his lips. "But I'm afraid new business is going to take me away for the majority of the day again."

I pouted, and he smiled with pleasure that made it all the way to his eyes.

"As much as I hate being away from you, it makes me yearn all the more with how much it equally displeases you." He laid his napkin on the table, a sign I recognized as his last move before standing.

I placed my hand on his arm and squeezed, finding it interesting that his gaze heated when he met my eyes. "I've been here a few days and haven't once been able to visit your gardens or feel the sun on my face."

The intensity of his gaze grew, and he clutched my hand. It was probably foolish to poke the bear, but I felt myself lean in. He grabbed the back of my neck and pulled me to him, his lips on mine, his tongue plundering for whatever treasure he thought he'd find. I couldn't prevent the enjoyment of the kiss or his possessiveness. Nor did I try to stop him when his hand reached under the table to squeeze my thigh before moving farther until his fingers scraped the edge of my panties.

I opened my mouth wider to accept his full passion as his kiss deepened.

"You are a temptress. I'm not sure which of us is caught in a snare."

I found his words odd, and it was difficult to pull back.

"I'll make sure Mrs. Newbridge allows for an hour in the sun. I like to see color on your cheeks." His smile was all-knowing as a heated blush came over me.

He stood and straightened his suit, stuffed his phone in his pocket, then leaned down and gave me one last intense kiss. "Behave while I'm gone."

The heat that suffused my body quickly dissipated when he left the room. It hadn't gone unnoticed that his last words were not said in a teasing tone but one that implied there would be ramifications if I stepped outside the lines that had been so rigidly drawn.

～

I TRAILED behind Mrs. Newbridge as she went through the house inventory. First, it was the kitchen pantry, then the linen closet, then the incidentals they kept on hand if the House was ever under siege. I was surprised when she confided that such a thing would be improbable with the entire estate being an island.

The statement triggered a mental discourse on what it would take to defend an island as well as attack one. Why my head went there instead of more domestic thoughts, I couldn't say. But I didn't fight it as I meandered behind her, asking a question here and there so she thought I was paying attention.

At this point, with my inane questions and random thoughts, she probably assumed I was a bit dim-witted, and that suited me fine. I continued to update my knowledge of the floor plan, picking up new information in changes to delivery schedules and staff rotations. The snooping seemed to come naturally, as did the ability to retain the information. But I pilfered another notepad and pen, and when someone stopped to talk with Mrs. Newbridge, I stepped aside to jot down quick notes.

Fortunately, Asshole hadn't come with us. On occasion I'd spot him somewhere, usually attending to other duties, but other times, I sensed his gaze on me—watching. I ignored him.

We had just finished lunch with the kitchen staff when Mrs. Newbridge sat back and gave me an evil eye. "The master said I had to take you on a garden stroll as if I'm your servant." She tossed her napkin on the table. "As if I have time for such pleasantries."

I lowered my head, playing the submissive mistress. "Sorry, I don't mean to be a burden. It's just been a long time since I've been outside."

She tsked, then seemed to brighten. I inwardly cringed, not wanting to know what made this woman smile. Her focus had turned to the door, and I closed my eyes. Please don't let it be Asshole. He was the last person I wanted to follow me around outside.

When I turned, ready to accept who was coming, I was

surprised to see a gorgeous redhead walking our way. This wasn't someone from the staff. Her abundant attributes were accentuated by a flower-print sundress and three-inch heels. She swayed toward us with the air of someone who was not only comfortable with herself but with her position within the Family. There wasn't any familial likeness to Lorenzo, so probably wasn't a sister. Maybe some other relation.

"Roberta, who do we have here?" The woman's voice was sultry, and her eyes pinned me like a butterfly for closer inspection. Warning bells sounded. This was not a woman to take lightly. And she was on a first-name basis with Mrs. Newbridge. Another sign to tread carefully.

"Miss Brigette, I heard you'd returned." She frowned at me before turning back to the stunning woman, who now stared down at me. "This is Cressa."

"Ah. Lorenzo's latest acquisition." Her full-on smile didn't quite reach her eyes.

And two things hit me immediately. She all but purred Lorenzo's name, which declared she was no relative because she'd slept with him—and probably still was. Second, and the thought made my blood run cold, was the term acquisition. Was I just another female to add to his harem?

"Hello." I would have rolled my eyes at the inane response, but when the woman's smile warmed, it dawned on me to play the same dimwit I portrayed with Mrs. Newbridge. If I gave this woman, who was most likely Lorenzo's current mistress, her due respect, she could be more useful than making an enemy of her, which was probably what she currently considered me.

She held her smile as she confirmed my suspicion. "I'm Lorenzo's mistress. I'd heard Lorenzo picked up a new Blood Ward. A damsel in distress from another House I believe."

If she'd been away and just returned, either Lorenzo kept her updated on his affairs or this island had a strong gossip mill. From what I'd learned about Lorenzo, I assumed the latter.

"It's nice to meet you."

"I assume you're being instructed on the rules of the House and the duties required to keep it running smoothly. Lorenzo is an exacting vampire and expects the highest performance and loyalty." She studied me and my clothing. "It looks like he has Millie picking out your wardrobe. Not one for fashion, are you?"

Her question wasn't meant for a response, but I shook my head, tired of hearing how exacting Lorenzo was.

"The master has asked me to take her on a tour of the garden." Mrs. Newbridge's frown returned. "Sometimes I don't think he appreciates the amount of work required to keep the staff in line and up to snuff."

"That's because you do a marvelous job." Brigette touched the woman's shoulder. "He has much respect for you."

I wasn't sure if Mrs. Newbridge beamed at the compliment or the touch. Most likely both. Then it hit me. Something I'd missed in my curiosity of the woman's position in the manor. Brigette wasn't a vampire.

She eyed me again, and something sparked in her eyes. "I'll tell you what. I've finished my unpacking, and my first appointments aren't until tomorrow. How about if I show our young Cressa around the gardens? I so missed the island; it would be nice to take a walk and check on the rest of the staff." Now I recognized the look in her gaze—mischief. She came home to find a new chew toy—me.

Instead of fear, a gauntlet had been thrown, and I was up for a game of who played their role better. I lowered my gaze and gave Mrs. Newbridge a submissive glance.

"Oh, Miss Brigette, I don't want to hand you such a burden."

I had to hold in a smile. Being called a burden wasn't the dig the old woman thought it was. It was a call to arms I'd gladly accept.

"Not at all. I think it's important our dear Cressa understands the role she's expected to play as a new Blood Ward."

Mrs. Newbridge stood, not taking a chance Brigette might change her mind. "It's such a joy to have you back. If you don't mind, I'd like to continue with this month's inventory."

"Never a problem, Roberta. You know you can come to me anytime." Brigette strode toward the outer door and snapped her fingers. "Come along, Cressa. You'll need to learn to keep up."

Like the Family's newest pet, I rushed to catch up, happy to play the submissive puppy. This bitch would learn the hard way that this puppy pissed where she wanted and hid a wicked bite.

Chapter Twelve

DEVON WATCHED Colantha contemplate the portrait on the wall. He'd selected the library after Colantha had returned everyone back to the study. Most took the experience in stride but, surprisingly, Simone appeared the most rattled and had asked to return to Oasis.

He released the rest of the cadre, who scattered quickly. Now, Colantha's vampires stood just outside the doors like sentinels. "I hope you don't mind the library, but I suppose any room would do since you could move us someplace more to your liking."

She gave him a small chuckle. "I don't dreamwalk as much as you would think. At least, not for personal reasons. I spend many hours training young and old dreamwalkers alike, and after a while, it's nice to stay in one place." She moved toward the bookcases and stopped on occasion to read the spines. "I must say you have a great deal of rich history here."

"My parents were the collectors. Now that Lyra is back with us, I imagine she'll pick up where they left off. It complements her painting."

"An artist? How marvelous. Are any of her works here?" Colantha scanned the walls.

"No. We considered it a security risk." When Colantha gave him a curious look, he indulged her. "Now that the Council is aware of Lyra, you might as well know the story." He waited until she took a chair across from him. "Lyra's presence in the manor was a guarded secret until she had to fill in for me."

"When you were addicted to the Poppy for a second time?"

He nodded. "Lyra was in the accident that killed my parents, along with her fiancé. I'd been away for several years, and with the death of everyone close to her, she fell into a deep depression. When she recovered, she claimed to hear voices and suffered from nightmares she was convinced were real. This went on for a decade, maybe longer." He ran a hand through his hair and stared at the decanter of scotch Lucas had left on the coffee table. "When the nightmares ended, it was just the voices, but the trauma left her in somewhat of a childlike state. I was concerned for her safety outside the manor, and I refused to put her in a sanitarium, though that's what the other Houses believe I did. All that began to change when Cressa arrived."

Colantha leaned over and lifted the decanter, pouring herself a glass. When she lifted the decanter toward him, he nodded, and she poured him one. "Tell me why you think that."

He sipped the scotch, running a hand along his pants, not sure how to explain it. "Lyra didn't come awake all of a sudden, but there were longer periods of coherent thought. She told me Cressa would save me from my beast. I hadn't believed her."

"She mentioned she'd dreamwalked before Cressa?"

He rubbed his eyes, sorry he'd agreed to the scotch. He was so tired. Lucas would need to call for another donor. His worry over Cressa was taking a toll. "That was news to me. I hadn't been aware of it."

"What about the dreamwalk she had with Cressa?"

"Lyra has a penchant for taking things that don't belong to her. It grew worse when she was ill. She never hid what she took and never apologized. When she was caught, she would smile and let us return the item to its owner. If she really wanted the item, she would just take it again. The medallion was one of those items. She found it in my safe and put it on."

"And she had no ill effects?"

"None."

Colantha leaned back and nursed her scotch, tapping a red-painted nail on the armrest. "Why did you believe Cressa was a dreamwalker? Our species is rarely spoken of. We keep our secret well-guarded."

He stared at the picture of his father over the fireplace. Had his father known of the dreamwalkers? He'd always wondered what it would have been like to sit in his father's study and discuss the myth of dreamwalkers over finely aged scotch. But that would have been impossible since Devon hadn't even considered dreamwalkers until after his father's death. It didn't make the desire any less real. "I believe I'd gone back east. Northeast I should say—Vermont. There's a small House that keeps to itself. Most vampires don't know how wealthy they are, but they do know how eccentric. Quite odd is what you would typically hear at vampire gatherings. But they're smart and, as far as I know, the first vampire House to have business partnerships with shifters.

"I'd met the House leader's youngest son, Charlie, when I was in Europe. We had similar ideas of how vampires could grow as a society, even with the decline of the fertility rate. After my father died, and I became House Leader, he invited me to his home. One night, we got drunk on absinthe."

Colantha laughed out loud. "No one ever believes me when I tell them it's possible to get a vampire drunk. I've always said they simply haven't tried hard enough."

Devon grinned, remembering the evening. "We snuck down to the cellar, looking for what we thought would be a decent bottle of wine when Charlie tripped over something on the floor. It was a carpet that covered a trap door. Being bold on drink, we found flashlights and followed the stone stairs. It wasn't nearly as dusty as I assumed it would be and, as it turned out, housed a comfortable room with electricity, fine Persian carpets, and aged leather couches. The walls were filled with books.

"We just happened to find one that mentioned dreamwalkers. There wasn't much. Just that long ago there was a species that could share their dreams. And if the vampire wasn't sufficiently prepared for the experience, they could go mad hearing voices, trapped in a living nightmare."

Colantha drained her glass. "And based on Lyra's behavior, it reminded you of what you'd read."

"I spent years looking for any reference to dreamwalkers no matter how minor. At one time, I thought I'd found something, but it was a dead end. Then Cressa walked into my life, and she unwittingly drew me into a construct."

"From what she tells me, that was the first time it ever happened."

He nodded. "Based on her reactions to those first dreams, I believe her."

"The one thing I've yet to understand is the strong connection between the two of you, but for now, we'll take advantage of it. I will create the construct, and you will be the anchor that draws Cressa out. We must use her bond with you to counter the mesmerizing. She'll require strong memories that can link to her reality. I'd like to meet with Lyra and Cressa's friend. Ginger, isn't it?"

Devon nodded. "When?"

"After dinner. From there, we'll decide when to make the attempt."

～

DEVON ENTERED Cressa's bedroom expecting a sense of loss to greet him. And it hit him like a brick. She'd been in the manor for less than three months and had been through so much. They both had.

He was angry for allowing her to stay at the condo. After he'd beaten the Poppy and settled the beast, he'd seen how angry Lorenzo had been. He wasn't privy to what was happening in the Council with the discovery of Magic Poppy in Gheata's basement, but rumors were beginning to leak. Whoever was behind the Poppy would have to put their plans—whatever the endgame was —on hold until things cooled down. And that could take several months.

The Sentinels, who would be put in charge of the investigation, were known for their slow and methodical approach, but even with that, he doubted they'd find the ringleader. His gut told him Lorenzo was the mastermind behind the Magic Poppy, and if he ever discovered what Cressa was, they might never find her. Devon's only hope was that their ruse of her being his Blood Ward was the only reason Lorenzo had bothered taking her.

After his meeting with Colantha, he'd gone to the safe house to check on Jacques. He was up and around, though his skin wasn't completely healed. But it wasn't his physical injury that kept him from being approved for full active duty. Jacques blamed himself for Cressa's kidnapping. No one faulted his actions that day, but only time and recovering Cressa would heal his mental state.

Devon knew all about blame. He'd made a huge blunder blaming Cressa for his mental fugue after the Poppy incident. And Madame Saldano, who'd been at the safe house with Jacques, seemed to relish chastising him for his impatience during his recovery. He assumed she did it for Jacques's benefit, especially since she'd been right.

His further discussions with Colantha had confirmed the healer's opinion. His fugue was an aftereffect of blending two blood types after a high-volume exchange. Colantha also believed he would carry residual dreamwalker blood in his system for some time. It wouldn't harm him but was most likely the reason he was able to reach Cressa in a construct. She'd been surprised he'd recovered as quickly as he had. When he'd confided his experience at the scene of Cressa's accident where, after a massive headache, instant clarity had returned, she'd simply nodded.

Strong emotions, like his anger and fear for Cressa, had pushed the final healing. She equated it to Cressa's intense emotions. More specifically, the anger and frustration she felt around him when they'd first met, which had sparked her dreamwalker abilities.

He stared down at the scarf in his hands, not remembering picking it up. It held her scent, but before he could fall back into the blame game, laughter made him spin around. He'd been so busy with his musings, he hadn't noticed there was anyone else in the room.

The laughter was coming from the closet. When he peered in, he found Lyra, Ginger, and Colantha huddled in the back, their heads bent close. Ginger was still giggling.

"Why are you all in here?"

The three women turned around at the same time. Their cheeks were tinged with blushes, even Colantha, and he was sorry he asked.

"Colantha wanted to know more about Cressa." Ginger held a pair of jeans in one hand and linen pants in another. "These two garments express a very different Cressa. During the day, she'd just as soon wear jeans or sweats, though she wears what's expected of her with these." She waved the arm that held the linen pants.

"I wasn't aware these other clothes bothered her." Devon had requested she wear clothes that reflected her status as a Blood Ward to fit the persona she'd agreed to play.

"Oh, don't get me wrong, she likes these other clothes, but they remind her of her days living with Christopher. But she has her favorites—things you bought her." She moved in a circle, taking in the entire closet. "If you were to look at the clothes you first bought her and compared them to your more recent purchases, you'd see they're not the same. Both represent the Blood Ward of a House leader, but the newer clothes fit her personality better. Maybe you didn't recognize it when you made the selections, but you did it just the same."

"I hadn't noticed."

Ginger shrugged, and she handed the linen pants to Lyra, who hung them in their appropriate spot. "I'm a fashion hound. Cressa, not so much. It's not that she doesn't like the finer stuff, it's just not as important to her. Like I said, she'd lounge around in sweats all day if she could."

Devon looked to Colantha. "And this helps you how?"

"I control everything in my constructs, down to the clothes a person wears, how their hair is styled, to what makeup they wear. We have to assume that, just like you, Venizi has procured a specific wardrobe he demands Cressa wear along with certain expectations of behavior. Knowing what I do of Venizi, he will be more stringent in his requests where you were willing to bend."

"You want to bring Cressa to a construct as she would see her true self. Not just in the environment but in her choice of clothing."

"Exactly."

"But we think Colantha might have to change constructs during the session." Lyra took the jeans Ginger had been holding, folded them, then hugged them to her chest. "Places that represent Cressa's personalities, as well as the world she lives in with us."

"You make it sound like this was just a staged play she's been living in." Devon didn't like what he was hearing. Had he forced Cressa to be someone she wasn't? Yes, he'd provided clothing befitting her role, but that was when she'd first arrived and their relationship was strictly business. Did he still see her in that role?

Worse, did she see herself like that? With no freedom to make her own decisions.

"Don't go there, brother." Lyra touched his arm.

Colantha chuckled. "Don't worry, vampire. I know how this must look to you. You're wondering if you've been controlling her all this time. You're concerned she sees life in this manor as restrictive as it must be with Venizi." She moved past Devon as she left the closet, the rest of them trailing after her.

She took a seat by the cold fireplace, and like good soldiers, everyone took seats around her. A tea service had been set on the coffee table, and Lyra poured everyone a cup.

Colantha sipped her tea and nodded approvingly. "Ginger shared Cressa's youth with me in addition to their life after they met. It was a hard life, but a happy one. One they felt comfortable with and had learned to bear. All of that changed when Cressa was caught by Sorrento and found her way here."

Devon braced himself for what was coming. When he considered the last three months, he grimaced. He'd been difficult, moody, and single-minded in his pursuit to destroy Lorenzo and regain his place on the Council. So he wasn't prepared at all for what Colantha said next.

"Cressa has found a home here. She's made friends among the cadre and with Lyra. You've allowed Ginger to be included in this new life, and she's reconnected with her mother on a more mature level. While you don't realize it, vampire, you've given her a place to spread her wings and become who she was always meant to be. You've allowed Pandora to come out when required. And yes, it was for your own gain, but having your censure removed in order to secure your vote on Council matters benefits all of us— vampires, shifters, and humans alike. It is in this environment, and only this one, that dreamwalkers can once again take their rightful place in society."

"We both benefit from Cressa."

She shrugged. "One could look at it that way, but Cressa isn't the only one required to make the world safe for everyone. All I'm trying to say is that this House, your people, and Ginger make up her world. One that is comforting to her, one she's willing to fight for. And that is what my construct must represent in order to break whatever tendrils Venizi holds on her."

He nodded as he considered her words. They made sense. If Colantha could provide such a construct, he believed Cressa would remember who she was. The question, as he glanced at Ginger and Lyra, was whether he was critical to the construct. He decided not to ask, refusing to consider how important the answer was to him.

"Do you have everything you need?" It seemed a safe enough question.

"I need to know the best location to use," Colantha answered.

"That's a tough one." Ginger scratched her head as she stared at the empty fireplace. "I've never known her to be connected to any one place."

"We'll have a better chance if I have three settings. I can work with two, but it adds more risk for success."

"The sycamore tree," Lyra suggested. "She's always seemed as connected to it as I am."

"Yes. The last construct we shared was made from several locations. She'd made it on her own and was quite proud of it." Devon leaned forward, his mood brightening. "The sycamore was there, and..." There was something more important, something that seemed private when she'd mentioned it. He snapped his fingers. "Newberry Park. It was the base of her construct. She said it was a place she used to run to when she needed to feel safe."

"Really?" Ginger seemed in awe. "It must have been when she was a kid and Christopher was on the warpath."

"Was there any landmark in the park?" Colantha asked.

"I think there was a fountain."

"We could drive there." Lyra refilled teacups. "It's not that far, and I assume we wouldn't want to make an attempt until after midnight."

Devon nodded, then his gaze shifted to Colantha. "I'd like to add one more location for you to visit, but it's not as close. I suggest we leave now."

Chapter Thirteen

BRIGETTE LED me through the manor, and I obediently followed, guessing at which room would come next, testing my memory of the floorplan. Ninety percent accuracy. For some reason, I kept forgetting about the portrait room. Or maybe the house was magical and it just kept switching locations. I'd have to review the floor plans again before I went to bed.

The solarium wasn't as grand as another one that came to mind, and I almost tripped when the thought hit me. Part of my memory seemed to be returning, like scattered pieces of a photograph that had been cut into dozens of pieces, but the critical sections had blown away in the wind. Frustrating at best.

"This is my favorite room of the manor." Brigette stopped by a large fern and broke off a brown frond, tossing it on the table for the house staff to clean up. "I'd prefer you avoid coming here. It's one thing to have you temporarily living in the manor. It's quite another to take what I consider to be mine." She gave me a cheery smile before exiting onto a stone path.

I didn't have to be told that her threat over what she considered hers also included Lorenzo. That was alright by me. There were still moments when I was ready to rip off my clothes and let him have his way with me, but I knew that wasn't the real me. There was another side of him—a darker side—that cooled those moments of promised intimacy. The only problem was that I doubted Lorenzo cared one whit what Brigette considered hers.

The path ran through floral beds, past a handful of fountains, and under canopies of trees before coming to an expansive, luscious green lawn. On the far side, to the left of the garden path was a fair-sized pool and hot tub. On the right, and within partial view of the manor was a two-story, bungalow-style building.

"What's this? Is it for guests?" There were several balconies on the second floor and patios at ground level.

She laughed. "You're either quite naïve or you truly have lost most of your memory." She made hand quotes when she said memory and winked. If that was in reference to the mesmerizing, I didn't think it was all that funny. "This is where the humans live. I have my own suite here, though I spend most of my evenings in the manor."

From what she'd said in the kitchen, she'd just returned from someplace to find the master's new plaything in the kitchen. I couldn't blame her for being jealous, as long as she wasn't dangerous. And somehow, even that thought didn't scare me. I could handle myself in a fight, though I wasn't sure I wanted to know why. Maybe it was the martial arts moves that came so easily, or the confusion when I hadn't found a dagger in my hand.

Brigette passed by the bungalow, and we continued until she turned off onto a gravel path. The vegetation grew thicker the farther we walked.

"How long have you been on the island?" The continued silence was becoming unnerving, and Brigette's easy stroll became more determined as she picked up her pace.

"Around six years."

"Are you a Blood Ward?"

She snorted. "Several years ago. I have the option to be made vampire whenever I want, but Lorenzo has asked me to remain human for a little longer." She gave me a self-satisfied grin over her shoulder. "He likes the taste of my blood—among other things."

Okay. TMI. I decided silence was the best option in this awkward situation.

I was beginning to question where she was taking me and whether there was a cliff on the island. Five minutes later, she rounded a corner, and an old stone building came into view. It looked decades older than the manor and the outbuildings I'd seen. The stones had been whitewashed some time ago, and time, salt, and stormy weather had worn some of the paint away, revealing the stone surface beneath. It was a single-story building with two windows, their shutters closed. The single wooden door with iron hinges had a small iron-barred window set at eye level that appeared to open from the inside. Waves crashed close by, and I imagined a cliff along the backside of the building.

A vampire stood next to the door and frowned when he saw us. "You know you shouldn't be here, Miss Brigette."

"I know, Arnold, but I was showing our new Blood Ward the island and lost track of where I was. We'll just follow the path that winds around the tidal pools if that's all right."

He nodded. "All quiet today, but it's best if you keep moving."

"Absolutely. My apologies again, Arnold."

"Not necessary for you, Miss Brigette."

I waited until we'd turned down a couple of bends in the path before asking the question Brigette had to expect I'd ask. "What's that building for?"

She continued for several more paces as if she hadn't heard me and walked through an opening in the foliage. A view of the ocean came into view. The mainland was visible, and I sighed. Not that far away but too far to swim. I'd expected as much.

Brigette sat on a stump that seemed perfect for the view and studied me again. "It's where he keeps his enemies. Vampires and others that won't be missed. Sometimes, an occasional human who didn't follow the rules. And, of course, there have been a Blood

Ward or two who simply didn't work out but weren't mentally sound enough to be on their own. Lorenzo took pity on them."

Blood Wards. Like me? "I don't understand."

"Some don't take the time to understand Lorenzo. How he protects us. Cares for us. They question his rules. I have to admit, Lorenzo can seem rather old school when it comes to his expectations of a lady. And I assume he hasn't explained his three-rule policy yet. Let's just say you never want to be reprimanded three times." She nodded at the path we came from. "It would be impossible to find a House that would accept a Blood Ward that didn't meet Lorenzo's exacting standards. So, when necessary, he keeps them as part of his collection."

I turned my back on her to stare at the mainland. A cold shiver ran down my spine, and goosebumps broke out. A blinding headache hit me, and I dropped to my knees, grabbing my head. It was like someone was poking around in my head, picking through a flash of memories. Some I recognized, others I didn't. A glimpse of a face in a mirror. It wasn't mine. It was a man. I couldn't tell if I was screaming out loud or in my head, but moments later, Brigette shook me.

"What's wrong with you?" She was yelling back. "You need to calm down and be quiet."

I must not have complied because she slapped me. Hard.

The headache subsided, and I sank back on my heels, sucking in large amounts of air. When my breathing normalized, I stood and rubbed my cheek.

"Just look what you did to your pants. That's mulberry silk. Lorenzo will be furious with you." She grabbed my elbow and dragged me down the narrow path until we reached the stone path. We were almost back to the manor when she stopped and spun to face me. "You won't say anything about our little detour off the main path. I promise you, you won't like the consequences."

I nodded. Who was I going to tell? All I wanted was my bed. A light pounding persisted, and I preferred not doing anything that made it worse. Maybe I suffered from migraines and didn't remember.

Before we reached the back patio, Asshole stepped out from a side path.

"Where have you been?" He looked angry, and it only got worse when he noticed the dirt stains and frayed material at my knees.

"We went for a walk through the garden and Cressa took a tumble. Heels don't seem to suit her. I'm surprised Lorenzo would have selected someone so unschooled to become a Blood Ward."

"Lorenzo has his reasons." He sneered at me. "Go to your room and get yourself cleaned up. Lorenzo will expect you for dinner this evening." His gaze moved over Brigette. "You're looking rather fetching this afternoon. The spa suited you."

"You are a dear. I had a very relaxing time."

"You should prepare as well. The master will expect you after his brandy and cigar." He grabbed my upper arm, squeezing it until the headache returned, and tears stung my eyes. "In fact, let me take this one off your hands. I'll see her to her room."

Brigette flashed a million-dollar smile. "You are the best to me."

Asshole dragged me through the manor and to my room where he opened the door and shoved me inside. I tried to catch myself but twisted an ankle when my heel caught on the rug. I went down —hard.

I glared at him.

He bent over and grabbed my chin. "You need to start doing what is asked of you. The master is not a tolerant man. If I say one word about the condition of your clothes, it could mean your first strike. So, remember this favor I give you. I'll expect you to return it when I ask."

He shoved me to the floor before walking out the door. It slammed behind him.

I crawled to the bed and climbed in, curled into a fetal position, and drew the covers over my head. I stayed that way until the pounding in my head ceased and the darkness came.

I WASN'T sure when the headache stopped and the dreams began.

At first, they were pleasant. A young woman running across a beach. Her dress was vintage, her hair cut in a bob, the age of flappers and Prohibition. A man ran behind her, catching her and twirling her around.

The scene changed to a picnic under a young sycamore tree. The woman seemed familiar, but her hair should be longer. The man's image brought memories of paintings—dozens of them. Some included his face, others just an outline, but they were all the same man.

The images grew darker—fire, pain, screaming. He couldn't dream, and he tried. Tried so hard. He lived in a cell where there was no light, and when they came to ask him questions, he went to an even darker place.

In a flash, the man was in a different cell. Light streamed in from a bare window. His hair was long, greasy, and tangled. A straggly beard hung to his chest, yet his eyes were as clear as a river stream, with no lines on his face to give away his age. He smiled. A beatific smile of another time and another place.

Then, his eyes refocused and stared at me, pleading. "Help me, Cressa. Help me."

I sat up and grabbed my head, but the headache was gone. The covers had been kicked off, and I was still in the torn slacks. My knees stung, and my upper arm felt bruised from where Asshole had grabbed me to drag me through the manor.

Brigette.

It was becoming apparent I wouldn't find a friend in this place. And I didn't know if the building she showed me was meant to terrorize me or prove a point. I was a threat to her. Lorenzo's new plaything. Was I living in a dream of cliches, or were all vampire Houses like this?

Memories of Trelane suggested otherwise. If he had been my abuser, assuming Lorenzo hadn't lied, why didn't I have night-mares of it?

I shuffled to the bathroom and stripped off my clothes then stood in front of the standing mirror. I turned to view my left side. There wasn't a mark anywhere I could see. I faced the mirror where the only visible blemishes were the bruising on my knees—the result of the fall from the blinding headache.

When I turned to view my right side, the bruising that covered my skin from shoulder to thigh was now an ugly yellow, tinged with a dark purple as they began to fade. Even so, the marking still appeared uniform. The only new bruise was the one forming on my upper arm, as I suspected.

What would leave a uniform bruising? A beating from an abuser or being thrown against something. It had to have been a violent movement for my body to slam against something hard enough to leave the marks. A vampire throwing me against a wall? Or an accident?

The shower was hot and luxurious. After drying off and taking care with my hair and makeup, I walked into the closet and did two things. I pulled out my secret floor plans and made updates based on my walk earlier in the day, adding the outside buildings and a general recollection of the paths. They weaved through the landscape, but the dimensions seemed right.

Then, I reviewed my wardrobe. Images of another closet super-imposed over this one. In addition to dresses, pants, and blouses, there were workout clothes, jeans, and cozy sweatshirts. I shook the other closet away and focused on the choices in front of me, pulling out a robin-egg blue sleeveless sheath dress and a light sweater. I ignored the four-inch neck breakers and found a pair of kitten shoes.

If Brigette wanted to play games, so be it. It was apparent I was on my own. Something nagged at me, convincing me this was far from the first time I'd been in this type of situation.

I'd just slipped on a necklace when the headache came again. This time, I found a chair before the images came.

"Stop it. Whoever you are, stop it. I'm here. I see you."

I didn't know why I said it, but it felt right. When the man's face first appeared with his unwashed hair, his gaze flitted about, wide-eyed. Then he was clean-shaven, and his gaze was clear but still pleading.

"Find a way, Cressa. Find a way to free yourself, and then free me. Tell her I love her."

The outer bedroom door burst open, and the image and headache vanished as if it never happened. Someone stomped around—most likely Asshole.

"What are you doing in here?"

Yep, it was him, and when I glanced up, he appeared surprised.

"I was getting dressed. Isn't it almost dinner time?" I stood and brushed off my dress and stormed past him, bumping his shoulder hard as I went past.

"I thought Millie was running late." He trailed behind me.

"I haven't seen her." With hands on my hips, I gave him a long look. "Believe it or not, I've been dressing myself since I was a little girl." When he just stared at me, I shook my head. "Wow. All of a sudden not a single witty response. You're beginning to disappoint me."

I took a last look in the mirror over the dresser and waltzed out the door not bothering to wait or get his permission. It was impossible not to smile as he hurried to catch up. I ignored him as I wondered what game Lorenzo was in the mood to play tonight.

Chapter Fourteen

DINNER WAS BECOMING A ROUTINE, boring affair. I ate with more purpose than usual, which made Lorenzo lift a brow as I accepted a second helping. My improved appetite was blamed on the fresh air from the garden. Since he didn't mention Brigette, I didn't bring her up.

We were drinking after-dinner cappuccinos when Lorenzo sat back and gave me a long look. "I hear you've been doing well with learning the house schedule."

That surprised me. "Really? I didn't get the feeling Mrs. Newbridge liked me."

He smiled. "Oh, she doesn't. But that doesn't prevent her from giving me the facts. She admits your etiquette skills are adequate. And don't pout. That's high praise from her. I also understand she's taken you through the main functions of the house."

"I didn't realize how complicated running a house could be. It got a little overwhelming at times."

"Well, it didn't seem to show." He clapped his hands and leaned toward me. "I think some form of celebration is in order. I have some free time before a late-night meeting. What would you like to do?"

From what Asshole implied, Lorenzo's late-night meeting would be Brigette. I really had to check my need for attention because I shouldn't be irritated that he was seducing me while having cozy nights with his mistress. These conversations with Lorenzo were a dangerous game, but spending time with him might provide valuable information. And one could never have too much of that.

I lifted my brows and gazed at the ceiling as if I were considering my options. The possibilities of what he'd allow me would be narrow, and no doubt his yet-to-be-revealed House rules would apply.

"I'd like a tour of the manor."

His brows lifted. "You must have seen most of it with Mrs. Newbridge."

I grimaced. "My feet would agree with you, but my days trailing behind her mad search for any drop of dust isn't the same. From my quick glimpses, you have interesting art and amazing heirlooms. The architecture alone is stunning." I lowered my gaze and shrugged. "No one can properly show off a house than the one who owns it."

I crossed my fingers that I hadn't gone too far. But the light in his eyes and the straightening of his shoulders revealed his pride leaking out.

"Ernesto, have our brandy served on the office balcony in an hour." He stood and held out his hand. "Let me take you on a historical tour of my home." His smile was charming. "I hope I don't bore you."

I stood, returning his smile as my skin warmed to his touch. "I don't see how that could be possible."

An hour later, I wanted to strangle myself rather than listen to Lorenzo pontificate on the glorious battles his ancestors fought in, his business prowess, or the rich artifacts he'd collected over his long life, which was somewhere around five hundred years, give or take a hundred.

The tour ended in his private office, which was elaborately decorated with dark-paneled walls and paintings of battle scenes. A massive wood desk was on the left with two bookcases behind it. On the right was a gas-lit fireplace surrounded by two leather sofas and four matching chairs. Twelve monitors filled the space on another wall above another sitting area. Next to it was a fully stocked bar. I expected an espresso machine, then sighed. Once again, other images were superimposed over reality, and I didn't know why. Was I seeing remnants from House Trelane or a different place?

He led me out to the balcony where the brandy had been poured. Instead of sitting, I picked up my glass and strolled to the classic stone railing made with an open framework design and peered out over the island. The sun had set, and dusk was settling over the landscape, but it was light enough to make out a boat leaving the dock, heading toward the mainland. I checked the watch I'd found in a jewelry box. It was nearing eight o'clock.

"You found the watch." He stood close enough for our arms to brush.

"Just this morning." I made a pretense of showing him. "The diamonds are a perfect touch."

"I thought so." He wrapped an arm around my waist.

"Doesn't it get old having to take a boat each time you need to go to the mainland?"

He turned his gaze to where the boat was already halfway across the small channel. "That's the transport for staff and cargo. I use a small yacht with its own office. The trip is about twenty minutes including docking and isn't much different than having to drive through traffic."

"And I'm sure a limo is always waiting dockside," I said in a chiding tone as I bumped his hip.

"Always." He set our glasses on the railing and turned me to him, lifting my chin. "Just another couple of days and I'll welcome you to my bed." He kissed me, his body more than ready as he pushed it against mine, the rail now to my back.

The vamp knew what he was doing as one arm held me against him as his hand roamed. Through it all, I could only guess why he was waiting. Was it a mind game? And then it came to me. He wanted me completely mesmerized. He wanted me to come to him, eager and willing. Then his mastery of me would be complete.

His hand moved to a more intimate spot, and I tried to relax, knowing I couldn't prevent his actions, when a chime made him stiffen. He didn't stop until the chime rang again.

"Damn it. I need to take this." He stepped away so quickly I had to grab the rail. I downed the rest of my brandy.

He was on the phone, and though I couldn't hear what he was saying, his tone was growing angrier by the second.

I ignored him and considered the railing and ledge before leaning over the side, which required placing a foot in one of the open spaces between the stones. I climbed up another step that put most of my body weight over the railing. The height didn't scare me. Instead, my gaze darted to the open stonework that framed the balcony, searching for hand and toe holds I could use to either climb down to the garden below or up to the roof.

I wasn't sure why I might want to do that, but a memory flashed of a climbing wall, then I was clambering up the side of a three-story house, running across a similar railing before grabbing onto a cornice and pulling myself up to the next floor. I used a knife to slip the latch and open the slider.

The room was dark, and I scanned it with a penlight, searching for my target. I had entered a condo where the owners weren't home. That couldn't be right. That would make me—what—a thief?

I jumped down from the railing and sat down hard on the patio chair.

I remembered that place. Not only did I break in, but I went directly to the safe that was hidden behind a portrait. Not a surprise. Many safes were hidden behind paintings. This particular one had been a disturbing sight, and I'd run my penlight over it several times before the timer in my head said to move on. I cracked the safe with the third code I tried, found the envelope I'd been paid to recover, and took a stack of money and a small bag of jewels. After shoving the goods into a backpack, I raced toward the entryway and slid into a closet. I waited five minutes before the door opened with a card key and two people stumbled in. Based on the sounds, they'd been in heavy petting mode.

A soft thud that might have been a purse hitting the marble floor. Something slammed into the closet door, and I held my breath. When the sounds grew distant, I cracked open the door. They were down the hall and turning into the master bedroom. A single shoe lay halfway down the hall next to what looked like a blouse.

I glanced down before leaving the closet and saw the other shoe. That must have been what had hit the closet. I quietly opened the front door, grateful they hadn't reset the alarm, though I knew the code. The outer hallway was empty, and I whipped off my face mask and stuffed it in the backpack. Once I hit the stairwell, I pulled off my black sweater and jammed it in the pack then ruffled my hair as I raced down the stairs to the first floor which had two exits—one to the lobby and one outside. When I opened the door, Lorenzo pulled me up by my arm, breaking the memory.

I held in my emotions as his angry face stared down at me. Had I done something wrong?

"I'm sorry to cut this short. Another matter came up that I must take care of personally. Can you see yourself to your room?"

"Yes." My voice was shaky as he led me to the door.

"I'm sorry." He brushed strands of hair from my face. "I didn't mean to scare you. It's nothing you did. I'll see you at breakfast."

He all but pushed me out the door, and I raced back to my

room. I tried to hide my excitement as I shoved Asshole away when he attempted to block my bedroom door.

"Lorenzo was interrupted by some business matter." I slammed the door in the vamp's face. I danced around the room, unable to hold in the elation any longer. I was Pandora, and I was a thief. A really good thief.

Now, if I could only remember more of Trelane and why I'd been living with him.

SERGI TURNED the limo down the unmarked dirt drive that led to Oasis. Devon wasn't sure they'd get this far after a long and heated discussion with Colantha and her vampire guards over the secrecy of the location. The only reason he relented in allowing her guards to come was Sergi's reminder that Colantha had allowed him to drive into her compound to retrieve Cressa. Now, they had shared secrets.

Lucas was in the front seat with Sergi. Lyra, Ginger, Colantha, and her two vampires shared the back with Devon. Simone wasn't pleased when he called before leaving the manor to advise of their visit. He assured her she didn't have to greet them, but some refreshments on the west outdoor patio would be appreciated.

Colantha made Simone nervous, and though he couldn't be sure, he expected it had to do with control and who had it. Simone might manage Oasis, but her background was security and tactical fighting, and she had no defenses while in the construct. The only reason Sergi wasn't as upset was his previous experience with Colantha. And it explained Colantha's fierce need to keep her bodyguards close at hand since she was just as defenseless. But the situation proved one thing: Devon had to find a way for his Family to leave a construct at will. Something he would discuss with Colantha.

He'd studied Colantha on the hour drive while Lyra and

Ginger kept her occupied with questions and stories. She appeared to be fully engaged in the conversation while staying aware of everything around her, including his steady gaze. She ignored him, and it reminded him of Cressa's similar ability to appear bored while capturing every emotion and object around her.

When the outer housing units came into view, Colantha moved her vampires out of the way so she could get a better view. She rolled down the window, and he half-expected her to jump out. When the main house came into view, she released a sigh. Her vampires glanced at each other, and he wasn't sure what to make of their slight grins.

Devon relaxed and looked to Lyra, nodding his head toward the window. She bent her head to see what he'd seen and smiled.

Simone stood on the top step just outside the door. The limo stopped at the base of the stairs, and Lucas jumped out of the limo and opened the passenger door. The two vampires got out first and scanned the area, taking in Simone and the other vampires of House Trelane. Sergi opened the other side door, and Devon stepped out in time to see Simone smile at her guests.

When they reached the top step, she held out her arms. "Welcome to Oasis, home of House Trelane."

Colantha bowed her head before turning to view the surrounding estate. "Quite impressive." Then she turned back to Simone and followed her into the manor.

They were led directly to the outdoor patio where refreshments waited. Once they were seated, Simone turned to leave, but Colantha caught her hand.

"You are very important to Cressa."

Simone appeared shocked then quickly schooled her features into a light nod. "She is a precious member of the House."

Colantha waved her hand, dismissing Simone, who glanced at Devon and compressed her lips into a fine line before leaving the patio.

Colantha raised her voice enough to be heard. "You can't fool me, vampire. I can plainly see what is in your heart."

Simone stumbled partway down the hall before veering off into whatever room came next.

"I didn't mean to annoy her." Colantha took the proffered glass of iced tea and closed her eyes. "Black peppermint tea. Exquisite." She turned to Devon. "She's a strong one. She'll make an excellent House Leader one day. But she needs some of that smugness knocked out of her."

Devon chuckled and changed the topic. He waved to the gardens that stretched out before them. "Cressa hasn't spent much time here, but we have a shared memory down by the edge of the lake, and over by the oak tree." He pointed toward the east. "But our most intimate dreams occurred in my private garden."

"What were her favorite things in the garden? Do you know?" Colantha asked.

He smiled as he remembered his moments in the dream. "We always met at the grotto. There are cascades of red roses, like those near the lake. She seemed to like them." He laughed. "She once commented on how she enjoyed the feel of the grass between her toes, and then she'd wiggle them." His laughter faded. "She enjoys the simple things."

She patted his arm. "Show me."

After the tour of the garden, they returned to the patio where a light refreshment was served with more black peppermint tea. They discussed Colantha's ideas for the base construct, and Devon was surprised by Colantha's desire to have the three of them—Lyra, Ginger, and himself—participate.

"If we break Lorenzo's mesmerizing, how long will it last? He'll continue to mesmerize her as often as he can for several more days." Lorenzo wasn't sloppy. He wouldn't stop the mesmerizing until Cressa was completely devoted to him.

"Once she realizes who she is, and what Lorenzo has been

doing, his influence will no longer work—now or in the future. She will subconsciously recognize it for what it is and block it."

"Dreamwalkers can do that?"

"Considering our current relationship with vampires, most have practiced the technique to prevent such situations. Although Cressa has never trained for this, she has great power, and I believe I can guide her through the basics needed to free herself of Venizi's hold."

They stopped at Newberry Park on their way home. It was a decent-sized park for being close to the heart of the city, complete with a small lake that allowed paddle boats in good weather. There were three fountains in the park, and after a quick review of them, Devon was positive the second one they'd visited had been in Cressa's construct.

Once back at the manor, they met in the library until Letty called them to dinner, where they discussed music, art, and Lyra's paintings. After dinner, they went to their rooms to rest, agreeing to meet at two a.m. in the library. Instead of going to his room, he went to Cressa's and locked the door behind him.

He strolled through her closet, stopping occasionally to smell a blouse or a dress, catching the soft remnants of her scent. They'd been through so much in the last two weeks. A true test of their commitment to each other. She had stuck with him, even when he'd blamed her for his fugue state. She might have backed off to give herself space from the cadre and him, but she hadn't planned to run away. Instead, she wanted to move to Oasis until they worked through everything that had happened. It wasn't fair that this would happen to her—to him—to them.

He picked up a quilt from a chair and laid down on her side of the bed. What was she doing at this moment? Dinner with Lorenzo? Something more intimate? He pulled the blanket close, her scent drifting over him. He turned on his side and tightened his grip on the quilt. "Wait for me, Cressa."

~

I WOKE with a start and sat up. No one was in the bedroom, but I'd felt a presence. I was sure of it. Minutes ticked by, and I sat quietly, barely breathing, waiting for someone to take a step. After five minutes, I released a sigh and fell back onto the pillow.

What had woken me?

I closed my eyes, trying to remember my dream. It seemed so real. There was a grotto with green grass, a stone bench, and a tangled hedge of roses. Deep red roses. Their scent was familiar, but I couldn't place from where.

The scene changed to a bedroom. Again, it seemed familiar, but where I'd seen it was just out of reach. A cold hearth was off to the right, a door that probably led to the bathroom on the left. In the center of the room was a king-sized bed with a man curled on his side.

Curious, I tiptoed around the room to get a better look at him. He appeared to be asleep, and, with the low light, it was difficult to discern his features. His clothing was casual but high-end, and his hair, which covered most of his face, appeared dark blond, maybe light brown. He hugged a blanket to his chest.

I suspected he was a handsome man.

No.

He was a vamp. I don't know why I thought that, but I was certain it was true. Something drew me to him, and I stepped closer—unafraid. This vamp wouldn't hurt me.

Open your eyes, pretty vampire.

For a brief moment, I thought it would happen.

Then the door burst open, and I sprung up, eyes wide. I must have fallen asleep again.

Lorenzo stood in the doorway, and he looked mad.

I scrambled off the bed. It was evening, and I'd laid down with a book and must have fallen asleep. My blouse was wrinkled, but my pressed linen plants survived unscathed.

"Lorenzo. I'm sorry you caught me napping." I held my hands clasped together in front of me. Guilt crept over me, but it had little to do with anything I might have done and more because of the dream.

He studied me, which only made me fidget. His steps were light as he strode toward me, scanning the room as he grew closer. When he reached me, he lifted my chin with a single finger, and I forced myself to remain still.

"I don't want you spending any more time with Brigette."

"Alright." My voice held a slight tremor. "I wasn't aware I was to avoid her."

"She returned early from a trip, so I hadn't concerned myself with those details."

I forced my shoulders to relax. "Can I ask why? She seemed nice."

At first, I thought he'd tell me, but then his face went blank. "It's enough that I said it. I won't have you questioning my orders."

I stepped back. "Of course."

He stroked my cheek, then marched out without another word.

I crawled onto the bed and grabbed a pillow, hugging it close. Something had changed, but I wasn't sure what. And only one word kept running through my head—run.

Chapter Fifteen

Colantha meandered around the library, moving from one artifact to another, perhaps preparing to create a construct. The fire blazed, and a tea service with light refreshments had been brought in along with a cooler filled with bottles of her special juice. Frederick and Jamison were stationed at the closed door but could easily reach any of them in seconds if the need arose.

Four seats had been moved to the center of the room, all facing each other around a coffee table. Lyra, Ginger, and Devon, dressed in comfortable clothes, nestled into the padded chairs. Colantha couldn't predict how long the dreamwalk might take and didn't want anything interfering once they got started. Everyone would remain in their position, eyes closed. It didn't matter if they napped or meditated, Colantha would bring them forward when needed.

She drank a full glass of juice, touched her medallion, then closed her eyes.

Devon glanced around. He wore a dark charcoal suit with a gray shirt and silver tie. It was one of Cressa's favorite color combinations. Ginger's dress was a bold pink with short sleeves. Her hair had been fluffed into wavy curls, and she appeared ready for a date with Lucas. She sat with Colantha at a table near the window. They each had a foamy drink in front of them.

They were in a San Francisco coffeehouse that Ginger and Cressa always stopped at when they went to the city. Ginger said it made them both feel as if they'd made it. Not rich, but comfortable enough to head down to the city when the mood struck just to have a latte and do some window shopping. Colantha had brought Cressa to this same place during her training session, and they'd decided it wouldn't hurt to have two different memories collide.

He had been positioned across the coffeehouse in an old leather chair. A demitasse cup of espresso rested on a side table, and a tablet lay in his lap. He was far enough away for no one to notice him, and Colantha assured him he would hear everything even through the crowded room.

A few seconds later, Cressa appeared at the table, sitting between the two women. She jumped, and when she saw Ginger she almost flew across the table to hug her. Then she fell back into her chair and held her hands in front of her face. "I'm so sorry. I didn't mean to do that. I—" She scanned the room, her eyes widened, and her lips curved into a grin, but then she frowned when her gaze landed on Colantha. "This is weird. Am I dreaming?" She waved her hand as if she could erase the image. "Never mind. That was stupid. Of course, I am. Either that, or I've finally snapped."

Ginger grabbed her wrist. "You're not dreaming. This is real. Can you feel the warmth of my hand?"

Cressa shrank back.

"We're here to bring you home. Or at least, try to help in some way. But you need to know what Lorenzo is doing to you."

Shock replaced the uncertainty. She turned to Colantha. "Who are you?"

The room shifted, and they were in a dark room where only a single candle glowed.

Colantha and Cressa sat cross-legged in the training pit, their knees touching. Cressa sprang back until her back hit the wall of the pit. Devon stood in the deep shadows of the room, once again, a silent observer.

"Where am I?" Cressa asked, squinting as she scanned the room, looking over both shoulders before completing the circle. She stared at Colantha. "You again. Do I know you?"

"Of course, you do. I'm the one who told you the mysteries of what you are?"

Cressa rubbed her face and wiped hard at her eyes. When she opened them, her shoulders dropped. Her head snapped up. "Wait. You said what I am, not who I am." When Colantha just smiled, Cressa's fierce face appeared. "What aren't you telling me?"

Devon stood in front of a fountain in Newberry Park. Sounds of splashing came from a fountain where water flowed from a sculpted mermaid. The sun was warm and the sky a brilliant blue, a typical day once the fog lifted.

Cressa sat at the edge of the fountain, wearing blue jeans and a soft white shirt that showed off her golden skin. The short tresses of her sable-colored hair rustled in the breeze. He walked up to her, and when his shadow crossed over the water, she looked up and lifted her hand to cover her eyes.

"Hello." Her voice was light, her mouth soft, but her forehead wrinkled. "Do I know you?" She laughed. "It seems I've been saying that a lot recently."

He considered the question. "May I sit?" He pointed to a spot on the fountain next to her. When she nodded, he sat facing the park, deciding on the best way to answer. "You do know me. My name is Devon."

The lines on her forehead increased. "I know that name. But I don't remember you."

"I know. It's there. It's being blocked."

"Says you." Her head dropped as she turned to stare at the water.

He chuckled and should have anticipated her stubbornness. He ran a hand through the water, cupping a small amount that he dribbled back into the pond. "Do you know where we are?"

Her head lifted, and she glanced around. At first, he didn't see any recognition, then he caught the exact moment she remembered.

"Newberry Park." She turned to the fountain and the water spurting from the mermaid. "And my favorite fountain."

"You shared this place with me only a few nights ago."

"I was running away."

The change of subject threw him. "You were in a car accident. You were on the way to the manor."

She shook her head. "I was beaten."

"No, Cressa. There was an accident and then a fire."

She began to rock.

The scenery changed, and she was sitting under a large sycamore tree, leaning against the thick trunk. Lyra sat next to her, pulling items out of a picnic basket.

"I wish we could have had a tea service, but I suppose it doesn't work as well at a picnic." Lyra passed her a blueberry scone.

"Oh, good. Cook remembered." She picked up the scone and bit off the end. Her eyes closed, and she hummed in delight. "Good god, it's been too long since I've eaten a blueberry scone."

"I'm glad we had the opportunity to do this," Lyra continued on as if she hadn't heard Cressa mention Cook. Cressa didn't seem to notice it, either. "House business has kept us busy."

"It's good to take a break between missions. It clears the mind for the next one."

"Is that Cressa's opinion or Pandora's?"

She snorted. "Pandora would want to race to the next job, but she's learned the art of patience—" She shook her head. "Wait. You know Pandora?"

Devon circled Cressa. They were in the training room at the manor. The climbing wall was on the far side, a section of mats lay in the middle of the floor with the ropes beyond. Cressa scanned her surroundings then focused on him. The confusion in her eyes cleared, and she began to move. At first, her movements were stiff, as if out of practice, and he kept his distance, waiting for her to loosen up, get comfortable, and remember.

They danced around each other for several minutes, taunting each other with a quick lunge or feint, her movements becoming more fluid. She was remembering her martial arts if nothing else. Then she smiled.

"Bring it on, vamp."

And he did. They hit, blocked, swept, and danced. Nothing too aggressive, not at first. But it didn't take long for the intensity to increase as Cressa remembered more moves and went on the offensive rather than waiting to defend herself.

That's right. Come to me.

On Cressa's next kick, Devon grabbed her leg and spun her around, temporarily disorienting her, before he leaped for a rope, swinging until he reached a second one, then kicked off a post to circle back to her. She was ready and took the full impact of his body as he released the rope to fall on top of her. They rolled, legs and arms tangling, until they stopped with him on top.

He smiled down at her. "You should have stepped back to let me land and then swept my legs out."

Her eyes searched his, and something shifted in them. A tiny spark of memory. She grinned. "And maybe I wanted to be caught."

He ran a hand through her hair. "And maybe I wanted to catch you." His head dipped, but with a strength he wasn't ready for, she pushed at his chest, wrapped her legs around his, and heaved until she rolled them over. She shoved away, kneeing him in the groin.

She stood over him, hands on hips, and a wicked smile on her lips as she watched him struggle for breath. "Is that all you got, vamp?"

He made it to his knees and lunged for her. Her laughter floated behind her as she dashed for the climbing wall.

~

ANOTHER GARDEN. Not the one on Lorenzo's island. Yet, this one was familiar. The stone path led me past vines, arbors, and a variety of lush vegetation. The scent of roses and honeysuckle teased my senses. If I could only remember.

The path urged me on, and I winced as I stepped on a pebble. I was barefoot and the workout clothes from moments ago were gone; I wore nothing but a silk nightgown. The warm night air skimmed my skin like an old lover. The burbling sound of a fountain piqued my interest, but someone waited for me at the end of the path. I ran and pushed giant tropical leaves out of my way until I stopped short at an overgrown grotto.

He sat on a stone bench dressed in shades of silver and gray. His hair was combed back into a ponytail, taming his long, silky hair that had brushed against my cheek on more than one occasion. The heat of a blush grew as his piercing blue eyes watched me.

I wiggled my toes and glanced down at the lush lawn. Soft blades tickled my feet as I flexed them, enjoying the splendor. When I lifted my gaze, my toes still doing their thing, he smiled.

His eyes changed, glowing the icy blue of his beast before they warmed. Like a fish who'd been hooked, I inched my way forward, unable to stop and not wanting to.

I paused a few steps shy of the stone bench.

"Do you recognize me, Cressa?"

I hesitated, remembering the other dreams. "You're Devon Trelane."

He stood and moved with a natural grace, and I was keenly

aware of the lean muscles under all that cloth. Just like I remembered from the gym. More than that. I'd felt those arms around me, my hands running over his shoulders, pulling him down to me.

I froze where I stood, anticipation sending shivers through me, tightening my belly. When he stepped up to me, the difference between him and Lorenzo was tangible. Where Lorenzo frightened me, even when some invisible force drew me to him, there was a calm that enveloped me when I looked at Devon.

He stared down at me as if he was the one snared. I didn't stop him when he snaked an arm around my waist and tugged me to him. His lips were soft and warm, his kiss tender, and my senses reeled. I gripped his arms, pulling him closer, not wanting him to stop.

This, I remembered.

The heat in his kiss, the strength of his arms, the taste of him—it felt like home.

I pulled back, my hands gripping my head. An intense pain hit me, and I dropped to my knees, my fingers digging past the grass to the soil beneath.

"Cressa?" Devon was on his knees next to me. "Are you alright? Is it a headache?"

"Give me a minute." The agony from seconds before receded to a soft thrum and then nothing. I blinked. And when I glanced up into Devon's terrified expression—everything rushed back.

I'd left the condo in a cheerful mood. There had been a strain between us after I helped put his beast to rest. "Jacques was driving me to the manor. We were resuming my training."

"Yes. What else?" His deep sigh signaled his relief.

I shook my head, piecing my memory back together. "I was in the back seat of the sedan." I stood on shaky legs and stepped away to pace across the lawn. "I wanted to move to Oasis until we worked through our difficulties." I smothered a cry. "Something hit the car. I slammed my head against the door." I began to freak out, and Devon rubbed my arms. He'd moved so fast.

"It's alright. You're fine, and Jacques is fine. Tell me what else."

"There was a fire. Jacques told me to let them take me. Not to fight. Then he screamed." I spun around and tucked my head into his chest. "Two vampires took me. I don't know if I passed out on my own or if they knocked me out. Either way, I woke up in a bedroom, and Lorenzo was standing over me."

The first few days with Lorenzo hit me like a baseball bat. Holding my hand while his eyes bored into mine. "My god, he mesmerized me."

"That's what we believe."

More images of Lorenzo made me pull away from Devon. I turned and raced blindly through the garden, knowing exactly where I needed to go. Devon's steps pounded behind me. He could have overtaken me, but instead, he followed me.

When I reached the fountain, I dropped to my knees and bent over the edge. I cupped my hands and drank, rinsing my mouth before spitting the foul water onto the grass that circled the fountain. After the fourth or fifth time, Devon pulled me away.

"What are you doing?"

I shook my head, not wanting to tell him.

He sat on the ground next to me and pulled me into his arms. It felt good to be there, and I was ashamed that I'd forgotten him. Pissed that Lorenzo tried to take this away from me.

"Tell me." His tone was soft and encouraging.

I grimaced and turned my head into his chest again. "I kissed Lorenzo."

Silence descended with nothing but the sound of rippling water. Then his grip on me tightened, and he kissed the top of my head. I closed my eyes and wrapped my arms around him.

"I don't know whether to laugh or let the beast release his rage. Either way, I don't blame you."

"I blame myself. I can't believe how weak I was."

He pushed me back and held my chin, forcing me to look him in the eye. "Lorenzo is very powerful. He wouldn't just mesmerize you once. He would do it whenever he could touch you, increasing his hold over you."

I nodded. "I began to sense when his pull was the strongest. He's been leaving the island every morning and not returning until evening. I began to question things. He said you'd been beating me. It explained the bruises on my side that were obviously from the accident."

"You have Bella to thank for Lorenzo's day-long absences." He pulled me to him and held on tight.

"I hate to break up this reunion, but we have business to discuss."

We both pulled back and stared at the woman.

"Colantha." I pushed myself up but shouldn't have bothered.

We were back in the coffeehouse, this time at a circular table. Lyra and Ginger were on either side of me, and I gripped their hands, their strength of conviction tamping down my fear of the situation I found myself in.

"Now that Cressa is back and the mesmerizing strands have been purged, we need a plan for her to return to where she belongs." Colantha nibbled a shortbread cookie. She dabbed a napkin at the corners of her mouth then leaned back in her chair.

"Before we do that, I need to know something." Devon decided not to wait until Cressa was physically home to get an answer regarding Colantha's hold over them in a construct. "What if someone like me doesn't want to be part of your dream? Is there a way for me to remove myself, assuming I'm aware enough to know I'm in a construct?"

She considered his question, tapping a bright-red fingernail on the table. "It depends on the strength of the dreamwalker and the one who doesn't want to be there. The construct is based on a psychic link. If someone has a strong mind and will, they can pull themselves out. The stronger the dreamwalker, the stronger the will must be."

"When you first arrived at the manor and you pulled us into a construct, you mentioned someone had a strong enough will to pull themselves free." Lyra pushed her cup aside and placed her arms on the table as she bent forward. "You were talking about Simone."

Colantha nodded. "Why did you think it was her I was thinking of?"

"Because she meditates daily," I answered.

"Ah. I thought so." Colantha sipped her cappuccino, licking the foam off her upper lip. "If she had moved into a meditative state, she would have found herself back in Devon's office." She chuckled. "I wonder what Frederick and Jamison would have made of that."

"Is it just the meditation or the fact she's vampire?" Devon asked.

Colantha narrowed her eyes as she considered the question. "Being vampire has its advantages. Your mind is more focused, so meditation comes easier. Your intelligence also plays a role." She glanced at Ginger. "For a human, it can be more difficult, but not impossible." When Ginger frowned and stared down at her cup, Colantha reached out and patted her arm. "Don't fret. There are exercises you can do to strengthen your mind. You have the ability; it simply needs to be awakened."

Ginger's shoulders relaxed, and then she laughed when our cups vanished to be replaced by mugs of hot chocclate complete with melting marshmallows. She wasted no time in sipping hers, and as Colantha had done earlier, used her tongue to wipe away a sticky marshmallow mustache. "I guess I have one more item to add to my training schedule."

Lyra poked at the marshmallow before sinking it under the chocolate with her spoon. Then she stirred and stirred until it had completely blended with the chocolate, then she took a long sip and closed her eyes.

Colantha turned her steely focus on Devon, who hadn't moved and appeared to be assimilating everything he'd heard. "Aren't you going to drink, vampire? I understand chocolate soothes the beast."

I was surprised when Devon copied Lyra's actions, stirring the marshmallows into the chocolate before taking a long drink. What happened at Devon and Colantha's first meeting? They appeared to be on friendly terms, a common ground, yet there was a play for control going on, and I suspected Colantha was enjoying it, while it irritated Devon.

"Perhaps we should get down to business then." Devon glanced at those around the table before resting his gaze on me. "Can you find a way off the island?"

I thought about all the information I'd been collecting, though I hadn't known why at the time. Even through the mesmerizing, Lorenzo couldn't block my true nature. "Lorenzo's security is pretty tight, but I think I found a way."

Chapter Sixteen

I STIRRED UNDER THE BLANKET, warm from the comfort of friends, the memory of being in Devon's strong arms, and the taste of his passionate kiss before Colantha ended the construct.

"What were you dreaming?"

I froze, then bracing myself, popped my eyes open. Lorenzo sat on the edge of my bed, staring down at me. Did he know? *Stay calm.* He couldn't possibly know. It took a moment to transition from the construct to reality, especially when I hadn't been prepared for it. Not to mention all I'd learned while there.

"Or was it a nightmare?"

My breath rushed out, and I dropped my gaze. He didn't know, but what the hell was he doing in my room while I slept?

"I can't remember." I rubbed my eyes.

He touched my cheek, and it took every ounce of determination not to flinch or turn away. I desperately wanted to back away. I preferred racing away, but not with this vampire. This one had to be cajoled and tempered, confident in his hold over me.

"Dreams are like that, Cressa. One moment so vivid—" He snapped his fingers. "The next minute gone."

I nodded. But I did remember the dream. I remembered it all.

The scent of the roses, the feel of the grass between my toes, having coffee with Ginger, my chat with Lyra, then the heat of Devon's touch on my skin, and the gentle scrape of his fangs on my neck after a passionate kiss.

"Why are you here?" My tone was soft and full of wonder. I tried not to gag.

"I happened to be passing by your room when I heard you scream. Perhaps it was a nightmare after all." And for the first time, I caught his lie.

It was there in his coal-black gaze. He laid a hand over mine and now came the time, sooner than I'd planned, to test Colantha's theory. Could he mesmerize me again?

It was a risk, but everyone had agreed I had to test it. They would give me thirty-six hours, and if I wasn't at the designated spot by then, they'd pull me into another construct to find out what went wrong.

He caught my gaze, and his vampiric spell worked its way over me—through me. "Kiss me, Cressa."

He didn't move, waiting for me to come to him. A test.

I caressed his cheek as I lifted my lips to his. My kiss was gentle, but his response wasn't. He dragged me to him as he pushed for a deeper kiss. I had no choice but to comply and hope he wouldn't take it any farther.

He pulled his head back and stared into my eyes. His arms wrapped around my waist, holding me close. I held his stare, my gaze unfocused, and smiled.

"You're a beautiful woman, Cressa. Soon, you will be introduced to my friends, and then vampire society as my consort." He ran a hand down my cheek. "One more thing I've taken from Trelane. He would have been better off letting the beast consume him." He kissed my forehead then whispered in my ear. "Tonight, my dear. You'll be mine tonight."

He stood, and I fell back, pulling the sheet with me. "You won't have a reason to be shy after tonight. But, until then—" He straightened his suit. "I have business off the island again. Mrs. Newbridge has work to keep you occupied." He lifted my chin. "You might share my bed tonight, but until you've become trained on every aspect of running this house, I can't introduce you to my friends. I'm planning a weekend gathering in a couple of weeks. Until then, you'll need to focus on everything Mrs. Newbridge tells you so you'll be ready to impress. Only the best for House Venizi."

I nodded and held my smile.

"Very good." He strode to the door. "Come, Stephen. I need to run through a few tasks with you. She'll be fine on her own until Mrs. Newbridge comes for her."

After giving them a full minute to be sure neither returned, I ran to the bathroom and immediately brushed my teeth before jumping into the shower, the water hot enough to turn my skin red. My heart didn't stop racing until I toweled myself off.

At least I could be grateful the mesmerizing hadn't worked, but playing Lorenzo's charmed mistress-to-be was more difficult than I'd imagined. Even with all the scrubbing, I still felt tainted by his touch, and one thing was certain. I had to expedite my plans. Whatever it took, I had to be off this island before Lorenzo returned.

I'D BARELY DRESSED before Mrs. Newbridge stormed into my room, once again not bothering to give me the courtesy of knocking. Would she treat me the same way as consort to Lorenzo? Not that I planned on sticking around to find out, but I was curious about the hierarchy in the House. It seemed some of the human staff had more power than the vamps.

I shoved my hands in my pockets as I followed her to the kitchen, my fingers playing with the edges of the hand-drawn map and time schedules I'd grabbed at the last minute. I wasn't sure if I was going to see my room again before I made my break, so I'd dressed in clothes that allowed better movement along with the lowest-heeled shoes I could find.

"Sit over there in the corner and eat your breakfast. I have several other tasks this morning and don't have time to coddle you. You have eight hours of work before Stephen returns to take you to the salon to prepare for our master."

I sat at the bistro table that was conveniently located next to the walk-in pantry. A bowl of oatmeal with various toppings waited for me, and I dutifully ate, not knowing when I'd eat again. Mrs. Newbridge must have been talking about me based on the pointed finger she kept flashing in my direction as she spoke to the cook. When she left, the cook went back to work, ignoring me.

While I ate, I mentally ran over the map of the island. It was too dangerous to take out my notes, but I had to confirm the dates and times of the shipments off the island. When I finished, the cook was literally elbow-deep in making dough. Keeping one eye on her, I crept to the pantry, heading straight for the delivery schedule. The dry goods only came once a week, but the fresh stuff came over daily, and I pulled out my notes to confirm the times matched.

I kept my movements subtle as I went back to the table, picked up my dishes, and shuffled to the cook, keeping my gaze down.

"What do you want, girl?"

"I wanted to go the restroom before you put me to work."

"Down the hall. I'm sure Mrs. Newbridge showed you where. You need to be quicker of wit or face the wrath of our master. Now go, I need to finish this."

I scurried from the room. What a dismal place to live, and I couldn't wrap my head around why these people were so loyal to such an asshole. But maybe their harsh behaviors were for my benefit, beating the new consort down while I was being mesmerized. A lesson to never question my place or duties until all I wanted to do was please the master for any tidbit of reward. Or maybe he just paid really well.

I raced past the bathrooms and turned left to the laundry room. I strode in like I belonged there and walked right to the corkboard. Once again, I sighed with relief that the times hadn't changed.

I ducked into the bathroom on the way back to the kitchen and took out the map, reviewing locations and the paths to the boat dock. Based on the schedule Mrs. Newbridge kept on her office wall, a boat came every afternoon at three. It left at four, which meant all the items to be loaded onto the boat would be picked up at scheduled intervals throughout the day. And I thanked the gods the schedule corresponded to the times listed on the kitchen and laundry schedules.

The dilemma I faced was how to get on the boat and keep everyone from looking for me until then. I had a few ideas but would need help from unsuspecting individuals. The first thing was to gather all the supplies I required, and I trudged back to the kitchen where the cook waited.

"It's about time," she huffed and led me to one of the sinks. A large basket of potatoes and a matching one filled with carrots sat on the counter. Next to them was a single vegetable peeler. I didn't need to ask to know how my morning was going to be spent, but at the same time, I held back a grin. Step one just became easier than I could have hoped for.

I SCREAMED as two vamps hustled me down the hall with the cook and one of her assistants trailing behind. The cook mumbled over and over, "I have no idea what that nitwit of a girl did. One simple task is all I asked."

Blood streamed from my wrist, and it hurt like hell. The tears weren't difficult to conjure up, and I kept them flowing as I continued to scream. I never realized how much screaming lessened the pain until I needed to breathe again.

It only took moments to reach the infirmary, and the single nurse in the room rushed over as soon as we entered. After she gave me a firm command to shut up, I clamped my lips together.

"Hold her still while I see what she did." The nurse gripped my wrist like it was a chicken wing she was preparing to rip off the carcass. And I took mild offense that she immediately assumed I'd been the cause of my injury. She was right, but it still stung. "This is deeper than a flesh wound, but she shouldn't require any stitches."

"Why don't you just give her blood?" one of the vamps asked.

The nurse looked up in horror, and even the cook and her assistant took a step back.

"You must be new to the island. One never gives blood to any of the master's property. That is his alone to give. I'll clean it and bandage it, then he can decide whether her actions deserve a pure healing from his blood or if she should keep the scar as a reminder of her foolishness."

The vamp bowed his head. "A teaching moment. Thank you."

The nurse seemed mollified, and she nodded toward a bed. "Put her over there, and then you can leave." She turned to the cook. "What happened?"

"I gave her a simple task to peel potatoes and carrots." The woman, who was always so stern, wiped her hands over and over, her face a mask of deep worry. Would Lorenzo punish her for my mistake? That wasn't what I'd intended.

"Don't fret, Phoebe." She placed a hand on the cook's shoulder. "It's a good thing you didn't give her a knife. She would have probably slipped and slit her own throat."

The cook seemed to relax. "And that would be such a shame."

The three of them laughed as the nurse followed them to the door. They did know I was within hearing distance, right?

"Now, don't worry. The master will only be concerned with

how stupid and incapable she is. And then we'll have to refrain from giving her anything sharper than a butter knife."

The cook and her assistant left, still chuckling.

When the nurse spun around, she stood with her hands on her hip as she studied me, a sneer on her face. She was no doubt wondering how someone could be so stupid as to cut themselves that badly with a potato peeler.

"Don't move. I'll get something to clean you up. And don't drip on the floor."

While she was gone, I scanned the room, grateful I'd remembered the details. The pharmacy was next to the janitor's closet, and the door was open. I laid back down and waited for the nurse to return. She carried a tray filled with a stainless-steel bowl, two bottles of liquids, bandages, gauze, and elastic wrap. When she turned to grab scissors from a side table, I knocked the tray over, and it crashed to the ground. The glass bottles shattered as the rest of the items scattered, the bowl rolling on its side until it hit a table leg and fell flat.

"What's wrong with you?" the nurse shrieked. "Look at this mess." She glared at me, the floor, and then my wrist. "Well, I can't let you leave with your arm like that, but I'm not cleaning up your mess." She pointed toward the janitor's closet. "There's a broom, dustpan, bucket, and mop in the closet. You'll need water. There's a sink on the other side of the pharmacy. Be quick about it while I replenish a new tray." She stormed off. "And try not to bleed over everything," she yelled over her retreating back.

Once she was out of sight, I ran to the closet and hauled out the bucket and, after a frantic thirty seconds, found cleanser and dumped some in. I dropped the bucket in the sink and started the water. After a quick glance across the room to where the nurse disappeared, I hurried to the pharmacy.

I turned in a circle, taking stock of all the cabinets. Mrs. Newbridge brought me here once after a long day of cleaning. She hadn't said anything, but I think I'd given her a migraine. After a second review of the cabinets, I spotted the one I wanted and, as expected, found the door unlocked. The second shelf was filled with vials of various colors. Mrs. Newbridge had taken one of the pink ones, which I knew was for headaches. I was betting everything that the purple liquid was the same sleep aid that Lyra used. I grabbed the vial and stuffed it in my pocket before racing out to the sink. The bucket was almost full, and I jumped when the nurse walked up behind me.

"What's taking so long?"

"I was waiting for the water to get hot."

"That's not necessary. There's already enough liquid on the floor to prevent anything from drying out. And using a little muscle never hurt anyone."

I grabbed the bucket and set it next to the broken glass. The nurse handed me the broom before sitting on a stool to watch me clean.

Thirty minutes later, I walked out of the infirmary with instructions to go to the library and start reading the stack of books Mrs. Newbridge had left for me. For the next two hours, I watched the clock as I turned the pages, waiting for Asshole to come for me.

ASSHOLE DRAGGED ME, which wasn't an exaggeration, back to my room at two thirty. He made sure to grab my injured hand and seemed to relish my squeal when he shoved me into the room. Mrs. Newbridge followed us in with my lunch tray and, as anticipated, a tea service for the vamp. She set it on the table, clucked her tongue at me, appeared to want to say something, thought better of it, and stormed out, slamming the door behind her.

I lifted the lid off the plate, pleased to see a roast beef and cheddar sandwich, which I immediately bit into, starving after only eating oatmeal at breakfast.

Asshole sat across from me and watched with an amused expression.

"Is something funny?" I asked between bites.

"I'm looking forward to seeing what punishment Lorenzo has in store for you when he hears what a troublemaker you've been today."

I gulped. The threat was real if my plan didn't work. I licked my lip to clean a spot of mayo and held back a grin when the vamp followed my tongue. He poured a cup of tea, his gaze barely leaving mine. I reached for my water and the glass toppled. We jumped up.

"Oh my god. I am so sorry. Let me get something to clean it up." My hand shook as I picked up the glass and set it aside.

"No. Stay where you are, and I'll get something."

I was already reaching into my pocket as he marched to the bathroom. I removed the stopper and added four drops to his tea. Lyra took six drops when she wanted to sleep through the night. She added two drops when she only wanted to sleep for a couple of hours. With Asshole being twice Lyra's size, I figured four drops was a happy medium.

I'd just returned the vial to my pocket when the vamp came out with a towel. I picked up the plate with my half-eaten sandwich and set it aside, moving other items out of the way to help with cleanup.

"Most of the water is on the tray." I held out my good hand. "Please let me clean this up. I've been a nervous wreck all day. I'm truly sorry. Sit and drink your tea. You shouldn't have to deal with my mess."

His expression softened, and he tossed the towel over. "When you say it that way, your clumsiness makes sense. Your first night with Lorenzo can seem scary but, from what I've heard, he's a generous lover as long as you follow his commands. He maintains control over his property, and you'll find it easier if you just do as he asks."

My hands shook, and this time it wasn't an act. Once I cleaned the table, I took the tray to the bathroom to dump the remaining water and wash out the towel.

When I returned, I pushed the plate of food away, no longer hungry.

The vamp seemed to take pity on me and poured me a cup of tea. His was half gone. We drank in silence until the teapot was empty. Then I got up and laid on the bed, turning on my side to keep an eye on him. I closed my eyes and ran through the rest of my plan.

My nerves were raw. I took a long, shallow breath, calming myself. This was a job like any other. I was in a castle with a huge moat and had to escape the dragon.

I could do this. Although time was tight, I was still on schedule.

After ten minutes of running over the remaining steps, I opened an eye. I blinked, grinned, and sat up.

Asshole was down, the teacup next to his head. I jumped out of bed and crept close, watching his breathing. Slow and steady. I bumped the table with my hip, but the jostled table didn't wake him. He was sleeping fitfully, though I didn't think his mood would be improved when he woke.

It was fortunate that the tonic worked so quickly, and I thanked the vamp metabolism for the assist.

Now, I just needed the potion to be as long-lasting as it was for Lyra.

Chapter Seventeen

I WAITED another five minutes for the sleeping aid to sink in, taking the opportunity to change clothes. I found a pair of pants with a bright floral print on a dark blue background, a matching jacket, and a navy-blue sleeveless blouse. I kept the same shoes, and when I passed a mirror almost laughed hysterically. It was the worst-looking outfit I could have found, but the busy pattern might be the difference between getting off the island or dealing with Lorenzo's harsh punishment for a failed escape attempt.

I slipped through the mansion, working my way through the least busy areas of the manor. When I ran into someone on the staff, I simply nodded and continued with my head down. No one called me out for being without my bodyguard or Mrs. Newbridge. At the back door, I paused. It had been a few minutes after three when I left my room. I glanced out the door and didn't see anyone. The building where Brigette stayed was to my right. The back way to the dock was to the left.

This was the most dangerous part of the plan—getting to the other building without being seen. I should have brought some type of cover to go over my crazy pantsuit. It was certainly unforgettable. An idea struck, and I turned right out the door, sticking close to the house.

The pool was on the way to the bungalow with the pool house off to the left. I heard splashing as I grew close and tiptoed down the rock path that led to the back of the pool house. I stuck my head in and paused, listening for anyone who might be changing. The only sound was the muffled splashing from the other side of the building. I grabbed a robe and pulled it on over my pantsuit, then wrapped my hair in a towel as if I'd just left the pool.

When I stepped back onto the rock path, I took a right, avoiding the pool, and followed the path that led to the bungalow. This was the danger zone. Humans came and went at all hours of the day. If I could get to the building without anyone seeing me, all the better.

I was just about to step out when I remembered my shoes. They were not something someone would wear to the pool, and they would be noticed. I took them off and stuffed them in the robe's pockets.

When I was a few feet from the building, the door opened and two people walked out—a young man and a woman who was probably a few years older. I lowered my head and stepped aside.

"Hey, how was the pool?" the man asked.

"Wet." It was all I could think of.

He laughed and then gave me a closer look. "Hey, are you new here?"

"Paul, we don't ask personal questions. Remember?" The woman grabbed his arm and pushed him on. "Have a good day."

I hurried through the door and moved through the main hallway toward the back of the building. I could have gone directly to my destination rather than take a chance in the building, but where I was headed was behind fencing. The only way to ensure access was to use the same door as the residents.

I had just passed the staircase and a hallway when a clear voice rang out.

"Cressa?"

Damn it.

I spun around. "Brigette. How good to see you?"

She glanced around. "Are you alone?"

There was no easy way out of this, so I gave her a partial truth. I turned around and loosened the robe. "I was trying to find someplace where I could be alone. Then I thought maybe you had time to talk."

"We're not supposed to see each other. Lorenzo's orders."

"Yeah. Why is that?"

She gave me a critical eye then glanced around, grabbing me by the hand. "Hurry. Keep your head down, and tighten your robe." She pulled me up the stairs, and we moved quickly to the end of the hall. She punched numbers and the door opened just before she shoved me through.

"Take a seat at the kitchen table." She walked to a cupboard and grabbed two glasses.

I took the towel off my head and laid it over a chair, tossing the robe over it.

Brigette took a step back, looked me up and down, then laughed. "No wonder you wore a robe. That's just hideous."

I grimaced, not sure what to say since I'd picked the outfit for a specific reason.

"Don't tell me. Millie dressed you again. That woman has the worst taste."

"Yeah. I'm not great at fashion, but I think I could have done better."

"God, I hope so." She pulled a bottle of vodka out of the freezer and set it down with the glasses. "I'll give you five minutes, and then you have to sneak out the back. Some of the humans snitch on the others, hoping for more privileged status."

"Sounds cozy."

Brigette laughed and poured the vodka, sliding one over to me. "That's the only downside to the island—constantly watching your back. So, I'll give you one piece of advice: do what Lorenzo says exactly the way he wants it and when he wants it. You'll survive long enough for him to get bored and find a new piece to share his bed, then he puts you out to pasture and things get easier." She took a long swallow and waved her glass around the expensively furnished apartment that was almost as large as the condo Devon bought for Ginger and me. "You live in luxury with less stringent rules. At some point, Lorenzo will ask if you want to stay and serve a minor role or get your freedom back, assuming you're still human. He mesmerizes you, gives you a bit of his blood, then tucks you into a nice condo someplace close. When you wake, you have no idea who he is, but you have enough of an implanted story to blend back into society. No fuss, no muss."

A chill went through me. Was this how other Houses did it? I'd never asked Devon about his blood donors.

"I'm guessing you decided to stay."

"I know this world and understand my role in it. I'm allowed to leave the island when I want, go where I want, and it's all paid for. As long as I continue to follow his rules and his requests, I'm well-pampered. But not everyone is cut out for this, so I'd think long and hard about where you want to end up when Lorenzo tires of you. Never kid yourself. We're possessions—nothing more."

I finished my vodka and leaned in, turning the glass in circles while deciding how to approach the change in topic. There wasn't an easy segue. "Do you remember showing me that building where a guard stands post?"

She refilled the glasses, her mood shifting with the topic. "That's not a place you want to go."

"Who's in there?"

"I don't know. I'm not sure there are many that do." She gripped the glass, her eyes unfocused. "I remember walking by there one day, not really thinking where I was going. I thought I heard screaming, but only in my head." She downed the glass and wiped her mouth. "I never go there anymore." Her eyes searched mine. "I only took you there to scare you, and I'm sorry I did."

I felt time slipping by and finished the second vodka, wiping my lips as she did before standing. "I'm sorry to put you in jeopardy by stopping by." I slipped on the robe and wrapped my hair in the towel. "No one will see me leave."

When I got to the door, I turned. "Take care of yourself, Brigette."

I shut the door with her still sitting at the table, staring into her empty glass.

Her words bothered me as I worked my way down the hall to the outer door that led to the dumpster in the back of the building. I worried I'd spent too much time with her and lost my single opportunity. No one was in sight. I took a moment to close my eyes and pray to whatever gods might be listening that I wasn't too late.

The rumbling of a motorized vehicle broke the silence. It was close. I lifted the dumpster lid and looked inside. It was three-quarters full. I used the robe and towel to prop the lid open while I scrambled over the edge and slithered inside. God, the smell was atrocious and there was nothing stable to stand on—just squishy stuff. I pulled the robe and towel in with me, sorry I couldn't wear it, but if anyone checked the dumpsters, because Lorenzo could be just that paranoid, the white fabric might give someone enough reason to check further. I pushed them under the garbage at the far end of the dumpster while I pulled the floral jacket over my head, covering my face, then pulled the trash over me as the gate to the trash bin was opened.

I heard banging and then came the jostling of the container. The day before, I'd had an opportunity to see a metal laundry bin being pulled by a small four-wheel vehicle down one of the side paths. What I didn't know was what happened at the dock. Were the containers loaded onto the boat or were they dumped into a larger container already onboard? I'd considered hiding in the laundry bin, but that seemed too risky.

Trash was another thing. It was more likely the trash would be emptied into a larger container, and if that was the case, I'd have to tuck myself into a ball and hope no one saw me tumble out. If luck was truly on my side, they simply exchanged a full container with an empty one, and I'd have to worry about getting out on the other side. But at least I'd be off the island.

The container moved several feet then stopped. It was overly warm, and the smell made my stomach lurch. I swallowed. The last thing I needed was to add fresh vomit to the mix. It already stunk like it.

The container began to move again, picking up speed. One more step achieved. I lifted my head, trying to find fresh air that might leak through the gap between the lid and bin. It would only be a few minutes to the dock, but before I could plan for what might happen once we reached it, a blinding headache hit me.

I COVERED my ears as words repeated over and over, "Don't leave me here. Don't leave me. I won't survive much longer. Please. Don't leave me."

The voice was male and filled with such deep anguish that my heart clenched, and tears pricked at my eyes. The words filled my head then ended with a pitiful wailing.

"Who are you?" It was all I could think to say. "I don't know who you are."

"I'm like you. I've touched your mind before." Whoever it was sounded sane. Was it another dreamwalker?

"I don't have the means to save you. I can barely save myself."

"You can't leave me here. Please. Don't leave me."

I had no idea who this person was, but I had a good idea where they were being kept. "Do you know where you are?"

"I don't remember. Please. Don't leave me."

"I'll be back. I need to get help. I'm only one person. I don't know how to find you."

"Venizi." Then the headache stopped.

"Are you still there?" My question was greeted by silence. Whoever it was, and wherever they were, they were out of my reach. Every fiber shouted to jump out and get to that building. But it would be suicide by myself.

For one crazy moment I considered jumping out and racing for my room. Maybe it was better to stay and find a way into the building. But then I remembered Lorenzo's words. I was supposed to sleep with him tonight. And that was going a bit too far in my book. He would definitely have to mesmerize me for that shit to happen. Thank god he couldn't do that anymore.

I had to stick to the plan. And as the container was removed from the vehicle and pushed over grates, then rolled across a rough surface, my own freedom became more important. It killed me to think I was leaving a dreamwalker behind. And tears fell as I felt the subtle rocking of the boat.

This was the hardest part. The minutes ticked slowly as I waited for the boat to depart. I expected shouting and a mad search at any moment. With any luck, Asshole would still be asleep.

After minutes of sweltering heat and grasping for whatever air I could get, the boat began to move. We were barely away from the dock when I heard what I thought was another boat. The motor faded as the boat I was on picked up speed as it crossed the narrow channel. Had that been Lorenzo returning home?

Once he found me gone, they'd search the island. How soon before he thought to have the boat searched? That wouldn't be good. I'd expected him back later. Maybe it was someone else, but it was best to plan for the worst.

When the boat slowed and came to a stop, I heard the yelling. Whether it was from Lorenzo alerting his vamps to have everything searched or from some other problem, I didn't know. But I had to wait for the container to be unloaded before I could climb out.

From what Devon had shared, there were at least a dozen vamps that ran the boat launch. I should have thought to bring a knife. The infirmary would have had a scalpel. My martial arts would have to be enough.

The sound of squealing wheels made me think the container next to mine was being moved. A lid opened, a minute went by, then the lid dropped shut. Either someone dumped more trash, or they were searching.

I moved deeper into the sludge, pulling whatever I could reach over the top of me, using the sleeves of my jacket to grip items, hoping not to get stabbed or cut by anything. Then, my container was being moved, and my heart was in my throat when the lid was thrown open. Even deep in the muck, I could sense the light streaming in. Garbage was moved around, and items above my head shuffled. A pole or something similar poked my side before I shifted enough to let it pass. If they moved it just a few inches to the right, they'd find something with more mass. Then the lid slammed shut, and I would have sighed with relief if I had enough air in my lungs.

The container was rolled a fair distance. If they emptied it into a dump truck, that would be problematic. The trucks had hydraulics that compressed the garbage. I needed to get out before that happened, but I had no idea if the container was shoved into an area that wasn't monitored or if it was sitting out in the middle of the activity.

A bark came from my left. It was a high-pitched sound that went abruptly silent. Then it yipped again. There was muffled yelling, and I thought I heard running. It was impossible to tell, and I dug my way out to the top of the heap. With all my strength and nothing stable to stand on, I managed to push the lid open enough to see.

Fresh sea air hit my face, and I sucked it in. The yelling

increased, as did the barking. When I peeked out, a dog was being chased. It zigged then zagged as vamps, which I assumed based on their speed, tried to corner it. The dog was faster.

Something seemed odd, and it took a moment before my garbage-addled brain caught on. It wasn't a dog—it was a wolf.

I scanned the area before glancing back at the wolf. There was a second one now, and everyone was focused on it. Something lay on the ground. It looked like a bag from one of the sandwich chains in the city, the big blue and red lettering clear on the packaging. Did the wolves take someone's lunch?

No one seemed focused on the containers, and from what I could tell, the unloading of the ship had stopped once the wolf action began. I smiled as I gathered items to shove between the container and lid to lift it high enough to squeeze through. It wasn't easy, as I couldn't find anything firm enough to stand on to help with the height I needed to pull myself up.

I scrounged around, wiping sweat off my face with the inside of my blouse, until I found a couple of compacted trash bags then laid pieces of cartons on top of them. Once my footing was stabilized, I pulled myself up until I got a leg out of the container. I kept an eye on the wolf and vamp action as I pushed my muscles past the limit to shift my body to the outside of the container so gravity could do the rest. If I had better shoes, like something with traction, it would have been easier.

I was still heaving, my eyes watering from exertion and the stench, as I watched the wolves find a gap in the fencing when arms grabbed me and hauled me out, depositing me on the ground.

"Keep quiet."

I thought I recognized the voice but must have been delirious from low oxygen and the stink of rotting everything. The garbage that held the lid open was pushed back in, and the lid quietly closed.

A hand gripped my upper arm and pulled me up. I didn't make a sound as I was dragged away, half stumbling as one of my shoes slipped off. I tripped over ropes and buoys, the sea air now filling with the scent of decaying fish, which smelled better than me.

I was beginning to focus on my surroundings when I was shoved toward a large box freezer. The lid was open.

"Get in."

I balked and turned. "Simone?"

"Do as I say. We only have minutes."

I did as she asked and watched the lid shut. I wasn't going to have air for very long, but then I noticed a spot of light. I twisted around, trying to find a comfortable position, and noted the back wall had three one-inch-sized holes. Air. I closed my eyes as the freezer was lifted and then pushed across something.

An engine started, and the vehicle—which I assumed was a truck or van—slowly began to move. The yelling continued as the truck inched its way along. My foot pressed against the freezer as if I were stomping on the gas peddle, forcing it to move faster.

Instead, the truck slowed and came to a stop. I heard a door squeal open, and a tailgate dropped. The sound of scraping nails and a shift in the truck bed made me smile. We'd just picked up the wolves.

The truck crept along for what had to be another fifteen minutes before it slowed again. The bright light from the air holes grew dimmer. Doors slid shut with a bang.

I heard something that sounded like grunting and whining. The freezer jostled as it was moved off the truck.

When the freezer was settled on the ground, the lid opened. I blinked against the light, dim as it was, and stared up at four faces —Harlow, Simone, and a man and woman I didn't know. They were all smiling.

Then Harlow took a whiff and waved his hand against the putrid stink rolling off me. "Hello, luv. It's good to see you in one piece, but there's no way in hell you're traveling in the same car as me."

Chapter Eighteen

I SLIPPED into the warm water until my head was completely submerged. After three steaming showers and now soaking in my second hot bath, the stench of my escape through the garbage bin had finally been purged. I sat up, the water streaming down my face, and breathed in the scent of oranges and spice. Ginger didn't say where she found the bath salts, but I'd need a dozen more jars for the sheer sensual pleasure.

Lyra asked if I could join the Family for dinner if I were up to it, and I couldn't see a reason to say no. I'd been through a trauma, and they understood, but they were vamps. If they had been in my position, they would simply accept what happened and carry on, eventually deciphering the wisdom of their journey.

Humans weren't built to absorb emotional impacts as easily as a vamp. We had to stew on it, wondering if the entire experience could have been avoided if we'd only changed one element of our day. But second-guessing ourselves wouldn't change the eventual outcome. It all boiled down to the individual—their past experiences, ability to talk about it, and so on. But then again, I wasn't entirely human. And I couldn't imagine Colantha hiding in her bedroom while she internalized her emotions.

After Harlow had opened the freezer lid, I'd been so relieved that I'd accomplished a job, which was how I'd viewed the escape. But there was more to it this time. I'd had my memories taken from me. My control. And while I seemed to have hidden it from everyone at the docks, it shook me to the core. But now, only hours later, I was mad, and the rage was building.

Maybe Simone had something to do with my enlightened focus. It had been a surprise to see her there. Ginger had shared in confidence that once the plan had been developed, Simone had demanded to be at the docks when the boat arrived. Once I was out of the freezer, she'd whispered, "It annoys me I feel the need to hug you. Thankfully, your smell forces me to keep my distance."

I had to hold in a snort and almost kissed her when she handed me a set of gym clothes. I'd slid behind a stack of crates in the warehouse and stripped off the horrid floral pantsuit. The leggings and thin sweatshirt comforted me more than words. Most of all, my feet reveled in the woolly socks and tennies. Simone had my back.

My second surprise was meeting Elijah and Raquel, the alpha and beta of the Humboldt pack, who I'd met before, but not in their human shape. I knew them in their wolf persona as Mr. Black and Ms. Gray, the two wolves who'd helped me get into the papermill to find Devon and put his beast to rest. And while they didn't comment on my oddball discussion with their wolves, the winks they gave me at our departure from the docks told me they remembered it.

"Hey. Are you decent?" Ginger's voice rang through the bedroom and into the bathroom. "Are you still in the bath? You must be shriveled by now." She pushed the bathroom door open. "Wow, it smells a ton better in here." She carried a basket with flowers, a variety of lotions, and a woman's magazine, which she dropped on the counter. Her nose sniffed the air again. "By the time you lather some lotion on, you'll be presentable." She picked up the magazine and sat on the toilet as she flipped through the pages. Her dark hair shone with red highlights and curled about her head. She wore a blue sundress with a huge yellow sunflower splayed across the front. Her persona rang of an innocent, which she continued to embody. No one would suspect that daily sparring lessons with her dagger made her a deadly adversary. It still shocked me at times.

"Lyra will be upset if we're late. She's still bummed out about the special dinner she'd arranged after you rescued Devon. And I know you had your reasons, but can you not disappoint her this time?" She closed the magazine and leaned toward me, her eyes sincere. "I feel bad that the cadre still looks to Devon for approval on most things. He should say something. If he didn't want to take House leadership back, then he should tell the cadre to stop going around her."

I could only stare. My mouth might have hung open. When had she become entrenched in House politics? "I'll be ready in plenty of time."

She sat back. "Oh. Okay then." She glanced around the bathroom then stood. "I'll find you something to wear."

I considered her as she sashayed out of the room, and I pulled the plug on the tub. Ginger was known to get frazzled when steeped in high emotions. My kidnapping had to be a major event for her, and while we could talk about it, sometimes the nonverbal worked just as well.

After drying myself off, I kept quiet when she handed me clothes. I didn't complain when she made me sit on the toilet as she blow-dried my hair and used gobs of gel to give it a spikey look. I had to admit, I looked ready to hit the clubs and snickered to myself at what Lorenzo would have thought.

I grabbed her hand as we stared at my hair in the mirror. "It looks great." We stayed like that for a moment, then I added, "I didn't mean to worry you."

Her eyes teared up, but she held it together and smiled. "For the first time, I had friends to help me through it. But I think Devon should put a tracker on you."

I laughed and searched my closet for shoes. "I'm sure Lorenzo's vamps would have removed it before taking me to the island."

"I don't mean something in your clothes or a piece of jewelry. I'm thinking one of those under the skin type."

"You mean a subcutaneous implant?" I cringed at the thought of my every movement being watched.

"Yeah, that's it." Her words held a haughty tone. "And I think he'd agree with me." She grinned before almost skipping out the door.

I followed her, giving my room a last glance. It was good to be home.

IT WAS MORE a party than dinner. A long linen-covered table had been set up in the solarium, covered with fine china and crystal goblets. Floral arrangements had been interspersed between the candelabras. This gathering was more than Devon, Ginger, and the cadre.

Elijah and Raquel were there along with The Wolf, Harlow, and Trudy. I took a double take at Harlow, who wore a tailored suit. I needed a picture. I winked at Trudy for the fine job she did in dressing him. But it was Jacques that brought tears to my eyes. I strode toward him before anyone else, and when he noticed, he dropped his head. He didn't look like he'd been burnt, but from what Ginger had shared in her recap of events during my second shower, he'd made a remarkable recovery with the help of the healer.

I put my arms around his shoulders and hugged him. He stiffened, and I worried I might be hurting him, but when I glanced at Bella, who'd been standing behind him, she nodded when she saw my expression. So, I kept hugging him until he finally relaxed and his arms went around me. After several seconds, they tightened.

"I'm sorry I didn't protect you."

"From what I hear, you did everything you could. I'm so thankful you're alright, and I'm sorry you had to deal with so much pain because of it."

When he didn't respond, I pulled back but kept my voice low. "Vampire morality won't allow you to forgive yourself, but I forgive you. It's easy enough to do since the accident and my abduction wasn't anyone's fault. Sometimes things just don't work out. If anything, it was my fault for not staying at the manor."

He nodded, and while he still appeared morose, there was a light in his eyes that hadn't been there before. It was a start.

Harlow didn't waste time giving me a hug while squeezing my ass. "I won't mince words. You had Trudy and me worried."

Trudy pushed him out of the way and pulled me into an embrace. "This Lorenzo is a real piece of work. There's a special place in hell for vamps like him." She reached for a cocktail from the table and handed it to me. "Vodka martini, just how you like them. We get to spend the night, so drink up."

"That's right, luv. We're here to get shitfaced." He leaned in. "I hear there's going to be a breakfast meeting to discuss what happened and plan revenge."

Trudy elbowed him. "Not revenge. Go get another drink. You think better drunk."

He smiled and kissed her cheek. "Just what the Trudy ordered."

We laughed, and I glanced around the room. "I had no idea Devon had called in the troops." Colantha was in a corner speaking with Lyra while Frederik and Jamison stood behind them. I'd wait until tomorrow for a heart-to-heart with the dreamwalker. I squeezed Trudy's arm as we split up, and I headed for Remus, his two wolves, and Decker.

"Cressa." Remus held out his arm, and he engulfed me in a bear hug. "You have an uncanny ability to find yourself in trouble more than anyone else I know."

"And all it seems to take is me minding my own business."

It wasn't long before we were called to dinner, and I forgot my troubles as we listened to Devon and Remus share stories that sounded more like tall tales. When Decker and Harlow added their own adventures, the group laughed so hard that Bella began to snort, which made everyone howl more.

We were like soldiers who'd faced a battle and came away winners. But it was a charade for our true feelings, the deeper cuts, and the tender bruising to our egos and souls.

When Cook brought in a four-tiered, dark chocolate and raspberry cake, a voice called out to me. It was faint and, glancing around at the smiling faces, was meant only for me. It was ever so sorrowful and wrenched my gut.

"Don't forget me. Save me."

THE GUESTS HAD GONE HOME or staggered up the stairs to the guest rooms. I stared at the cold hearth in my room, wondering why Devon hadn't found time to talk to me since I'd returned, although everyone at the party told me how driven he'd been to find me. He'd even flown to New Orleans to seek out Colantha, a story I wanted to hear more about.

I couldn't imagine what went through his head when he'd seen the burnt husk of the sedan. Then again, maybe I could. When the beast had risen after Devon's readdiction to the Poppy, my world had collapsed in so many ways. But the possibility of never seeing Devon again had cracked something in me.

If he'd been willing to move heaven and earth to find me, why had he avoided me all night? I shoved the quilt from my lap and changed from my shorts and tank top to one of the silk gowns he'd bought me. I grabbed my favorite satin robe, tying the belt as I marched down the hall toward his room.

I rapped lightly. Not hearing a response, I tapped a bit louder.

"Come."

I opened the door, surprised to see the lamp shining brightly from his writing desk. He was bent over, scribbling a letter with a fountain pen, and as irritated as I was, I smiled at the vamp who believed in the promise of the future yet was still unable to shed some of his traditional ways.

"I'll have this letter ready in a minute, and then you can get a messenger to send it."

After a minute, he glanced up, and his gaze widened. "Cressa."

I paced with my hands behind my back as I studied his room. I'd been there several times, but usually in his bed, and I'd never taken the time to appreciate his selection of paintings and strategically placed art pieces. The furniture was old and most likely antiques, and I wondered if he'd changed it much since his parents had died.

"You've been avoiding me." I meandered to a side table where a bottle of scotch had been opened. I poured myself a couple of fingers and took the bottle to the desk. I lifted the bottle and, when he nodded, I refilled his glass.

"I've been busy monitoring Lorenzo in preparation for a counterstrike. Decker, Remus, and Elijah wanted to review strategies for possible retaliation."

"I hadn't considered Lorenzo would move so swiftly."

He set the pen down, folded the letter, and slid it into an envelope that had already been addressed. He stood and leaned against the desk. "And I wanted to give you time to rest. A lot happened today. You risked a great deal escaping the island only to face a room filled with friends where you had to show how strong you were."

"I agree I need time to wrap my head around everything that's happened. I'm probably in some delayed shock, but..."

He was in front of me in two quick strides, tugging me to him. I wrapped my arms around him, unable to get close enough. Devon was my haven, my safety net, and knowing he'd put as much effort into finding me as I did in calming his beast shattered all the petty issues I'd piled between us.

They were nothing in comparison to the threat that faced us. Lorenzo wouldn't be happy to find me gone, and he would rage the next time he saw me standing with Devon. Santiga Bay might be large enough to hide in, but the vampire community wasn't.

Devon took a step back and waited for me to meet his gaze. Where most people would be terrified when his eyes glowed an icy blue, it made my insides quiver when they melted to a silver blue. He ran a finger along my lips then brushed my hair back.

"I thought I'd lost you." His voice was thick with emotion.

"I'm sorry I didn't listen to you. I should never have gone to the condo."

He shook his head. "You shouldn't have to worry about where you stay. It was my responsibility to keep you safe."

I snorted. "You can't keep me in a gilded cage or drive me around in an armored truck."

His brow lifted. "Now, that's an idea."

I poked him in the ribs. "You know what I mean."

"I do. And let's not talk about that. Right now, I don't want to talk at all." He kissed me. It was slow and sensuous, tempting me to ask for more, but I let him continue at his own pace, taking time to enjoy the feel of his lips on mine, the warmth of them, and the growing heat between us.

How could someone have made me forget this vampire? I wrapped my arms around him and pulled him closer, not wanting him to end the kiss. The world around us ceased. He was all I needed, and I let everything else go.

He picked me up and carried me to the bed. His hands were gentle as he removed my clothing, his touch electric where his fingers skimmed my skin. He stepped back and removed his clothing, but he was taking too long. I wanted his touch, his skin on mine, and our bodies entwined.

He complied as if he'd heard me scream my demands out loud.

He covered me with his lean physique, his knee pushing my legs apart as his lips returned to mine for a quick kiss before running his fangs down my neck. A ripple of need rushed over me. He continued a path around my breasts, over my tummy, and lower still until I arched with satisfaction.

I forgot the days we'd been apart and my stolen memories. I never thought someone would love me with such passion. The idea that we could have lost this so easily drove me to a decision. But then I felt the beast in him rise, and the thought slipped away.

It might have been minutes or an hour when I cried out as the orgasm hit, shaking me to my core as wave after wave crashed over me.

His thrusts increased until the intense pleasure rippled through me again. He howled like a wolf—or perhaps the beast was calling out its satisfaction as his body shook and his final strokes slowed before he collapsed next to me, rolling me with him.

We fell asleep in each other's arms, my last murky thought repeating over and over in my head—I'll never forget again.

I WOKE in a place of darkness. What little light there was came from a crude window cut out of stone that was covered with a crosshatch pattern made of vertical and horizontal iron bars. Stars shone in a dark sky, and waves crashed against a shore from somewhere below.

I spun around at the strike of a match. A small oil lamp sat on a table in a large room, its edges barely visible. But the flame was strong enough to reflect the stone walls. Stacks of books were piled high on the table, and behind it were two wooden bookcases so old they appeared to lean against each other for support. They were over-stuffed with more books and collections of papers wrapped in string. Rolls of parchment were gathered on a top shelf, held in place by thick tomes.

I shuddered when I noticed the iron shackles on the wall next to the bookcase. Two were placed about shoulder height and two near the floor. A quick image flashed of a man held in the manacles, spread eagle against the wall. Then it was gone.

A cot was set against another wall. It was two feet off the floor, and a single blanket had been shoved aside, a limp pillow at the head. There was a second table with a wooden chair where a tin plate and cup perched next to another lamp, this one unlit.

In a corner, a sheet hung from the wall, and I guessed from the stink that it hid some form of bathroom I was happy not to see. Next to it was a wooden door inset with a speakeasy door made of vertical iron bars. At the bottom of the door was another opening, this one much wider but only twelve inches high. Another image hit me that showed a tray of food being passed through it. This was a dungeon cell.

Hooks had been drilled into the wall where ragged clothing hung. Hand drawings had been taped to the walls—garden scenes, night skies where the stars were linked together into astrological shapes, and dozens with the face of a woman. The same woman.

I stumbled back. Lyra. There wasn't a doubt in my mind.

Another sound made me spin around. A man stood by the bed. He was painfully thin. His clothes were threadbare, and his greasy hair fell past his shoulders, almost the same length as his scraggly beard. But it was his eyes that reflected years of torment, loneliness, and a bare sliver of hope.

"Don't forget me. Save me." His voice was rough from unuse. As if he'd been sleeping for years and just woke.

And if what I'd already seen wasn't horror enough, a ghostly figure hovered in the corner. It faded in and out. At first, it was nothing more than a white outline, then as its features filled in, it turned to full color.

It was a woman.

She knelt on the rough stone floor and cried as she rocked back and forth. My first instinct was to go to her, but instead, I glanced at the man who, even with his heavy beard, now seemed familiar. He was staring down at the woman, and a trail of tears sparkled in the dim light.

My gaze flashed back to the woman, and I took another step back. I tried to scream but all I could do was shake.

Lyra.

She was dressed in the same tunic and pants she'd worn during the party. The man shuffled a step toward her then turned his gaze to me. His eyes were pleading, his arms outstretched.

"You're my only hope. Save me. Save us."

I sat up and stared into another dark room. This one was Devon's, and I released a tormented sigh as I jumped from the bed, scrounging for my nightgown and robe in the pile of clothes at the foot of the bed.

Devon must have sensed my movements. "What's wrong?"

"Lyra. I need to get to Lyra."

He moved with vampiric speed, tossing my robe to me as he pulled on his pants. We raced down the hall to the stairs as he slid his shirt on. We pounded up the steps to the third floor. Her bedroom door was already open.

We burst in to find Colantha soothing Lyra on one of the couches. The expression on Colantha's face should have stopped me. She was angry and fiercely protective. Frederick and Jamison stood sentinel near the wall—watching and waiting.

"Did she see it, too?" I asked as I dropped to the floor next to Lyra, my hand instinctively rubbing her arm.

Devon stood near, but not close enough to cause Colantha's vamps to take any action.

Lyra was still rocking as Colantha murmured words I didn't understand. They were a foreign language, perhaps French or Creole. Or maybe dreamwalkers had their own language I wasn't aware of.

Lyra calmed and pulled away from Colantha to stare down at

me. "You saw. You were there. Hamilton is alive. I'm not crazy, right?"

Devon shot me a look I couldn't decipher as it was mixed with too many emotions.

I continued to stroke her arm. "Yes. I saw. Hamilton is alive. And Lorenzo has him."

Chapter Nineteen

DEVON SET LOGS on the fire then stepped back to ensure the new logs picked up the flames. It was mostly a ruse. He needed time for this new information to soak in. Hamilton, Lyra's boyfriend who had died in the accident with his parents a hundred years ago was still alive. On the surface, that made no sense.

But it did. It made perfect sense.

He'd always had a suspicion that his parents' death weren't an accident. A long-lost intuition that had been triggered by Cressa's accident and the staged fire. They'd wanted him to think she'd died in the fire like his parents. But why? This went way beyond Lorenzo's need for one-upmanship. Had it been more than just taking his Blood Ward from him?

None of it explained why Lorenzo would have taken Hamilton. And how could he be alive after all this time? Too many damn questions. He turned when the door opened, and Sergi led the rest of the cadre in. Simone had decided to stay another couple of days before returning to Oasis. And Jacques, who had healed enough for light work, trailed behind Bella as usual.

Colantha had moved Lyra to the sofa in front of the hearth, and Cressa sat on her other side with Ginger next to her. Frederick and Jamison took positions at the door, and the cadre took chairs around the fire. Devon glanced at the antique marble clock that rested on the mantel. It had been a gift from their father to their mother and fit Lyra's whimsical personality. The chime had just signaled four in the morning.

Lyra had wanted immediate action—storm the castle in search of the lost prince. But they only had Cressa's word—no—that wasn't right. She only suspected Hamilton was being held on the island, if it was truly him. Cressa had never met him, yet all one had to do was look around this room and anyone would recognize him, even with a full beard. If anyone fit the adage, the eyes are the window to the soul, Hamilton would be the one. From what Cressa said, it was the first thing she'd noticed.

The whir of an espresso machine from the kitchenette would be Lucas making drinks for everyone. At this point, there wouldn't be any more sleep, and he already had a long day planned for everyone.

"I'd like to wait until Lucas finishes before I start. It's important for everyone to hear the entire story." Devon ran a hand through his hair and wished they were in his office so he could pick up his father's crystal to roll around in his hands. It provided an excellent focal point.

"Let Jamison finish the espressos. I'd prefer we get this done so Lyra can get some rest." Colantha waved a hand over her head, and Jamison strode toward the panel that hid the small kitchen.

A moment later, Lucas walked out carrying the first of the drinks, which he passed around before finding a seat.

"I'll give you the short version as I remember it." Devon glanced at Lyra.

She nodded and looked at the others. "I'll add anything that might be pertinent." Her head lowered, and she stared at her hands, her fingers curling in and out of fists.

"It was the summer of 1925, and our father and mother had driven to San Francisco with Lyra and her boyfriend, Hamilton. I believe they went to meet with the curator of the Renaud Library."

"Was it open to the public back then?" Simone asked.

When Devon didn't seem sure, Lucas answered the question. "Not exactly. You could arrange a tour or request a visit for either scholarly pursuit or to search for Family ancestral documentation."

"Father knew the curator." Devon kept the details brief. "He was an old family friend. They had dinner and, on their return home, they were hit by an erratic driver. Their car burst into flames before they could get out. Some helpful bystanders were able to pull Lyra from the car, but our parents and Hamilton weren't as fortunate. The driver of the other car had left the scene. Since there was no registration found, we weren't able to locate the owner of the vehicle."

"The other car didn't catch fire?" Simone asked.

"No. My understanding was that there was peripheral burning from our House car. It had been hauled away before I returned home, and at the time, I didn't see a reason to investigate further."

"It sounds like an accident, but, if I remember correctly, you didn't believe that," Sergi said. For once, he hadn't pulled out his tablet.

"Not then. It was sometime later when I contacted Teller, one of Father's cadre. He made a comment about Father being secretive for several days leading up to the accident. He had brought on a human assistant for what he referred to as a special project."

"That isn't particularly unusual," Simone offered. "Vampires have been using human assistants for centuries. Why was this one different?"

"Because Hamilton was the gardener." Lyra picked at her dress with a trembling hand. One might think it was because she was scared or on the verge of tears. She'd have every right to either emotion. But he knew his sister, and it was much more than that. She was angry. Blow the roof off the house raging mad, but somehow, she had the strength to hold it in. He glanced at Colantha and wondered if the dreamwalker had the ability to mentally calm Lyra's beast.

"A gardener?" Simone asked. "Well, that would have caused some gossip."

"He was more than that." Lyra's face lit up, and she laughed. "He called himself a landscape architect and designed the gardens for the manor. He's the one that planted the sycamore tree." Her gaze became unfocused as she stared out one of the windows that overlooked the tree, the tips of its branches nothing more than a shadowy presence in the dark sky.

"From what Teller told me, it was obvious to the cadre the man had more training and intelligence than to be a simple gardener." Devon kept an eye on Lyra as they discussed Hamilton. "What concerned the cadre were the secret meetings behind closed doors and the assignments Father sent Hamilton on. But Teller couldn't tell me any more than that. Since I had no proof to say the accident was more than it was, and with Lyra's injuries and dealing with such a great loss..." He glanced at his sister.

"I had already slipped into my madness." The light had gone out of her eyes, but she gave him a weak smile. "There's no other pleasant way to say it."

"Why did your Father go to San Francisco without his security detail?" Bella asked.

"According to Teller, everything had been quiet for months. Even the Council had taken down time for the summer." Devon preferred not to dwell on this part. He had no reasonable explanation for a man who'd spent centuries with one eye over his shoulder to take his family but no security. His cadre didn't have a better explanation, and the truth was, they'd become lax.

"It does appear similar to Cressa's accident." Sergi took out his tablet, and Devon held back a smile. Sergi would be aggrieved to know he'd become so predictable. "There would probably be very little online regarding something that happened so long ago, but it might be worth digging through old newspaper files. The House was a large part of the community at the time. I can check if there's anything available."

Devon nodded.

"If it was more than an accident, what would be the reason?" Lucas asked. "Guildford..." Lucas stopped and glanced at Colantha. "That was their father, and he was on the Council. Was there a political issue going on at the time? There had to be a reason he met with the curator, even if they were old friends. Or maybe it was poor timing that gave his adversary an opening."

"Father was quite influential on the Council," Lyra answered. "He had his enemies, Lorenzo being the main one. Although shortly before the accident, Lorenzo had suggested an alignment of our Houses."

Devon's head shot up. "I wasn't aware of this."

Lyra shrugged. "I don't think Father gave it any consideration. Lorenzo wanted to join the Houses through marriage, and thankfully, Father wouldn't hear of it."

"Marriage? To Lorenzo?" Cressa asked as her face contorted to a mix of disgust and confusion.

"From Lorenzo's traditional values, it would make sense." Simone shifted in her seat as everyone turned to her. "This was a hundred years ago, and since societal changes in vampires move slowly, it wasn't unusual for Houses to be aligned through marriage. But I agree, this normally happened with Houses that had similar interests and beliefs. To bring two great Houses together with such dichotomy was only seen during times of war as a step toward peace."

"You mean peace by one House consuming the other." Lucas was nodding. "There are many Houses that no longer exist due to that. Winner takes all in exchange for saving lives."

Cressa turned to Lyra, and Devon knew her well enough to see the wheels turning. "I know the Trelane and Venizi Houses have been estranged for centuries but, from what I know of Lorenzo, the proposal seems odd, even for him."

"I agree with Cressa." Sergi laid down his tablet and picked up his espresso. "There had to be more to it. Something else was going on."

"What was your relationship with Hamilton?" Colantha's tone was firm but sensitive. Her hand stroked Lyra's arm, and if his sister was aware of it, she didn't seem to mind. "Was it more than a passing fancy with a human?"

Lyra's face took on an ethereal expression. "It was much more. We were in love. Not a simple love, yet not complex. There had been an instant attraction from the very beginning. It blossomed after the first time we spoke at a gallery opening in South Rim. He was a sculptor, and I was showing my paintings."

"I wasn't aware you showed your paintings." Devon took a seat near her. "Mother never mentioned it in her letters."

Lyra shook her head. Her expression reminded him of when she was a young Sangui Genu—a true blood—stubborn and rebellious. "Father and Mother were angry that I went. Avery, my best friend at the time, helped me sneak the paintings out of the House." Her face clouded over. "After the event, Mr. Sutton, the gallery owner, told me one of the paintings had sold. Then I discovered Lorenzo had bought it. And while he might have taken some fancy to me, I think he was more irritated by my flirtation with Hamilton. It was at that event he seemed to take a particular interest in me."

"Because Hamilton was human?" Simone asked. "It would make sense to Lorenzo that it would be beneath vampire etiquette."

"And a reason for Lorenzo to believe Guildford had become weak," Lucas suggested.

"And his first step at proving Guildford wasn't fit for Council," Sergi agreed.

"Maybe it was deeper than that." Colantha patted Lyra's arm. "Were you aware that Hamilton was a dreamwalker?"

She nodded. "He brought me to his dreams a few times." The

ethereal expression appeared again. "It was the most amazing experience."

"Did anyone else know?"

She shook her head. "He made me promise not to tell anyone, and I didn't. Who would have believed someone like that existed? Though I always wondered if Father knew more than he let on. Though I don't think Hamilton said anything to him."

"Something's nagging at me." Lucas picked up his cup and glanced at Jamison. "Would you mind?" When the vampire nodded with a smile and returned to the kitchenette, Lucas continued. "You mentioned Guildford was good friends with the curator at the Renaud Library. What was the man's name?"

Devon shook his head. "I don't remember. Father had many friends, and I was a son with no thought of running the House but had gone on my required sojourn anyway. At that time, I'd been in Europe for several years. It was one of the Renauds, that much I do recall."

"It was Philipe Renaud," Lyra said. "They were getting together to discuss a book. I believe it was something Hamilton suggested Father should read."

The room fell silent as Devon and the cadre glanced at each other.

"It wasn't the *De første dage*?" Devon asked.

Lyra tilted her head. "That sounds familiar. Yes, I'm sure that was it. How did you know?"

"ARE YOU MAD? His island is a fortress." Simone stared at Devon as if he'd lost his mind.

They had adjourned from Lyra's room once the book was mentioned, and the group had lapsed into more questions than anyone had answers for. Devon had sent everyone to their rooms to rest before he'd entertain any more discussion. Colantha had remained with Lyra, and Cressa fell face-first in her bed and would probably sleep for several hours.

A great deal had happened since Cressa's return and her discovery of Hamilton being alive. He hadn't spoken to Colantha yet about how Hamilton could still be alive after a hundred years; he remembered questioning her age the first time he'd seen her in New Orleans. But that could wait. They had more important issues.

He'd called for the cadre and Decker a couple of hours after sunrise. He let them talk amongst themselves as he settled behind his desk and picked up the white crystal, finding the warmth of the stone comforting. He'd never asked his father where he got it. It just showed up on his desk one day, and like him, his father would pick it up when he needed to think. Whether the crystal was meant to center him, focus him, or just give him something to do with his hands, it didn't matter. It did what it had always done for him— allowed his mind to sketch the beginnings of a plan. One that required the cadre's expertise in helping to shape and hone.

"He might consider it an act of war." Sergi's words might sound as if he was against the idea, but the light in his eyes reminded Devon of their early days just before they went into battle.

"It's definitely bold. I love it." Decker's laughter filled Devon's study. "I wouldn't mind seeing him taken down a peg or two. He must have been raging mad to come home and find Cressa gone with no explanation of how she did it."

"His first thought would be inside sources." Bella's lip curled in disgust. "Anyone who'd been around her will be thoroughly interrogated. And he'll expect a possible raid."

"That might keep him occupied for a time, but it won't last." Lucas watched Bella pace. "He can't stay on lockdown forever, assuming he'd choose to do that. And he didn't hear one word from Devon after the accident. He has to be wondering about that."

"Maybe he thought Devon considered her a runaway after the crash." Bella nodded, warming up to the idea. She stopped by Jacques, placing a hand on his shoulder. "If she was trouble for Lorenzo, maybe he'll believe she was a handful for Devon and he's thankful she's gone."

"His thinking her a handful wouldn't be wrong," Simone said.

They all laughed. The group continued to discuss Devon's crazy notion, but Lucas and Bella turned silent, both in their own world, most likely running through scenarios. Bella had always been itching to go after Lorenzo. Lucas would be mentally listing a pro and con analysis, considering ramifications from the Council.

But the Council wouldn't care. They were aware of the long-standing animosity between the two Houses, and as long as no other Houses were impacted, and the human world was none the wiser, the Council would look the other way. They preferred Houses to take care of their own problems.

"Alright. Let's focus." Devon attempted to bring the cadre to order, and it took another minute before they quieted. "I'm not planning on storming the island tomorrow. In fact, I'd prefer a plan where he didn't know it was us. And we have to ensure anything we develop has a high probability of success."

"How do we know for sure this Hamilton is really there?" Simone asked.

"Most of you have dreamwalked with Colantha." Devon smiled when Simone shivered, and the others shifted in their seats. "You only witnessed a glimpse of what she can do. She'll try to reach him on her own, and then most likely with Lyra and Cressa. If they all agree it's him, and he is, in fact, on the island, then we need to rescue him if we can."

"You think Lorenzo knows Hamilton is a dreamwalker?" Decker asked.

"I do. Or perhaps not a dreamwalker but someone with blood that interacts with vampire blood. I don't know how he knew about Hamilton or why he saved him from the fire. At this point,

I'm once again questioning my parents' accident—why they were targeted, why Lyra was saved, and why Hamilton was taken."

"I haven't been able to find anything online regarding the accident." Sergi typed in his tablet. "I'll work through my contacts with SBPD, but I still think reviewing back copies from newspapers of the time will prove most useful."

Devon nodded. "Track down Yun if you can. He took charge of the House investigation and might have a different opinion once he considers Hamilton might have been the possible target, and my parents' deaths an extra benefit.

Sergi nodded. "We need pictures of the island, maps of the channel, schedules of the boats. I want to know every possible way on and off that island."

"Remus keeps wolves around the dock." Decker pulled out a bag of black licorice and bit into one. "He owns a couple of the warehouses, and one of his wolves owns a combo food shack and bait shop near the boat launch. A few of them work at the boatyard. They keep track of the schedules. It shouldn't be a problem to run closer surveillance and track any changes in security."

"Can you connect me with one of their contacts?" Bella asked. "I'd like to get a sense for the area and see what we can use for possible diversions."

Devon glanced at Simone, who had quieted, but he spoke to Lucas instead. "I need you to make a run to the city. Philipe Renaud had been in the Renaud Library with the *De første dage* at the time of my parents' accident. I want to know what happened afterward. At some point, Philipe left San Francisco for the Los Angeles library. He either did that because of the accident, or it was a simple coincidence with the opening of the SoCal branch."

Lucas brightened at the thought. "It might give me an idea how to track where he is now."

"My thoughts exactly. He had the book, and it was apparently in the Los Angeles library for some time. The Renauds keep excellent records. We need to dig deeper."

Lucas nodded. "And I have an idea how to approach them on it."

"You're rather quiet, Simone." There could be several reasons for it, and Devon could take the time to guess, but it was sometimes easier to poke Simone and see what happened.

Not many could do that and come out unscathed, but while Lyra was still considered the House Leader, preparing for an attack was his specialty. His father had honed him from an early age to be a strategist. This mission would be no different than any battle. His original plans to remove his censure from the Council had taken a very dark turn and had uncovered more to Lorenzo's plan than he could ever have thought possible. But he sensed everything coming together. There were still dots he hadn't connected, but they were getting closer. They were on the right track.

"We need to know Lorenzo's schedule." Simone's posture didn't change, but her fangs dropped enough for the tips to be seen through her sneer. "Not just when he comes and goes from the island, but something that's part of his usual routine that might give us an edge. Something so normal, he won't see us coming."

"And how will we go about determining that?" Devon asked, knowing she was already thinking of something.

"We need to socialize. See what the aristocracy is humming about."

He chuckled. "And you believe that's something you should be tackling?"

Her sneer grew to a smile most would run from. "You always said I needed to make friends with other Houses. What better time?"

"And what will you be doing?" Sergi asked Devon.

"I'll be working with Colantha. I want to see if she has a trick or two we can use to our advantage."

"And Cressa?"

"I have plans for her," Simone responded before Devon could, but she nodded to Devon. "When you're not in need of her, of course."

"I'm afraid much of this will come down to Cressa. She's had an insider's view of the island. We need a solid plan with concrete information. If we miss this opportunity, and Lorenzo has any idea what we're up to, he'll either move Hamilton or decide he's become too much of a risk."

Chapter Twenty

I STARED AT THE CEILING, having slept as long as I could, knowing Devon worried about my recovery. I'd be lying if I said I wasn't bothered about being kidnapped and mesmerized. It wasn't easy knowing someone had taken control of my thoughts and actions. If Ginger and I still lived alone in the old apartment, I'd probably be rolled up in a ball, unsure how to protect myself. Even though I was away from Lorenzo, I would be looking over my shoulder for some time, terrified someone could do that again without my knowledge.

Another vamp had mesmerized me when I'd first come to the manor. It was during the tea party at Gruber's, and Devon had immediately brought me out of it. And one time I'd watched him mesmerize someone who'd broken into my old apartment. I didn't seem to mind mesmerizing when it worked toward my benefit.

Where did one cross the line in controlling another's thoughts? Good question, but this wasn't the time for philosophical debates. Lorenzo's mesmerizing wasn't used just once to gather information. He'd used it whenever we were together with the goal of permanently putting me under his control. And yes, I was traumatized by the event, but I was more than that. I was incensed. Neither emotion was healthy, but I didn't have time for a psychiatrist, so I decided to just go with the rage. And rescuing Hamilton out from under his nose would go a long way in tempering the trauma.

After dressing, I found Colantha in Lyra's room and was surprised to find Ginger there, too. They were in front of the hearth where a low fire burned. Colantha sat with Lyra on the couch while Ginger was curled up in one of the stuffed chairs next to them. Frederick and Jamison stood by the windows rather than the door. While they wouldn't leave Colantha's side, they appeared to have relaxed enough not to hover as closely.

The coffee table was filled with a coffee urn, artfully painted mugs that I assumed came from Lyra's collection, and platters of brunch items that had been cleanly picked through. My stomach growled at the sight. When Ginger noticed me, she waved and grabbed her cell, making a quick call and keeping her voice too low for me to hear. Hopefully, the call was for more coffee. Lyra's kitchen would be well-stocked, but she was more of a tea drinker.

"Cressa." Lyra seemed surprised to see me. "Devon said you'd be resting."

I snorted. "Lying in bed and remembering the last few days isn't entirely restful." I dropped into the other stuffed chair and gave Ginger a grin. "I'm surprised you aren't sleeping in."

"Are you kidding? With everything that's going on, I'm not going to miss a moment."

Colantha studied me for a while, and I found it almost as unnerving as one of Lorenzo's mesmerizing stares. It didn't last long, and she sat back, seeming comfortable with whatever she saw. "Ginger has been telling us how the two of you came to be part of House Trelane."

"I thought I shared that with the two of you before." I found a clean mug and lifted the urn, pouring out the last dregs that gave me half a cup.

Colantha snickered and picked at the sweatshirt she wore over leggings. Not the clothing I would have expected from the prim and proper lady from New Orleans. But everyone had to let their hair down occasionally. "I have to say, Ginger tells a more engaging story."

Ginger beamed, and I raised my mug in salute. Colantha wasn't wrong.

I gave Lyra the same studied review Colantha had given me. She looked tired, and I doubted she'd gotten any sleep. Vamps didn't need to sleep, but it increased how frequently they required blood. She would need a donor soon, and if she didn't request one herself, I'd have to squeal to Devon. He would be keeping an eye on her, but with a new mission underway, it could slip his attention.

"I was hoping you could tell us more about your time on the island." Lyra's gaze was hopeful, and while I'd known this was coming, she wouldn't get the answers she sought.

Lyra wouldn't be the only one who'd want to hear it again with more detail. Devon was most likely in his office with his faithful cadre around him, reviewing my tale. I didn't begrudge his time with the cadre. They were his guards, his sounding board, and his friends. Devon was a man of action when the time came, but he was primarily a strategist. He wouldn't allow his emotions to force an unwise move. He'd been after Lorenzo for too long, and I'd come to learn that Devon was a patient vamp. That in itself would drive Lorenzo crazy as he waited for Devon's next chess move.

I took in a deep breath, ready to share what little more I could provide when a knock interrupted me.

"Come," Lyra called, though she'd barely raised her voice.

The door opened, and Cook waltzed in with a tray. It was unusual for him to leave the kitchen except for the occasional stop in the dining room to bring a special entree. My gaze fixed on the coffee urn, but the scent of fresh food brought another growl from my stomach.

His eyes shined with amusement when he caught my singular focus. "It's so good to have our Cressa back with us. I thought you could use something special from the kitchen."

I grinned and drained my mug, jonesing for a fresh cup. "You know me too well. And you've already fed this crowd once."

He set the tray down while Frederick brought in a fresh teapot. The vamp set the pot down in front of Lyra and picked up the soiled dishes, giving Cook space to unload four fresh place settings and several plates with silver domes. He lifted the lids, and my eyes glazed over. Blueberry scones, scrambled eggs, and bacon for me. The other plates were a mix of crab rolls, a selection of finger sandwiches, and strawberry tarts with dollops of whipped cream, no doubt freshly made. He placed a hand on my shoulder, and I patted it.

I blinked back tears. "Thank you, Cook. This means a great deal to me."

He squeezed my shoulder and, after giving a small bow to Lyra, scurried from the room.

"He missed you." Lyra poured a fresh cup of tea and took a finger sandwich, nibbling the edge.

"Well, I can't tell you how much I missed all of you." I filled my mug and, in between bites of food, told them everything I could remember of my time on the island.

The moments of Lorenzo's mesmerizing were the most difficult to share, but Colantha felt it was important to understand how it was done, and I couldn't disagree. Though it was a definite weakness, Colantha thought I'd been building an immunity to it from the start. It began with the tiny moments of odd images that were superimposed over reality. The first one that came to mind, which almost made me laugh, was when I'd walked into Lorenzo's kitchen expecting the immense coffee urn that Cook always kept filled. And while Lorenzo had a strong hold over me while he was mesmerizing me, it began to dissolve as soon as he was out of sight.

"Did Hamilton only reach out that once?" Lyra's voice cracked a bit, but she remained calm.

I bit into the blueberry scone, closed my eyes for a second as I recalled the headaches, then shook my head. "I remember at least one other attempt, maybe it was two, but they weren't nearly as clear as the last one."

"I want to try reaching out to him myself." Colantha caressed her medallion in what appeared to be a reflexive action. "It can be tricky when it's a dreamwalker I don't know in a place I'm unfamiliar with. From what you've shared, I don't believe he built a construct. It sounds like he brought you to his exact location. Whether that was on purpose to prove he was a prisoner or because he's too weak to do anything more than that, I can't tell you.

"I can bring him to one of my constructs with you as a conduit. He recognizes you as a fellow dreamwalker. While I'm much stronger, he might not be as willing to come to me."

"I want to be included in that attempt." Lyra straightened; her stubbornness was taking the lead on this. "I might not be able to call to him like you can, but I think he'd be more comfortable if I was there."

I wanted to protect her, worried about how much she could take. "He might not want you to see him in his current state. He seemed distraught when he saw you in the last dreamwalk."

"I understand your concern, but I've been seeing him for decades. Sometimes glimpses, sometimes more. Years of torture, pain, and lost hope. I want him to know that I still believe in him." Lyra's words were defiant, but then she crumbled. "That I still love him."

Colantha rubbed Lyra's back. "He knows that. Otherwise, he wouldn't continue his attempts to reach you."

"I'm sorry, Lyra." Sometimes, I said the most awkward things. "Of course, you love him, and I believe he knows that. You can't blame me for worrying about you."

She took the tissue Colantha handed her and blew her nose. "I know. I'm trying to be strong, but every time I think about how long he's been there, I get so angry."

"That brings up something I'd like to know." I turned to Colantha, who conveniently glanced away. "Exactly how long do dreamwalkers live?"

Colantha reached for a strawberry tart, licking the whipped cream off with her tongue before eating the bite-sized morsel. After taking her time to relish the taste, she gave me a mischievous smile. I returned it with one of my own. The woman still scared me at times, but there was no way she was leaving this room without answering. Her two vamps wouldn't be enough to block me from getting answers. I was confident Lyra could keep them at bay.

"It's complicated."

I snorted. "You can do better than that."

She stared at the ceiling and sighed as if she'd shared the answer dozens of times. "It's not the same for us as with vampires. Unless they get their head chopped off or burn in a fire, there isn't much that can kill them. As long as they don't get any one of the rare diseases that occasionally kills one, receives enough blood when needed, and don't take their own life out of boredom, they can live for centuries.

"Dreamwalkers have more weaknesses when it comes to killing us. That's why it was so easy to decimate millions of us over the centuries, even after the initial purge. A well-placed bullet, several types of diseases, severe blood loss, or our head conveniently removed from our bodies—any of those will shorten our life span. But it's more than that. Genetics plays a role, as does whether a person is a full dreamwalker or half. From a social perspective, we don't care whether they're full-blood or part. There's no shame in only having a small percentage of dreamwalker blood, but it does play a part in longevity. Then add in a dreamwalker's individual power as well as their ancestors'—" She shrugged. "Some of us have strong connections to vampires, even after the purge, and if there's blood sharing, that will play a role."

"Is there, like, an average life span you could share?" I was used to Colantha's attempts to divert from answering questions, but I believed her when she said it was complicated. It might sound like subterfuge on her part, but I didn't think she did it on purpose. At least not for this specific question.

She sipped her coffee as she considered the question. "Some have lived for centuries, and for others, they live what would be considered an extremely long human lifespan. But I would say most live a couple of centuries. I don't know Hamilton or who his family was. But I can sense his power. Even locked away for a hundred years in stressful, torturous conditions, he continues to call to others."

"Being locked away doesn't necessarily weaken a person."

We all turned toward the door where Simone had quietly entered. I was still wrapping my head around the average dreamwalker living for two centuries, but it faded to the background as she strode toward the group, nodding at Colantha's vamps before dragging over a chair. "Except physically, of course, depending on the conditions they're kept. But if one has a strong enough mind, the physical doesn't become as important. That's not right." She shook her head. A rare moment indeed for her to backtrack a statement. "The physical is important, but a strong mind can keep the body conditioned, which in turn helps to maintain their mental faculties. The important thing is to eat what is given to you and perform a daily exercise ritual to stay limber."

She poured coffee into a clean mug then sat back, apparently done with her sharing time. I didn't know anything about Simone's past, but she obviously had one. But I didn't think her story was something she shared with just anyone. She seemed to have first-hand knowledge of the topic of confinement, and anything more would be too personal to share in mixed company.

"Is Devon finished with the cadre?" I asked.

"For the most part. You didn't miss anything. He's not planning on storming the island." Her gaze shifted to Lyra, whose lips pressed into a thin line.

I nodded, expecting nothing less.

"Cressa provided more details about her stay on the island." Colantha watched Simone, who ignored the dreamwalker. Simone was uncomfortable around the woman, and I understood. She was a control freak.

"Anything of interest?" Simone kept her gaze on me, and like the others, gave me a once-over to evaluate my condition.

"No. It was more about Lorenzo's mesmerizing routine and when his hold began to weaken."

"Probably small moments from the beginning, but most certainly whenever you dreamwalked."

My gaze widened, then narrowed when Simone sniffed at my response. I'd never considered she might have insights on this.

"Mesmerizing is a mental skill. So is dreamwalking. It's not surprising one would weaken the other."

Colantha nodded. "That's correct."

The two women stared at each other, then Simone nodded at her, accepting Colantha's agreement. Simone must be dying to know if Colantha ever sparred with her bodyguards. It would be interesting which of the two would come out on top without using dreamwalking skills.

"So, what are Devon's plans?" Ginger had been quiet for most of the discussion but had apparently been soaking everything in. "I would think he'd need to know more about the island and this building where Hamilton is being held."

"That's part of it," Simone agreed. "Sergi can get satellite images, but they don't provide the best resolution. And we need details."

"We'll need the best pictures we can get for the building and the surrounding landscape," I said. "It looks like it's one story, but there might be a basement."

"Can we get one of those flying things?" Ginger asked. When everyone stared at her with quizzical expressions, she sighed. "You know. Those drone things."

"I'm not sure how close it could get." It was an interesting suggestion. "They can be noisy."

"If the surf is up, the breakers on the island will distort the sound," Simone said. "But they would see them."

"Not until they got up close." Ginger perched on the edge of her seat. "One time, someone flew one where our old apartment was. We could hear it, but we had a devil of a time finding it. It was gray or silver and blended into the sky. Greco was pissed from what Bulldog said. He thought it was one of the other drug lords trying to get into his territory, and he had it shot down. Turns out it belonged to some geek who was into remote-control stuff a couple of blocks over. He actually had the nerve to find out who destroyed his drone and got right in Bulldog's face."

"When was this?" I asked.

"Oh, a few months ago. We were still living in the neighborhood, but I think you were out of town on a job."

"I can ask if Sergi knows someone," Simone offered.

I shook my head. "I have a better idea. Let me check with Harlow. I bet Roxie has an idea or two on that topic."

Simone shrugged. "Let's check with both and keep our options open."

"May I ask what my brother has you doing?" Lyra's voice was cold, but Simone ignored the tone.

She sighed and looked aggrieved enough for the tips of her fangs to show. "That's part of the reason I'm here. I don't say this lightly when I say I might have taken on more than I can handle."

"Oh?" I found this more than interesting and couldn't help smile when Simone squirmed.

"I told Devon I would socialize and see what the word is on Lorenzo's activities."

I glanced at Lyra, then at Ginger, then back at Lyra. The

tension with Lyra broke, and much to Simone's shame, we all broke out in laughter.

Chapter Twenty-One

SERGI FOLLOWED THE STEEP, winding road as it curved its way to the mountain peak. It had taken some time to find Yun after multiple attempts to locate Guildford's old cadre. There were four at the time of Guildford's death, and they'd scattered after Devon took over the House and brought in his own team.

There had been hurt feelings, and Devon discovered quickly that he'd handled the transition badly. One of the cadre, a young vampire by the name of Teller, was the only one who seemed to have understood Devon's inexperience enough to speak with Sergi.

Teller had found a new position with a small House in Chicago. He was the only one of the four Sergi had been able to easily find, and they agreed to meet at a coffee shop with a view of Lake Michigan.

"Thank you for meeting with me." Sergi centered his cup of cappuccino and set his tablet to the right. He studied the young vampire, who by now was closing in on two hundred years, which would have made him quite young to be part of a cadre back in the 1920s, but the same could be said of Lucas and Bella. The vampire was broad-shouldered, tall, and muscular. And maybe it was that muscle that Guildford liked to have close by.

Teller gave him the same measured study. "I heard Trelane got himself into some trouble lately." There wasn't any animosity in his tone. He was fishing. The House he belonged to was considered an ally to House Trelane, but that was because they were tied to a larger House that was fully committed to Devon. Whether his House was a true friend to the Trelanes might not matter to Teller. Members of a cadre held to a certain standard, a loyalty that could transcend House politics. One reason for a leader to hold their cadre close.

"The complexities of the Trelane and Venizi Houses go back centuries, as you know."

The vampire nodded, a frown creating wrinkles on his forehead. He sipped his coffee. "Venizi hasn't given Devon any rest since his rise to House leader. But he seemed happy enough with Devon's censure. If the rivalry is heating up, then Devon must be pushing for something."

"He wants the censure removed."

Teller nodded. "And Venizi knows Trelane's vote would tip the Council away from Venizi's old-world thinking. I can see where that would be enough for him to take action against Devon. With his censure, Devon should be an easy target."

"One could make that assumption." Sergi scanned the coffee shop as he sipped the cappuccino. It was a small place and not very crowded. Other than the one vampire that came with Teller, and a possible shifter, the rest of the customers appeared human.

Teller laughed. "And that could end up being a fatal mistake."

Sergi eyed him but said nothing.

Teller relaxed and gave Sergi another smile. "I know there were hard feelings among Guildford's cadre when Devon took over. He'd been away for some time, and the cadre thought he'd keep us around while he settled in. We felt abandoned. We'd been dealt a great loss when Guildford and Irene were killed and Lyra injured."

"There was hurt and mistakes made on all sides. Devon tried to make amends."

Teller gave a half shrug. "By then, it was too late and too fresh. We were concerned for his struggles, his addiction, but it wasn't our place to help." He played with a stir stick, picking away fine strands of wood. "And though we don't share it outside the old cadre, we were all proud of his return; his unwillingness to be beaten even after his censure. The others would probably never admit it, but we watched his rise in the business world—the partnerships he's made with the shifters and humans."

"You've been watching him?"

Teller grinned. "Of course. Whatever you or Devon might think, we still have loyalty to House Trelane and Guildford's Family. We watched Devon and Lyra grow up. And while some of the hurt still remains, Devon's loyalty to his sister and his House is everything Guildford would have done." He leaned over the table. "Devon has his father's patience. We know he's building up to something. We thought he'd been dealt a fatal blow with this mess with the Poppy and Boretsky's murder. But he's a sly one. He has many of his father's leadership qualities and he's battle-tested. Because of that, Venizi believes Devon handles a House like his father and the other ancients."

He fell back in his seat and snapped the stir stick in two. "The other thing none of us will admit was that Devon made the right choice in selecting a new cadre." He held up his hand before Sergi could say anything. "We still believe it could have been handled better, but we would have held him back. Devon might be five hundred years old, but his focus is set firmly to the future. And he needed a cadre with that same drive. We would have hampered him in finding his own footing."

"Devon still wants to make amends. The cadre's departure still bothers him."

"Now that sounds more like his mother."

Sergi chuckled—the first crack in his defenses. "Now that is something I never considered."

"So, what made you fly to the Windy City and track down old Family members?"

"Ever since Devon has started his crusade to remove his censure, he's discovered tidbits of information that make him believe that his parents' deaths weren't an accident."

Teller's face grew red, and his hands that had been resting comfortably next to the coffee cup fisted. "We'd suspected, but there wasn't enough evidence. And with Lyra's injuries and Devon's arrival, we had no choice but to drop it."

"I've searched old newspapers, but there's not enough information to lead me anywhere. I've asked for the files on the accident from the police, but I don't expect them to be of any help once they find them."

"Why now after all this time?"

"There was another accident a week ago involving a Family member who is quite dear to Devon. It has the same feel as the one that killed his parents."

"And you suspect Venizi?"

"We know it was him. The passenger was kidnapped, and the driver burned in a suspicious fire. The passenger ended up on Shadow Island but managed to escape."

"Now that is someone I'd like to meet. I didn't think anyone could get on or off that island without Venizi's permission."

"And I imagine that it's still driving him mad."

Teller finished his coffee and pushed the cup aside, resting his elbows on the table. "As much as all this makes me happy, I'm not sure what I can do for you."

"I'm trying to locate Yun. He was my predecessor. I'm hoping he had insights that might help with our investigation."

"Venizi is too good to leave enough evidence worth taking to Council."

"It's not evidence we need, and we have no plan to take it to Council."

Teller's brows rose. "Devon plays a dangerous game."

Sergi's devilish smile should be enough to let Teller know how serious House Trelane was in this endeavor. "And he has every intention of winning."

Teller did know where Yun was and texted the vampire, who immediately agreed to meet with Sergi.

Now, Sergi was driving to the top of a desolate mountain where a private monastery hid deep in the backcountry of British Columbia. From what Teller told him, the monastery was non-denominational. Anyone interested in pursuing their own beliefs was welcome, but they took their privacy seriously.

Sergi had tracked down preliminary information on Yun, who had also moved to a smaller House but, after twenty years, was offered a cadre spot in a larger one. He spent forty years there before turning rogue to focus on his studies of ancient Japanese religions and martial arts.

From the outside, the monastery was everything one would expect. Stark walls that looked centuries old with little adornment. With the building sitting above the tree line, vegetation was scarce and what little was there were nothing more than scattered bushes hardened to withstand the snowy winter months. Being summer, the grass was green, softening the severe building that covered a city block.

Once inside, everything changed. The first thing was the sound of chirping birds and a waterfall. The immense entry hall had a marble floor, tall ceilings, and white walls, which were bare with the exception of an occasional watercolor of herons or swans in mountain and lake landscapes.

Low couches ran along two walls, and a large double door that rose from floor to ceiling was the only entrance to the rest of the building. He found one additional wall hanging by the door where an internal map of the structure had been hand-drawn. The simple rectangular building was divided into three levels of multiple rooms and hallways. In the center, a long space had been carved out for a garden area in addition to sectioned-off areas that ran alongside the interior building walls.

He didn't have long to peruse the map before the doors opened and a short man of undetermined years with a slight bend to his back and wearing a navy-blue yukata shuffled through the door and bowed.

"Brother Yun is expecting you." He spoke with a clear British accent that surprised Sergi. When the man turned and walked back through the door, Sergi followed.

The door shut quietly behind him, and he decided not to dwell on how the door closed when no one else had been present. They traversed down a long hall with doors on either side, then turned right at the end to follow it three-quarters of the way down. He considered suggesting a movable walkway, then decided the occupants wouldn't be bothered by how long it took to get from one place to another.

He doubted he'd survive long in this stark environment.

The guide pressed a button, and a faint melodic chime could be heard on the other side of the door.

A long minute later, the door opened to a wiry man of average height, dark intelligent eyes, and a blank expression. He wore a dark-colored gi, and a light sheen covered his brow.

"Thank you, Lee. That will be all." Yun waited for the man to bow and exit before turning his gaze to Sergi. "I was just finishing my morning meditation. You'll need to excuse my dress."

"It is I who has taken you away from your daily rituals."

The vampire snorted and turned to lead Sergi into a room that wasn't too dissimilar to the entryway of the monastery except in size and with more wall hangings. There were watercolors in addition to scrolls and pedestals with sleek sculptures.

"I thought we could have afternoon tea in the garden."

Sergi expected gray cement walls and a single table and cot with this being a monastery. Instead, the fully decorated room was the size of a one-bedroom apartment with a wall dividing the sleeping area from the living area. A movable panel hid the kitchen.

On the far side of the living area was a sliding glass door that led out to an enclosed garden. It was similar to a greenhouse with glass on all sides including the roof, which opened using levers. Plants of various heights and textures filled the space. A small section to the left was nothing but sand with a single stone bench. On the other side was a small waterfall and pool where three fish swam. Songbirds twittered, jumping from one branch to another.

While the stark exterior of the building was too harsh for his liking, Yun's environment was someplace he could live should he ever leave the cadre. A place of peace.

Yun strode to a bistro table near the waterfall where a tea service had been set with two small plates of sushi.

They settled down and ate quietly. Once they were finished, Yun refreshed the tea then sat back. "I haven't spoken to the cadre the last two times they got together. I find it more difficult to leave these days."

"I can understand after seeing this for myself."

Yun nodded. "It's not your normal monastery, but there's no reason not to have comfort while dedicating yourself to the perfection of mind and body."

"I would agree."

"I understand from Teller that all is well again with Devon and that Lyra has made a remarkable recovery."

Sergi suspected Yun knew more than what Teller told him, but he wasn't there to interrogate. He wanted whatever answers Yun might be able to provide, and this was his turf, so Sergi would play by his rules.

"Devon has recovered from the attempt on his life."

Yun's brow rose. "Assassination by addiction isn't the most expedient or assured."

"No. But with Devon's past history with the Poppy, and a new delivery system, the assailant made sure the beast would be difficult to overcome."

Yun nodded as he sipped his tea. "And as I said, not without risks. Devon recovered."

"He did."

"I suppose the more amazing feat was Lyra's recovery."

"The House Trelane has been very fortunate indeed."

Yun gave a slight bow. Neither was willing to give up any more information than was necessary. Not without some negotiation.

After some time went by while the two drank tea and watched the songbirds, Yun stood and went to a side table where a metal pot was plugged into a socket. He refreshed the teapot and returned with a small plate of shortbread. They drank more tea and ate the cookies. When they were done, Yun turned his attention to Sergi.

"I believe the saying is 'it's your dime'."

Sergi liked this vampire of few words. He brushed crumbs from his pants and told Yun of the recent accident, Cressa's kidnapping, the artificially set fire, and Cressa's eventual escape from Shadow Island.

"If you came to ask why Venizi did this, I can't help you."

"We know why he did it. We're more concerned about how similar this accident was to the one Devon's parents were killed in."

If Yun was surprised by the statement, he didn't show it. And Sergi didn't think the vampire was that naive. Yun stretched out a hand, and after a minute, one of the songbirds settled on it. It sang a soulful sound then flew away.

"We suspected Venizi from the start, but there wasn't any evidence to point to him. This was long before forensics were available, and the fire took care of any fingerprints. Venizi was in the vicinity at the time, but it would have been foolish to question a Council member.

"Do you believe it was Guildford they were after?"

"Who else?"

"What can you tell me about the gardener?"

Yun gave a soft chuckle. "After all this time, I'm not sure what Guildford saw in him. He was sharp for a human, always respectful, and anyone could see he was infatuated with Lyra. From what I remember, she returned the feelings. And, of course, that was easily seen after the accident and her collapse. But I'm not sure why Venizi would go to such lengths for a mere human, though at the time, he had his own infatuation with Lyra."

"Really? I had no idea." In fact, he already knew that from what Lyra shared with the cadre. But he needed a way to pull more information from this vampire, and playing dumb was one option.

"He'd asked Guildford for an alignment of their Houses with Lyra the sacrifice."

"Marriage?"

"Yes."

"Do you know why the four of them traveled to San Francisco that day?"

"It was for the book."

Sergi was surprised Yun knew about the book. "All that way for just a book. Couldn't they have sent it by messenger?"

"From my recollection, it was considered a rare book that wasn't allowed out of the library."

"And he felt the need to take the gardener along with his wife and daughter?"

Yun smiled. "Guildford thought highly of Hamilton and knew his daughter was in love. But Irene was against her daughter's involvement with a human. The trip was a way for her to get to know Hamilton and see how happy the two were together. It was a fatal relationship. Hamilton would grow old and die while Lyra remained young and beautiful.

"But Guildford would do anything to keep Lyra happy. Besides, it was Hamilton who told Guildford about the book. And after several phone conversations with Philipe Renaud, he became obsessed with seeing it for himself."

"What was so important about it?"

Yun shook his head, his expression turning pained. "I don't know. Guildford refused to talk about it, concerned that no one should know about it until he'd seen the book for himself. We had no idea what could be in a single book to create such paranoia. But I believed it must have been something that could create an even deeper divide amongst the vampires." Yun's expression was earnest and regretful. "To this day, I wonder if more of us had known what was in that book, Guildford, Irene, and Hamilton would still be alive today."

Chapter Twenty-Two

I STARED at the parking lot and the entrance to the tea house. "I don't think I can do this anymore." This was the second tea house of the day for the third day in a row. "I guess going to a tea house wasn't as much of a thing with them as I originally thought."

When Simone asked for recommendations on how to uncover Lorenzo's social calendar, Ginger suggested we find a place where there was a lot of gossip. Simone had insisted vamps didn't gossip, which produced an eye roll from Ginger.

Lyra had recommended the tea houses, and then I remembered three vamps I'd met at Gruber's tea party. It was the same night that I'd pulled off my first heist for Devon, even though he hadn't sanctioned it. I'd used the vamps as a shield for my getaway. We'd had a nice chat, and they seemed to be aligned with Devon's House, though I hadn't realized the importance of that at the time.

I remembered their names—Rachel, Red, and Naomi—but I knew nothing else about them. Ginger wouldn't know them, Lyra hadn't been out of the house in decades, and Simone wasn't a socialite. Since Gruber was an ally of Lorenzo's, we couldn't ask him.

The three vamps had mentioned tea houses, so we agreed to try all the tea houses in Santiga Bay at varying times for four days. If that didn't work, we'd have to do the unthinkable—attend another tea party. It was risky because we could run into Lorenzo, and we didn't want any contact with him until after the rescue mission.

The tea houses weren't any safer since Simone and I had run into Lorenzo at one not that long ago. The plan was for Bella to go in and scout the place for the vamp then give us the green light if he wasn't there. Once inside, she'd watch the front in case he showed up before we left.

There weren't that many tea houses in the city, and we'd have to visit each at least twice at different times. I suggested three per day.

Lyra had agreed. "Unless things have changed since the last time I was at a tea house, the regulars stay for hours. We could stop in for their special small-course meals and still make all three within a reasonable time frame."

We'd had high hopes on the first day, but now that we were at the second location on the third day, our excitement had deflated. Lyra watched the park across the street. I was in the back seat keeping an eye on her. I was pretty sure her mind was on Hamilton, but it had been a long time since she'd visited a tea house, and she seemed to put him aside once we entered each establishment.

I rubbed my stomach and groaned. "I don't think my belly can survive another bite. And with all the tea, I'm going to be peeing the rest of the afternoon."

Lyra chuckled, her focus still on the park and whatever memory she'd conjured up. Simone grunted, which was pretty much her entire vocabulary between the tea houses.

My cell chirped, and after checking the name of the caller, I answered. "Did you make it?"

"Oh my god, Cressa." Ginger's excitement was almost tangible. "Luke got us a room at the Ritz. Can you believe it? The Ritz. I keep pinching myself. Whenever we were in the city, we couldn't even afford a drink at the bar." She giggled. "It's a suite, Cressa. A suite."

A muffled voice sounded like they were calling Ginger. She said something back, but it sounded like she'd covered the mic. "Sorry, about that. Luke ordered a tea service. We're going to meet a friend of his for drinks and dinner this evening. And then...you know."

I slapped a hand over my face. "TMI."

She giggled. "I just wanted to let you know we're here. I'll check back in tomorrow."

"Try to behave yourself."

"Sure. I'll give it some thought."

I was still smiling when I stuck the phone in my pocket. "Luke made it to the city."

"I wonder if he'll get any work done." Simone drummed her fingers on the steering wheel, waiting for Bella's signal. "It was a mistake to take Ginger with him."

"Oh, I don't know. Ginger can be serious when she needs to be. She's been around us long enough to get by, and she's quick when—" I stopped when Bella walked out the front door, scanned the parking lot, then walked toward a nondescript car near the entrance.

That was the signal the place was clear, and she'd wait in her car until we were done. If Lorenzo had been in there, she would have left the parking lot and taken a long route back to the sedan we were in.

Simone drove into the parking lot, and rather than let the valet park the car, she chose a spot toward the back of the lot. Easier for a fast exit if Lorenzo showed up.

We were on our way to a table in the back when I spotted them. They looked different without their party clothes on, but it was them.

"The table on the right. The three women." I whispered it as close to Simone as possible, hoping no one could hear me as we approached the women.

Simone stopped the host for a moment, who nodded and continued on to their table where he would wait. Then she steered us toward the women and let me take the lead. I stumbled as I passed their table and grabbed on for support.

"Oh my god, I'm so sorry." I glanced up at the trio's leader —Rachel.

She stared at me as if I were a clumsy idiot before she took a double take. "I know you."

I stared back, looked at the other two, considered them for a moment, and snapped my fingers. "The tea party. I'm sorry, I don't remember your names. It was a crazy evening for me."

"I'm Rachel." She nodded to her two friends. "Red and Naomi. You're Trelane's Blood Ward if I'm not mistaken."

"That's right." I stood aside. "Where are my manners? This is Simone, first of the House Trelane cadre, and Lyra Trelane, leader of House Trelane." I would have loved a video of the three women as they straightened in their seats and fluffed their hair.

"It's an honor. I'm Rachel McLeod, youngest daughter of the House McLeod, and these are my friends, Leslie Nelson of House Nelson—but we call her Red—and Naomi Walker of House Walker."

"The honor is mine," Lyra said. "They're all fine Houses."

"We just ordered." Rachel glanced around as if searching for someone. "But we'd be happy to have the first course paused if you could join us." When Lyra looked at Simone, she added, "Of course, we understand if you can't. Perhaps another time."

Simone shrugged. "It's up to you, Mistress."

I turned away as if searching for someone, worried I'd bust out laughing. Simone was playing it a bit over the top, though it was the proper salutation. Anna would be so proud of me.

The host that was seating us rushed over as he waved for a server, who immediately had additional chairs brought over. Fortunately, the table was large enough for six. From what Simone had mentioned on the first day of our search, it wasn't unusual for friends to arrive unexpectedly and decide to join a table already working through the courses.

I had to hand it to Rachel and friends. They were respectful but weren't afraid to be themselves. Simone was friendly enough, but Lyra was the hit of the afternoon. We were finishing the fourth course before Lyra took the lead in directing the three women down our planned path.

"I'm sure you've heard the rumors that I haven't gotten out much over the last few decades." Lyra placed a small spoon of duck pâté on a biscuit and nibbled the end while the three women glanced at each other.

"You know vampire society," Red said. "It would take more than a century for anything to change much."

Lyra covered her mouth and swallowed her bite. "That is so true. I suppose it's good some things don't change. I haven't found time to add my name to the social register. Well, you know, with all that trouble with the Council."

"I can't believe anyone would believe Devon Trelane capable of murdering a Council member." Naomi sipped her tea and glanced around the room before leaning in. "Most people around here despise Lorenzo. I wouldn't be surprised if he did it."

"Watch your tongue, Naomi." Rachel turned pale.

"That's alright." Simone tapped her nails on her teacup. "No one has gotten in trouble with the Council for speaking their mind. Just don't say such a thing while in Council chambers."

"Of course, not," Naomi said. "It just slipped out."

Lyra, who was sitting next to her, patted her hand. "It happens to the best of us. So, tell me. What balls are coming up?"

Red snorted. "They say timing is everything. It just so happens, Lorenzo is throwing a huge fantasy ball next week. I hear he's opened it up to all the aristocrats."

"Was this unplanned?" Lyra asked. "Usually something like that has to be scheduled weeks in advance."

"Oh, it has been," Rachel responded. "The invitations went out a month ago."

Lyra smiled at Simone. "I suppose ours got lost in the mail."

The women laughed, but then Rachel got a wicked twinkle in her gaze that gave me goosebumps. I had a feeling we were going to get our payday. "I know several people who won't be going. I'm pretty sure they still have their invitations."

From what Anna had told me about these private balls and gatherings, invitations went out to specific Houses. The invitation was required for entrance, but the staff couldn't possibly put faces to names, and it was rare for security to question the vamp holding the ticket.

"I know several Houses that won't be going," Naomi chimed in. "I'm pretty sure I could get my hands on however many you need."

"And why would you do that for us?" Simone asked.

Red looked straight at Lyra. "If we had to bet on House Venizi or House Trelane as the last one standing—" she picked up her teacup as did Rachel and Naomi, "—our money is on the one led by powerful women."

Chapter Twenty-Three

Devon's office was dark. The only light glowed from four candles. I sat in a comfortable chair next to the cold fireplace. Colantha sat across from me, our knees almost touching. The candles had been placed in the standard pattern of north, south, east, and west. Jamison and Frederick were close for whatever Colantha might need.

We didn't know if this would work. We didn't know how long it might take. A bottle of juice cooled in a champagne bucket. We'd already drank one glass.

Devon and Lyra sat across the room. Lyra had wanted to be part of the dreamwalk, but Colantha refused. If this was Hamilton reaching out to me, Colantha was concerned that his early breaches into Lyra's mind, purposely or not, might impact her in unknown ways. And while it did make sense to use Lyra as a focal point, it might create another problem. Additional emotions, brought on too soon, could fracture Hamilton's grasp if he was unstable. His pleas for help aside—which anyone would be asking for if they'd been incarcerated for a hundred years—he could be mentally impaired and still harness great power that could end up damaging whoever was in the construct.

The simplest approach would be to reach out to him and attempt to pull him into a construct of our own making, but one that was somewhat familiar to him. It was best to take things one step at a time.

Since Hamilton had reached out to me on the island, I was someone familiar. Colantha, while unknown to Hamilton, had the power to maintain the construct and control Hamilton if needed.

To say I was a bit unnerved would be an understatement. There was a great deal riding on this. I didn't want to disappoint Lyra, but most importantly, we needed to know if Lorenzo was aware Hamilton was a dreamwalker.

I breathed deeply, focusing on the candle that had been set on a stand behind Colantha and a few inches above her head. There was a similar stand behind me. We'd been meditating for the last ten minutes, and my mind was beginning to wander. Fortunately, with Devon and Lyra being vamps, they could hold still for hours without making a sound, which helped, but I still knew they were there, and it was unsettling being watched.

"Ready?" Colantha's soft voice barely reached me.

"Yes." My medallion, while comforting, rested heavily around my neck, and I was thankful to be wearing it again.

We decided to use Devon's office, which used to be his father's study. Devon provided the details of the study from his recollections, adding bits from Lyra's memories. Hamilton spent many hours with Guildford in this room, so Colantha agreed it was our best option.

With nothing more difficult than the flick of a switch, the room changed. The fireplace was still to my right, but our chairs changed to something more appropriate for the 1920s, and a third chair had been added to our left rather than the sofa. The bar that Devon had added was gone, replaced with a side table that displayed an array of alcohol in decorative glass bottles. It was bordered on both sides by tall bookcases. Across the room where the espresso machine should be were more floor-to-ceiling bookcases.

With the construct in place, it was my turn to find Hamilton and bring him forth. I tried several times, but something unexpected happened. Other dreamwalkers reached out, none of them Hamilton. Almost all were imprisoned in some fashion— restrained in a family home, confined in psychiatric facilities, detained in human prison systems, or enslaved by others for reasons I'd rather not know.

I couldn't help them, and I pushed them away.

We stopped after an hour to drink juice and walk around. Ten minutes later, we were back at it. Colantha wanted to attempt bringing Hamilton forth, but she didn't have any better luck than I did. After a brief discussion with Colantha, who approved, I changed tactics.

Rather than bring him to us, I went to him. I focused on just the man and where he was located. The first image that came to mind was the building. A vamp guard stood outside the door. I moved past him into the building and immediately found myself in the room where I'd seen Hamilton.

The switch from moving into the building and then to Hamilton's cell jarred me. Did it mean Hamilton wasn't in the building but someplace else? Or did I jump directly to his room because I'd never seen what was beyond the front door?

On my fifth attempt to connect, exhausted and a severe headache threatening, something changed because he was right in front of me—haggard and wild-eyed.

"Who are you?" he demanded. "Why are you chasing me?"

"You called out to me. When I was on the island. Don't you remember?"

The confusion in his gaze softened, but he was still suspicious. "I remember. You left me."

"I had to leave so I could get more help. Lorenzo is too powerful for me alone."

His gaze cleared, the edges of his own turmoil receding like a veil being lifted. "You're a dreamwalker."

I nodded and held out my hand. "Come with me to a safer place where we can talk. I want you to meet someone."

He hesitated, glanced around at his cell, then took my hand.

The ragged clothes he'd been wearing changed to a suit from the 1920s, his hair in a style fit for the era. Colantha and I wore similar clothes.

He tried to slip away when he recognized the study, but I could feel Colantha holding onto him. I gripped his hand, squeezing it.

"You have nothing to fear from us. Colantha is my mentor and a powerful dreamwalker. She's here to help. We're searching for you, but we're not positive of your exact location, so we wanted to bring you to a place where you might find some comfort."

He tore his hand away and broke down. His thin body shook, and tears flowed from what seemed a bottomless well. Colantha hummed a soft melody, her voice strong, warm, and inviting. Several long minutes passed before Hamilton settled.

He rubbed his arms before curling into himself, his gaze darting between the two of us. "I don't know who to trust."

"That is understandable, young one." Colantha's voice continued in a soothing tone. "You have been gone from us for a long time. You are still in peril, and your mind knows it, regardless of the construct we share."

He wanted to believe us. I could see it in his eyes. He was searching for help or for someone to put an end to his suffering. "I'm not sure."

"Does this place look familiar?" I asked. "Take your time and look around."

He did. And within a couple of heartbeats, his weeping continued, and he shook his head. "No."

Then he vanished.

~

I FELL BACK against the chair. My breath heaved, and my arms hung at my sides. I was exhausted and disappointed. Colantha appeared as fresh as when we'd started, which only added irritation to my emotional fatigue.

"What happened?" Lyra grabbed Devon's arm.

"Let's give them a minute." He placed a hand on hers, and she settled back into the sofa, but her expression was filled with anxiety.

"If it's truly Hamilton, which I believe it is—" Colantha gave Lyra a soft smile that was neither good nor bad, "he's afraid."

"Of what?" Devon asked. "Lorenzo?"

She shook her head. "He no longer has fear of his captor. And that isn't always a good thing. In this case, I believe it's a sign he's given up." She leaned over, her focus pinned on Lyra, who had paled. "I don't mean to hurt you, child. But you need to understand. He's been calling for help for a long time without success." Her expression softened, and her shoulders slumped. "I believe he was tortured during the early years of his captivity. That's why he hasn't been able to connect with anyone. His torment would have made his constructs dark and terrifying."

I watched Lyra, as pale and still as stone, but after a moment, she nodded. Was that acceptance of Colantha's interpretation or that Lyra had been aware of the earlier torment, but was never aware of who was receiving it or creating it? What if she'd been pulled into a construct and had experienced everything Hamilton had lived through? If that was true, it was amazing she'd been able to break out of her psychosis.

"But now we have the means to rescue him." Devon seemed to sense Colantha's shake of her head before it happened.

"He's convinced himself he won't be freed. His contact with Cressa on the island was out of habit. When she left, it reinforced his inability to find help."

"That's great." I didn't look at Lyra. It was bad enough that I'd made matters worse, I didn't want to see it reflected back at me through her eyes.

"Stop it." Lyra's tone was sharp. "I don't blame you if that's what you're thinking. None of this is our fault. It's Lorenzo's."

Lyra always found a way to surprise me. Instead of reacting to the worst, she'd doubled down on finding an answer. "When can you try again? I want to go this time."

"Not yet," Colantha said. "If he were to see you now in his current state, he might become lost to us. Once he accepts the reality and that we aren't a hallucination, we can help. That will be the time to bring you in." She accepted the glass of juice Jamison handed her. "We'll use it as the final push he needs to reengage. Then we'll see what he can tell us about his prison."

We decided to rest for a couple of hours and then retry. Colantha sat with Lyra and the two fell into a whispered conversation, oblivious to the rest of us.

I stood and stretched, wincing as the tension in my muscles released. "I guess I'll get some rest."

"I think you should eat something first." Devon took my elbow and steered me toward the door.

"I think the juice is still working its magic."

"And that will help with your mental fatigue, but your body needs fuel, which in turn feeds your brain." He steered us down the hall toward the back of the house. "You can rest afterward."

He took my hand and led me down a second hallway to the servant's staircase. When we passed the third floor and kept going up, I recognized where he was taking me—the widow's walk.

Perfect.

A fuzzy sun greeted us, and the cool sea breeze washed over me, cleansing the strain from the last couple of hours and recharging me. We stood next to each other for several minutes, our arms brushing, before he stepped away. I stayed a minute longer until I heard the clank of dishes.

I turned toward the sitting area where a tray of lidded plates, a coffee urn, and two mugs waited. "When did you have time to do this?"

"I can't take credit for it. All it took was a brief call to Cook." He lifted the lids to reveal blueberry scones, bite-sized quiche, and bacon.

He sat and filled the mugs while I put plates together.

"Come sit with me." He tugged me to him, but it felt awkward holding my breakfast plate and a mug of coffee. "Let me hold your coffee." When I hesitated, his lips turned into a boyish pout. I didn't know he could do that, and my stomach did a flip. He was too damned cute. "I could use some personal touch right now."

Ah, hell.

I handed him the mug, then slowly slid onto his lap, keeping the plate steady as he wrapped an arm around my waist. Once I was settled, I set the plate on my lap and took back my mug. I snuggled against him, tore off a piece of scone, and moaned as the blueberries squished in my mouth.

We ate in silence. The warmth of his body was a perfect balance to the cooling temperature. Once we'd eaten most of the food and were on our second mug, he pulled me tighter.

"Was it bad?"

It took me a moment to consider his question. "I'm not sure how to put it into words. If I had to choose one, it would be tragic. He'd been imprisoned for so long. When he connected with me a couple of days ago, I saw the room where he's being held. It was filled with books and writing materials that passed the time, but he was so alone. He's lived more than one person's lifetime in a prison with no hope of leaving. And then Lyra, thinking him dead all this time."

I set down my mug and burrowed into his arms, my head resting on his chest. "He doesn't have control over his dreamwalking and doesn't have his medallion. If it had been on him at the time of the accident, Lorenzo would have taken it. I know he's been tortured, but I wonder if he's been drugged. Maybe he still is."

"I hadn't thought of that." Devon ran a thumb over my wrist, the effect calming. "He was most likely mesmerized, but from what we've learned from your experience, that wouldn't have lasted long. Which might have forced Lorenzo to try drugs. He could be using sedatives, hallucinogens, or some homegrown concoction from the Blood Poppy."

I sat up. "I never considered the Blood Poppy. I wonder what impact that would have on a dreamwalker. I mean, it's on our medallions. We're supposed to have some connection with it."

"As are vampires. But the only knowledge I have of the Blood Poppy is from its derivative the Magic Poppy."

I shivered. "And that couldn't possibly leave a positive impact."

"Remus's lab is still trying to determine what other ingredients make up the Poppy, but they're not having much luck."

A funny feeling made my gut twist. It couldn't be that simple. Surely Remus's lab would have tested it, but maybe they required a pure sample, rather than from what had been found in Devon's system. The blending might have thrown off the results.

"What's wrong?" Devon brushed my hair from my face. "You're chilled. We should go in."

I glanced up at him. "What if Lorenzo knows Hamilton is a dreamwalker, and he's using his blood?"

Devon shook his head. "But your blood cured me of the Poppy. If Lorenzo was using it to make the Poppy addictive and bring the beast out, wouldn't your blood have made my condition worse, possibly permanent?"

That shocked me. I had been so sure my blood would cure him. What if it had done exactly what he proposed? I could have locked Devon within his beast forever. "I don't know. Maybe it has to do with the ratio of vampire to dreamwalker blood. Or maybe there's another additive. But why else would he keep Hamilton imprisoned for so long? Lorenzo must be getting something out of it. If it was a simple grudge, it should have died out decades ago."

"All I know for sure is that we're not going to figure it out today. And we need Colantha for this discussion. Maybe even Remus." He stood while I was still in his arms, and I wrapped my arms around his neck. "You need a nap before your next session."

He carried me down the stairs to the second floor, then straight to his room.

I grinned. "I thought you said a nap."

He chuckled. "And that's exactly what I mean. But there's no reason you can't sleep while in my arms." He stripped us both down until we were left in our underwear, and then he pulled me into bed, throwing the covers over us. "We've had little time to hold each other over the last couple of weeks. I need to feel you next to me."

We spooned, and when he threw an arm over me, I tugged it to me, holding on tight, surprised by how quickly sleep took over. My last muddy thought was if Lorenzo had a Blood Poppy, who gave it to him?

Chapter Twenty-Four

AFTER A DEAD-TO-THE-WORLD NAP, we were back in Devon's office, the four of us in our same seats. I had just polished off a glass of Colantha's juice, which knocked away the cobwebs from my nap.

We didn't waste any time as Colantha created the construct of Guildford's study, and I reached for Hamilton. His face appeared almost immediately, but he turned away from me, unwilling to listen.

Instead of trying harder, I relaxed. "Keep the construct open. I'll go get him."

I focused on him and his room. We needed to map a complete layout of his prison, and as much as I wanted to get a start on it now, this wasn't the time. He had to be removed from this environment and see what awaited him. There wasn't time to coddle him. I had to take a chance, so I grabbed his hand and tugged him into Colantha's construct.

"Come, Hamilton." I walked along the bookcases, reviewing the spines. "Guildford had so many books, but many appear to be in other languages. Were you able to read these?"

Silence answered me, and I thought I'd already lost him. But then a light whisper reached me.

"Only a handful. I preferred the ones in Greek." Hamilton's figure appeared ghostlike, a transparent figure that trailed behind me, his fingers grazing over the books as he passed.

I ignored Colantha, who sat in one of the study chairs as her gaze followed Hamilton.

"How many languages do you speak?"

"Five." He paused and squinted at a thick tome. He chuckled, and the sound startled me. "Six if you count Latin."

"Why wouldn't I count Latin?"

He shrugged. "How many do you speak?"

"One."

He laughed. "You're young, aren't you?"

"Trying to guess my age?" I teased.

"You seem new to dreamwalking."

"I only recently discovered what I am. What I can do."

"Are you real?"

I laughed. "Oh yeah, I'm real. My name is Cressa, by the way. I don't think I ever introduced myself." I stopped. "But you knew that already, didn't you? Did Lorenzo tell you, or did you find out some other way?"

His shape began to dissipate, flickering as if he'd disappear altogether. "I might have dipped into his dreams."

"Can you call him into one?"

"I never tried. I didn't want to give him any more power over me."

"I'm sorry."

"Don't pity me."

"You seem stronger today, but you're fighting me. Why won't you speak with Colantha and me?"

He stopped and turned, noticing Colantha for the first time. His figure solidified then lightened to a filmy white transparency. He stood next to her, his clothes ragged but clean.

"Do I know you?" he asked.

"No, child. We've never met, and I'm sorry for that." Colantha wore a red silk pantsuit with a simple white shirt underneath. Her medallion hung around her neck for all to see, and Hamilton stared at it while reaching for his own necklace.

His hand fisted when he found nothing there. "I feel drawn to you for some reason."

She nodded and waved to the chair next to her. "I am Colantha, Heiress to the Seven Tribes, daughter of Adelice, and holder of the Seven Veils."

I stared at her. She never told me any of that. Was she making this shit up? But when I glanced at Hamilton, he stared in awe before bowing his head and dropping into the chair.

"I've only heard of the Seven Tribes through rumors and our small resistance group."

"It must be kept secret."

He looked horrified. "Then you shouldn't have told me. He might not visit me often, but he can pull information from me. I've been able to control how much I give him, and in small nuggets that mean nothing on their own. I'm still a puzzle he can't figure out."

"Which I imagine is why you're still alive after all this time. He has no idea what you are or what you're capable of. If he did, he'd be terrified."

I was grateful Devon and Lyra weren't in the construct with us. Devon was already irritated by Colantha's power to drag a vamp into a construct against their will. Whatever her version of terrified might be, it wasn't something he needed to hear.

Hamilton chuckled, but it turned bitter. "I assume I need my medallion for that."

"Does Lorenzo have it?" I blurted it out without thinking.

"No. But he'd seen me wear it. I'm not sure when. In the first days, it was all he could talk about. He kept asking where it was, how he could get to it, but I refused to tell him, which only made him angrier."

Colantha touched his knee. "Don't let that trouble you. Those days are behind you. You're with us now."

Somehow, her words settled him, and his anger lessened until his features softened, and he gazed at her with a reverence that made me uncomfortable. I thought it a bit much, but after she rambled off all those titles, I wondered if I hadn't been giving her enough respect.

She continued on, holding his gaze. "I can typically hear when another dreamwalker is in peril, but only if they are wearing their medallion. If not, they have to be close for me to hear their call. I imagine the dreamwalkers who could hear you were either unable to help or assumed you were one of many others who live in asylums, untrained and unaware of their abilities. They will sometimes call out during their dreams, unaware of what they're doing."

He leaned back and stared up at the ceiling. His eyes closed, and Colantha waited. Maybe giving him time to assimilate everything he'd been told. "I was foolish and impatient."

"None of that. We must focus on the here and now." Her gaze roamed the room. "Do you know this place?"

He opened his eyes and glanced around. "It's Guildford Trelane's study. He's dead, isn't he?"

"Yes."

He hung his head. "My fault."

Colantha's slap was so quick, I jumped. Hamilton touched his face, at first startled, and then anger burned in his gaze.

She stood and stared down at him. "I won't say this again, so it would be best you paid attention." Even from where I stood near the bookcase, her raw power rolled over me.

Where I would have been cowering, Hamilton straightened in his chair, his attention focused. Apparently, Colantha could play good cop and bad cop all at the same time.

"Bringing the truth to light is an act of bravery. Our truth has been hidden for far too long, and while you might have acted prematurely, it's not your actions that are in question. Although the result created great tragedy within House Trelane, it is due to one vampire. And one day soon, he'll pay for that."

She turned to me, and I gulped. I'd been perfectly fine being kept out of this conversation. My head was already spinning.

"It was written long ago that dreamwalkers would live through a long period of dark times, but that a Trinity would awaken and bring us into the light."

Hamilton nodded. "Yes, but the book—"

"Is not of your concern now. Your only task is being freed from your incarceration. And we need your help for that."

He nodded, and he fell back against the chair.

"You're tired. We all need rest. Sleep, Hamilton, and we'll call you back soon. There are others you must meet in order for us to be successful. Do you understand?"

"Yes." He was already fading.

"We are real, Hamilton. We will return."

"You're real. This is real." Tears leaked down his face as his shape faded like vapor.

I blinked and was back in Devon's office. I stared at Colantha as if I'd never seen her before today. Her sharp glance told me to be quiet about what she'd shared. For now, I wouldn't say a word. But soon enough, she had some explaining to do.

"WAKE UP, CRESSA."

I snuggled deeper into the warmth and scent that was all Devon. He shook me, and I burrowed deeper. "No." The single word was muffled by covers and Devon's body, but that vampiric hearing was good enough to pick up my refusal.

"You won't like the alternative."

"Go away." That didn't sound petulant at all.

Weight shifted on the bed. Good. He took the hint.

A second later the cover was stripped from the bed, and goose-bumps erupted from the chill of the room.

"Give them back." My arm snaked out, flailing in the air as if I could snatch a corner.

Warm hands grabbed my ankles, and I was dragged across the mattress, my fingers digging in. It was useless against the strength of the vamp who I was about to kick the ass out of as soon as I had enough strength to sit up. Standing might be out of the question for the foreseeable future.

He caught me in his arms before I landed on the floor and carried me into the bathroom. He tried to get me to stand in the shower, but I clung to him, the tile floor frigid against my bare feet. He pried my fingers off his shirt, and I dropped to the floor.

The water hit me. At first, frigidly cold before the heat warmed to just below scalding.

My arms and legs kicked out as I tried to stand, but the tile was slippery. I was aware enough to hear the shower door slamming shut.

"You're an asshole!"

"I told you you wouldn't like the alternative. I've been trying to wake you for the last hour."

"Maybe that's because I'm exhausted."

"Understandable, but it's been four hours."

That couldn't be right. I felt like a slug. The juice never impacted me this quickly, and I'd only drunk a couple of glasses. Had Colantha upped the dosage of whatever she put in her concoction?

"Colantha didn't want you to sleep any longer."

Now that I was more awake, the hot water was doing the trick as my muscles relaxed. I ran my hands through my hair, washed and conditioned it, then soaped my body.

"Do you need help?" His tone was full of amusement.

"Not unless you want to lose a hand."

He chuckled. "Are you keeping your dagger in the shower these days?"

"No. But it sounds like an excellent idea."

I finished rinsing but stayed under the water, the harsh beads soothing the tension in my back. "How long was our last session? I don't remember walking up to my room."

"It was a little over half an hour, and you didn't walk to your room. You and Colantha gave us the highlights and then you passed out. I carried you up here."

Yikes. No wonder he was concerned.

I shut off the water and opened the door. His hand shot out with a towel, which I wrapped around my hair. Another towel was in my hands before I knew it, and I dried off as I stepped out.

He was smirking, and before I could think of a sharp retort, he helped me with my task, rubbing the towel against my skin. He dried my arms, my breasts, my belly, and then my legs. When he stood, he grabbed my face between his hands, the towel dropping to the ground as he kissed me.

There was nothing gentle about it, and he lifted me up and tossed me on the bed. He stripped in record time and joined me, bringing the covers with him as his body covered mine.

"Is this what Colantha had in mind after you woke me?"

"She wasn't specific. Just that you should wake up and get nourishment."

He ran a hand down my body, not stopping until he reached between my legs.

"And what do you call this?"

"Appetizers." His head disappeared beneath the covers.

My head fell to the side. The drapes were parted enough for me to see it was still daylight, but the sun would be gone soon. My eyes fluttered shut to the touch of his tongue and the wicked emotions he evoked. I don't know when we'd become a couple. It seemed we'd taken that next step without talking about it.

A low groan escaped me, and all thought disappeared. Whatever we were to each other, and as hot as the sex was, something deeper had developed without my notice. How the hell had that happened?

Then I screamed when he nipped me, dragging my thoughts back to the other Devon. Not the one who was burrowing his way into my heart, but the one who was giving me such intense pleasure it scared me. I gripped his hair and arched my back as waves consumed me.

Then he was inside me and nothing mattered. His own release came sometime later. I wasn't watching the clock. I wasn't even aware of the concept of time. For all I knew, Devon stopped time when we were together.

He rolled, bringing me with him, and I laughed. He always did this, yet each time was a surprise when I ended up on top, the cool air drying my back. It was like lying on a slab of stone—all hard edges and lean muscle. But he was warm and smelled so good. The heat poured off him as a warm tingle slid over me. My arms lay at my side, and I stroked his hip with a relaxed tempo that matched the beat of his slowing heartbeat.

"I'll ask Cook to have something sent up while we shower. Maybe some of his special egg and brie souffle."

"That takes like an hour."

"Turn the shower back on and get it hot. I'll keep us occupied."

Chapter Twenty-Five

Lucas watched Ginger as she piled fresh strawberries onto her waffle. He was going to take her out to breakfast, but they'd gone out for dinner, and after an amazing night, she wanted to take advantage of the upscale room. So they'd spent most of the morning in bed working up an appetite.

Besides, room service looked good on her. She piled two tablespoons of whipped cream on top of the strawberries, crammed a slice of bacon in her mouth, and chewed as she determined the best way to cut into her waffle masterpiece. After the first bite, she ran a tongue over her lips to clean the whipped cream away, and he dropped his gaze; otherwise, they'd spend the rest of the day back in the bedroom.

"I have the appointment at the Renaud annex this afternoon." Lucas refilled her coffee cup then took a bite of the hashbrowns. They were good, but nothing compared to Cook's food.

"I know." She licked whipped cream off the side of her hand. He had no idea how she managed to get the topping there, but he dropped his gaze again when he caught a spark in her eyes and one of her sexy grins.

"I'm not sure how long I'll be. I want to wander through the stacks a bit before asking if the current curator has time to speak with me."

"That sounds reasonable." She licked her fork and then fell back with her hands folded over her stomach. "I think we should save some of this for an afternoon snack. There's room in the fridge and the microwave will do in a pinch to warm it up."

"Or we could call the kitchen to pick up the trays as is."

Her nose scrunched up. "And waste all this food? I know I come from humble living, but it's not just about the money. I don't think food should be wasted. Not with how many hungry souls are out there." She perked up, perching on the edge of her seat. "Maybe we should ask for take-out boxes then hand them out to any homeless we see. I know the hotel can't do it, but nothing says we can't."

Lucas grinned. It was hard not to. She had such a different way of looking at things, many times surprising him. But through it all, she was a generous person, even when she had little herself. She now shared a condo with Cressa in a safe neighborhood, though Cressa chose to live at the manor. Either way, Devon ensured they always had money in their bank accounts, but it grated on her. She never said anything, but it was obvious that she only took what was necessary to survive, not wanting to take advantage of Devon's hospitality.

He had tried to convince her that Devon didn't care, but when there had been a real possibility that the House might have been lost to Lorenzo's meddling, she became more aware of how precarious her status was. He'd discussed her finding a job with Devon before, and he'd been agreeable, but then the issue with the Poppy and Cressa's disappearance had forced Ginger to stay at the manor. A job would have been impossible under heightened security concerns. Until Devon finished his business with Lorenzo, Lucas would find a way for her to feel useful and worthy of being part of the Family.

"So, is this annex a library or just a large storage facility?"

Ginger pushed her plate aside and turned her attention to her coffee.

"It's a library. They allow visitations upon request, but if they have special projects or events scheduled, the requested date tends to be renegotiated."

"And do they allow humans in with their vampire friends?"

He sat back and shook his head. "You would be bored."

"Are you kidding? Cressa told me about the library in L.A., which she says doubles as a museum. There are tons of books to browse." She leaned back and stared at the ceiling while pulling at her lower lip. "Though I imagine lots of them are written in languages I can't comprehend, but still, there should be enough written in English."

He considered her request. His first inclination had been a hard no because in most cases, humans weren't permitted. "There's one possibility, but I'm not sure you're going to like it."

She narrowed her gaze and frowned, her tone testy. "If you don't want me to go, just say so."

"I would. That's not what I'm trying to say."

Her mood instantly improved. "Tell me."

"I could get you into the library and possibly increase my chances to meet with the curator if you were introduced as my Blood Ward."

She stared at him, and he braced himself for an explosion.

"Your Blood Ward?"

He nodded slowly.

Her grin returned. "Is that all? That's no big deal."

"Are you sure?"

"What would they know?" Her head tilted, and he braced himself again. He relaxed when she gave him a mischievous grin. "I think after the library, we should come back and continue the role-playing." She winked. "We'll just have to make sure the Do Not Disturb sign is out."

GINGER STRODE across the parking lot in black leggings, a blood-red silk shirt, a black lace scarf, and ankle boots. A small purse hung from her shoulder. She wasn't a tall woman, but she walked beside him with purpose—her head held high, her oversized sunglasses only removed when they reached the front desk. Her gaze swept the room without landing on anything until it reached Lucas, and then she smiled at him.

Not once in all the time he'd known her had he seen her so stately. She'd obviously watched the other vampires because she had their moves down so well that the receptionist gave one appreciative glance her way and then ignored her.

After receiving the lengthy introduction the receptionist always delivered upon entering the library, Lucas thanked her and took Ginger's elbow, directing her into the building.

"How am I doing?" she whispered.

"You're perfect."

She beamed as he continued to guide her through the first floor. A quarter of the floor held shelves with the most widely requested books, which were updated every couple of months. The rest of the floor included a small tea room, two meeting rooms, a banquet room, and general offices.

They took the stairs down to the third floor where the rarest of books and journals were stored. He decided to leave the second floor, which was the largest selection of books, for Ginger to peruse while he spoke with the curator.

They worked their way around the stacks until Ginger stopped halfway down an aisle.

"Maybe we should see if they have the book listed in their database or files or whatever system they use to keep track of the books."

Lucas couldn't hide his confused expression. "Why? Cressa

and Simone already confirmed it had been in the Los Angeles library."

"All they confirmed was that the book was out for restoration. Who knows when that happened? And wasn't it once in this library? It would be interesting to see if it's still considered part of the inventory."

Lucas ran a hand through his hair and stared at the floor. He couldn't see how a Renard would make that kind of mistake. But they weren't far from the card catalogs. "Let's take a look."

Ginger forgot about her role as she bounced on her toes while he thumbed through the handwritten cards in the Da through De drawer.

"I don't believe it." He pulled out the card labeled *De første dage*. Ginger's warm breath sent shivers through him, and he slid an arm around her waist and kissed her cheek. "You're amazing."

"I know." She squeezed him back. "Where does it say it is?"

He glanced around at the labels displayed in bold lettering on the ends of each row. He nodded toward a stack to their left. "Somewhere down that aisle."

She grabbed his hand and led him toward the bookcase. "So they're listed by title rather than author?"

"Yes. Many of the books have authors, but just as many don't, their creators lost through time. Most vampires are more interested in the subject, not who wrote it. We're close." He slowed and ran a finger down one shelf, then checked the one below it. "Here." He knew his voice was filled with more excitement than it should be. As soon as he pulled the book down, he could tell there was something wrong with it. The spine reflected the name and was weathered like an old book. But it was nothing more than a sleeve—no— it was a box.

He opened it and stumbled back until he hit the next row of bookcases. Ginger reached out for him. It was a note similar to the one in the Los Angeles library. "Out for restoration."

"Just like in SoCal."

"But why?"

"Maybe it's more than just these two libraries. What if they put that in every library?"

He racked his brain. "Some type of ruse, a misdirection."

She nodded, pacing up and down the aisle. "I suppose it depends on when it was done. But think about it. Devon's father had traveled here to discuss this book. We know he met with Philipe Renaud. Then, on their way home, they have a fatal accident. What if it spooked Philipe?

"Whatever was in that book just became dangerous. So, he needs to hide it, but he's a Renaud, right? You've told me dozens of times how important their role as Keepers of Knowledge is to them. So, he can't destroy it, and he can't remove it from the inventory."

Lucas stumbled out of the stacks to a sitting area. "If the book was added to the Los Angeles library it's possible he did the same in every library. He adds the book to the inventory and then immediately records it out for restoration."

He dropped into a chair, and Ginger sat on the arm, taking the box from him. She smoothed back his hair while he closed his eyes, grateful he'd brought her with him. Not just for her insight but her ability to calm him. "He's made it impossible to determine which library the book is in."

"And I doubt it's in any of the restoration rooms."

"He would have hidden it somewhere in the inventory, but where?"

"Do you think he's the only one who knows?"

That was an excellent question. If the book held secrets so important others would kill to keep it hidden, it would go against everything a Renaud believed to hide it away forever. That was the purpose of the libraries in the first place—to share all knowledge of their history. Was it possible a Renaud, or more than one, forgot that? Or was paid enough to overlook it?

"We have to believe there's at least one other that knows. If he kept it to himself, he'd leave some form of breadcrumb so his family would eventually discover it. How do we even begin the search? I've built a list of his known friends from over the decades. My original idea was to speak with each of them and see if I could track down Philipe."

She handed him the box with the note in it. "I don't know what your plan was with the curator, but maybe this is a good starting point."

He stood, opened the lid, and stared at the note. "Will you be alright by yourself?"

"I'll stick to the second floor, but if I get bored, I'll be in the tea room."

He smiled. "Remember, no sugar in your tea."

She grinned. "I know—sacrilege!"

He kissed the top of her head and went in search of a custodian, who he found scurrying down a row of stacks. "Can I bother you for a moment?"

The custodian turned, and his harried frown turned into a smile. He was of a slight build with wire-rimmed glasses and a timeless face. "Of course, I didn't see you. I tend to get distracted. What can I assist you with?"

"I was wondering if the curator was in. I'd like to ask them about this book and how much longer it will be in restoration."

The custodian took the box, read the spine, then looked inside. "My, we haven't used this form for quite some time."

"Really? Do you know how long?"

The vampire scratched his head. "At least fifty years. Maybe more." He placed the note in the box. "Now as to the curator. She was in a meeting when I last stepped by her office. But let me see what I can find in the inventory files. Follow me."

It was the logical next step, and it provided a reason why he'd want to see the curator for a deeper explanation.

Lucas followed the custodian to a door on the same floor that opened into a massive file room. "I thought you might keep the files in a database."

"For everything from the 1980s on, everything is immediately added to the database. We've managed to scan and transfer previous files back to the early forties. It's a continuing project that will take another few years to complete, but it's just as easy to come to the file room. Most of our requests still come through paper forms." He stopped at a computer and glanced at Lucas. "The majority of the vampire community prefers paper over computers." He looked over his glasses with a curious gaze. "I assume by your earlier statement you're not one of those."

Lucas chuckled. "No. I prefer to keep step with the times."

The custodian nodded his head and sat in front of the computer. The software was hi-tech and seemed odd surrounded by the files and cabinets that were painstakingly free from dust. The vampire typed in the name of the book and then frowned. "That's interesting. Our rarest books are typically listed in our main inventory."

"And that's unusual for what we're looking for?"

He shrugged. "Not necessarily, but items being restored are typically added to the database once work has begun on them. It's not surprising for some of the oldest books to require time to care for, but I have to say, fifty years is somewhat unheard of. It's possible the file was added incorrectly, but that would be even more unusual."

He turned off the computer and shuffled toward the file cabinets. "Come. Let's check the files."

Lucas considered the long aisles and followed the vampire three-quarters of the way down the line of old wood cabinets, occasionally slowing to read the labels on the cabinets. They were alphabetical if he was reading them right.

"Here we are." The custodian pulled the drawer open and filtered through the folders, most of which were bent and frayed. "Hmm. That's strange."

"What is it?" Lucas looked over the vampire's shoulder and instantly saw the problem.

"The file isn't here. I suppose the curator could have it, but after seeing the age of the note, it would be an unusual coincidence."

"Perhaps she's available now to ask?"

He agreed, and Lucas followed him up to the first floor. From what Cressa had said, in the L.A. branch, Philipe had kept an office on the fourth floor next to the restoration office, so he was surprised to be led upstairs to the curator's office.

Meredith Renaud was tall and willowy and looked to be in her mid-thirties by human standards, but there were lines at the corners of her eyes that he didn't think came from a jovial personality based on the deep frown she presented on first introductions. The frown deepened further after hearing the dilemma the custodian presented.

"Let me check the inventory. I'm sure it was simply a mistype." She turned to her computer, and Lucas glanced at the custodian, whose own expression appeared doubtful. "Yes, here it is."

The custodian grimaced, and Lucas drew close, but Meredith kept the screen from their view. "It looks like it required special handling for restoration and was transferred back to the home library."

"Which one? New Orleans or France?" Lucas hoped it was still in the States.

She hesitated, then said, "New Orleans."

"I apologize, Ms. Renaud, I must have typed something wrong." But the custodian's gaze narrowed a bit in what Lucas read as suspicion before turning blank.

"It happens." She smiled, though it was formal and didn't reach her eyes, which were cold and calculating. If he was Sergi, he would consider her a vampire with something to hide. "Now, I'm sorry, but I have another meeting. Is there anything else I can help you with?"

Lucas held her gaze. "Can you tell me when it was transferred?"

Her gaze turned flinty, and her smile became wooden as she turned back to the computer. "Quite some time ago. Ah, this makes sense. It was 1906. Probably the result of the Great Earthquake."

"Really?" Lucas gave her a quizzical look. "Is it possible it might have gone to a different library, like maybe the one in Los Angeles?"

"That would be impossible. The Los Angeles library didn't open until the mid-1920s." She turned away, busying herself with shifting several files on her desk. She was lying, but there wasn't anything he could do about it. "Now I really must get to my meeting."

"I'll show you out," the custodian said, and he nodded to the curator. "I apologize for bothering you. I should have checked a second time."

"It's no trouble." She gave Lucas a last look. "Thank you for your visit. I'm sorry I couldn't be of more help."

He followed the vampire toward the entrance where Lucas stopped him. "I have a friend I need to find. I left her on the second floor."

"Of course, sir."

"May I ask how long Ms. Renaud has been the curator here?"

"About a year, maybe less."

"I see. And who was the curator before that?"

"That would have been Claude Renaud."

"And where is he now?"

The vampire lowered his gaze. "He returned to his homeland."

"France?"

He nodded. "Now, I must return to my duties."

"Of course." Lucas gave him a small bow. "Thank you for your work here. It's very important."

"Yes." He started to walk away but turned. "Please be careful."

And with those cautionary words, the vampire continued a quick pace toward the back of the library as Lucas watched him go. Meredith Renaud had lied, and the custodian knew it. This was unheard of. In all his years, he'd never heard of any impropriety with the Renauds and the libraries. Why now? And was it only with this particular location?

He stopped at the tea room and found Ginger sitting primly at a small bistro table with a cup of tea and remnants of crumbs on a plate.

She stood as soon as she saw him, and when he reached her, she took his hands and placed a kiss on his cheek. "We need to get out of here. Now."

He pulled her close and scanned the room. There was a group of four females at a table across the room, laughing as one poured more tea. Two other tables were occupied with vampires in earnest conversations. It wasn't difficult to spot the vampires who seemed out of place—two in the corner and another two at a table by a back door. There were cups in front of them, and though they faced each other, they weren't talking.

"How long have they been here?"

"Two followed me up from the second floor, and the other two showed up about ten minutes later."

He took her elbow and led her to the front door, keeping to a normal pace. He kept his voice low. "Do you have your dagger?"

"Yes." She didn't seem scared, but he felt the tension radiating from her.

He stopped at the front desk, which gave him the opportunity to see if they were being followed. The four vampires had followed them and now split into two different directions.

"I was wondering if you had a map of the library. I would like it for further training for my Blood Ward."

"Of course, sir. I apologize for not handing you one when you first came in."

He smiled. "I've been to so many of the libraries, I didn't think about it."

She smiled. "We appreciate your patronage."

He put Ginger's arm through his as he led her toward the exit. "We're safe inside, and should be while on the property, but you need to be prepared."

"I'm already gripping my dagger."

He glanced down and saw her hand in her purse. "Stay close to me, and if we get surrounded for any reason, remember..."

"Back to back in a fight when you find yourself surrounded. Focus on those that have direct access to you, and trust your partner to watch your back."

He stopped before they exited, and he pulled her into a hug. "Have I told you how amazing you are?"

"Not lately. And if we make it back to the hotel, I expect a very expensive dinner at the fanciest restaurant you know. I've been saving a new dress."

He smiled and gave her a sound kiss.

"Is that appropriate for a Blood Ward?"

His smile widened. "On occasion."

She poked his stomach. "Good to know."

"Ready?"

"Yeah, I'm hungry."

"I saw your empty plate."

"One cookie doesn't make a meal."

The sunshine hit them as they went through the doors. No one was outside, which gave Lucas some comfort that the vampires following them probably weren't from the Renaud Family. They were halfway to the car when Lucas heard the doors open and the quick footsteps.

They moved quickly. Not quite a run, but as fast as Ginger's shorter legs could move. The vampires caught up to them as they reached the car. Lucas had time to hit the button to shut off the alarm and unlock the doors. There were only two vampires, which made sense. The parking lot was public, and there were visitors in the building that could come out at any time. And others could unexpectedly drive up.

Two vampires could be swift and efficient, leaving little evidence behind. But four could get messy and would be more obvious. He stayed with Ginger but didn't have time to open the door. They spun around in perfect synchrony, and Lucas moved toward the one on their right. He didn't want to leave Ginger's side, but they were in a position where they had to work one-on-one. Ginger's skill with the dagger had greatly improved. She'd almost beaten Sergi on two occasions, and even with the number of fails, she was still impressive.

Since there weren't many better than Sergi, she should be alright, but one mistake, one second of hesitation could be her death.

His best option was to kill the one in front of him as quickly as he could.

He attacked, surprising the vampire who must have thought Lucas would first seek conversation.

He ducked the vampire's swing, barely missing the edge of the blade. When he came up, he pivoted on one leg while kicking out with the other. His strike hit the vamp just below the knee.

The vampire didn't go down, but he stumbled, and Lucas swung up with his knife. His strike was true, and the blade sunk into the vampire's stomach. It gave him time to check on Ginger.

Lucas turned to find her facing the vampire as he rushed her.

They must have been staring at each other while the vampire considered Ginger, assuming her a mere human—nothing more than a Blood Ward. It was rare to find a Blood Ward who'd been trained for battle. That occurred after they became a vampire.

So, when the vampire advanced, Ginger waited until he was ten feet away. Her knees had been slightly bent, and she took a step before jumping straight into the air, swinging her right leg out and hitting the vampire mid-chest. The air rushed out of him as he was thrown back.

A grunt from behind made Lucas spin back toward his own foe. The vampire made it to a standing position, but it was clear Lucas had hit a vital spot. Not enough to kill. The vampire took a step toward him, dagger raised, but he doubled over on his second step. Lucas took advantage and kicked out, his leg swinging high and wide as it struck the vampire's chin. He went down.

Lucas spun around and moved toward the vampire who was advancing on Ginger.

Her blade was out. She stood in a standard vampire stance the other vampire recognized. It slowed his steps. He was probably wondering why a Blood Ward would have been trained for that particular stance. It wasn't one of defense but of attack.

When the vampire noticed Lucas approaching, his knife already bloody, the vampire glanced at his fallen partner and ran. He didn't run for the library but toward the far side of the parking lot where the other two vampires waited in a black sedan.

Why hadn't they come to help their friends?

He glanced at the library where the four females stood just outside the doors. They had stopped a few yards from the entrance as one searched her purse. Their attackers hadn't wanted to create more of a scene. The only reason the fight hadn't caught the interest of the females was because they were talking and laughing, but it wouldn't be long before they headed for their cars.

He turned back toward the downed vamp. He was gone.

"He was still in pain, but he ran off that way." Ginger waved toward the street.

"His friends will pick him up. Let's get out of here." He waited for Ginger to get in the car, then shut her door before running around to his side.

They were through the gates before she asked. "Who were they?"

"I don't know."

"How did they know we were here? Or do they work for the library?"

"I don't know that, either. But something is very wrong."

Chapter Twenty-Six

I TRAILED behind Devon with mixed feelings about another round with Colantha. My body was in good shape, but my head was still fuzzy. I would have preferred lounging in bed with Devon, watching an old black-and-white movie, and munching on Cook's multi-flavored popcorns. Something with Katherine Hepburn and Cary Grant. But Devon preferred war movies. Go figure. Perhaps *From Here to Eternity* would be a decent compromise once this was all over.

He glanced over his shoulder. "Are you up for this?"

"Haven't gone off the deep end yet."

"That's not funny."

It was, but I thought it best not to irritate him. He seemed all cool and calm while I dreamwalked, but it bothered him. I was someplace he couldn't reach me—at least not easily. I understood, but it didn't change what we had to do.

I rubbed my stomach, stuffed with Cook's souffle and glazed asparagus paired with a lovely Bordeaux, then finished with an espresso and chocolate almond flan for dessert. Colantha would be pissed if I nodded off in a food coma.

Everyone was waiting for us, and Colantha gave Devon a stern look that rolled off him. We took our places, and I caught Lyra's anxious smile. I nodded, returning my own, hoping this construct didn't end badly. I slurped down the juice Jamison handed me and settled against the chair.

"The last meeting with Hamilton went well." Colantha set down her empty juice glass and straightened her jacket. "I thought we'd need another session or two to convince him we were his best hope, but I was pleasantly surprised to find his sanity well intact. He has a quick wit, and it's time for him to see Lyra."

"Has he asked about me?" Lyra asked.

My heart ached at the brave face she tried so hard to hold onto.

"I need you to prepare yourself," Colantha continued. "You must be ready with whatever honest emotion you feel for him. He hasn't asked about you, but he did ask about your father. I believe he thinks you're dead, and as long as he doesn't ask, then whether you're dead or not, you're still alive in his heart."

Lyra's hand went to her mouth, and it was obvious she hadn't considered Hamilton might think she'd died in the accident. I hadn't been wrong. This was all so tragic.

"He needs to know you're alive. From there, we'll have to see how it unfolds. There's no way to know how this news will affect him."

Lyra nodded. "I'm ready."

"I know you've been in constructs before, but you might not be aware of how fast a construct can change. I don't expect that to happen tonight, but if it does, just relax into each one. Don't focus on where we land. Keep all your attention on Hamilton."

"Alright. Let's do this."

"Frederick. Please bring another chair for Lyra. And you might as well bring one for Devon." She turned to him. "Cressa and I will complete the construct and bring Hamilton to it. If he has accepted what we've discussed, I'll bring Lyra in. I don't know if you'll be needed, but I'd rather you be prepared. I might bring you in but give you a signal for silence. Do you understand?"

"Yes." Devon sat in the chair to the right of me with Lyra across from him.

Colantha's gaze turned to me. "Are you ready?"

I bent my head to the left and then the right, like a boxer waiting for the bell. If I'd been standing, I'd be bouncing on my toes. "Let's go."

In an instant, the landscape changed to Guildford's study.

"You're becoming quite adept with accepting the change from reality to construct."

"I don't even have to think about it. It's like one big puzzle. I might not know the individual pieces, but I can picture the full image. I have to focus harder on the individual pieces when it's my construct."

"That will change with time and practice." She glanced around the room, seeming to make a decision about something. "Bring him to the chair across from us. Let him be comfortable."

I was still learning the best way to bring someone to a construct. With Hamilton, he tugged at me, like he held one end of a long string, and I held the other. If he was stronger, he could probably pull me into a construct. Instead, I pictured him resting comfortably in one of the study chairs, then pulled the end of the string—hard.

Hamilton blinked and glanced around. He nodded to Colantha then set his hooded eyes on me. "I thought you'd call me to the construct sooner, but I appreciate the extra rest. I'm a bit out of practice."

"I slept for four hours, and to be honest, I could use another six."

He laughed, and the man in Lyra's paintings came to life. His smile changed him. A man with a future and hope. A man who hadn't been forgotten. And I understood why Lyra still loved him after all this time.

"How do you feel about what we've told you?" Colantha asked.

"I'm beginning to remember who I was before the accident." He blew out a deep breath and ran his hands up and down his thighs. "It's hard to explain. When I woke up after the crash, I only remembered bits and pieces of it. Over the years, chunks of memory returned, but others remained elusive, as if they'd been stripped from me. I was a dreamwalker but there were certain memories that slipped away."

"Lorenzo must have mesmerized you." I couldn't believe it. He must do that with all his captives.

"I'd wondered, but it shouldn't be surprising." He hung his head.

Colantha clucked her tongue. "I'd like to move to the next stage now that you know your mind isn't playing tricks on you." She nodded to me, and I stood to move to a chair near the door.

"I don't understand." Hamilton's expression changed, his gaze once again hooded as it darted between us.

"I want someone else to join us, and Cressa is simply giving up her chair. Is that alright?"

"Sure." His knee began to bounce.

"Prepare yourself."

Several seconds later, Lyra appeared in the chair I'd vacated. I had a perfect line of sight of the two of them as they laid eyes on each other for the first time in a hundred years.

Lyra's eyes brimmed with tears. "Hamilton." She reached out a hand.

Hamilton jumped up and stumbled back, knocking into the chair. "No. It can't be. You're dead."

She shook her head. "I was pulled from the wreckage before the fire spread. My arm had been broken, and I was in shock. I passed out and woke in my room with vague memories of that night."

He studied her for several minutes, perhaps comparing her to the vampire he remembered from decades earlier. I was beginning to feel like a voyeur.

He took a tentative step forward, then another. Before I knew it, he was on his knees in front of her. "It's really you?"

The tears broke through the dam, but through it all, Lyra smiled. "It's me." She sniffled and ran a hand under her nose.

"I thought you were dead."

She laughed. "And I thought the same of you. Even so, I had no idea you could live this long, and you don't look any older." Her eyes dropped before they locked on Colantha's. "Did you change his appearance?"

"You see him as he is today, though a bit cleaner. It's the only image Cressa has of him."

"Other than my paintings."

"This is the man I saw when he called to me while I was on the island." There wasn't much more I could say. "At first, I didn't recognize him with his beard, which Colantha has removed from this construct. But it was his eyes that convinced me he was Hamilton."

She stood, grabbing his hands and forcing him to stand as well. For a moment, all she did was stare at him, as if confirming each feature of his face was as she remembered it, then she wrapped her arms around his waist. He laid his head on top of hers and closed his eyes. It was so easy to see—he was home. There was no doubt this man held a deep connection with Lyra.

I glanced to my left, surprised to see Devon standing in the shadows. His gaze was locked on the tableau in front of us. I couldn't read his expression. He'd locked them down, and I was dying to see beyond his facade.

A long time passed before Hamilton stepped back, his hands still gripping Lyra's. "What do we have to do to make this real?"

Lyra released his hands and, somewhat reluctantly, they returned to their seats. Once they were both sitting, she leaned toward him. "You need to tell us what you can about where you're being held."

He shook his head. "I don't know much."

"You'd be surprised how much you might remember," Colantha said as she rejoined the conversation. "Start with a basic image, and then we'll help you fill in the blanks. But you both need to be aware that this effort will require a great deal of time and energy. We won't accomplish everything in one visit. You need to let me know the minute you begin to feel tired. Don't try to hold on. It only makes it worse. Then you'll require more rest between attempts rather than if we stop the moment you feel a slip in energy."

She gave each a mother-superior stare, and they glanced at each other before nodding.

"Alright. Let's start at the beginning. Tell us about the room where you're being held."

I glanced down and found a pen and pad of paper on the side table next to me. I began writing. My written notes wouldn't return with me, but writing everything down would make it easier to remember once we left the construct.

When I glanced at Devon, he was sitting, his own pen gliding over paper as he listened to Hamilton describe his prison.

"In the beginning, I woke in a room with cement walls. The only window was the grated one in the door. I was injured with a broken tibia, and they left me like that for several days as Venizi hounded me with questions. He asked about the medallion and what I knew of Guildford's defenses. Once he got what he could out of me—" He looked at Lyra, his gaze beseeching. "I only gave him information that with a small bit of effort on his part, he could discover on his own. I knew little of the security, always depending on Yun's ability to keep us safe. Fortunately, Venizi was satisfied for the moment, and I was given vampire blood to heal my leg. I was kept in that room for the first few years with little food and water. The beatings were daily, except for the days when Venizi would visit, and those days I don't remember."

Lyra's gaze became fixed as she listened to Hamilton, and then she began to sway. She'd told me once of the horrible nightmares she'd had her first years after the accident. Now we knew what those nightmares were.

I glanced at Devon, barely able to listen as Hamilton described the torture. His gaze had been on Hamilton at first, but now it was on his sister, and before anyone would admit to being tired, he signaled Colantha to end the session.

We'd heard enough.

Chapter Twenty-Seven

I SAT under the sycamore tree with Lyra, our backs against the trunk as we gazed out to sea. The remains of a picnic lunch scattered around us, and we sipped the last of a bottle of merlot Cook had sent with the basket. We needed it after our last session with Hamilton.

He'd been shaky in the session where he began to describe the room he'd eventually been moved to—the one he'd been in for the last ninety years. Colantha modified the construct as he gave us more information. As details began to fill in, he settled into a pattern of providing a description, waiting for the construct to change, then providing the next one.

Lyra made Hamilton sit with her on the sofa, and they held each other as Hamilton honed the details—where the door and window were, what he saw when he looked out the window, and what he remembered of the hallway he'd been taken down when he was moved from his first cell.

After that, he needed a break, and we met back after an hour. He continued with the hallway he stumbled down when he was taken upstairs several decades earlier for what he called Lorenzo's sessions, which he remembered being the first floor. Then he provided a snapshot of a door that we suspected to be the main entrance into the facility. Slowly, the building I'd seen on the island began to take shape.

It was during this last session that Hamilton was introduced to Devon. He seemed hesitant around Lyra's brother and what his intentions might be, but it wasn't long before he fell under Devon's magnetism. It reminded me of how old Devon was and the battles he and Sergi spoke of during Family meals or evening drinks in the library. He'd commanded battalions, something I couldn't quite wrap my head around—hundreds if not thousands of men following him unquestionably into battle.

Once, Hamilton had called Devon "Guildford," which had stopped the conversation. Then Devon smiled, seeming to take it for the respect with which it was given, and the two seemed to find common ground. When Devon began to ask more detailed questions, suggest weak points, then wait for Hamilton's opinions, the rest of the session moved rapidly.

Not long after that, Colantha put a stop to the construct.

It had been two days since we began the sessions, and while it was taking a toll on me, Lyra grew strength from it.

"This has to be hard on you." I picked at a blade of grass and watched a small caterpillar make its way over a small stretch of dirt.

"Even harder for Hamilton." Her tone was bright and cheery, which seemed at odds with their situation.

"You believe we can get him out."

"Don't you?"

I nodded but refrained from looking her in the eye. "It won't be easy. We need to wait for everyone to report back and see what plan we can piece together, but in the end, we have to try."

"It would be easier if Colantha could bring Lorenzo into a construct and tie him in chains."

"If only. But Devon's right. Unless Lorenzo has a willing dreamwalker working with him, making him aware of what we can do, we need to keep our abilities a secret until we need them. I don't know what Devon has planned after we rescue Hamilton, but his larger mission with Remus is still the ultimate goal."

"I know. Though I still say it would be cathartic if we could each have ten minutes with him."

I laughed, not able to disagree with the sentiment. A sailboat headed north along the coast with four people visible on the deck. It stuck with me for a reason I couldn't explain, and I tucked it aside to consider later. I changed topics, ready to ask a question I'd been putting off.

"Hamilton seems to be accepting all this rather easily."

"I don't know. I think it was difficult for him in the beginning. From what he's shared with me, he didn't know what to make of you and Colantha, but he was aware of being in a construct. He thought Lorenzo might have found another dreamwalker and this was a new form of torture."

I winced. "It was pretty obvious he didn't feel comfortable. I think he was a bit freaked when he found himself in Guildford's study, but at the same time, it seemed to bring him comfort. But I'll never forget his face when he saw you."

"Everything seemed to click at that moment. Maybe it finally became real and gave him an ounce of hope." Her voice cracked a bit, but she shook it off, her gaze seeming to focus on the same boat I had. "I swear it was like those hundred years never happened." Tears rolled down her cheek, and she wiped them away. "I'm sure he didn't see the same frivolous creature who cared about parties and fashion. He says I'm stronger, more assured. He pointed out a small wrinkle." She laughed. "I was devastated."

And that made me laugh.

"But it was meeting Devon that solidified our intentions. He sees my father in my brother. I never looked at Devon in that same light. Certainly not as clearly as Hamilton sees it. This might sound strange, but I feel like I've been in the same prison as him." She glanced up at her third-floor apartment. "I've been locked away in the same room for as long as Hamilton's been in his prison. The only difference was that mine was self-inflicted."

"That's not entirely true." I ran a hand down her arm. "In fact, I'm positive it's not true at all. You were in an accident that took everyone you loved. Then, before you could make sense of it, you were brought into nightmare constructs that twisted your reality. No one knew what Hamilton could do. No one even considered the fact he could still be alive or that someone kidnapped him. If you didn't have your painting and midnight walks, you might still be locked away in your mind. That's not frivolous or self-inflicted. You were a victim as much as Hamilton was."

Lyra took my hand, her tears once again brimming on the edge of her lashes. "You're a good friend, Cressa. As I've said before, you were always meant to be here. You're our salvation."

DEVON CHECKED THE LIBRARY, theater, gym, and widow's walk, then made a second visit to the kitchen before running up to Lyra's room. As a last resort, he circled the outside of the house, but he couldn't find Cressa anywhere.

He checked his office before climbing the stairs to the second floor, kicking himself for not checking the solarium and pool, but was too tired to go down and confirm. It seemed foolish to call her cell to find out where she was in the house. He should install an intercom system. He grinned. She'd probably be averse to wearing a GPS tracker.

Instead of turning right toward his room, he turned left on impulse. He should have checked her room, but she had wanted to move about because she said the manor felt confining. He knocked lightly, not expecting an answer. He held his ear to the door and heard breathing. He'd found his thief.

He cracked the door open. She was on the bed, mostly dressed, lying on her belly. Her head faced the hearth, and a few tresses stirred with each long, slow breath she took. She had to be mentally wiped from the last two days. Though she had drunk less juice than when she'd been in New Orleans, the extra sessions with Hamilton and withdrawal from the juice should have prepared him for her eventual crash.

He kicked off his shoes and lay on his side next to her while he watched her sleep. Somewhere, early on, she'd become more than an asset to help him reach his goal. She'd become an integral part of the Family and his cadre.

He remembered their first major fight. It was the night of Gruber's tea party when she took it upon herself to steal a document she'd overheard Gruber talking about. Devon had been upset she'd taken such a risk. If she'd been caught, it could have jeopardized his mission, yet she'd discovered an important document that was one of several required to remove his censure. She'd done that for him. She could have just as easily told him about it after he'd returned from the impromptu Council meeting. He knew she did it because she'd been bored and her instincts to snoop were too great to ignore, but at the same time, she wouldn't have done it unless it was something that would aid his cause.

It was also her way of showing him her worth. Her fear of being returned to The Wolf, or worse, Sorrento, had plagued her. He could smell the scent of her fear and uneasiness in those early days. But still, it had touched him. They'd been through a great deal together, and there was so much more to come.

Lyra said she was meant to come to them. To save them. He didn't know what that meant or how Lyra would know such a thing. Perhaps it had been her own relationship with a dreamwalker. He'd spent decades searching every minuscule link to the fable of dreamwalkers, and now he found himself surrounded by them.

Had his father been the first step to the discovery of dreamwalkers? Was it House Trelane's predetermined destiny to bring vampire society to the brink of civil war? Or would it be the dawning of an age of enlightenment for their species?

He brushed the strands of hair from Cressa's face and listened to her soft breaths. If he removed all the reasons she was here—her Pandora persona as a tool for removing his censure and her dreamwalker species that could revolutionize the future of vampires—would she still hold such a vise grip over his heart?

He scooted closer until her body touched his, then he laid his head down and closed his eyes. What they had now was enough. She knew she belonged here, and through everything that was yet to come, he'd make sure she no longer questioned it.

"Hey. Wake up."

Something nudged him, and he groaned, a pleasant dream slipping away too quickly to remember. Tendrils of soft hair fell across his bare chest. He didn't recall taking his shirt off. Ah. Now he remembered. He'd wanted to feel the warmth of her skin against his.

"Why are you in my bed, vampire?" Her tone was light, and though he suspected she'd attempted a sultry voice, there was enough humor for him to understand the game.

He moved so fast, there was a quick intake of breath followed by a gasp as he rolled her over until he laid on top of her.

"I'm here to do your bidding. What would you ask of me?"

Her smile brightened the room, but then her lips turned to a pout. "If we only had the time. Sergi and Lucas are both looking for you, and it's just a matter of time before they think to look here."

He grinned, unable to pull away from dark amber eyes that sparkled with mischief. When he squeezed her butt, she rubbed against him.

"Okay. I give." He rolled away and stood before it went any further and searched for his shirt.

She sat up and crossed her arms over her chest. "Well, that was rather quick."

He chuckled as he buttoned the shirt, then looked for his tie. "I am a vampire."

"Yeah. But you could show a little respect. I did let you sleep with me."

His brow lifted. Her lips twitched. "I believe the keyword there is sleep."

She walked up to him, and this time her sultry was working just fine. She wrapped her arms around his neck, bringing him down for what he hoped would be a kiss. Instead, she whispered in his ear.

"Let's see if you can manage something a bit more than sleep next time." Then she patted his backside and walked out the door.

He picked up his shoes and headed for his room, meeting Sergi as he bounded up the stairs. He fell in behind Devon, and when they reached his room, Sergi dropped into the chair at Devon's writing desk.

"What is it?" Devon had to ask if he wanted the information now. Otherwise, Sergi would assume he was distracted, and he'd wait for what he considered the proper time to divulge whatever he had to share.

Today, he wasn't in the mood.

Sergi leaned back and crossed a leg over his knee. A casual position that said there wasn't anything critical to report. "I take it you know Lucas has returned."

He nodded as he stripped off his shirt on his way to the bathroom. "Cressa told me." He couldn't see Sergi but pictured his brow lifting at that. "I don't know whether she heard it from him or Ginger." He took a quick rinse in the shower, ran his wet hands through his hair, then grabbed a towel.

Sergi waited until he was walking to his closet. "Remus has asked for a meeting."

"Did he call or his beta?" Devon asked.

"His beta."

Devon walked out of the closet in his brown-striped suit pants, his blue shirt still open, a tie and a pair of socks in one hand, shoes in another. "Ask Decker to set something up here at the manor. Have we had any visitors?" He sat down to put on his socks.

"A few drive-bys and a handful of discreet individuals roaming the neighborhood around the safe house."

"What about Cressa's condo?"

"Someone has posted three vampires around the building."

"It must be driving Lorenzo mad wondering how she got off the island." He buttoned his shirt and added a pair of gold cufflinks.

Sergi chuckled. "And he can't find a trace of her anywhere."

"Now that Ginger is back, it should be easier to keep Cressa at the manor."

"But for how long?"

He stood and pulled the tie around his neck, quickly tying the knot before going back to the closet, appearing seconds later with his suit jacket. "Let's see what the cadre has for us. Make sure Bella keeps Lorenzo's vampires busy when Remus comes. I don't want anyone to know he was here."

"Wouldn't it be easier to meet someplace else?"

"Maybe. But I doubt Colantha would feel comfortable with that."

Sergi stood. "You plan on introducing them?"

Devon pulled at the cuffs of his jacket and straightened his tie. "We're going to need allies to break Hamilton out. And we can only guess what the fallout will be after that. It's time for full disclosure."

Sergi followed him out of the room, and Devon smiled when he heard him mutter, "It's about time."

Chapter Twenty-Eight

DEVON STROLLED INTO HIS OFFICE, more relaxed than he'd been in some time. He was dog-tired, but instead of feeling the beast nipping at him, the harmony between them had returned. Most of his cadre was in attendance, but he was surprised to find Simone straddling a barstool. She'd gathered vital information for their mission, but rather than returning to Oasis, she'd apparently remained here in case she was needed.

He bent and placed a kiss on her cheek. "Thank you for being here."

"I heard Lucas had returned from the San Francisco annex." She shrugged under his intense perusal. "I love a good mystery."

"No, you don't." He kissed her cheek again. "It's still good to have you here."

He turned to where Lucas and Ginger sat on the couch. Lucas's expression was grim while Ginger appeared detached, but she held her head high, an arm wrapped around Lucas's. Devon wasn't sure who was holding who upright.

"Why do I have the feeling you have bad news?" Devon sat in a wingback chair and crossed his leg. He scanned the room. "Where's Bella?"

"She's finishing her guard patrol." Sergi glanced at the clock. "She'll be here as soon as she finishes."

Devon had expected Cressa. Simone might not like mysteries, but it would be difficult to keep Cressa away from one. But she might have already gotten an update from Ginger.

"Let's get started. Did you discover anything new?"

Lucas shared the events at the library and what they'd learned about the book. He started with the fake book that held the same restoration note as the one in the L.A. library, the chilling reception with the curator who'd lied about the book, and the vampires who appeared to have been waiting for them. Though he agreed they might have been followed, either way, they had been attacked in the parking lot during broad daylight.

It would be impossible to know which Family the vampires belonged to. It was easy to blame Lorenzo, but since it was typically him, he'd earned the suspicion. The vampires, whoever they were, might have assumed House Trelane would show up at the annex or they were somehow tracking them, but it was thin. He wasn't aware that anyone outside the House knew of the book's existence or his interest in it.

"So, what do you make of this business with the restoration?" Devon asked. "Do you think it was just an honest mistake, or are they hiding something?"

"It would only be a guess until we visit a couple more libraries, preferably farther east. It would give us some indication of how far the disinformation has spread."

"I think the home library should also be investigated." Simone plucked at her violet caftan before smoothing it. "That's the only way we'll know how widespread the conspiracy is."

"Conspiracy?" Lucas glanced at the others. "That seems to be a leap."

Devon shrugged. "I agree we should keep an open mind. It's possible the Renauds made an honest, if unheard of, mistake. But the curator said the book was moved from San Francisco in 1906, and we know Philipe Renaud showed it to my father in 1925. The question remains of who placed the false books in the inventory. That could give us an indication of whether a conspiracy is afoot."

"Are you thinking there are more people involved than just Philipe?" Lucas asked.

"That remains to be seen, but the curator's lie and the vampire attack makes me think Philipe wasn't alone in this. The question is whether Philipe hid the book on his own or with his family's approval. The other libraries need to be checked."

"There might be someone else that can help, assuming you can find them."

Everyone turned to the door where Lyra stood. Cressa hovered behind her, and she shrugged her shoulders. Devon rose and waited by the sofa as she entered the office, smiling at the cadre.

"I thought you were napping, or I would have told you of the meeting." Devon frowned at her appearance—pale and fragile. It had to be difficult knowing that all her early trauma wasn't a fractured mind but someone pulling her into their own personal nightmare. He wanted to blame Hamilton for all he'd done, but it hadn't been his fault. There was only one vampire to blame, and he'd get his due.

"Cressa told me, and I was going to let you deal with this, but I've been thinking about that evening in San Francisco quite a lot since discovering Hamilton is still alive." She sat and pulled Cressa down to sit beside her. "I have to admit, the last few days have been a bit of a whirlwind, and I'm still trying to make sense of it all. I'm beginning to see bits and pieces from that time in the city and then the accident."

"She's been dreamwalking with Colantha." Cressa ignored Lyra's glare. "They have to know. They can help. You know this."

Lyra rolled her eyes like a petulant teenager. "It could be my imagination. My mind grasping for answers in a sea of confusion."

"Explain, Lyra." Devon remained still, trying to absorb this from his sister's perspective.

She scratched her head and glanced around the group. Everyone watched her—some with curiosity, the rest with doubt. "As I said, little bits of memory have been coming back, but, after all this time, I didn't know if they were actual memories or fabrications. They became more vibrant after the dreamwalks with Hamilton. When I told Colantha, she thought a dreamwalk of that day might yield more answers."

"Wasn't that dangerous?" Simone asked.

Lyra shrugged. "Colantha mentioned there could be some relapse if it triggered the trauma from the accident."

"For Christ's sake, Lyra, why didn't you have one of us with you?" Devon's fists clenched, and he forced himself to relax.

"This was about me and Hamilton. Not the cadre. I didn't know anyone in this room but you back then, and I needed to remember it as if it was yesterday. I don't expect you to understand, but this was the only way I could make the memories fresh."

There was grumbling, mostly from him, but Devon did understand. With Colantha's ability to build a construct that would be as real as Lyra could describe it, something might be gained by it. But still, was it worth the risk to her sanity?

"You discovered something." Sergi, as usual, got right to the point. He, out of all of the cadre, including himself, had always treated Lyra differently. He was patient and supportive, but never treated her as a child, even at her worst moments. He also pushed her harder, and she never rebelled against his actions.

"I think so."

"About the accident?" Simone asked.

"No. The library. When we arrived, Philipe Renaud met us at the front desk and took us on a tour. It didn't take long for the men to start talking about the book—the *De første dage*. But I noticed this custodian, a woman, who followed Philipe everywhere. He was very secretive around the other custodians when he spoke of the book. But he wasn't concerned about this particular custodian."

She gazed off to some spot above the hearth and a soft smile touched her lips. "I remember thinking there was a personal relationship behind their side glances. They both seemed excited about someone else knowing about the book. Someone they trusted."

"Who was this custodian?" Lucas asked.

"She was young, pretty, but bookish, you know?"

Lucas smiled. "I've met one or two of those." Then he glanced at Ginger, who lightly elbowed him.

"I can't remember her name. Colantha tried to help me remember, to no avail. But I would think the library must have a record of her employment, assuming they're willing to provide the information."

"There are other ways to find out." Lucas seemed more confident than Devon felt, but he'd proven his resourcefulness many times over.

"Maybe she still works there," Ginger offered. "Or maybe she moved with Philipe to the library in L.A. and then ran away with him." Her eyes took on a dreamy look. "So romantic." Then she sobered. "Except for probably having vamps on their tails."

"This needs to be checked out, but not now." Devon glanced around his office at the cadre's expectant faces. He shook his head. "I know you all want to jump on this, especially Lucas. But it needs to wait. Our first task is retrieving Hamilton. Then we'll decide how to proceed with locating this custodian and the book."

He pulled Lyra up from the sofa and hugged her. When he stepped back, her face was set in stone. She knew what was coming. "Thank you for the risk you took. I still would have preferred knowing about it first, but it's done. However, worry over Hamilton and all this dreamwalking is taking its toll. Simone will call for a blood donor, and I won't take no for an answer."

"Maybe we should ask Hamilton." Simone typed into her cell, then laid it on the bar. She would have sent for a donor. "He might remember more about this custodian."

"I don't think it's a good idea to ask Hamilton yet." Cressa's brows scrunched. "Hamilton has held up remarkably well to this point, but that doesn't mean he's not fragile. If dredging up memories of that day was a risk to Lyra, it would be for him as well. I don't think we should take the chance."

Everyone turned to Lyra, who'd sat down. It took her a moment to become aware of the eyes on her. She sighed. "I don't know. He seems well, but his whole focus is on how to free himself. It might be the only thing holding him together at this point. If I had to choose a path, I'd select the one with the least risk."

Devon nodded, seeming satisfied. "That's my thought as well. We have time to dig into this further once we get Hamilton off the island." He looked to Lyra, and she nodded in agreement, then laid her head on the sofa and closed her eyes. He considered having Cressa take her to her room, but there wasn't any reason she couldn't listen to the rest of the conversation. "Simone, have you discovered a way for us to get onto the island?"

"Lorenzo hosts what he refers to as a fantasy party. It's in four days. And from what we were told, it's so daring, that many wear masks to protect their identities. Although I imagine some wear a mask for the kink."

"What's the plan?" Devon asked.

"I have a couple of thoughts. But we'll need more than vampires to succeed. As well as several diversions," Simone said. "I've secured six invitations to the party. Getting in will be easy; getting out is a different story."

"With Cressa's intel on the island, we have a decent floor plan of the manor." Sergi tapped a few buttons on his tablet, and the LCD screen above the hearth came alive with the image of Shadow Island. "She had limited access outside of the manor, but the details she provided match fairly well with the satellite images we were able to obtain. But it was Ginger's idea of a drone and the assistance of Harlow's team that gave us details on the island's defenses we haven't had before." He pushed another button, and the image zoomed in. "Based on previous surveillance we've performed, Simone and I have identified various security teams which are marked with circles. The red, blue, and yellow lines are what we believe their current routes to be. We assume security will increase for the day and evening of the ball; however, there are several landmarks we feel our inside teams should be aware of."

"We could use help from the shifters if The Wolf is so inclined," Simone added. "Decker has a couple rogues that could prove useful. If The Wolf can provide access to the buildings he owns around the marina's dock, it would assist with our exit strategy."

"I have a meeting with Remus tomorrow night. I think we'll be able to secure additional resources." Devon stood and approached the screen. "What's this area here?" He tapped the screen. The island was mostly cliffs with a small bay where the dock was located. On the opposite side of the island was a cove with what appeared to be a narrow stretch of sand.

"It's a beach." Cressa seemed surprised. "I never heard anyone talk about it. Do you think there's access to it from the manor?"

"Is there any other place on the island to dock or beach a boat besides the main dock?" Devon asked.

"I haven't seen anything on the images from the drone," Simone answered.

Sergi nodded in agreement. "I've reviewed all the recordings. The drone did an amazing job, and this small stretch of sand is the only other place to land a small craft. I also searched for possible cave entrances, but the terrain only allows limited views. That doesn't mean something isn't there. As we know, the island is a jut of land from the mainland that remains well above tide levels year-round. These pictures were taken close to low tide."

The group quieted as they stared at the monitor. The island told them part of the story, but the vampire that owned it shouldn't be discounted.

He smiled at Sergi. "Have you ever known Lorenzo not to have an exit strategy?"

Sergi met his smile with one of his own. "He would never own a piece of land that didn't have more than one exit."

"You think there's a cave that leads to the beach?" Simone asked.

"We'd be foolish to ignore the possibility." Devon stared at the image. "We have a couple of days yet. Let's see if we can get more footage around this area."

"I'm surprised you haven't studied the island before," Cressa said.

He considered her comment. The cadre had gathered general information, and they had cruised as close to the island as they could get without stirring the island's defenses. But that had been several years ago when Devon had first planned his long-term mission to remove his censure from the Council. His focus hadn't been specifically on the island but on Lorenzo's defenses.

He shook his head and stared at the island on the screen. "It's a waste of time to learn too much about an opposing House. Like us, they change their defenses frequently. Other than keeping track of his schedule, anything more can become an obsession."

"That makes sense. What's next?"

"The same as any other mission. We continue to gather intel and double the training hours to include practice drills. I also want repeated reviews of the manor inside and out until everyone knows it as if they lived there." His focus turned to Lyra. "You need to work with Colantha and continue your dreamwalks with Hamilton. We need him strong enough to walk off that island."

"AGAIN." Sergi paced along the rubber mat in front of the wall. Ginger gave him her best evil eye before she shook out her arms and began her climb.

I watched her, amazed at how quickly she'd picked up her climbing skills, but I could see she was weakening. Her timing was slower, and her moves less coordinated.

"What are you waiting for, sunshine?"

I glared at Sergi and leaped up to my favorite handhold, scurrying to the other side of the wall where a rope hung from the top. My legs burned, and my arms shook. I was faster than Ginger, but I'd been climbing for years. I grabbed the rope, gripping tightly so I wouldn't let go too soon. My arms had a different thought, and when I swung around to grab the other rope, my fingers locked up and the rope slipped from my grasp.

Sergi had his eye on Ginger, who was slowly crossing the top of the wall to the other set of ropes. It was unfortunate for him because when I let go, I used what momentum I had to fly toward him. He looked up, but it was too late. I was like one of those cat memes—arms and legs spread wide as I landed on him.

I heard his grunt, and I returned one of my own when his elbow dug into my kidney. He rolled me, trying to pin me to the floor, but I intertwined my legs with his and held on, forcing the roll to continue.

A loud scream, high-pitched and sounding eerily like a blend of hell cat and Tarzan. We both looked up in time to see Ginger flying at us, her hand raised with her wooden dagger. Now it was Sergi's turn to try to keep our roll going, but we'd lost momentum, and I ducked my head, waiting for the impact.

Ginger landed on us and began stabbing with the dagger. Fortunately, she kept stabbing Sergi rather than me, but I let my guard down, thinking the drill was over. When Sergi gave the signal he'd been defeated, Ginger turned on me and began slamming the dagger down. Thankfully, the dagger was on its side, but it still hurt.

A whistle blew and we fell back, sprawling in different directions.

"That's enough for one day." Devon strode over and stared down at us.

Simone stood next to him, her fangs peeking out of her wide smile. "Never would I have believed that Ginger, a mere slip of a woman, could shame the two of you so well."

"I wasn't part of the drill," Sergi muttered and pushed my legs off him as he jumped up.

Devon laughed. "You were in the marked zone. Cressa might not have noted that when her grasp on the rope broke, but Ginger, as weak as she'd become after all the climbing, had the presence of mind to stay focused, even when exhausted." He put out a hand to Ginger, which she gladly took.

I growled as I got to my hands and knees, and after several long breaths, managed to stand, though my legs trembled. I'd started the drills an hour before Ginger, but I had to give her credit. She kicked our asses but still bumped her fist into mine. I managed to take down Sergi, so it was a team effort.

Sergi scowled. "Humans are unpredictable."

"Especially women," Simone added, her smile not diminishing in the slightest.

"This shouldn't be news to you, but let's hope Lorenzo's vampires have the same blind spot." Devon tossed towels and bottles of water to us. "You have an hour to clean up and rest. Then back to the conference room to review the plan."

Ginger moaned. "Again? I'd almost prefer another drill."

Devon's brow raised, and he glanced at Simone.

Ginger raised her hand. "Don't even think about it. It will take me most of the hour to climb the stairs."

I put an arm around her shoulder. "Let's go to the pool. We can shower there then jump into the hot tub for a few minutes."

I dragged her away, each of us a support for the other. "We need to get out of here before they think of some other form of torture."

The vamps laughed, even Sergi. We waited until we moved into the hall before our grins came out, and we fist-bumped again.

"I can't believe I'm still standing. How long have we been at it?"

I glanced out the windows as we shuffled into the pool room. "It's close to sunset."

Ginger's head popped up. "We've been at it for what, almost four hours? No wonder I feel like my bones melted."

We took turns in the shower, then spent fifteen minutes in the hot tub before another quick shower. We went back to our rooms to dress for dinner. I waited ten minutes before giving up on a nap and, feeling restless, left my room. Ginger was already a few steps ahead of me.

"Hey, wait up." I hurried to her, and we walked down the stairs, opting for a celebratory glass of wine in the library. Surviving a four-hour training session with vamps and still being able to walk around and crow about it was worthy of a whole bottle.

We had just poured the last of the bottle into our glasses when Simone sauntered in.

"I'm glad some of you have time to relax." Her tone suggested otherwise.

"Don't blame us. We'd be happy to assist if someone gave us a task. But my only worth seems to be drop-dead drills and practicing constructs with Colantha." I should have let it go, but I was suddenly in the mood to test buttons. "It's not our fault you're a workaholic."

She stared at me, and Ginger kicked me without the convenience of having a table to hide it. Subtle it wasn't, and Simone caught the gesture.

I ran my hands through my hair then lifted the empty bottle of wine. "Sorry. I'd pour you a glass if we weren't already drinking the last of it."

She dropped into a nearby chair and smoothed her peach-colored caftan. "Everyone has been showing signs of stress. It's fortunate I'm able to maintain my normal mood."

I held back a snort and sneaked a glance at Ginger, who suddenly needed to examine her scarf for signs of who knew what. But when I thought about it, Simone was right. Sergi and Lucas had been short-tempered. It had been a shock to hear Sergi laugh after our last drill. Even Devon seemed to have difficulty keeping his emotions in check.

I took a gulp of wine. "We need to release this build-up of stress."

"The Wolf is coming in a couple of days, right?" Ginger asked.

Simone nodded.

"Let's make it a social gathering. Drinks before dinner then some entertainment after. Devon has a huge gaming room with a pool table, darts, and all kinds of things. We can make it seem more like a pub." She sat up, pulling her legs underneath her. "Devon and The Wolf can do their private business, and the rest of us can blow off steam."

Simone gave us a smile that made me shiver. "One thing I know to be true. I've never seen a shifter pass up a game of pool."

<h1 style="text-align:center">Chapter Twenty-Nine</h1>

THE NEXT TWO days were a whirlwind of activity similar to when the House had been threatened with sanctions. In addition to their duties for the mission, Devon tasked Lucas with the additional task of preparing for a siege at the manor. It was a great deal of effort, but with each stab he gave Lorenzo, the more likely a retaliation.

Cook was busy creating frozen meals, while the pantry, infirmary, and armory were restocked. These preparations weren't required for rescuing Hamilton, but for Lorenzo's retaliation when he discovered Devon had stolen his prize prisoner.

Drills and reviews of the mission became a constant. Harlow brought Trudy and Roxie by once a day to join them in going over the plan, offering suggestions where warranted. Their role might be small, but it was crucial for success as well as dangerous. Cressa had been surprised when Harlow agreed to it, but the amount Devon was willing to pay for their help was difficult to walk away from.

Devon had driven to Oasis earlier that morning, meeting with Simone to review last-minute preparations for a possible siege at his private estate. All housing on the property was being made ready as a safe house for the Family and shifters requiring assistance.

Rather than using the main drive to the estate, which could expose their location, he wanted to make the two back entrances available, but he faced opposition.

"You put all of Oasis at risk by revealing our exits." Simone, who wasn't a pacer, proved she was rather good at it as she walked along the floor-to-ceiling windows that overlooked the back of the property.

"We have to trust our allies. And increased traffic through the front gates will be too suspicious." Devon understood her concern. It was one thing to trust your allies, but the more shifters and vampires became aware of Oasis, the more difficult to control the information flow, leaving a weakness for the primary emergency exits.

"It's too great a risk. We should make changes to the safe houses to accommodate extra casualties. We could also open one of the other properties."

"We won't have time to increase the security. They weren't planned as safe houses."

"This is only our first strike against Lorenzo. It will become more difficult after this. It's time for more than one safe house."

He couldn't argue her logic, and he'd been thinking along the same lines. There was too much to do and very little time to do it.

"Select one of the properties to prepare as a safe house in time for this mission. Then, add two others to be upgraded once this mission is complete. Share the details with me and the cadre, but you have my permission to begin on the first site immediately. Do you have one in mind?"

She nodded and went to the table where they'd started their meeting. After scrolling through her tablet, she pushed it toward him. He smiled, anticipating this would be the one she'd pick. It was an old apartment complex at the edge of an even older industrial section just south of the Hollows. It was accessible from various routes, there weren't many homes in the area, and even less traffic.

It had been their first safe house twenty years ago and was still maintained. It was where Devon gave rogue vampires a roof when they came to town before they decided whether they were interested in joining the Family or living alone, assuming Devon approved it. It looked like crap from the outside, but three units were upscale and comfortable with all the modern conveniences. The other apartments had minimal features but were more than comfortable. The lobby had been retrofitted with state-of-the-art surveillance and security systems that protected the complex, including a fifty-foot perimeter. But it would require additional cameras and monitors to be considered an official safe house again.

"I agree with your choice, but I'd still like one of the entrances to Oasis cleared for this mission." He held up his hands. "We'll provide a diversionary access point. Arrange for unmarked and varying types of vans at pickup locations. We'll keep the entrances secret. Let's use the buildings farthest from the main house for anyone not part of the Family. Will that meet your concerns?"

"Yes. I'll contact Sergi to help with the selection of pickup points and the teams."

Once he was back at the manor, there was a string of vampires waiting to discuss problems. He farmed a few to Sergi, others to Lucas, and a couple to Bella, and then worked through issues with the remaining handful before going up to check on Lyra and Colantha.

Devon and the cadre were included in one construct a day so they would be more comfortable, but contact with Hamilton was left to the two of them. Lyra slept between constructs, and he always expected her to be weaker each day, but she appeared to be healthy. He shouldn't have doubted Colantha's training techniques.

Jamison and Frederick had developed a fondness for Lyra and became overly protective when others came into the room, including the cadre. While it was odd, Devon allowed it. Should they face a siege, he knew Colantha and Lyra would be in good hands.

He checked in with Cook, ordered a pot of coffee and a meal to be brought to his office, then checked on Sergi before shutting his office door. Delicious scents overwhelmed his senses, letting him know Cook had already delivered the meal. In need of some time alone, he locked the door.

A smile lit his lips when the back of his office chair slowly turned to reveal Cressa.

"There you are." Her dazzling smile breathed energy back into him. "Everywhere I looked for you, someone said you'd just left."

"Yet somehow you arrived here before me."

She shrugged and stood, patting the chair in invitation. "I ran into Cook, who was headed this way. You must have made a detour somewhere."

Devon strolled around the desk, eyeing the food that had caught his attention when he'd first walked in. Then he put an arm around Cressa and gave her a kiss. He sat and welcomed the soft leather comfort. He leaned his head back and closed his eyes.

The soft scent of her perfume further relaxed him as she stepped behind the chair.

"You're tired." Her hands caressed his temples.

"I just need some food."

"What you need is blood." She trailed a hand over his shoulders as she moved around him. Then she was in his lap, and his arm instinctively wrapped around her waist. "Why won't you take my blood?"

His eyes popped open. There was hurt in her gaze, and he shook his head. "It's not what you think. If it was just me on my own, I'd risk it to see what happened when the beast was asleep. But I'm not alone. I have the House to think of—my Family. We're heading into dangerous times, and I can't risk my mental faculties."

She considered it and, though obviously disappointed, she nodded. "I understand."

"I might reconsider if Remus could provide a definitive answer of your blood's impact."

"His lab hasn't discovered anything?"

"It seems they've found plenty, and that appears to be the problem. The lab is having difficulty sorting through the data in search of common markers."

She was quiet for a long moment, her hand stroking his arm. Then she tapped a finger and sat up, his arms preventing her from rising. "I'm not sure why I didn't think of it sooner." She gave him a long look, and worry spread through him. What crazy idea was she plotting? He'd laugh if it wasn't such a critical topic.

"Would it help if I gave him some of my blood?"

Not so crazy after all. He had planned on asking but then the accident and everything snowballed. He took her hand. They were small hands but not dainty. There were small scars from training and callouses from working with her dagger. But they were the most beautiful hands he'd ever seen.

"You'd do that for me?"

She snorted, but her tone was soft honey. "Of course. It's for the cause, right? And it's about time I understand more about who I am. And that includes my blood. What if I ended up in the hospital someday and the doctors freak about my strange blood?"

He laughed. "As long as you have your priorities. I'll arrange for Madame Saldano to come tomorrow. She wanted to perform a last health check on Jacques."

"I feel bad I haven't asked about him more."

"He's back on full duty, but Bella has been giving him light assignments. He's looking forward to the healer's report to prove he's ready for more."

"She's rather protective of him."

"Hmm. Too much, I think. Anyway, the healer can take your blood while she and Remus are here on the same evening."

"Excellent planning. Two birds, one stone sort of thing."

"Let's eat. Afterward, I've saved some sofa time with you."

Her brow rose. "Oh, really."

"Two birds, one..."

"Just stop. You're too much. But I'll make you a deal. I'll agree to some couch time if you promise to get blood before the night's over."

It was such an easy request. He'd promise anything for sofa time with his thief.

THE FOYER of the building was typical for any middle-class home, though it was currently marred with the bodies of two vamps. Since they still had their heads, I assumed they were alive regardless of the amount of blood pooling beneath them.

Devon grabbed my arm and dragged me down the hallway—living space on the left, an office on the right, kitchen in the back. The building must have been a staff bungalow many years before. A second hallway appeared to be bedrooms, and Devon left to check and confirm no other vamps were on the first level while I moved back to the kitchen.

The door next to the pantry led down to the next level. We moved quietly and quickly until we neared the bottom and Devon held up his fist. Two voices confirmed more vamps in the basement, but there could be more.

I held my dagger in front of me as we crept down the last two steps, listening for a change in voices that could signal they were aware of our approach. Devon gave me the signal to stay put, but I shook my head. The vamps' tone changed to whispers. Devon had taken out the upstairs guards in less than a minute, but they might have heard something unexpected.

We could wait for them to come to the stairs. The wall

between the staircase and the room prevented them from seeing us but was an equal disadvantage on our side.

I tapped his shoulder and whispered directly into his ear, "Let me go first. It will confuse them."

Based on his furrowed brows, he didn't like it, but he eventually nodded. I held my hands behind my back, dagger still at the ready.

I stood, my black body suit not exactly attractive but still showed off some of my attributes. I did my best saunter as I cleared the last step and moved into the next room.

"Hello, boys. Since you can't join the ball, Lorenzo thought you might like to have your own party."

I didn't see any more than the two vamps, who stared at me, a questioning gaze passing between them. They seemed to be wrestling between the Lorenzo they knew, who would never allow such a thing during guard duty, and the fact they were probably bored out of their mind babysitting a long-time prisoner.

"What's the matter, boys? I know it's a bit unorthodox, and I'm only human, but if you're not interested, I'll go find someone who is."

I turned for the stairs, but before I reached them, one of the vamps lunged at me. He didn't have a weapon, and when he was almost on me, I swung my dagger slicing across his throat. It was enough for him to stagger and fall to his knees. I kicked out with my right leg which sent him sprawling backwards.

It was an unfortunate circumstance for his friend, who hadn't expected his comrade to fall, and he tripped over the body. He was able to keep his footing, but it left him in a poor position to fend off Devon who had made his move before the first vamp went down. In seconds, the fight was over.

"Don't say it," Devon said as we moved past the fallen vamps and raced down the hall. "I'll have to consider the honeypot trap in future scenarios." The doors along the hallway were closed with bars across the doors. When they reached the one on the end, Devon pulled off the bar and yanked the door open.

Hamilton jerked to a stop. He appeared to have been pacing, a ragged backpack hung over one shoulder.

"Come on. We're behind schedule." Devon waved him forward.

It was a surreal feeling as I gave a quick glance around the room. The construct Colantha had made based on Hamilton's description was almost perfect.

Hamilton followed Devon back down the hall and up the stairs to the first floor. I brought up the rear. We slowed before moving back into the kitchen, but all was quiet.

The two vamps were still down in the foyer, and we stepped around them, careful to stay out of the blood. The last thing we needed was to leave a trail.

Devon scanned the outer perimeter before hustling us out, taking the path to the right. We'd taken a handful of steps when a bright light hit us.

Seconds later, the sound of automatic weapons filled the air as Devon's body jerked for what seemed like an eternity. I screamed as he dropped. He struggled to get up but fell back, twisting in agony. Silver bullets.

I shoved Hamilton to the side and used a hand to shield my eyes from the light in an attempt to make out how many were out there.

From behind the spotlight, Lorenzo walked out of the darkness. He held a long silver sword.

I still had my dagger out but didn't hear the vamps that sneaked up from behind. They grabbed my arms, and my dagger was wrenched from me. I struggled, but they forced me to my knees. I gave a quick glance to Devon, but he was fighting off the effects of the silver.

"I have to hand it to you." Lorenzo moved around Devon, watching him writhe. "Quite the daring bravado to invade my home and steal from me. I always knew the House Trelane never played by the rules."

Two vamps were leading Hamilton away, but Lorenzo waved them off. "I want him to see firsthand there's no escape for him."

He glared down at Devon then turned his glowing red eyes on me. "I've had my eyes on you all night, wondering why you looked so familiar behind your masks. At least, you've come to me rather than making me come for you."

He lifted my chin. "It's past time you shared my bed. And you will come willingly."

He turned his back on me as he circled Devon again, who was on his knees, attempting to stand.

"Remember who your true master is."

Lorenzo lifted his sword and swung.

I screamed.

"Cressa. Cressa." Someone was shaking me. "Cressa, wake up. Wake up."

I opened my eyes to see Devon kneeling over me, a concerned expression in his warm gaze. I glanced around. We were in his room.

I sat up and clutched him to me. His arms circled me as he rocked me back and forth.

"It's alright. It was only a dream."

The bedroom door burst open as Sergi and Lucas rushed in.

"It's alright. It was just a dream," Devon repeated as he continued to hold me, but I pushed back.

Tears streaked my face and wouldn't stop. "No. Nothing is alright. Our plan won't work."

DEVON FUSSED with his tie until it laid perfectly then pulled on his jacket. Cressa had left his room an hour earlier after a long nap, and while she appeared excited for the evening, the dream still bothered her, as it did him. Her last words before walking out the door were something about doing her hair and makeup with Ginger, and she'd meet him downstairs. He'd be surprised if either of them was on time.

While she was sprucing, he'd have time to meet with Sergi and Simone. They'd been working on an alternative strategy based on Cressa's prescient dream. He'd experienced two with Cressa before, both of them ending in blood, and both coming true. He wasn't going to take a chance with this one, and he rubbed the back of his neck, recalling her vivid retelling.

He found Sergi and Simone in his office, pouring over a map on his desk. "Have you settled on the necessary changes?"

Sergi grunted. "We've considered her description of the building's interior. It might not be accurate, but it's more than we have."

Simone gave Devon one of her withering stares before arching to stretch her back. "It would have been helpful if she'd had the dream a few days ago before we spent all our time reviewing the original plan."

"No one wishes it more than her. While her skill at creating constructs has increased under Colantha's tutelage, neither she nor Colantha can explain her prescient dreams or why they appear when they do."

"Or so she says." Sergi was still focused on the map, and when it grew quiet, he peered up at Devon. "Not Cressa, Colantha."

Devon nodded. "I had hoped she'd have more insight into them."

"Perhaps she feels the dreams have warned us enough in advance," Simone muttered.

"Or perhaps I haven't been able to study her dreams long enough to give you any other advice."

The three of them turned to find Colantha staring at the espresso machine for several seconds before she began tinkering. "Prescient dreamwalking has only been studied on the surface. We can document the dream, how much of it comes true, and the timing of the dream to the actual event, but they've never given consistent results, not even with the same dreamwalker. And those with the ability are quite rare and, for many, their sanity becomes questionable over time."

"What does that mean?" Devon's question was drowned out by the sound of the machine, which seemed excellent timing on Colantha's part.

Once the espresso was poured into a demitasse cup, she glanced at the group. "Anyone else for an espresso?" When they shook their heads, she picked up her cup and approached the desk, staring down at the map.

"Don't worry about your dreamwalker, vampire. I would say the same is true of Hamilton."

"He's also prescient?" Sergi asked, finally taking his eyes off the map as he sat back in his chair.

She nodded and found a seat. "Not as much as Cressa, or perhaps it's more that it's not prescient in the same manner. What Hamilton perceives in his dreams are happier days or positive moments in time. Or they had been before his abduction. He hasn't had a single prescient dream while under Venizi's less-than-pleasant accommodations, but he's had one since we've connected."

"And what did it tell him?" Devon asked, not sure he wanted to know the answer.

Colantha sipped her coffee as she considered her answer. "I'd rather not go into specifics without his permission. Dreamwalking is still a dream and can be quite personal. But I'll share this small piece. He sees himself free of Venizi, but it can only happen if a roadblock is removed. Now, at the time, even with my tutoring, he couldn't define what that roadblock was."

"When was this dream?" Sergi asked.

"Now that's the right question. It was before Cressa's dreamwalk, and before you ask, I didn't tell her anything of Hamilton's prescient dream. I've told no one, not even Lyra. These are still early days for removing his trauma and allowing his natural dreamwalking abilities to recover, which I might add are healing at a remarkable rate."

"And Cressa knew nothing of this?" Simone asked.

"She's had little time to do any dreamwalking with us. When she has, they've been focused on Hamilton's memories of the island, validating his previous details or discovering slight tweaks in his memories. It is possible that during those dreamwalks, she subconsciously found something that triggered her prescient dream, or it's just as likely it had nothing to do with them at all. Did her previous prescient dreams suggest a connection to anything she'd been doing prior to the event?"

Devon shook his head before thinking it through, but he considered each dreamwalk before he spoke. "The first one was when she fell through the window at a ball. We'd been training earlier in the evening, but she'd never been to Raul's house and wouldn't have knowledge of the stained-glass window, nor the construction material left at the side of the house. Yet her dreamwalk provided those specific details, including my decision to give her my blood to save her life. The second dream was a horrific event with the shifters that neither of us could have imagined."

Colantha shrugged. "Cressa told me the same thing, and Lyra agreed with the second dreamwalk, which she had somehow become a part of."

"She'd been wearing Cressa's medallion at the time," Devon offered.

She grinned. "Which only makes it more confusing. I came here now, not to interrupt what must be difficult decisions, but to tell you of my dreamwalk with Hamilton an hour ago. He's had another prescient dream. It appears the roadblock has disappeared, but there's still a darkness that hovers. After he revealed this information, I told him of Cressa's dream. We are in agreement that a change to the plan is necessary for success. We also believe the darkness remains because you've yet to determine your final course."

"That's hauntingly cryptic." Simone glared at Colantha, who simply nodded.

"Hamilton did offer one piece of advice that I don't understand but thought you might."

"And what's that, dreamwalker?" Simone refused to give her an ounce of leeway.

"The answer is in the cave."

Chapter Thirty

AFTER FINISHING HER ESPRESSO, Colantha left Devon's office, walking out the door without another word. None was needed. The team had already been wondering about a cave, and now they were just handed proof one existed with no resolution on how to find it.

They hammered through final personnel assignments for another half hour but were no further along on the cave or how to garner more information. Lucas could research old survey maps of the island, but Lorenzo had owned it for a long time, and it could take weeks to gather information that would be questionable at best.

The constant influx of data coming in so late into the planning grated on Devon and the cadre; none of them pleased with making so many last-minute changes. He glanced at his watch. They'd run out of time to discuss it further.

He entered the foyer and found Cressa waiting for him, staring up at one of the family portraits as she fiddled with the strap of the evening dress she wore. It was an emerald-green silk that fell to mid-thigh, enough to show off her long legs. The neckline was modest, the thin halter straps allowing for a low cut in the back that showed off a lean, muscular figure, the result of hours of training.

When she turned, her eyes sparkled with excitement. She sauntered over in surprisingly low heels, but it would be a long evening, and he had to be satisfied with her not showing up in leggings and an oversized sweatshirt.

"What are you smiling about?" she asked before standing on tiptoes to plant a soft kiss on his lips.

"How lucky I am."

Her warm gaze switched to curiosity. "You're a smooth talker."

The doorbell chimed, giving him an easy out as he led Cressa to the door. "Let's greet our guests."

Rafael opened the door as they approached, revealing The Wolf on the other side.

Devon beckoned him in. "Welcome to our home. Please come in."

The Wolf nodded as he entered, leading a small entourage. Directly behind him was Braden, his beta, Elijah, the alpha of the Humboldt pack, and Raquel, Elijah's beta. Decker trailed behind, hands in his pockets and a warm smile on his face.

When Remus stopped in the middle of the foyer, he made a slow circle as he took in the fresco painting on the ceiling and the tiered crystal chandelier that cast rainbows when the sun hit it. "Stunning as ever."

He gave Cressa a long look. "I haven't been here since the night I came to deliver a package."

Cressa blushed and glanced at her feet.

Devon couldn't fathom the relationship between these two that made Cressa blush whenever she saw Remus. She wasn't shy, and he wasn't jealous, but he'd admit he was insanely curious.

"And it was a fortuitous day for the House Trelane, which has only strengthened our bond." Devon shook The Wolf's hand. "Let's go to the solarium and have drinks while enjoying the sunset. We can discuss the mission after dinner."

~

THE CONVERSATION in the solarium ended with a brief discussion of the mission. I was positive Devon and Remus would talk past the call for dinner, but it was Decker, who'd been out of town until earlier that day, who kept the conversation going as he was caught up. They agreed for the teams to meet at one of Devon's downtown warehouses to review the mission a few more times before everyone left for their final assignments.

Then, the shifter stories began with the vamps trying to outdo them. It was all in good nature, and while the alcohol didn't have an impact on them, Ginger and I giggled at pretty much every-thing. Though most of my focus was on Devon.

He'd taken blood earlier that morning, and he looked so much better. Not in the hot way—even low on blood he was gorgeous—but healthwise. And with it, his mind became sharper, and I listened to the requests made of him throughout the day including issues with the mission, security for the manor and the safe houses, to more personal matters. Every decision was made quickly with each requestor seeming satisfied when they left. It never got old watching how well he led.

Dinner was the standard meal served when welcoming an ally. Endless days of Anna's training regarding etiquette and the proper place settings once again paid off. And Cook outdid himself, with several threats to steal him away.

Ginger and I reduced the wine intake throughout dinner so we'd be ready to show off our skills when the group retreated to the game room. Ginger warned everyone off allowing me to handle the darts, and then proceeded to kick everyone's ass in the process. On the other hand, I showed off my skills at air hockey, but playing against a vamp older than a hundred years was near impossible, so I wasn't shamed when I beat most of the shifters.

The finale was the pool contest between the vamps and shifters. In the end, the shifters won three games to one. Vamps had excellent eye-to-hand coordination that made their shots smooth and decisive, but the shifters understood how to run a table, and they held the edge for bank and trick shots. I'd rarely seen anyone in Devon's gaming room, and for some reason, I had the feeling shifters used their gaming table for talking through business in addition to friendly Friday night gatherings. It was like anything else: the more you played, the better you got.

We ended the evening in the library, where comfortable chairs had been rearranged with the sofas to form a half circle so everyone had a clear view of the display panel where a painting used to hang. Lucas was at the controls, and Devon gave a ten-minute overview of the recent changes made to the mission.

"And why this sudden change?" Elijah asked.

Devon glanced at me, and I nodded. I'd agreed to give part of my secret away but not everything. He rubbed his hands together then took the glass of cognac Bella handed him as she continued on with a tray of snifters.

"Cressa occasionally experiences prescient dreams."

Braden snorted, then looked aghast as he turned to me. "I apologize."

I laughed. "Please. That was a rather large drop of information for anyone to take seriously. But I'm afraid it's true."

"Do they all come true?" Remus asked. He was the only one of the shifters who knew about dreamwalkers, and Devon told me he shared my prescient dreams with him. He had a great poker face, which was probably necessary as The Wolf.

Devon nodded for me to continue, and I stared at the half glass of wine in my hand.

"The two I've had have both come true. One exactly as I dreamed it, the second one—" I pushed the visual of the shifter slaughter back into the dark recesses and cleared my throat. "The second one was close enough."

"And this recent dream was specific to the island and the

recovery of Hamilton?" Braden had been watching me carefully and seemed to be a thoughtful man, similar to Sergi.

I nodded and twisted around so I could see everyone. "The rescue attempt failed shortly after we pulled Hamilton out of the building. We were heading for the docks when Lorenzo's forces overtook us."

"And what exactly do you propose that makes the new plan more effective?" Elijah appeared doubtful, and I fidgeted under his dark stare.

"We modified assignments and have devised secondary and tertiary routes to the docks," Sergi said.

"I suggest the inside teams make every effort to avoid Lorenzo." I still recalled Lorenzo's statement of seeing beyond the masks. "We have to remain inconspicuous and shouldn't rely solely on the masks."

Devon tapped the small section of beach on the image of the island. "And we've been told there is a cave that might provide additional options, but we don't have a way to validate the information. Hamilton believes he knows where the entrance is, but it's been decades since he's seen it. We believe this piece is critical to our success. If we miss this opportunity, it's impossible to know when we'll get another."

Remus rubbed his chin, and the shifters glanced at each other before turning their focus to their leader. "I might know of someone knowledgeable about the island who would know of the cave."

"Cato," Braden said the word with reverence.

Remus nodded. "Cato once worked on the island. Not by choice. Long ago, Venizi had the discreet pleasure of owning shifters."

"The Council banned that practice long before Venizi bought the island," Sergi said.

"They might have banned it, but there was a time when they

turned a blind eye to certain aristocrats who refused to bend to the Council's rules. Even members of the Council."

Sergi pushed his tablet aside. "I remember now. This must have been almost two hundred years ago." He looked to Devon. "When we were in Prussia."

Devon nodded. "When my concerns laid elsewhere at the time. Go on, Remus. What happened to this shifter?"

"Venizi had troubles with a lesser house who decided to strike out. As you can imagine, Venizi hit back hard, and though the lesser house eventually lost, they put up a good fight, weakening Venizi's defenses. Cato took that moment to stage a rebellion while the bulk of Venizi's forces were away. They killed most of the vampires that remained on the island. The majority of the men stole ships from the main dock, while the rest led the females and cubs to another ship that was moored on the other side of the island. The only access was through a cave."

"And is Cato still alive?"

The Wolf sipped his cognac and pulled a cigar out of his pocket. He held it up, and Devon nodded approval. He took his time lighting it, and after a couple of puffs he gave us what we wanted. "He lives in the forest outside Middletown, near Clear Lake. He only leaves his cabin once a week to shop for supplies and doesn't appreciate visitors."

"I had no idea shifters lived that long." I slapped a hand over my mouth, but the shifters laughed.

"We're not immortal, and our longevity isn't assured. Many things are fatal to us, but with fewer wars, we survive longer than our ancestors. Most people aren't aware that Cato still lives. Venizi most of all."

"Will he be willing to share what he knows of the cave?" Devon asked.

"Normally, I would say it's doubtful. But you plan a strike against Venizi for the express reason of taking something of value to him. Cato won't be able to say no."

"Why haven't you done something with the information before?" Devon asked.

The Wolf rolled the cigar in his fingers. "It was too much of a risk."

"And do you think this mission is too risky?"

"We're planning to remove one individual, not take the island. And this time, it's not only shifters taking the risk."

Devon nodded with a cagey smile. "No. It isn't."

I LEFT the group an hour later as Devon ran the group through the new plan, tweaking it as they went. But it all came down to finding the cave, and it was decided that Devon and Remus would go together in the morning to find Cato. As crazy as it seemed, the group was eager for the mission to proceed, even without knowing the location of the cave. They were self-assured, or too arrogant, to believe they couldn't find someone who could be mesmerized or otherwise encouraged to divulge the necessary information.

I jogged up to the third floor to Lyra's room, planning to knock and see if Madame Saldano had arrived to find the door half open. Multiple hushed voices came from deep in the room. I crept in, not wanting to disturb the speakers.

Frederick and Jamison gave me a quick glance from the windows as I approached the living space. The healer sat next to Lyra, who was lying on the sofa. Colantha stood next to them, her eyes closed, her lips moving, and her voice hushed. She spoke in an unfamiliar language and gently swayed.

I circled around the tableau and stood near the fireplace. Lyra's eyes were closed, and a light sheen covered her brow. The healer's hand rested on hers, and, with her lids closed as well, appeared to be in some type of trance.

Colantha had done something similar the day before. She claimed to be strengthening Lyra's abilities within a dreamwalk. I wasn't sure what the healer was doing, but before I could ruminate on it further, the healer's eyes popped open. I leaned back, caught off guard. Her eyes were white. Not a milky white, but a solid shiny white. She blinked, and they shifted into their normal pale green.

A moment later, Lyra's eyes fluttered open at the same time as Colantha's. Lyra smiled when she saw me and sat up, shifting her legs off the couch.

"Cressa, come sit by me. Madame Saldano is ready for you."

I stayed where I was. "What were you doing? You all seemed to be in some sort of trance."

"We were in a construct." Colantha moved to a chair and rubbed her temples. I only saw her do that when she'd spent too much time in one.

Madame Saldano picked up her bag and pulled out an array of bottles in various colors. I recognized the bottle of clear liquid with rainbow sprinkles, which was what she'd given Devon when he was healing from his time with the Beast. She poured some into a vial, topping it with a stopper, and set it aside.

"I was performing a psychic test on Lyra both before and after a dreamwalk." The healer glanced at me. "And now I understand what happened to you when you fell into your psychic coma."

She mixed a blue, green, and pink liquid together that somehow created a turquoise-colored potion. That shouldn't have happened, but no one else thought the results of the color combination was odd, so I didn't say anything. The liquid went into another vial. Then she picked up pink and purple vials I was familiar with.

She looked to Lyra. "You know what to do with these two." She laid the pink and lavender vials on the table in front of her, then picked up the one with rainbow sprinkles. "This one heals the psyche and should be taken after each dreamwalk. This last one —" she laid the turquoise vial next to the other three, "—will strengthen your psychic abilities and should be taken no less than thirty minutes before a dreamwalk. An hour if possible."

Colantha watched with interest, and I stepped toward her, lowering my voice. "Who told her about dreamwalking?"

Her gaze never twitched. "I did. With the permission of your vampire."

I dropped into a nearby chair. "Really? He never mentioned it."

"He didn't make his decision until right after dinner. The juice doesn't have the same impact on vampires. With as little as Devon has dreamwalked, it doesn't take a toll, or at least nothing that blood won't cure." She played with the medallion at her neck. Her thumb rubbed back and forth over its surface. "For this mission, it's possible Lyra might need to traverse multiple constructs. I can increase her psychic tolerance over time, but time isn't something we have. I had hoped Devon might have a solution, and he did. I met with Madame Saldano before I made the final decision to share our secret."

I let that sit for a while. If anyone had the right to make the call it would be Colantha. "Alright." I moved to the sofa and sat next to Lyra, taking her hand. She drank a small portion of the vial with rainbow sprinkles. "How do you feel?"

"A bit tired. But I'll feel better in the next half hour or so. I'd like to say goodbye to Remus and his family."

I turned to the healer. "I guess I'm ready."

"You're sure you want to do this?" she asked.

"Sure. It's just blood."

She cringed. "I wouldn't let too many vampires hear that. Blood is extremely important to them, as you can imagine."

"As it is to dreamwalkers," Colantha added. "However, this blood sample is important. After speaking with The Wolf, I find him to be trustworthy. He's the leader of a species facing the same problem dreamwalkers faced centuries ago. Please proceed."

Madame Saldano nodded and took out long plastic tubing.

"Please roll your sleeve above your elbow. Or if that's not possible —" She glanced up and blinked at my bare arms and the sleeveless dress. "Never mind. I wasn't paying attention."

I held out my right arm. "No problem."

She wrapped the tubing around my arm, and the needle stick was quick and painless. A single vial filled in seconds. It was red. I shook my head. Of course, it was red. I'd seen my blood numerous times from cuts and scrapes, but suddenly, it seemed to be its own entity. What if there was nothing special about it? But a quick glance at Colantha told me this simple act would have long-lasting ramifications.

Lyra and I went down to meet Devon and Remus in the foyer as he and his shifters were preparing to depart. Decker hung back with Bella and Jacques. Apparently, he was staying with us, most likely eager to reengage with the mission reviews now that he was back in town.

Devon stopped in the middle of the foyer when he saw me and Lyra on the stairs. I strolled to his side, welcoming his arm around my waist as I smiled at Remus.

"Before you go, I wanted to give you something." I held out my hand, then turned it over, palm side up, revealing the vial of blood.

Remus stared at the vial, then at me. When I nodded, he picked it up. "You have my word no one will know where it came from."

"I trust you."

Three simple words and with it, I felt the energy in the room change. The shifters seemed to stand a little taller, their expressions full of purpose. I probably imagined it, but Devon squeezed my waist.

I would have to ask Colantha what she thought of the relationship between House Trelane and the shifters. It might be nothing, but something deep within me said it could be a game-changer.

Chapter Thirty-One

THE SUN HAD BARELY RISEN when Devon drove out of the manor in one of the cars from the Family garage. It had been difficult to pull himself away from Cressa, whose warm body had nestled next to him the entire evening. He drove to the northeast side of town, near a busy industrial park. Two fast food restaurants were already busy with early morning workers. Devon turned into the parking lot of a nearby diner and found a spot close to the entrance.

He glanced around the lot but didn't see any cars that might belong to Remus. A couple of minutes later, the shifter walked out the door with a brown bag under his arm and two to-go cups. He stopped next to the passenger side and placed one of the cups on the roof before opening the door.

Remus stuck his head in and handed Devon the other cup. He retrieved the one from the roof and climbed in. Once he was settled, he opened the paper bag and turned the open end toward Devon.

"Best breakfast burritos this side of town."

Devon peeked in and took one. He sipped the coffee, surprised at the bold flavor. "This doesn't seem your type of haunt."

"I have a warehouse not far from here."

"And you hang out at the diner?"

Remus laughed after swallowing a bite of burrito. "It's owned by a shifter."

"Now it all makes sense."

They finished their breakfast and coffee in silence. On the way out of the lot, Devon drove by a waste can and tossed their debris. Their drive would take a couple of hours. It wasn't time Devon wanted to waste, but it could mean lives saved if the shifter was willing to share what he knew about the cave.

Two hours later, Devon pulled into Middletown, a small mountain town northeast of Santiga Bay.

"Do you know where this shifter lives?" Devon pulled into the line at a drive-thru coffee hut.

"Yes, but I want to talk to someone else first. They'll be at the hardware store."

Once they had fresh cups of coffee, Devon found the hardware store a block away. The town had been rebuilt after a devastating fire a decade earlier and, being close to Clear Lake, attracted tourists interested in hiking, fishing, and boating in the nearby rivers and lakes.

"Do you want me to stay here?" Devon asked.

"Would you mind?"

"No. I understand the reluctance."

Remus left his coffee and marched into the store with his usual stride that had several women rubbernecking. Even the men took a double take. Remus definitely stood out, and Devon maintained a constant vigil in case they'd been followed and he'd missed them.

Fifteen minutes passed before Remus exited the building, scanning the area as he returned to the car.

"Let's go." He picked up his coffee and took a couple swallows, keeping his gaze straight ahead. "Take a right at the next corner and drive. Cato's about ten miles out of town."

"Did that have to do with our visit, or was it something else?"

"I have a contact that keeps an eye on Cato and knows if he's up for visitors."

"You make it sound as if he's in a retirement home.

Remus laughed. "He's an extremely old wolf, but don't let his age or appearance fool you. He can kill within seconds. He has periods of time when his memories of the island overwhelm him. A local healer drops off a special herbal tea blend when she gets wind of his troubles. It usually does the trick, but it can take a few days for him to be safe around non-shifters."

"And today?"

"He's been in one of his better moods all week."

"It's a shame we'll be the ones to destroy it."

SIMONE STARED out the window from Devon's office chair, the sun still making its way over the fir trees before spreading its rays on the flower beds. She'd tuned out the team hovering over maps and schedules in front of the fireplace. The cadre and Decker had been reviewing it for an hour before Braden and Elijah joined them. They continued to make minor adjustments on timing, costumes, and boat placements.

Harlow, Trudy, and Roxie would join them in an hour to review their portion of the plan. Cressa and Ginger, who were in the training room, would take a break and join them as well. It was all coming together, but everything hinged on what information Devon and Remus brought back with them.

She hadn't wanted human involvement in any of their plans, but after Cressa had involved Harlow's team to assist in bringing down Gheata and gathering the evidence to exonerate Devon in Boretsky's murder, she had to admit they had skills that couldn't be overlooked.

Devon's move against Lorenzo would be the humans' most dangerous mission yet, so their involvement would be minimal but crucial. Roxie had been instrumental in handling the drone, which provided invaluable information on the island and Lorenzo's defenses. In a series of shots taken over three days at four different times each day, Simone and Sergi had a fair idea of Lorenzo's security, only to discover he'd gotten lazy. Perhaps being on an island where the only approach was by boat or helicopter, he'd come to consider himself unapproachable. But even an island could be overrun.

The question was whether Lorenzo would change his security measures when he opened his home for his party. The team's consensus was that any security build-up would be at the dock and around the manor, extending into the main garden. Sergi doubted they would increase the guard at the building where Hamilton was located, and she had agreed. It would only draw unwanted attention should a guest stray that far.

On the other hand, his guest list were aristocrats, who cared little for intrigue. Was Lorenzo aware of how careless his guests were with his invitations? They couldn't leave it to chance, so the planning and drills all assumed that Lorenzo would be waiting for anyone who might challenge his security. A worst-case scenario was always the best way to plan.

"I think we're ready to have Colantha and Lyra come down and review their part in the plan." Sergi was typing away on his tablet, and she was always curious about what required so much attention. It wouldn't surprise her if he captured each suggestion and question from every meeting. He was a master strategist, honed by years as captain of the guard during his days with Devan and his battle campaigns. She'd lost track of how many times she found him in his office spending hours reviewing meeting notes. If fussing with his tablet made his plans and consultations as invaluable as they were, she wouldn't question his methods.

"Lucas, can you gather them and retrieve Ginger and Cressa from the training room?" Simone pushed her empty espresso cup aside. The second one had left her jittery. "Let's get one full review in before our other guests arrive for lunch."

Lucas had barely left when the siren sounded and her phone chirped.

Everyone jumped up while she grabbed the phone.

"What is it?" she demanded. "We're on our way."

"What's wrong?" Sergi asked.

"It's the safe house."

THE ROAD to the house weaved through the forest and probably felt safe to the shifter, leaving him plenty of room to run. When they broke out of the trees, Devon thought they had the wrong address. He'd been expecting a rundown shack surrounded by tall weeds and siding that barely warded off the weather.

Instead, the building was a quaint cottage that could belong to any grandmother, complete with window boxes filled with colorful late-spring blooms. More flowers surrounded the house and trailed down a stone path that led from the driveway to the front porch. Two outbuildings stood off to the right. One was a barn and the other a small shed that was most likely the well house. A propane tank was off to the left.

The car rolled to a stop as Devon stared at the structure.

"Not what you were expecting?" Remus chuckled.

"Not exactly."

"He's a recluse, not a derelict. He's adapted to the times, rarely eating off the land except for the food he grows in his garden, which is behind the house. He works as a handyman around town for food and to pay the taxes and utilities. Once a week, he goes to town for groceries and dinner at the local bar where he sits in the back, keeping to himself."

"And the town accepts him?"

Remus scanned the yard. "There are a few rogue shifters in

town and, other than looking out for each other, keep their own company. The townspeople have nothing to fear—other than his occasional bad temper." He got out of the car and stretched.

Devon studied the yard and woods a last time before following Remus to the house.

Before they reached the door, Remus gave him a side glance. "I might mention that he's not too fond of vampires."

Devon glared at him as Remus knocked on the door, and before he could respond, the door opened.

"Remus. What the hell are you thinking bringing a vamp to my door?" The grizzly old man was a couple of inches shorter than Devon and just as lean. His long gray hair was tied back in a ponytail, and his equally long beard was surprisingly clean if not in need of a trim. A black patch covered his left eye, and his right eye, the color of onyx, was clear and filled with intelligence and anger.

"He's a friend. This is Devon Trelane." Remus waved toward the older shifter. "This is Cato."

Cato stared at Devon, his good eye squinting as he took him in. Then he grunted and turned around, shuffling into the warm house. "Shut the door behind you, and don't let the cat out."

Devon's brow rose. His Family never had house pets, though he'd been fond of his horses. Even so, he wouldn't have thought a cat and a wolf would get along. He followed Remus as they moved through the house toward the kitchen. A comfortable seating area with a couch and two chairs faced the fireplace where embers slowly burned. Even with the days approaching summer, the forest air was cool.

"I just put coffee on. I wasn't expecting company."

"We won't take much of your time." Remus ignored the kitchen table and took a seat on a barstool at the counter that overlooked a fairly modern kitchen.

The handyman business must be good, or he had a side job Remus didn't feel like sharing. Fair enough. He was only there for information.

"I suppose you stopped to see Hank."

"Yes. He didn't seem very happy."

Cato grunted as he pulled down two mugs from a cupboard and then a plate. "Loretta left him again."

"Ah. How long?"

"About three weeks so far. The pool at the bar is up to four hundred dollars on when she'll return." Cato opened a canister and placed cookies on the plate.

"Hank suffers from PTSD," Remus explained to Devon. "He's fine during the day when he has to be around people. But the nights can be hell when he forgets to take his medication. Loretta puts up with as much as she can then leaves him when it gets too rough. Then Hank goes back on his meds, and Loretta eventually returns."

Cato poured coffee into the mugs and passed them to Devon and Remus, sliding the plate of cookies toward them. "They're oatmeal and raisin. And we drink the coffee straight in this house."

Devon bit into what appeared to be a homemade cookie, nodding his approval. Then chased it with the coffee. "That's truly exceptional."

Cato grunted and wiped down the counter. A cat the size of a small poodle jumped onto the counter. It was a hefty, stocky thing with long gray hair and bright green eyes. It sat on its haunches and stared at Devon, its lazy tail wrapped around its front legs, gently flicking as it judged him.

Cato drank his coffee and stared at the cat. After a minute, the cat stretched its long body, licked its lips, then jumped down. It trotted toward the couch, where it jumped up and curled into a ball.

Cato scratched his jaw as he gave Devon another look. "Wasn't expecting that."

Devon wasn't expecting any of this, either, but his only response was to finish the cookie and take another sip of coffee.

"As I said," Remus started. "We won't stay long, but what we've come to ask won't be an easy subject."

The older wolf scratched his chin then rubbed his eyes. "It's that important?"

"It's the next step in our mission against Venizi."

Cato's gaze turned hard, his fist tightening around his mug until his knuckles turned white and Devon was convinced the mug would shatter. His grip eventually loosened but his eyes lit with an amber glow for a quick second.

Remus didn't move a muscle, and neither did Devon. If Cato was going to attack, this would be the moment.

"What do you want to know?"

Devon felt Remus relax at the same time his own defenses stood down. Remus nodded to Devon. This was his dime.

"We'll be infiltrating the island during a social gathering this evening in order to extricate a prisoner who was kidnapped a long time ago. We can get onto the island without a problem, but a safe exit is proving challenging."

"You want to know about the cave." Cato looked Devon in the eyes, and he didn't flinch from the shifter's steady stare, once again lit with amber.

"Yes."

Cato grunted then ran a hand over the back of his neck. "It's been well over a century since I've been on the island. He might have men down there for security. But with the current technology, he probably replaced the men with cameras and other security nets."

"We expect that and have it covered." When Cato's brow rose, Devon gave him a wicked smile. "We only need to know how to access them."

"You have a hacker?"

Once again, Devon was surprised by the shifter. He wondered which of them would be left standing if Remus hadn't been with him. He nodded at the question. "She's human."

Cato dropped his mug to the counter and let out a long, deep laugh. After several seconds, he wiped his eyes. "A vamp that's working with shifters and humans. I never thought I'd see the day." He pulled a pad of paper and pen from a drawer. "I guess I shouldn't expect anything less from Guildford's son."

"You knew my father?"

"I met him once, the morning after the island rebellion. He was with Graylord, the lead alpha before Remus, at the meeting place where the shifters were in hiding before being transported out of Venizi's immediate reach. I never thought I'd see a vamp help shifters. But Graylord spoke to your father with an ease he'd only give an ally.

"I've heard rumors over the years of shifters and vamps partnering in business ventures. But I also know vamps who would prefer to put their boots on the necks of shifters once again."

Devon nodded. "More than I care to admit."

Cato sketched out the island on the pad. Some of the landmarks Devon recognized from their own plan, but others were new. Cato laid down the pen and tapped a finger at a square that would be the building where Hamilton was being held.

"This building has three floors. Your friend will most likely be on the second floor, but it's possible they could be on the first. The third floor was for storage. There's a door toward the back of that floor. It leads to one of the entrances to the cave." He pointed to another structure halfway between the prison building and the manor. "This is the pump house. There's a door in the basement that leads to the second entrance." He tapped his finger on an X on the far side of the manor's back gardens. "There's a small path at what used to be a hedge of roses. Not sure what's planted there now. If you can find it, it leads to a stone statue of an angel. The statue is probably grown over with vegetation by now. It was the weakest entry point and was too exposed. Venizi might have had that entrance boarded over. All three tunnels converge at the cave that opens to the cove."

"He might have decided the tunnels are too risky and boarded them all up." Remus continued to study the map.

"Maybe," Cato said. "For all his bluster, Venizi falls back to the old ways. His strategy is textbook, and one thing you can be sure will never change—Venizi always keeps a backdoor open for a quick escape. That you can bet on."

Devon and Remus remained quiet on their way to the car. When they were inside, Devon stared at the house.

"He seemed pretty normal to me."

"Today, yes." Remus stared along with him. "Tomorrow, who's to say?"

"Well, luck must be with us that today was a good day." Devon picked up his cell he'd left in the console. His brows knit. "I have several urgent messages." He scrolled through them and found the last one from Simone.

"I have several as well. All from Elijah. Your safe house was hit."

Devon spun the car out of the driveway. He hit a button on his cell. Dread filled him at the sound of endless ringing that played over the interior speakers.

Chapter Thirty-Two

Simone strode through the front door, the cadre on her heels.

"What's happening?" Cressa asked, having to jog to keep up with her. "Is the safe house under attack?"

"Yes," she snapped.

"What can we do?" Elijah had come up quickly from her left.

"Stay here." She stopped at the first of several sedans pulling in front of the manor. She glanced around. "Lyra."

Lyra was dressed in khaki cargo pants and a long-sleeved T-shirt. Colantha was only steps behind her. "I'm here."

"Protect the manor. There might be a secondary attack coming. Elijah, can you stay and help?"

He nodded. "Where do you need Decker?"

Decker seemed at odds. It was apparent he wanted to go to the safe house, but his glances at Elijah told her what she'd always known. He might be a rogue, but his first loyalties would always be with the shifters.

"Keep him with you. He knows the manor well. You'll lead security while we're gone." She turned to Lyra. "If that's alright with you." Lyra was still the current leader of the House.

She nodded vigorously. "Of course."

Simone scanned the cars, the security detail filing into them. She snapped at Cressa, "Get in." When Ginger followed Lucas to the second car, she was about to stop her but thought better of it. Ginger had shown grit during her training that Simone hadn't expected. Taking her into a full attack was dangerous, but so was her role in Hamilton's upcoming rescue. If Lucas had a doubt, he wouldn't have allowed her to go, so she turned her thoughts to the safe house.

Giving the manor one last glance before sliding into the front passenger seat, she closed the door seconds before Sergi stepped on the gas, leading the caravan down the drive.

The safe house was five minutes away, but it took five minutes to get everyone in the cars. Ten minutes was a long time in a vampire attack. Simone texted instructions to the teams during the drive. Before they reached the house, which was on a ten-acre property at the end of a dead-end street with several acres of nature reserve behind it, three cars diverted down a road to the left, which led to a little-known trailhead. They would park the cars and run to the back of the safe house.

The two other homes on the street, almost a quarter mile away from the gate to the safe house, were owned by older couples that Devon paid well for their silence. The safe house itself had been built at the backside of the property.

Sergi led the remaining cars well past the other houses until they were almost on vampire land before pulling the cars into a blockade formation. Vampires scurried from the cars, scattering and immediately racing off into the woods in pairs. The drivers stayed with the vehicles to catch any vampires running away. The exception was Sergi, who ran with Simone straight up the drive.

On an average day, there could be up to ten vampires, maybe a couple more, in residence. It was meant for vampires who had been on missions for the House but needed a place to heal from an assignment or hide until the heat was off. But since the tenuous relationship between House Trelane and House Venizi had deteriorated in the last few months, the number of vampires at the safe house had more than doubled, leaving the current count closer to twenty-five.

Three headless bodies lay inside the main gate, which had been pried open. She recognized one head as part of their security detail, but she didn't recognize the one she stopped at. She glanced at Sergi, who stared down at the third one and shook his head. Not one of theirs.

They jogged on, Simone scanning the area as she ran. Cressa and Mateo followed ten yards behind. As they drew closer to the safe house, the sounds of battle reached her, and she increased her pace.

A vampire sprinted from the right, and Cressa ran to meet him. Crazy human. Simone was tempted to follow, but the vampire smiled when he recognized a human coming for him. He lowered his short sword and slowed as Cressa approached. He looked haggard but didn't have any blood on his blade unless he'd cleaned it off, which was possible.

A few feet from him, Cressa launched herself and hit him in the chest, riding him to the ground like a surfboard—Cressa's words. It was a technique she'd accidentally used once but had honed into her favorite move when approached by a vampire who thought her harmless. Simone couldn't blame the vampires for falling for the trap, there weren't many humans that went up against a vampire, and even rarer a female. But neither did she pity them.

Simone's last glance over her shoulder was of Cressa stabbing the vampire in the throat over and over. Cressa refused to carry a short sword, but after today, Simone expected that to change.

No longer worried about Cressa, she moved on and found one of their security guards. His left arm hung uselessly at his side and blood from a deep cut just below his rib cage dripped on the dirt. He continued to battle two vampires.

She raced toward them, her sword lifting as one turned in time to come at her. He was no match for her blade work, and she took him down with the second swipe of her sword. The second one, a female, was better trained, but not good enough when it was two against her. She turned to face Simone, ignoring the badly injured vampire now behind her.

The guard's anger and lust for vengeance drove him past his injuries. He stepped up behind her and, with his only good arm, swung his blade and severed her head before dropping to the ground. She couldn't stop to check on him and continued on.

Sergi was attacked by two vampires who had run from the house. After watching the fight for two seconds, she moved on. These weren't Venizi's best vampires, and if she had to guess, most were probably halflings. None with the experience of Devon's Family.

This was what she'd expected to find. A test of Devon's security. They couldn't allow any of them to escape.

She crossed the threshold of the house. The place was a mess of destroyed furniture and bloody bodies, most of them headless. Someone sprang from a closet where they'd either been hiding in fear or waiting for some unexpecting vampire.

She felt the slice across her right arm, cutting muscle. The pain was intense, but she compartmentalized it and moved her sword to her left hand. She twisted to the right, and with both hands on the hilt, blocked the sword aimed for her neck.

The vampire had a wild look in his gaze, one she'd seen before. He was on the Poppy. They crossed blades, and she pushed him back. She dropped her sword for a second, which unbalanced him, and kicked out. Her boot hit him in the chest, sending him sprawling. She dispatched him quickly and took a moment to check her injury. She'd taken blood two days prior and smiled when she felt the muscles knitting back together. Her arm would be ready for a sword within the next few minutes.

Though she doubted she'd need it by then.

With the vampires Simone had brought, the fight was over

quickly. The number of vampires Venizi had thrown at them equaled the number housed at the safe house. They lost three total, and based on the reports from her team, not one of Venizi's had escaped.

The drivers left at the gate were now searching for abandoned vehicles, but the attacking force might have been dropped off. Any survivors would be expected to find their own way home or, more likely, Venizi hadn't expected them all to live. The primary goal would have been to take out as many of the Trelane Family as possible.

The vampire they lost at the gate had held it for as long as he could, giving the other two guards the time they needed to alert the house. There hadn't been time to call anyone except the manor's security office. Their other two losses must have fallen at the beginning of the battle or because they'd been cut off without backup.

All of the remaining survivors had some form of injury—some minor, others much worse. Simone had called for the healer and blood donors as soon as the last enemy fell. When she walked back out to the front porch, she abruptly stopped.

She blinked back the tears that unexpectedly stung her eyes.

Cressa was kneeling over the vampire Simone had first come upon with the almost severed limb and bad belly wound. Her wrist covered his mouth as he drank.

When she glanced to her right where another vampire was on the porch, unable to stand, Ginger was doing the same thing.

"What are they doing? Devon would never allow this." She started for Ginger, but Lucas came out of the house and grabbed her arm.

"They're only giving small amounts to the most critically injured until the blood donors arrive." Lucas's grip tightened when she tried to shake him off. When had he become so strong? "It was their idea, their offer to help. Don't take that away from them."

Simone relented and took a step back. "Devon won't be happy."

"Maybe. But it's not his call, is it?"

She caught his gaze and shook her head, resting a hand on his shoulder. "No. Every team member gives what they're able."

Lucas grinned, but it quickly turned to a grimace as he kicked one of the dead vampires in front of him. "Some of them looked to be on the Poppy."

"Yes. Were they all halflings?"

"I don't know. Some might have just been young."

"The Wolf's lab could tell us if we supplied him with some blood." Sergi stepped up behind them. "Lorenzo was testing us."

"Or testing his vampires. Maybe both." Lucas watched Ginger, who was smiling, pat the vampire on the chest before standing. She never glanced their way but followed the porch toward the back of the house, her head turning as she scanned the area for fallen vampires.

"The healer can collect blood from the dead," Simone said. "Did you check on the manor?"

Sergi nodded. "Decker said a couple of cars drove by, but they didn't slow. There was only the driver in both of them."

"Their pick-up?" Lucas asked.

"Most likely," Sergi answered. "I guess Lorenzo hoped for some of them to return."

"And isn't that a bloody shame?" Simone turned to Lucas. "You need to get back to the manor. You have an appointment with Colantha and Hamilton." Simone watched Cressa approach, her face pale. "You've given too much blood."

Cressa shrugged. "I'm still standing. He was the last one but was the worst off." A smile twisted her lips into a mocking smile. "But you better keep an eye on some of them."

"Why is that?" Simone asked.

"You know. In case they go crazy from the tainted blood."

Simone rolled her eyes. "You're just not going to let that go." Cressa had been hurt when Simone had shut her out of cadre business when Devon's beast had control. She'd apologized, but Cressa continued to remind her when the opportunity suited her. Devon told her it was a human thing, and Simone put up with it because it was Cressa. And maybe because she still felt a wee bit guilty.

Cressa patted her shoulder as she passed her on the way into the house. "Still a bit too soon not to."

Simone's phone buzzed, and she glanced at the caller ID. Devon. And he'd apparently left several messages.

"Hello, Devon. It's over. We lost three. There are no surviving enemies. Cressa is fine. Don't rush home, clean-up will take a while." She hung up without waiting for a response. He'd be pissed, but it would stir his beast for their mission.

Chapter Thirty-Three

I STARED out the window at the late afternoon landscape. Long shadows stretched across the yard, and the branches of the sycamore tree swayed with the coastal breeze. I was still in my robe, but my hair and makeup were done.

My fingers traced over the medallion that hung around my neck. It had been a tossup whether to wear it. If I was caught, Lorenzo would find it and take it from me. But Colantha felt it was worth the risk. It was a weapon as much as the dagger that I'd wear in a thigh holster.

If I was caught in a situation where the dagger was of no use, then I'd call Colantha. She would build a construct to include whatever threat surrounded me. It was tricky as we'd have to build the construct together, and it would be quicker with my medallion as a focal point. We tested it a couple of times and it worked. The question was whether I had the control and nerve to close my eyes against the bad guys when they were standing in front of me, swords in hand.

I jumped when the bedroom door swung open, and I spun around.

Devon held his hands up. "Sorry. I didn't mean to startle you."

I gave him a wistful smile. "I'm just jumpy in general."

"It's a good plan, and I'll be with you every step of the way—or most of them."

The plan was for both of us to assist with taking out the guards where Hamilton was being held. Then Devon would circle back and advise the team to start their way toward the boats transporting guests to the mainland.

I didn't like being separated, but it was the fastest way to keep the rest of the team updated. It was too dangerous to wear mics.

"We'll be successful."

I gave Devon a more thorough look. He looked amazing in his tuxedo. His shirt was a silver gray so the color of the thin bodysuit he wore underneath, something each team member would wear, wouldn't show through. The dark color showed off the gold streaks in his hair and brought out the icy blue of his eyes. The effect sent shivers through me, tightening my middle.

If we only had the time.

"What are you smiling at?"

I hadn't realized I was until he mentioned it, and I grinned wider. "You're always so confident before a mission. How do you do that?"

He considered the question, taking it more seriously than I'd intended. Now, I was curious about his answer as he held his hands behind his back and slowly paced the room.

"I've commanded hundreds of missions and have experienced myriad emotions before each one. Most I knew in advance would be an easy victory or a possible defeat based on my assessment of the size of the army or the experience of the opposing commander. The missions now are typically covert, but judging the success of one isn't much different. There is much risk in this plan, but with our latest changes, I feel even more confident of our success."

"And what happens if the other commander is equally assured of their success?"

He smiled and stepped close, his arms pulling me in. "You have to believe in your success to the final moment. Until you can see the defeat in your enemy's eyes. Even when all else seems lost, never give up. Lorenzo has one weakness. He prefers surprise attacks, the hit and run, and when his back is to the wall, he only cares about his own safety. He'd rather scurry away and let his cadre take the hit, or find their own way out. That's not a leader. He depends on strength in numbers and never seems prepared for guerilla tactics. That's why I know we'll be successful. Especially in a room of aristocrats who'll scatter like roaches in the light."

His kiss was urgent, passionate, and demanding. When he pulled back, leaving me a little weak in the knees, his smile was predatory.

"This is our night. Time to take back what was taken from the House Trelane a hundred years ago. I won't disappoint Lyra."

And there was truly nothing more to say after that.

An hour later, after he helped me into my gown made to fit over my bodysuit, we walked downstairs where the team waited for us in the foyer. They looked stunning in their gowns and tuxedos, all of them made to appear similar yet different, right down to the masks that covered half their faces.

The idea was that if someone, specifically Lorenzo, spotted one of us and became curious, the next time they saw us, it would most likely be one of the other teams. The goal was to stay off his radar, but with the expected crowd of guests, it would be impossible for us to have eyes everywhere. Two of the inside teams were assigned to monitor Lorenzo, providing the other two teams the chance to sneak out to the garden.

We had originally planned to meet at a central point to go over the plan one last time with the entire team, but with the meeting with Cato and the raid on the safe house, we ran out of time. We had already reviewed enough that everyone knew each other's part as well as their own. But with the inside teams gathered in the foyer, we walked through it one more time, each person repeating their part to play. Colantha and Lyra, who would remain at the manor, repeated their part once the team reached Hamilton. When Devon was satisfied, we piled into the various sedans that would take us to the docks south of town.

When we arrived, we spaced our cars in between the other arrivals. The private dock that serviced the ferry to Lorenzo's island was on the far end of a string of docks that supported fishing boats and personal crafts. Lorenzo owned two of the buildings surrounding the dock and paid the harbor master to keep other crafts away.

But The Wolf owned several buildings and businesses along the same waterfront. Their purpose was two-fold: keep an eye on who came and went from anywhere along the docks, but also to keep an eye on Lorenzo, the shifters' greatest threat on the vampire Council.

Each of the Trelane sedans carried two vampires and two wolves, except for the ones with me and Ginger, the only humans in the group. Of the four in each sedan, one vampire and one wolf were dressed for the party. The other two wore black camo and would remain behind to aid in the escape, if needed.

Ginger was dressed for a party, but she also wore a bodysuit underneath her gown. She would be one of several diversions that Bella and Jacques had created for the evening. Jacques would oversee the diversions since Bella would be Sergi's date for the evening, while Elijah would be Simone's escort. That made five vampires, two shifters, and myself as the partygoers.

Besides Ginger and Jacques remaining behind at the docks, Remus's businesses along the waterfront housed dozens of vampires and wolves that had been brought in over the last two days in preparation for the evening. Quarters were tight, but from what Decker reported, everyone was getting along, which he deduced was their combined commitment to deliver a devastating blow to Venizi.

Braden, Remus's beta, waved for Devon from beneath a covered tent that had been set up in case of rain. Since the weather was spectacular, the guests lined up closer to the dock as they waited to board the ferry. With a nod from Devon, Sergi, Bella, Simone, and Elijah moved into the crowd to leave for the island.

Lucas and Raquel stayed by the sedan and kept their heads down as if in private conversation.

Devon led me to the canopy.

Braden was dressed as a fancy chauffeur, hat and all, and got right to the point. "Harlow and Trudy's boat left an hour ago. Trudy radioed that the party has started."

That was the signal that they had begun their long distraction that was meant to keep Lorenzo's security watching their boat as a possible threat. It wasn't unheard of for boats to anchor along the coast to watch the sunset, especially on such a lovely evening. Had it been raining, Harlow's team would have dressed as diehard fishermen, but with the lovely weather, drunken partygoers were a better distraction. Music would be blaring, and everyone would have a beer or plastic cup with what observers would assume was an alcoholic drink, especially with a bar in plain sight complete with blender. Harlow and Trudy were well protected with the addition of four vampires and two wolves on the sixteen-foot cruiser. They would remain on the water until they received news that Hamilton was off the island. Then they would head back to one of the southern docks to moor.

"Keep in touch with Harlow. Especially if Venizi's security sends a boat to check on them," Devon said.

"I'm pretty sure Harlow's drunken sailor routine will dissuade anyone from getting too close." I shrugged. "He actually pulls that off pretty well."

Devon smiled. "Of that, I have no doubt. What about Decker's boat?"

"They left shortly after Harlow," Braden answered. "They'll cruise straight for the horizon until they can barely see the island, then make their way north. They'll start their slow approach to the island once dusk settles in, making their final approach once they have the full cover of darkness. They'll be running dark and cruising slow, allowing the sounds of the shore to mask their approach, just as we discussed."

Devon nodded. "Excellent. Are you our main contact?"

Braden nodded. "Unless we have an urgent problem, then you might hear from Harlow or Decker directly."

I'd learned this tactic from Harlow and was a little surprised that Devon used it as well. It was how we'd pulled off the Gheata heist. One person is the earpiece. They monitor all the teams, so there's no cross-chatter or worries about being on the wrong channel. One channel, one central point. But if one of the teams got into trouble, it was faster and safer for the team leader to speak directly with whoever would talk them out of their situation.

We remained under the shelter, a couple of guests with their chauffeur. Nothing too out of the ordinary. After twenty minutes, Braden nodded to Devon and tipped his hat, having received a signal from one of the shifters. "Your first group is on the ferry. Time for you to line up. The second ferry will be docking as soon as this one departs."

Devon shook Braden's hand. "To success."

"To success."

Then Braden strode toward the sedan, where Ginger waited in the backseat. I wished I'd said more to Ginger before departing the manor. But she'd been in Lucas's arms waiting with the others in the foyer, their foreheads almost touching as they gave each other a pep talk, reminding each other of the little details for their respective roles. I didn't want to disturb Ginger getting her game face on. She'd waved at me as she stood by the sedan, a huge grin on her face before Lucas guided her inside.

I took a deep breath as Devon took my hand and led me to the line of guests waiting their turn for the ferry.

DEVON HUGGED Cressa close as they boarded the ferry. Lucas and Raquel had been at the front of the line and would exit first, leaving them the last of the teams to arrive. Cressa's hand trembled when he led her up the path to the manor.

"What's wrong?" Devon asked.

"I never saw the dock before. Not this close. I woke up in the manor and left in a garbage container. It's just bad memories."

He squeezed her hand. "There will be better ones after tonight." He wasn't sure she believed him, but she squeezed back, her grip tightening, and that was enough.

When they reached the manor, they paused, as did several other couples. The sight was breathtaking, and he had to give Lorenzo credit for his ability to grandstand. Spotlights shone from the ground and the roof, providing an amazing, and somewhat otherworldly, view of the landscape and intricate architecture of the manor.

"I never saw it from this view, not at night. And I'm sure I would have seen the bright lights from my windows. This must be just for the event."

"Not surprising. Come, we have time for one slow circle through the crowd to find the other teams. Then we need to get in place."

He breathed a little easier once he handed over his invitation and they moved past security, who appeared to be looking for weapons rather than faces, but there were one or two who searched the crowd, seeming to look beyond the masks. But more guests wore masks than not, which worked to their advantage.

Devon led Cressa through the throng of people who had arrived on two previous ferries. The ballroom was enormous, so it could fit more, but several groups of guests had clustered, making it difficult to get around them. Sergi and Bella were with that group, appearing engaged but not speaking. They both gave slight nods of recognition.

For her height, Simone was surprisingly difficult to find. She had selected flat-heeled shoes, so the women in tall heels were her same height. This was the idea since her height in heels would be a red flag for Lorenzo. Elijah had his arm around her waist and was speaking with another couple, who seemed to hang on his every word. She didn't seem in distress and gave him a gentle nod, so Devon continued on.

He didn't see Lorenzo and knew Cressa would be scanning the crowd for any sign of him. By the time they'd circled back to the entrance, there had been no sign of either Lorenzo or Lucas. They made a left down the hall where other guests were coming and going and wandered through the smaller rooms, spending a great deal of time stopping to kiss. It was their best opportunity to perform quick scans of the room as well as keep their faces hidden as often as possible.

"Thank god," Cressa said when they reached the solarium. "I don't think I could take the stress of another room. At least this one will give us more privacy."

"Except for the voyeurs," he teased.

"I'm going to assume Lorenzo is too busy playing host to join in."

Devon chuckled. "You can never tell who might be in this room of pleasure. Lorenzo allows pretty much everything."

She giggled and tapped her champagne glass against his. "We just need to find the perfect spot in the garden."

Her voice had risen, which gave him the signal that someone was coming. At the same moment, he spotted Lucas across the room. Raquel was glued to his side, his arm was around her waist. She grasped the back of his neck, bringing him down for a long, slow kiss. It was fortunate Ginger wasn't there, and he wondered if Cressa spotted them.

Devon felt a tap on his shoulder and turned to find an ethereal young vampire dressed as a fairy, complete with pointy ears and wings. He thought the pointy ears were supposed to signify elves, but he wasn't up to speed on fantasy, though he'd heard rumors of fairies for centuries but had never seen one. He supposed the same could be said of dreamwalkers, and yet he was standing next to one.

"Is there anything I can do to make your evening magical? Perhaps something in Lorenzo's gardens?" Her provocative smile suggested she'd heard Cressa's comment, which played into their plans.

"It's such a beautiful night, what better place for pleasure than under the stars?" Cressa's tone took on a dreamy quality. "But there are four of us." She covered her mouth and glanced around, lowering her voice. "We like our privacy. We'd prefer no one else joining in."

The fairy vampire nodded in understanding, a twinkle in her gaze. "I have the perfect spot." Then she looked around. "You said there were four of you?"

Cressa glanced around then up at Devon.

He kissed the top of her head. "They're at the door, waiting for us." He nodded to where Lucas and Raquel chatted with the occasional tongue-swallowing kiss. Cressa frowned before quickly replacing it with a smile.

She leaned toward the vampire. "They're not very patient."

The fairy vampire grinned. "On a night like tonight, who can blame them? You'll need to try the punch. It will stimulate all the right places."

"I think we're stimulated enough," Devon added dryly. He kept his tone light, but showed an eagerness to move along, which the hostess quickly picked up on.

"Please, follow me. We'll grab your friends on the way."

Lucas and Raquel came up for air as they approached, and they smiled, their hands continuing to roam each other. If Ginger caught wind of this, Devon wasn't sure who would pay the consequences. Quite likely all of them.

Devon showed Cressa increasing affection that made her giggle all the way to the secluded spot the vampire had led them.

"You'll want to come back to the manor in an hour or so. Lorenzo has a special erotic treat for the crowd." She gave them a wicked wink, gave the males a long perusal, then left.

They held their roles until Devon was able to confirm the vampire was gone.

Devon checked his watch. "We're five minutes early. Do you know where the building is from here? I think it's down that path we walked by."

Cressa nodded. "That's right, but we don't have to backtrack. There's a dirt path the gardeners use that will take us back to the one we want. It will take us by the staff apartments, so it's best to follow the hedges to the left of the path."

The others nodded, and Cressa took the lead. They ran into human staff near the apartment and ducked below the hedge until they passed by. When the building where Hamilton was kept became visible through the bushes, she stopped and pointed to the left and right.

Keeping her voice as low as possible, she said, "If my dream was correct, there's one guard to the left and one to the right."

Devon and Lucas nodded, and, quiet as the night, they split off, going around and coming in from different directions. Devon moved quickly, surprising the vampire guard and putting him in a headlock until he passed out. He dragged him to the entrance of the building, meeting Lucas, who dragged his own vampire.

"Any others?" Devon asked.

"Not that I saw."

Devon whistled lightly, and Cressa and Raquel appeared through the brush. They crouched next to the fallen men as Devon opened the door. It opened quietly, and he rushed in, Lucas behind him. There were two more guards, both knocking their chairs over as they stood, but they weren't fast enough. Devon leaped for one as Lucas jumped for the other. It was over in seconds.

They found a room on the same floor that locked from the

outside. They dragged all four into the room, confirmed there were no other exits or communication devices, and slid the lock home behind them.

Cressa and Raquel were in the kitchen, the door going to the lower levels already open.

Lucas led the way down the stairs with Raquel following him. Devon went next but stopped Cressa before she could take a step.

"Keep an eye out, just in case. I'll only be a second to ensure the cave entrance is open."

She nodded as her foot began tapping.

The stairs led to a large central area with a kitchenette, a table with four chairs, a sofa, and an LCD display mounted on a wall. To the left was a long hallway.

Devon found the door leading to the lower floor and raced down the steps, Lucas and Raquel following. He found the entrance to the tunnel that led to the cave at the far back wall, right where Cato said it would be. The tension that gripped the back of his neck since stepping onto the island released.

He turned to Lucas. "You know the signals."

Lucas nodded. "We'll get him out."

Chapter Thirty-Four

LUCAS AND RAQUEL stared after Devon as he ran up the stairs, then they glanced into the dark tunnel.

"It's a good sign there wasn't anyone down here guarding the door." Raquel stripped out of her gown, leaving her in a long-sleeved bodysuit. A belt and sheathed dagger were at her waist, and another dagger was in a thigh holster. The daggers surprised him. He hadn't fought alongside wolves before and had assumed they shifted to fight. It seemed he had a lot to learn.

"They could be waiting for us on the beach."

"Are all vampires so negative?"

"That wasn't negative, it was considering all possibilities."

"Uh-huh." She stuffed the gown behind one of the storage shelves. "Let's get the package." She didn't wait for him and took the stairs two at a time.

"Slow down." He shouldn't have to tell her more security could have shown up. When he reached the second floor, she was coming down from the first. She was faster than he expected.

"It's clear, but who knows how long before someone notices the outside guards missing."

Lucas turned down the hall that led to the cells. There were three doors on each side with a viewing port to peer inside each room. He opened the first one, and though no light flickered, he could tell it was empty.

Raquel opened the one across from him, and they checked the next two, all of them empty. He waited for Raquel to check the last room on her side, and she turned to him, shaking her head as she moved to stand next to him, pulling out the dagger at her waist.

He'd expected the other cells to be empty, but if someone had been in there, Devon had given him the decision whether to release anyone they found.

Lucas opened the last viewport, his eyes moving directly to the candle flame burning on a small table in the corner, then to the chair next to it that faced the dark window. The outline of a man huddled there. How many times over the decades had he stared at a world of sky and sea, perhaps occasionally seeing a ship pass by, sailing to places he would never go?

Until now.

Lucas tapped lightly on the door, not wanting to scare him. He'd only met Hamilton once in a construct, and though he'd been helpful and appeared strong, that was only a dream.

"Hamilton. It's me, Lucas. You remember meeting me?" He waited, seconds they probably didn't have ticking away. He was ready to ask again when Hamilton finally spoke.

"Of course. It was only yesterday, wasn't it?" His voice was scratchy from disuse but sounded strong.

"I have a friend with me. Her name is Raquel, and she's here with me to help get you out."

He turned his head, and even in the low light, Lucas's excellent vision could make out the question in his gaze. The man might think he's still dreaming all of this.

"This is real, Hamilton. I'm going to open the door."

Without waiting for another word, Lucas removed the bar over the door. He glanced at Raquel. "Stay by the door unless I call you over."

She nodded then turned back to face the hall, the dagger still in her hand.

Lucas opened the door and stepped inside, pausing for a moment to scan the chamber. The construct Colantha had created was almost a complete replica. The bed was against the wall to his right. A table with a single chair next to an overstuffed bookcase and a screen in a far corner that hid the chamber pot completed the scene. Except for the chair where Hamilton sat.

The room smelled of mold, earth, and human waste. They probably only cleaned out the buckets once a day, if he was lucky. The room was chilled with no fireplace.

Hamilton kept a wary eye on him as he approached.

Lucas kept his hands out, palms open to show he carried no weapon and meant no harm.

"I don't mean to push, but we have a bit of a time crunch in order to make it to the boat."

Then Hamilton's expression partially crumbled. A single tear rolled down his cheek.

"Are you dressed and ready?"

Hamilton stood, and though he was thin, he appeared strong, or strong enough not to require assistance. He held a bag that appeared stuffed. What the man could be bringing with him, Lucas didn't know and wasn't going to question. As long as it wasn't a pile of suitcases, the man could take whatever he could hold.

Lucas waited for Hamilton to come to him, then he held out his hand. "It's a pleasure to meet you in person."

Hamilton's reach was tentative, but he took Lucas's hand, his grip firm, and another tear escaped.

"I can't begin to know what you're feeling, but you need to hold it together until we get to the boat. Can you do that?"

Hamilton nodded.

"I hate to break up the meet and greet," Raquel's voice filtered from the hallway. "But we need to get moving."

Hamilton wasted no time heading for the open door with Lucas sticking close behind. Hamilton slowed when he peeked out the door, and only seeing Raquel, stepped out, glancing back to Lucas, possibly for assurance.

"Raquel, this is Hamilton."

She gave the long-term prisoner a nod with a bit of a smile before it turned into a grim line. "Nice to meet you. I'll take the lead. You need to stick close to me. Can you do that?"

Hamilton gave her a long look. "You're a shifter." His voice was scratchy and raw.

A touch of surprise lit Raquel's gaze, and she nodded. "Is that a problem?"

"Of course not. Just a surprise."

Lucas thought she grinned before she hurried down the hall. He shut the door behind him and placed the bar over it. It might slow down whoever followed them if they bothered to check the cell.

He rushed to catch up with the two who were already at the top of the stairs leading to the lower floor. Raquel had grabbed an oil lamp from a table and was lighting it with a match from a nearby box. She stuck a few more matches in her pocket and moved quickly down the stairs.

Hamilton concentrated on each step, a hand braced on the rough wall as he clutched his bag to his chest. When Lucas reached the bottom, Raquel was already at the open door to the tunnel entrance. Lucas kept shutting doors behind them as they went in hopes of making Lorenzo's security pause to question their route. They'd moved twenty yards down the dark tunnel when the siren sounded.

Raquel stopped and looked back. "Was that us?"

Lucas checked the walls and floor behind him. "We must have triggered something our security hack didn't catch. Let's move."

Raquel's progress quickened, and Hamilton stayed close on

her heels until they were all running. Lucas caught Hamilton any time he stumbled.

The tunnel was estimated to be a couple hundred yards long, and it twisted around curves on its downhill trajectory. Before he knew it, the tunnel emptied into a small cave, and they were assailed by the scent of sea air and damp earth.

He thought he heard Hamilton give a small cry, but he pushed the man forward until Raquel stopped at the edge of the cave.

"I don't see anyone." She doused the lamp before taking a step outside, staying low.

Hamilton and Lucas stepped out from behind her. The boat should have already been there. He took a few steps then stopped short when he saw a figure in the dark.

"It's about time. You're ten minutes late." Decker's tone was urgent. "Looks like you got the package. Watch your footing, it's pretty rocky."

Raquel took a few seconds to relight the lamp. She walked next to Hamilton, lending him an arm as they worked their way over the uneven ground toward the water and what Lucas could now make out beyond the light as a small wooden boat. Two shifters stood next to it.

He followed behind Decker and was almost to the boat when Raquel called out with a grunt. She dropped to one knee, Hamilton falling hard against her. She stayed upright and managed to stand, using Hamilton as a prop.

Lucas turned around to see vampires running for them. Lots of them. Too many.

Decker grabbed Hamilton, tossing him over his shoulder. Lucas took Raquel's arm, and she grabbed on, dropping the lamp as they ran. By the time they reached the boat, which was only a few footsteps away, Decker was in the boat with Hamilton. Raquel leaped in, and Lucas pushed with the two shifters to get the boat in the water.

Once the boat was away from shore, Decker started the motor

as the shifters picked up oars to row them into deeper water. Bullets pierced the side of the boat. When another spray of bullets came, the shifters returned fire. Lucas threw his body over Hamilton as he pulled Raquel down. She grunted in pain.

"Are you hit?" Lucas asked. He glanced over at Decker, who bent low as he steered the boat, keeping his eyes forward. A shifter, blood dripping down his arm, kneeled next to him. He changed magazines and continued to fire as the boat moved away from the island and the range of the vampire's weapons.

"It's the knife." Raquel leaned on a hand as she reached for her back, but she wasn't able to reach the handle of the knife Lucas hadn't seen.

"Is this from when you first dropped?" He asked.

She nodded.

Lucas held a hand on her back, keeping her low so he could see where the knife had lodged. It hit her shoulder blade and must be stuck in the bone.

"Take three large breaths," he commanded, and she turned her head to give him a growl but did as he asked. On the second breath, he pulled the blade out.

"You said count three." She panted, and he waited for the blood, but it was nothing more than a trickle.

"I did."

"Asshole." This time her growl was deeper, and, for a minute, he thought she might shift, but she held on until the boat hit the side of the cruiser.

Another shifter and vampire waited on the cruiser and began pulling them from the boat. One of the shifters had taken a stray bullet, and one of the other shifters took him into the salon.

Once they were all on the cruiser and the boat tied on, Lucas settled Hamilton and Raquel near the injured shifter. Then he met Decker at the cockpit.

"We can't stay for Devon and Cressa."

Decker took the controls and turned the cruiser north, the

lights from the island fading behind them. "They'll have to find their own way off the island."

DEVON RACED up the stairs toward me and when he drew closer, he had a quirky smile.

"Was there a problem?" Though I wasn't sure why he'd be smiling about it.

"I was just noting how ravishing you looked."

I rolled my eyes. Of all times to notice. "Did they get Hamilton out?"

"I don't know. But the entrance to the cave was exactly where Cato said it would be."

He moved past me to the front door and glanced out. All was clear, but my heart raced, remembering the dream. He shut the door behind us, and this time turned left back toward the staff apartment. I held my breath as we ran, waiting for the spotlight and sound of gunfire.

When we reached the spot where the fairy vampire had left them, I stopped to catch my breath.

"Are you alright?"

I nodded. "Catching my breath. I had to get past the point of my dream—" I straightened and shrugged. "Just needed to get past it."

Devon watched me for a moment and then took my hand. "We changed it. We're okay."

All I could think was—for now. We walked hand in hand out of the garden, straightening our clothes from our run, but anyone else who noticed us would think we'd just returned from a dalliance.

The first team I spotted was Sergi and Bella, who loitered inside the solarium behind a potted palm tree. We let them leave first and trailed a good distance behind them. Simone and Elijah were still in the ballroom, and Devon nodded as we passed them.

When we were in the thick of the crowd, Sergi and Bella grew close.

"I've seen Lorenzo a couple of times, up on the second floor." Sergi turned when Bella tapped him on the shoulder and accepted a glass of champagne. "There seems to be a lounge up there and probably another bar where he entertains his friends. He comes to the balcony with a redhead every fifteen minutes or so to look over the crowd, waving at some, and calling others upstairs. We'd just moved to the solarium before you arrived. Simone and Elijah always seem to find a large group to hide in."

"Has Lucas signaled yet?" I shifted from foot to foot, my gaze shooting around the room, watching for any sign Lorenzo's vamps might be on to us.

"It's too early yet. He was going to wait until he made it to the boat." Devon put an arm around me. "You need to settle down, you look as nervous as a rabbit waiting for the hound to dart in."

I leaned against him, but I couldn't help lifting my gaze to the second floor. "Has anyone seen Lorenzo anywhere but the second floor?"

Bella shook her head. "Not while we were here."

Devon checked his burner phone. I was probably making him nervous. They quieted as they watched the crowd.

After a few minutes, Bella asked. "How about a drink?" She stopped a passing server and handed glasses to me and Devon. No one drank, but I agreed it looked odd without having one.

Then I spotted two vamps climbing the stairs to the second floor. They appeared to be in some disagreement, and then I chuckled.

"What is it?" Devon asked.

"Those vamps heading up the stairs." The white-blond hair was a dead giveaway. "I think that's Erik and Ulrik."

"Who?" Bella asked.

"The Oslo twins."

Sergi and Devon both turned to look. When the twins reached the second floor, they leaned against the railing and gave the crowd a slow scan. They were smiling, and whatever they'd been arguing about no longer seemed important. I would lay odds they were betting on something.

Then their gazes stopped on our group. Erik lifted his glass half filled with a clear liquid as if in a toast. Vodka, if I had to guess.

He smiled. Neither brother wore a mask, which didn't surprise me. It was difficult to hide that blond hair. Then they set their drinks on the railing, and each pulled something out of their pockets and shook it out. They held a thin black mask, and they slid them on.

Erik crooked a finger at me.

"What could they want?" Sergi asked.

"And how did they spot you?" Devon glanced around, his grip around my waist tightening.

"Will they cause a scene if you don't go?" Bella asked.

"I don't know, and I don't think so. They've helped me out of situations before." I glanced up at Devon. "I think I should go up and see what they want."

"That's not a good idea," Sergi said.

Devon kept his gaze on them, then he glanced at the phone. "Five minutes. No more. And stay where I can see you."

"Promise."

I took my time climbing the stairs, managing to find a couple to walk with. I complimented her on her dress and mask as a way to make it appear we were friends.

When I reached the top and approached the brothers, Erik grabbed me as if we were long-lost family. He whispered in my ear, "Venizi knows you're here."

Chapter Thirty-Five

ERIK'S WORDS had barely registered, and I didn't have time to look down for Devon when the sirens sounded. The room silenced in seconds as the guests looked at each other then up to the second floor where Lorenzo should be. He wasn't anywhere I could see, but he had to be close.

"How did you know?" I managed to stammer.

"We've been schmoozing with him since we arrived in the States."

"What?" I'd pulled back. No doubt my face had to be a combination of shock and betrayal. But then, neither brother had declared their affiliation with Devon. And I'd never bothered to ask.

"Don't fear us, my lovely Cressa. We were sent to gather information on the state of the Council and news of the Poppy. Do what you need to do and get out quickly. And tell Trelane, the House Aramburu sends their regards."

Then, the two disappeared into the crowd. Vamps who looked suspiciously like security began closing ranks as the guests stood around like a herd of cattle. Then someone—did I recognize that voice?—shouted fire, and all hell broke loose as a stampede started for the multiple exits.

I scanned the area, searching for Devon. Some guests were fleeing through doors and even windows, yet others had turned their back to the crowd and faced the security forces as fights erupted throughout the ballroom.

I searched for my own exit and narrowly missed a vamp running for me. I recognized him as one of Lorenzo's, although I couldn't recall his name or most likely never heard it. I ducked as he made a grab for me, then came up swinging as I kicked, aiming for his knee but catching his thigh instead. He cringed but didn't stop as he swung a fist. I blocked it and brought my knee up, clipping him in the groin. He bent over enough for me to land a solid hit to his chin with the heel of my palm. Blood flew. He must have bit his tongue. Taking advantage of his momentary pause, I kicked the outside of his knee, and he went down.

Not waiting for him to get back up, I raced for the stairs, and my blood turned cold. Devon was fighting off two vamps, and a third was approaching through the crowd from behind him. From where I stood, it was easy to see his focus was set squarely on Devon. I caught the flash of silver. A dagger. Or worse, a sword.

I glanced around, knowing I'd never make it down the stairs and through the crowd in time. A jump from the second floor wouldn't be wise. My gaze caught on the drapes that had been tied against thick columns that rose to the ceiling. They were held back by a thick cord that curved around them, making a lovely design. Then I saw the rope used to release the fabric.

I yanked the skirt off my ball gown and pulled the dagger from my thigh holster. I cut the rope, and the drape unraveled, freeing the cord. I quickly estimated the length I'd need and jumped onto the railing.

The vamp was getting closer to Devon, and he did indeed have a short sword.

I jumped.

I undulated my body to pick up speed and give me time to direct my swing. I was going to miss him by inches. I stuck my arm out, dagger in hand, and sliced along the vamp's back. It wasn't enough to kill, but he stumbled, falling into two other vamps who appeared to be fighting each other. One of them saw the sword and kicked it out of the vamp's hand.

As I flew by, I was able to see that Devon had managed to cripple one of his adversaries and had stabbed the other one in the heart. Neither were dead but would be down for the rest of the night.

Unable to stop my momentum, and with no safe place to land, my wide arc was taking me right into a group of Lorenzo's security. Most of them weren't paying attention, too busy deciding what to do with the unruly crowd. With my dagger clutched in one hand, I managed to pull my legs up, my stomach muscles and left bicep screaming, and slammed into the center mass like a bowling ball hitting the strike zone.

The vamps who didn't fall were pushed off balance, giving me space to work with. I released the cord and hit the floor, somersaulting and rolling back up to my feet. I had to admit, Simone's grueling training was paying off. Once on my feet, I kept moving, not taking the time to look back. When the vamps regrouped, I wouldn't be able to outrun them. I had to get space between us.

One thing we all agreed on before starting our mission was that we all had our roles, and we knew our specific exit routes. We would run the game, trust each team member could get their job done, and find a way off the island.

I ran down a short hall then made a right, heading for my assigned exit. I sighed with relief when I spotted Devon and Sergi at the other end.

As I drew closer, Sergi pulled out a dagger and shouted, "Drop."

I didn't hesitate, hitting the deck sideways and keeping my legs straight, my arms crossed over my chest as my forward momentum rolled me down the hall for several revolutions. When I stopped, I took a quick look behind me. A vamp had been chasing me, but he'd stopped to grab his throat where a blade stuck out. He dropped to his knees.

I pushed myself up and scrambled for the door that Devon held open for me. I cleared the door in time to see Sergi swing his sword, taking the head of a vamp in the black colors of the security team. Several fights had broken out on the wide expanse of lawn and another inside one of the plant beds, crushing petals and leaves.

"This is where I leave you, friend." Sergi held out his arm, and Devon clasped his forearm as Sergi gripped his.

They pulled each other close. The only thing missing was thumping a fist on their chest like some ancient gladiators. But the sentiment was the same. My gut twisted, understanding hitting me. They were acknowledging that either of them might not get off the island. I blinked away the burn in my eyes and blew out a breath.

Sergi looked my way. "See you on the other side."

I nodded, unable to gather enough spit to respond out loud. But he understood. He turned and ran, glancing right and left as he disappeared into the darkness of the garden.

Devon grabbed my hand, and we ran. And as we dodged down different paths and through hedges, only one thing rang in my head. Please let the entrance to the cave be there.

GINGER HAD WATCHED LUCAS, Cressa, and the others board the ferries that took them out of her reach. There was to be no phone chatter. Each team would be on their own to perform their tasks and then find their way off the island. An island that belonged to a vile enemy. She glanced around the sole limo they'd brought and noted the bar.

One little drink wouldn't hurt. Besides, the scent of alcohol on her breath would only help later. She opened a cabinet and found what she was looking for on the first try. Tequila should do the trick. She hugged it to her as she opened a second cabinet. Several types of glasses greeted her, and she grabbed a short scotch glass. She poured a quarter glass and set the tequila back in its spot. The soft leather seats were heavenly, and she pulled her legs beneath her before taking her first sip.

The door across from her swung open, making her jump, somehow managing not to spill a drop. Jacques climbed in and shut the door.

He glanced at the glass and sneered. "You shouldn't be drinking."

"How do you know it's not tea?"

"I can smell it."

She slammed the heel of her palm against her forehead. "Of course. Well, I'm just a simple human, so I forget these things." Her sarcastic tone was for relieving her own stress. She'd been around the vamps long enough to know they tolerated humans and their strange behaviors.

"There's nothing simple about you." He sat back, leaning his head back, his eyes unblinking as he stared at the ceiling.

She wasn't sure if that was some type of compliment or a dig, so she ignored it. "You're worried about her."

"She knows what she's doing."

"So does Lucas, but I worry just the same."

She thought she heard a grunt, which she took as acceptance, and turned to stare out her side window. Remus's warehouse was starting to get busy. A couple of cars pulled into the lot, but only two or three shifters got out. She assumed they were shifters because they walked straight for the warehouse, bumping fists as they greeted the others. But single shifters were coming in as well, walking down from the main street or from farther down the marina.

Several minutes passed, her drink gone, and her nerves settled, she leaned down to glance out Jacques's window.

"Lorenzo's vamps seem to be restless."

Jacques turned toward the window, then sat up, turning his attention to the front windshield. "Remus's boats are coming in."

Remus had a dozen fishing boats that worked out of the marina, and having three come in at one time wasn't unusual for the end of the day. But these boats hadn't been out fishing. They'd been docked at a small harbor farther south. The only thing the boats held in their holds were shifters. At least a dozen on each boat. There would be about three dozen more in the warehouse.

"How many vamps are out there?"

"It's hard to tell. They come and go from their clubhouse. But at least a couple dozen, probably more. Venizi demands order."

She snorted. "Then he's not going to be too happy in about an hour."

Jacques laughed. "Let's get you in position while they're focused on the shifters."

They got out of the limo on her side, keeping them out of the main line of sight to Lorenzo's clubhouse, which was more a working warehouse similar to Remus's on the opposite side of the ferry entrance. The only difference was that a portion of Remus's warehouse was a small food stall that was busy all day long providing breakfast and lunch to the fishermen and tourists.

Lucas told her Remus had done that specifically so Lorenzo's vamps would have a difficult time harassing them if there were tourists around. Even without it, Lorenzo would have to be careful not to attract attention, especially with him being on the Council. But with it being past time for most boats to have returned, and the shops closed hours ago, it would be rare for a tourist to be out.

And tonight, security was tight on the vamp side of the dock.

The two of them walked slowly to the far side of Remus's warehouse where a baby blue VW Beetle waited. It was a sad shame.

"I think the tequila will add realism." Jacques conceded as he opened the door for her.

She climbed in and adjusted the seat and the mirrors. Then she turned on the radio and tuned it to a 1980s station. She glanced around.

"Where's my purse?"

When something bumped her shoulder, she found Jacques smiling at her as he handed her a clutch purse.

"Thank god. An actress isn't believable without her props." She opened it, plucked out the red lipstick, and applied it. Then she rubbed part of it off. She pulled her shirt off at an angle so a bra strap showed, and mussed her hair so it looked good but a touch damaged. Then she rubbed her eyes gently and looked at Jacques. "Well?"

"Rub your eyes one more time."

She did, and then he nodded his approval. He sat on a nearby wall and waited. She turned the music down low, left the car door open, and waited for the signal.

Fifteen minutes crept to thirty, then an alarm sounded. It could have been a car alarm, but Jacques checked his phone. "The ferry is on its way."

"I thought we had another half hour."

"Something must have gone wrong." He was on his phone, typing then reading, then typing more. "Decker was in place but no signal as to whether they retrieved the package."

"Someone must have been caught." She tried to keep her tone level but based on Jacques's raised brow, she wasn't successful.

"Not necessarily. Lorenzo probably has security alarms set, some most likely in places no one would suspect. We stick to the plan."

Ginger nodded and rubbed her stomach. It was fortunate on her part she hadn't eaten anything more than oatmeal for breakfast and an apple and chips for lunch. But the tequila was sitting on an empty stomach.

They waited another twenty minutes until the ferry arrived. While it was mooring at the dock, Jacques closed her door then bent to talk to her through the open window.

"Hit as many as you can."

She nodded. "I was pretty good at bumper cars." She turned up the music to blaring and rolled up her window.

She backed up and turned the vehicle toward the main road then made a sharp left that took her to the docks. She rolled down the window as she began her drive down the slight incline to the parking lot. The loud music drew the attention of several vamps.

The guests were just walking off the ferry, and several of them appeared panicked.

Selecting the best spot for the most damage and with the least amount of risk to her, she tightened her seatbelt and pressed down on the pedal. She drove straight into two cars that had been parked nose to tail. The force of the hit slid the cars into the next two rows.

She was prepared, and though the hit was forceful, no airbag deployed since the shifters had removed it. The seatbelt would cause a righteous bruise, and all she could do was hope it helped the cause. She opened the door and tried to get out, but her seatbelt was still on. By then, a swarm of vamps surrounded her while she tried to undo the seatbelt.

"God dammit." She slurred her words a bit. "It won't let me go." She slammed her fists on the steering wheel.

A vamp leaned in with a knife that spiked her angst, but he used it to cut her seatbelt.

"Hey, you ruined it." She pushed him back and started to get out but gagged as if she might throw up. The vamps backed up ten feet. Then she managed to get out but staggered as she glanced around. Almost a dozen vamps surround her. Not bad.

"Where's the reception?" When no one responded, she continued, "You know. Married couple, big white dress, I think she might be stumbling." She winked at them. "We had a few drinks before the wedding and then another couple before we left for the reception. Nerves and all."

She pushed her way through the vamps and stumbled to the front of the car. "Oh no." She bent over the undamaged part of the hood in a drunken hug. "My baby." She looked up. "What were all these cars doing here? The reception isn't supposed to have that many people."

An arm grabbed her. "What were you thinking?"

Ginger looked up into the eyes of a gorgeous man. Actually, a shifter. The vamps must have known, but they all backed up except for one, who eyed Braden suspiciously.

"You know this woman?" the vamp asked.

"Yes." Braden ran a hand over his head, ruffling his hair. "She was supposed to wait for me to drive. I had to find another car before I could catch her. Apparently, too late." He pulled her away from the vehicle. "Come on, sweetheart, let's get you in my car so you can rest while I take care of this."

"Just give me your name and number," the vamp asked.

Ginger noticed another vamp taking a picture of her license plate from the back of her car before taking one of Braden's plate. Fortunately, both vehicles had been bought from a used car dealer with fake identifications. Lorenzo would get nothing from this interaction, but as she was dragged to the other car by Braden, she glanced over and saw Elijah and Bella hurrying from the ferry. They ran toward a vehicle close to the shifter's warehouse, their masks still on but being stripped off as Elijah held Bella by the arm as if trying to get away from Lorenzo's disastrous party.

Braden put her in the car and gave the vamp a business card she assumed had the fake address of their fake persona.

The fleeing guests had the vamps riled up when an explosion rocked the dock. One of the boats on the far side of Venizi's dock had exploded. The vamps forgot all about them, and Braden jumped into the driver's side and pulled out of the parking lot.

"That was perfect timing." Ginger ran her fingers through her hair, trying to pat down the earlier mess she'd made of it. When Braden grunted at her comment, she rolled her eyes. "I wasn't sure we were getting out of that. They knew you were a shifter, right?"

He nodded, turning down the street after driving around the block. "They can smell us."

"You mean your doggy scent?" she teased.

He shook his head. "Lucas warned me about you." He drove toward the warehouse that opened as they approached. He pulled the car inside and drove to a spot toward the back where a large cargo van waited with a ramp. After he drove up the ramp and put the car in park, he shut off the engine and turned in his seat.

"The vamps can smell everything. The perfume you're wearing, what you ate for lunch, and the tequila you drank to ease your nerves." He glanced down at her body. "And other things."

She swallowed. "I guess I knew that. You know I didn't mean any disrespect. My mouth gets ahead of me sometimes. But I know what Remus, Elijah, and Raquel are doing for Cressa and Devon."

He grinned. "If that's the worst you can do, no one will take offense. But I wouldn't suggest saying it to Remus."

She felt her face pale. "I'm not completely daft."

"I don't know. You're a human in the middle of what's becoming a vamp and shifter war. You can't be normal."

She relaxed and laughed. "Now that I can agree with. Shall we see if our teams have returned?" She opened the door and squeezed out of the small space between the car and the van.

They walked to the far side of the warehouse where Elijah, Bella, and Jacques waited for them.

"Your explosive was perfect timing," Braden said. "I think the vamps were getting suspicious."

"They're checking everyone that's coming off the ferry," Bella replied. "I don't think we would have gotten by them without it."

"Where's Simone and Sergi?"

"Simone was waiting at the meeting spot and didn't want to

leave without Sergi." Bella had slipped her arm through Jacques's. "They'll have to find a different way off the island."

"Which is exactly what we did."

The group turned to see Simone striding across the warehouse. Sergi walked several paces back, talking with Mateo.

"How?" Elijah asked.

"We found another boat. I believe they call it a go-fast boat."

"Lorenzo won't be happy about that," Bella said. She smiled, something Ginger never saw her do much. She turned and gave Sergi a long look. "What's wrong?"

"Decker got Lucas, Raquel, and Hamilton off the island. But Lorenzo's security showed up and they barely got away."

Simone frowned. "Which means Devon and Cressa are on their own."

Chapter Thirty-Six

I PEERED through the leafy hedge and recognized the wooden structure, never knowing it was a pump house. Although I had no reason to have known. Two vamps were stationed by the door. Devon had left me where I was while he checked the perimeter.

"There are only these two." Devon slid next to me. "We need a diversion."

"I can do that." I ran my fingers through my hair, messing it up to what I hoped was something akin to bedhead. Then I rubbed some dirt on my face before pushing my way through the hedge, limping and holding my side, as I heaved for my next breath. An old iron bench caught my eye, and I made to sit down before glancing up and pretending I'd just seen the vamps. Instead of sitting, I backed up, then trotted away, accentuating the limp. I'd pulled my mask off once we were outside. At this point, I was pretty sure Lorenzo knew who had busted up his party.

As predicted, whether they recognized me from being on the island before, or they'd been ordered to detain anyone they found, they came after me. I thought one would remain by the door, and I'd have to deal with them. I grinned when they both came at me.

They were almost on top of me before the first one was tackled and stabbed several times in the lower back—a kidney shot. He'd be down long enough. The second one turned when he heard his mate making gurgling sounds, but Devon was already on his way to him, and he stabbed this one in the heart and twisted the knife, once again immobilizing the vamp. He would need a great deal of blood to heal completely.

We ran back to the pump house. Inside, it was larger than it appeared with massive water tanks that must be filled weekly with water brought from the mainland. That would explain why most of the laundry was sent out for washing. Water would be a precious commodity on this small island if they weren't able to drill a freshwater well, though there were large cisterns on the far side of the island that were probably used to store rainwater.

I found the door that led downstairs, where several dim lights lit the place. Huge generators pumped electricity for the island. I glanced at Devon. This would be one way to make life more difficult, but Devon shook his head. I shrugged as I remembered vamps and shifters had excellent eyesight in the dark, so I'd be the only one who suffered.

No one guarded the scarred wooden door at the back of the basement. Devon pried it open, and the first thing that hit me was the damp, earthy smell of what I imagined a grave would smell like six feet under. I thought I picked up the scent of the sea, but my imagination was playing tricks.

"Stay directly behind me, and I'll help you around any obstructions. Otherwise, just walk normally." He took my hand and led me into the darkness.

"Do you know how long the tunnels are?"

"A hundred yards or so. Maybe a bit longer."

I checked my watch. We were behind schedule, and Devon moved quickly but cautiously. He slowed several times to talk me over or around obstacles, and I tripped over small rocks, but Devon kept me upright.

It seemed like we were walking forever before he came to an abrupt stop.

"Are we there?" I whispered, not sure if there were vamps or some other impediment, but then I smelled it. The salty air. And if I listened, I could vaguely hear the sound of waves. He moved slowly now as we crept toward the exit to the beach.

A low light emanated from the entrance, the quarter moon providing enough light for me to make out shadows and rocks.

"Stay close to me. I can't see them, but I don't think we're alone."

"Decker and Lucas?"

"I don't think so."

Great. More vamps. Lorenzo must have been expecting this, or just covering his bases. Did Lucas, Raquel, and Hamilton escape, or were they lying dead on the beach?

We crept out, keeping to the side of the cave, and then once outside, stuck close to the wall of the cliff that ran straight up. There would be no exit that way without climbing gear. I squinted where I heard the soft waves hit the shore but didn't see a boat.

Two shadows raced from the far side of the beach, dodging around rocks, and Devon ran to meet them. I followed and whipped out my dagger, preparing for their attack strategy, and almost face-planted into the rough terrain.

One of them turned toward Devon, who had taken a defensive posture with no weapon. Pure brute force was his only offense. It typically worked.

The second one sported a sloppy grin if I was seeing him well enough in the low light. He looked like someone who'd drawn the long straw and I was his reward. He ran full bore, not slowing the closer he got. I stood my ground until his smile began to fade, no doubt wondering if I knew something he didn't. I did.

When he was within striking distance, I dropped to dodge his grab and twisting to my left, swung out my right leg, tripping him. I hated the move because it would leave a lovely bruise on my shin, but it was effective. I jumped up and slammed my foot on his back, wishing I'd worn more substantial shoes. But it did the job, and I stabbed his lower back, aiming for a kidney. He went slack, and I assumed I hit my mark.

I turned to find Devon rushing toward me, but when he was within a couple of feet, he turned around. And I saw them.

A dozen vamps came at us. There was no way we could beat back that many. They didn't rush but branched out to circle us. I glanced at Devon, and he nodded.

I wish I'd practiced what I was going to do with more than a handful of willing vamps. But I had to believe, so I sheathed my dagger and reached for the necklace that hid beneath my bodysuit. I grabbed the medallion in my fist and, taking a deep breath to settle my nerves, closed my eyes and called for Colantha.

Within seconds, a construct appeared.

We were in a dark circular ceremonial room. Long, narrow black tapestries hung on the stone walls and circled the room, each with a large red graphic symbol that repeated in threes—the Blood Poppy, an ibis, and a dagger. Spotlights were above each tapestry, illuminating the symbols. The floor was stone, and the only furniture were fifteen tall-backed, heavy wooden chairs that repeated the circle formation in the middle of the room. Colantha, Devon, and I took up three, and Lorenzo's vamps occupied the other twelve.

The vamps were wide-eyed as their eyes bounced around the room, maybe searching for a door where there wasn't one. The only way in and out of this construct was through Colantha. Not that the vamps could move. They were held against the chairs as if some invisible force were at play. And in a way, that was a fairly accurate assessment.

Colantha's eyes were pure white. I'd never seen that before, but she must be using a massive amount of power to hold the twelve vamps in place. Suddenly, one disappeared, and a minute later, I screamed as something slammed down on my right hand, and I heard the crunch of bone. Tears sprang to my eyes as I comprehended what had happened. One of the vamps had somehow escaped and must have stomped on my hand or slammed a rock on it. But if they'd hoped to pull me out of the construct, I refused to give them the satisfaction.

Seconds after I'd given the blood-curdling yell, Devon disappeared.

"Stay with us, Cressa. Trust in Devon."

I held my breath, then released it in short gasps as the pain throbbed mercilessly, and when I glanced down, several fingers were clearly broken, already swelling along with tinges of a bruise. Then the pain was gone.

My gaze flashed to hers.

She shook her head. "I can't heal you, but I can remove the pain, at least temporarily."

I nodded. I'd take whatever relief she could provide.

"Can they talk?" I pointed my chin toward the vamps.

"No. Nor can they hear. Well, that's not exactly correct. They can't hear us; they're currently listening to static white noise. It will give Devon the chance to sneak up undetected."

"Did you release Devon?"

"Yes."

"Do you know if Lucas got Hamilton out?"

"I don't. Everyone has been radio silent."

A soft gurgle from my right made me turn my head. A thin line of blood appeared at the neck of one of the vamps. And he disappeared with a pop. Then a second one, and a third.

"What's happening?"

"Your vampire is removing the enemy from the playing field."

With increasing speed, each vamp's neck began to bleed, and then they disappeared with the same popping sound. I assumed that was an indication the vamps were being sucked out of the construct as Devon either maimed, or mostly likely, took their heads.

When the last one was gone, Colantha caught my gaze. "Prepare yourself. The pain will return."

Then I was back on the beach, and I was screaming.

Devon staggered to me. "Let me see."

I didn't want him to touch my hand. I held it against my chest as I bent over and rocked in a vain attempt to lessen the agonizing pain.

"You need to get up. We need a place to hide in case Lorenzo sends more security."

I glanced around and cringed at the number of displaced heads.

"I didn't have a choice. The one that disappeared must have strong mental control to have escaped the construct. He used a rock."

I didn't respond, concerned I was going into shock. But I had to know. "I assume the boat left without us."

"I checked the burner. The signal came in twenty minutes ago."

Thank god. At least something went right.

"Any word from anyone else?"

"No. But there wouldn't be." He tried to get up, but his legs wouldn't hold him. Then he pushed off again, wobbled, then steadied himself. He grabbed me under my armpits and lifted me, careful not to jostle my hand. I grimaced through the pain, not wanting to pass out.

We shuffled toward a group of rocks that were damp from sea spray but clear of standing water, and we fell onto a patch of sand. Devon leaned against a rock, and I snuggled as close as I could. The pain had subsided to a constant pounding. The occasional sharp pain, like someone driving a nail through my hand, brought tears and fogged my head. I lifted my good hand to swipe my hair back and noticed the slick fluid coating my hand.

I sat up, looking to see if my injured hand was bleeding. I felt along my bodysuit but didn't feel any injuries, but when I pulled my hand away, it was stained red. I twirled to Devon.

"You're injured."

"It's nothing."

"Like hell. Not with this much blood. Where is it? Let me see."

The pain in my hand was all but forgotten when I felt how wet his bodysuit was. It was more than wet, it was drenched. Way too much blood had been lost.

"You need blood."

"I'll be fine."

I glanced around. "Will Decker risk coming back for us?" I knew the answer. Decker would take Lucas, Raquel, and Hamilton to a small dock on the north side of town. Far away from Lorenzo. Even if Decker attempted to return, it would take more time than we had. Once the guests were ferried off the island, Lorenzo would have security check every inch of the island.

"It would be best if we found another way."

I snorted. "Right. You can't fight. You can't even walk."

He struggled as he tried to sit up.

"Stay where you are." Why do men never listen?

"I'm not going anywhere." His fangs punched out, and he sliced a cut in his thumb.

"What are you doing?" I almost shrieked it. He couldn't afford to lose any more blood.

"You need the blood. It will heal your hand."

Now that he mentioned it, the pain that my endorphins had been masking came back with blazing fanfare. But I had a better idea.

"You first."

"What?"

I pulled my hair back and bent my head to the side. "You need blood more than I do."

He stared at my neck, then glanced away. "You need to fix that hand."

"You think my blood is tainted somehow."

"No." He spoke a little too fast.

"You think you'll end up in a fugue state again. But I think that had to do with the beast, and you drank a lot of my blood. You only need a few sips to heal this time."

"After you." His eyes drooped.

"No. Dammit. Stop being so obstinate. Isn't it better to risk a temporary fugue rather than die?"

He didn't say anything, and I shook him, thinking he might have passed out, but he growled. Then his fangs dropped again. I leaned in, bringing my neck down to him. There was a slight hesitation then he pulled me to him. The first pierce of fang was a quick, cold tingle then immediate warmth. A pleasant warmth, and he hugged me closer. Then it was over. Way too soon in my opinion.

He wiped his mouth clean then pierced his thumb again. He held it out to me.

I licked his thumb. My eyes widened. That was heavenly, and a flashback hit me of when I'd fallen from the window and Devon gave me blood to heal. I didn't think I would remember the taste of his blood. But I did. And I sucked on his thumb until he took it away. I moaned, not sure if it was from pleasure or pain, but then the healing properties of his blood went to work.

I'd been close to death when Devon shared several drops of blood with me after the fall through the window. And now, as the new pain of quickly mending bones made me want to screech, I was grateful I hadn't been conscious to feel the healing of multiple bones and ligaments the first time.

I must have blacked out. A voice was calling from someplace far away.

"Cressa, luv. Wake up."

Someone shook my shoulder, and I swung an arm to push them away but there was only air.

"Pandora, get a shake on. This is no time for a nap."

The use of my street name shook me awake, and I sat up, my elbow hitting a soft spot, and I heard a grunt.

"Devon?"

"You've lost your marbles. It's me. Now, let's get out of here before more of these vamps show up."

My mind cleared instantly, and I swung around. I must have elbowed Devon in the gut. He was sitting up, shaking his head, and then he pulled the blood-stained bodysuit away from his skin.

I twisted around. "Harlow?"

"Yes. Now let's go."

"What are you doing here?"

He rolled his eyes and glanced back at two vamps, who stood by a small boat. "Come help me get them up."

The two vamps ran to us, probably not realizing we might need it. Devon was already up by the time the vamps reached them, and he pointed to me. I would have been faster on my own without two vamps pawing at me while Harlow provided directions.

We moved as fast as humanly possible to the boat. I was helped in first while the men pushed the boat back into the water as they took turns jumping in. A couple vamps rowed until a motor started, and the boat sped up.

Devon shook Harlow's hand. "We didn't think anyone would be coming."

"Trudy and I were getting ready to head back to shore when Roxie sent a text that your GPS locator was stationary and still on the island."

"Did Lucas and Hamilton get off the island?"

"Yes, along with the lovely Raquel. They pulled into the northern docks about ten minutes ago."

"What about everyone else?" I asked.

"We haven't heard from anyone, but according to Roxie, yours were the only two trackers she picked up."

I fell back against Devon, who put an arm around me, and I squeezed Harlow's hand. "You're the best."

Harlow's grin turned devilish. "That's what Trudy tells me every night."

Chapter Thirty-Seven

I WOKE when Devon nudged me, and I popped up, rubbing my eyes and glancing around. I was still in the limo, and we were at Oasis. I didn't remember falling asleep, but I recalled the boat mooring at the northern docks. Decker's team had already left, and according to the shifters that patrolled the area, all members of the team were accounted for, including Lucas, Raquel, and Hamilton.

We'd also been told the other teams had checked in with no casualties. I'd been so relieved to hear the news, I'd hugged Trudy, and then Harlow, who'd given my ass a squeeze. Devon led me to the limo where he helped me in before turning to talk with Harlow. They'd shaken hands, and that was the last I remembered before waking.

"Why am I so sleepy?" I put on a smile when Mateo opened the door and helped me out.

"It's good to see you home and safe, Miss Langtry."

"For the hundredth time, Mateo, it's Cressa."

He smiled and nodded. "Of course."

I squeezed his arm. He'd never call me by my first name, but it was fun trying. "Thank you for this evening. I hear Ginger is alright." It wasn't a question, but I watched his expression for any sign our earlier information had been wrong.

"She's in excellent condition, and demonstrated superb acting skills."

I smiled. "She could have been a star." Mateo loved old black-and-white movies, and I assumed he'd catch the reference.

He chuckled as he turned to Devon. "The Family is waiting for you in the library."

"Tell them we'll join them in fifteen minutes. Has the chef prepared food?"

"She's waiting for you."

"Buffet style in the library with plenty of coffee."

Mateo bowed before leaving to get things in order.

I lumbered up the steps to the front door, and Devon put an arm around me. "I feel like I ran a marathon. I'm so lethargic. If I remember from last time, I had tons of energy."

"But it didn't happen right away. You'll feel better after a quick shower and clean clothes. You need a good night's rest. For some reason, while vampire blood heals you, your body requires more rest after healing than a normal human. You'll be buzzing around the manor before you know it."

"That won't be helpful in a fight. I wonder if Colantha has any thoughts on that."

"I have no doubt she does."

With Devon's help, and after another five minutes of sleep while Devon showered, I was washed, dried, and dressed in a loose turquoise caftan. If I read Devon's heated expression correctly, he would be more than willing to make the Family wait another hour. I didn't know if it was the shower or his expression, but I was feeling much better.

For this evening, the Family meant all the team members who had participated in the evening's mission, including the shifters but minus Harlow, Trudy, and Roxie. Remus had joined the group and was speaking quietly with Sergi, Mateo, and Decker in a far corner, drinks in hand.

Colantha, along with her bodyguards, sat near Lyra and Hamilton. Hamilton leaned against Lyra while she stroked his arm. I was sorry to have missed the reunion, but it wasn't difficult to imagine.

Lyra would have been waiting on the front steps, probably from the time she'd heard he was safe and on his way to Oasis. She would have raced down them the minute the sedan pulled up, yanking others out of the way until she could reach him. There would have been tears, and the two of them holding each other. Even though Hamilton was unwashed and bearded, the kiss would have been long and endearing. It was all there in her shiny gaze when she looked at me.

I hurried and knelt in front of them, holding my hand out to hers. Lyra grasped it tightly. I glanced up at Hamilton. His beard and mustache were gone, his hair combed back and put into a ponytail. He was horribly thin, leaving stark cheekbones, but his smile was weary and bright.

He took my other hand. "I can't thank you enough for what you've done." Tears gathered, and a couple leaked out. "I didn't think I'd ever see my Lyra again."

Lyra stroked his cheek. "Of course, you did. Remember the last time you brought me to your dream? You said there would be dark times ahead, but that in the end, we'd be together."

He rested his forehead against hers. "I remember. I suppose in the back of my mind I always remembered. But I couldn't see the path. If I'd been able to build a construct, I would have been able to draw you to me."

"My guess is that Venizi has been feeding you something that doesn't allow you to focus." Colantha turned her gaze to me. "You've taken vampire blood to heal your injury."

"News travels fast."

"Perhaps. But it's nothing I've been told. I can sense it in you."

That surprised me. "What do you mean?"

"I feel it, too." Hamilton shifted to sit straighter. "Many things are becoming clearer. I forgot how good the nectar tasted."

"The nectar?" I pinned Colantha with a steely gaze. "He's talking about the juice, isn't he?"

"A discussion for another time." She got up and moved to the sideboards where platters of food were being placed.

"I hate it when she says that."

Lyra laughed. "There's much to discuss, but considering the evening, I'm sure Devon has another agenda."

"We'll talk more in the morning." I stood to offer thanks to the others, but hadn't missed the relief in Hamilton's gaze, and how tired he truly was. He was putting on a brave face for the crowd, but he would need rest and Madame Saldano's special potions to fully recover. That, and Lyra's special care. I had a feeling the voices Lyra had been hearing would be gone. I'd have to ask Colantha, but I believe the voices she'd been hearing had been Hamilton's, possibly mixed with other dreamwalkers. But Hamilton had been the conduit. He'd been connected to Lyra more than he knew.

Once everyone had food, I made the rounds, thanking each person individually. Then I found a seat between Remus and Decker, my eyes locked on Devon as the others slowly turned their attention to him.

He stood in front of the hearth and his gaze swept the room, touching on each person. He looked relaxed, but I could feel the energy coming from him. The Family had pulled off the impossible, but we were far from done. Everyone knew Lorenzo would retaliate.

He lifted a glass of scotch and waved it slowly around the room. "Tonight's success wouldn't have been possible without everyone in this room. And while Harlow and his team aren't here, I want to remind you that this was a joint mission between vampires, shifters, and humans. A combination of forces that will be required as we chip away at Venizi until he's done for good."

Everyone lifted their glasses, and cheers of agreement flowed through the room.

"We must remain vigilant against what is to come. Lorenzo won't take the infiltration of his island lightly. I'll be issuing orders in the morning for the entire Family that no one leaves Oasis, the coast manor, or any of our properties without a partner. Every member of the cadre will have bodyguards in the car in addition to a second security vehicle. This order includes Cressa, Ginger, and Colantha for as long as she stays with us.

"Oasis and the manor will be on lockdown until this is over, however long it takes. I would also caution our partners—" his gaze locked with Remus and then with Decker, "—to take the same precautions. I don't know if Lorenzo knows of our arrangement, but after he reviews the outcome of tonight's events, he'll know the shifters helped. He can't take obvious measures against you without repercussions from the Council, but we know he has the means to retaliate under the radar."

He paced along the hearth as he considered his next words. "For the next two days, the Family will remain within our guarded facilities to gather, rest, and enjoy time off. While security will remain on high alert, I want shortened duty hours, so everyone has time to restore and recover."

He glanced at Remus again, and it appeared The Wolf knew what was coming because he glanced at Elijah and Braden, who nodded at him before he gave the final nod to Devon.

Devon gave Remus a long head bow, then turned to the audience. "On the third day, we'll meet again. An official notification will be sent to the Council to inform them I have reclaimed my leadership of the House Trelane. At that time, we'll plan the final stages in our preparation for war."

Everyone glanced around the room, some a bit shocked, others with a gleam in their eyes. Simone stood first, her glass lifted high.

"To war."

Sergi stood, his glass raised. "To war."

Lucas, Bella, and Jacques followed suit, each one's voice louder than the last. Each vampire in the room responded in kind as energy built. The final vampire to stand was Lyra.

She wore a fierce expression I'd never seen before as she scanned the room. She lifted her glass. "I hereby pass the leadership of the House back to my brother, Devon Trelane. And I pledge my allegiance to House Trelane and the call for war."

Cheers went up amongst the vamps, and I turned an eye toward The Wolf, who remained quiet as he observed the room.

When everyone calmed, Remus stood and walked to the hearth. Devon stepped to the side, giving the floor to him. Remus scanned the room. "As you know, the shifters have no real standing with the Vampire Council. While we hold one seat on the Council, it's nothing more than an honorary token with no real vote. It's no secret that Venizi and his followers, if they were to garner enough votes, would turn back the hands of time to a point where shifters were nothing more than slaves. Venizi has been duping the Council and many of the Houses with the development and distribution of Magic Poppy. But those days are over, and soon all will become aware of his deceptions."

He turned to Devon. "There are many vampires who don't follow Venizi, but the path House Trelane has laid out for centuries. We must strive for a new day where all shifters and vampires are equal, and to a new Council with equal representation and new laws. I believe the time has come to demand nothing less. The wolves stand with House Trelane, and when the call is sounded, will join them in battle."

This time the wolves in the room stood and howled with excitement and the call for blood.

A chill ran up my spine. This was getting real. I glanced at Ginger to gauge her thoughts. Her hand was gripped tightly in Lucas's, and her eyes were glazed with the energy building in the room. Most of it was the rush from her part of tonight's successful mission. But there was a reverence behind it that reflected her devotion to Devon and all he'd done for her. But it didn't stop there. She seemed to hold the same reverence for Remus. I wasn't sure she knew what war meant for us humans, and that scared me. Until Lucas put an arm around her and pulled her close. Well, I was still scared for her, but at least I wouldn't be the only one watching out for her.

I turned my gaze back to Devon, who'd been watching me. He would have followed my stare, but now he was only looking for my reaction to his speech. It was an easy one to give him. I gave him my best smile and lifted my glass in the air.

I ROLLED over and rose up on an elbow, pushing a strand of hair from Devon's face. His eyes glittered with passion.

"Don't tell me. My blood has kicked in."

I grinned. "I think you can manage another round."

"In case you're counting, this will be the third time."

I ran a hand down his arm. "I didn't hear any complaints earlier."

"I was merely making an observation." He took my hand and kissed each finger. "It appears your blood has given me increased stamina."

"And your head?"

"The clearest it's been in a long time." He turned and leaned on his elbow so we faced each other. He was so close I could see the flecks in his eyes as they changed from their clear icy blue to a warmer shade. "I have one question."

"Mmm." His hand roamed down my side making my insides warm and tingly. "What's that?"

"Simone mentioned that when the fighting broke out in the

ballroom, several vampires turned on Venizi's security. She noted two specifically adept vampires with white-blond hair."

I nodded. "Erik and Ulrik."

"What's their game?"

I thought back to what Erik said to me, and I slapped my forehead. "With everything else going on, I'd forgotten." I knew how important his words had been. I was quite aware of who they appeared to work for but could only guess at the implications. "Erik said they'd been sent to get close to Venizi and determine the status of the Council and the Poppy. His last words to me before he ran off to fight was that House Aramburu sends their regards."

His eyes went wide. "Aramburu? No one has heard from them for decades, possibly longer."

"Maybe they've decided to come out from the shadows. And maybe they have their own suspicions about who's responsible for the Magic Poppy."

"It sounds like a visit to Spain is in order. Have you ever been?"

I shook my head and traced a line along his bicep. "I've never been outside the country."

"Do you have a passport?"

"No."

"Then we'll leave for San Francisco in the morning. We can get you an emergency travel passport."

"We're going to Spain?"

"It seems Aramburu is reaching out. It would be a shame to disappoint."

And then he rolled me over. His knee moved between my legs as his kiss invaded my senses. I didn't know what going to war meant in this time period. And I'd be foolish to think it would end without casualties.

Possibly my own.

What Devon didn't mention this evening, because he couldn't, was where Colantha stood. But we both knew. She was tired of hiding. She would want equal representation on this new Council that Devon and Remus envisioned.

Remus accepted her. Would Devon's allies?

That was a question for another day. For now, I ran my fingers through Devon's hair as he trailed his fangs down my neck. And when his fangs slid into the tender skin at the base of my throat, I almost wept for joy. He trusted me.

Fortune favored the bold.

~

Thank You For Reading!

BUT DON'T GO! Keep reading for more of House Trelane.

~

LUCAS

War is coming.
The outcome hinges on one artifact.

LUCAS MAYNARD IS cadre in service to House Trelane. He has one mission—locate an ancient text or find the curator who hid it. His secret task could bring two distant races together or propel vampire society into a civil war.

Ginger Morrison is a human living among vampires. Though humans in a vampire House are common, there are days when she feels like an outsider, made terrifyingly real when House Trelane was threatened with sanctions that could have put her back on the streets.

Her fears dissipate when Lucas asks her to join him on his mission. Though the assignment is dangerous, a couple of weeks alone with Lucas is enough to drive away any concern for her safety.

But trouble follows their every move, and their lover's holiday becomes a battle for survival.

How far will a human go to save the life of a vampire?

~

And now a glimpse...

LUCAS
Of Blood and Dreams: Cadre, Book 1

Lucas

I STARED at the front door of the hotel from the plush lobby chair, watching for anyone who might have followed us. This was the seventh, no, the eighth hotel Lucas and I had stayed in since leaving Santiga Bay a little over a week ago. I turned around to get a look at the vamp at the front desk who was registering for two nights under an anonymous name.

I smiled. We'd started a game at the third hotel where Lucas made me guess the name he used to sign us in. The game included an interesting form of strip charades, a bottle of tequila, and ended with laughter and hot sex.

It eased the tension of our days attempting to complete the impossible task Devon Trelane, Lucas's boss and leader of the House Trelane, had given him. The House Trelane didn't have the largest Family in the vamp world, but the House was sizeable enough with over seventy extremely well-trained vamps. Even the children learned martial arts at young ages. Well, for the number of children there were.

The vamp fertility rates had dropped drastically over the last couple of centuries, and no one knew why. But I digress. Cressa, my best friend in the whole world, would say I have too much to say so it just comes tripping out of my mouth. I'm still deciding if that was a compliment or not.

I've always had a hard time focusing. I don't know if I was born that way or whether I simply got bored easily. But that was also a story for another day.

"Ginger. Hey, are you daydreaming again?"

I glanced up, not realizing I'd been doing exactly that. His eyes were the color of a summer sky, and his hair was a sandy blond that looked streaked from the sun. He had the face and physique of a beach boy, who spent his day on his board waiting for the next big wave. A shiver shimmied through me at his knowing smile.

"I'm not sure I want to admit to that."

He laughed. "Come on. Dinner first, then some fun. But there's not a chance you'll figure out the name I used this time."

I stood on tiptoes to whisper in his ear. "I guess that means I won't end up wearing much clothing."

He lowered his head so his warm breath tickled my ear. "If I play it right, you won't be wearing any at all."

I pushed him toward the elevators, both of us laughing. "Do we have to do dinner first?"

We kissed on the ride up to the thirteenth floor. Our arms were locked around each other as we stepped out, an overnight bag hanging over each of our shoulders. I was staring into his eyes, wondering what it would be like for him to mesmerize me. Was it possible for me to be more attracted to him than I already was?

The whir of a blade sliced past the back of Lucas's head, and we both turned to see two vamps racing toward us. The one on the right held a blade in his hand, so it must have been the other one who'd thrown his.

The vamp on the right drew back his arm, ready to throw his dagger when a throwing star hit him in the base of his throat. I didn't have to look to know Lucas had thrown it. He was masterful with shurikens, or what most call ninja stars, and he constantly practiced new routines.

And, unfortunately for us, he'd demonstrated that skill several times over in the last ten days. Somehow, vamps found us again as if someone had given them our exact route as soon as we planned it. We assumed we were being tracked, but after several thorough searches, then dumping and buying new supplies, they were still one step ahead of us.

Satisfied the second vamp was incapacitated enough for me to handle, Lucas turned his attention to the first one, who'd already drawn another knife. But now, we were close enough for Lucas to launch himself as he kicked out, landing a solid blow to the vamp's chest as he fell back. Lucas landed, ready to swing a leg out, but the vamp was prepared and was able to block Lucas's kick, forcing him off balance.

From there it was vamp on vamp. Lucas had drawn a dagger, and the two fell into fighting stances as they prepared to dance.

I glanced down at the vamp who'd removed the knife from his throat. He was still on all fours but was beginning to rise. My first kick hit its mark in the vamp's midsection which knocked the air out of him. The next one hit his lower chin with enough force that I might have heard his teeth rattle. I grinned with a manic glee when blood dripped from his mouth.

I took a moment to check on Lucas, who was wearing his opponent down. The vamp had been cut in multiple places. Talk about death by a thousand cuts. I didn't think Lucas planned on taking that much time.

My vamp got a second wind. His neck had healed, and he was rising to his feet. I couldn't waste a moment. If I let him get up with his speed and agility, the fight would end up in his favor. I flung a throwing star that sliced into the side of his face. He howled.

The vamp had to know I was human, which might have been why he leaned back and howled again, this time in apparent frustration. A bad move on his part to leave his neck exposed.

The slice across his jugular startled me, though it shouldn't have. It wasn't the first time Lucas made the injury as grievous as possible, it he didn't outright kill them. Whatever it took to make a quick escape without pursuit.

The other vamp had the same problem. The slice to his neck was so deep it would take some time for it to heal.

Lucas retrieved my silver star which he wiped clean. "Your aim is becoming quite consistent."

"Well, you know what they say—practice, practice, practice. Though I have to admit, as much as I hate Sergi's training sessions, they do seem to be paying for themselves." I checked the hallway but no one else was around.

I used the bottom of his shirt, which had pulled out of his pants, to wipe the blood off his face. "You got us a room on the thirteenth floor? I mean, I didn't think hotels had a thirteenth floor."

"When did you become so superstitious?"

"After the surprise attack at the third hotel."

He picked up the overnight bags and handed me mine. "From now on, no more hotels with a thirteenth floor." With a last look at the two vamps, who would be strong enough to crawl away in the next thirty minutes, assuming hotel security didn't come call-ing, Lucas kissed my temple.

"We'll have our evening. Just not here." He swung an arm over my shoulder as we hurried toward the exit sign that would open to the stairs.

Next stop—hotel number nine.

Thank You For Reading

DON'T MISS out on the release of **Lucas**, Of Blood and Dreams: Cadre, Book 1

Coming Spring 2024

As a special treat, if you haven't already downloaded it, consider reading the free prequel to the Of Blood and Dreams series - **Lyra**. This novella is set one-hundred years before the start of the series.

Get your FREE copy!

The catalyst. The victim. The bridge.

The Roaring Twenties. The time of flappers and Prohibition.

For Lyra, a young vampire and aspiring painter, the world is her canvas.

When she meets Hamilton, a sculptor and her family's gardener, time stops. He understands her like no one else.

But he's a human. And he's not the only one drawn to her. An ancient and powerful vampire has declared his desire to seduce her.

A perfect storm that sets the stage for all that is to come.

MAKE sure you never miss a new release!

Join my FB Readers Group - Kim Allred's Heart Racing Romance

Join my newsletter...I'm pretty much unobtrusive.

Follow me at Amazon, Goodreads, or Bookbub

If you can't wait and want to check out my other series, visit my website.

About The Author

Kim Allred lives in an old timber town in the Pacific Northwest where she raises alpacas, llamas and an undetermined number of free-range chickens. Just like most of her characters, she loves sharing stories while sipping a glass of fine wine or slurping a strong cup of brew.

Her spirit of adventure has taken her on many journeys including a ten-day dogsledding trip in northern Alaska and sleeping under the stars on the savannas of eastern Africa.

Kim is currently working on a follow-on series in the world of Mórdha Stone Chronicles and the next books in her urban fantasy series — Of Blood and Dreams. Her new time travel series, Time Renegades, is on the horizon.

instagram.com/kimallredauthor

amazon.com/-/e/B07CQY2J8Y

bookbub.com/authors/kim-allred

pinterest.com/kimallredauthor